MANCHESTER BLUE

Also by Eddy Shah

Ring of Red Roses
The Lucy Ghosts

MANCHESTER BLUE

Doubleday

LONDON · NEW YORK · TORONTO · SYDNEY · AUCKLAND

TRANSWORLD PUBLISHERS LTD
61-63 Uxbridge Road, London W5 5SA

TRANSWORLD PUBLISHERS (AUSTRALIA) PTY LTD
15-25 Helles Avenue, Moorebank, NSW 2170

TRANSWORLD PUBLISHERS (NZ) LTD
3 William Pickering Drive, Albany, Auckland

DOUBLEDAY CANADA LTD
105 Bond Street, Toronto, Ontario, M5B 1Y3

Published 1993 by Doubleday
a division of Transworld Publishers Ltd

A catalogue record for this book is
available from the British Library.
ISBN 0385 404204

Typeset in 11/13pt Times by
Falcon Graphic Art Ltd,
Wallington, Surrey
Printed in Great Britain by
Mackays of Chatham PLC, Chatham, Kent

To Ardi, Tamsyn and Alex.

For keeping quiet when I try to write
and making me realise how important
and valuable family is.

I love you all dearly.

And also to the police forces and drug
enforcement agencies throughout the
world who have to combat this most evil
and relentless of modern crimes.

EARLY DAYS

1

SADDLEWORTH MOOR

Near Manchester
England
October 1965

THE YOUNG POLICEMAN STAMPED HIS FEET. IT WAS A DAMP TIME, that first biting chill of autumn dusk. He rubbed his bare hands together, then turned and watched an older colleague clamber up the grassy bank towards him.

'Anything yet?' he called out.

'They've found something,' came the reply. 'Bloody hell, this stuff's impossible to walk on.'

The younger man watched the other slither down the embankment once again, the soft under-earth sucking at his boots and trouser-legs as he fell through the brittle, half-frozen grass surface of the moor. He was glad he was standing on the road, on duty to stop any sightseers or reporters from getting too close to where the police were digging. The road, the A635 between the villages of Holmfirth and Greenfield, snaked across Saddleworth Moor into a sharp bend where the young uniformed man stood waiting for his colleague. There was no traffic; the road had been sealed off to any passing vehicles.

He heard the older policeman swear as he slipped again, then finally climbed to the top of the bank where the road ran.

'What do you think?' the younger man asked again. 'Is it what they expected?'

'I don't know,' said the other, stamping his feet and clearing the mud off his boots. 'Bloody stuff. Ruin my boots.' He leant confidentially towards the younger man. 'All I know is that it suddenly went quiet. Then they said they wanted the area cleared. They told me to come up here and help you. Make sure no-one came down.'

'Nobody'll get past here,' said the young policeman.

He glanced over to the nearby group of reporters and television crews, and when he was satisfied that they were content to remain behind the rope barrier, he turned and looked out across the moor to where the canvas screens were linked by wooden posts to form a square fortress.

Saddleworth Moor. No place like it in the world. A desolate, windswept bog moor that rolls into the far hills, lifeless to the watching eye; the sort of place where you could expect murder most foul to be committed. At night, with the wind hugging the bleak, rolling terrain, whistling and crying like tormented souls, the moor seems to hold secrets of the most hideous nature. Secrets long buried and best forgotten in the mists that shroud the emptiness of the place.

But this time, the moor was about to reveal its terrible secrets.

The young policeman sensed it; something calamitous was about to break. It was a sixth sense that would serve him well in future years, that fine instinct that all good police officers have of sudden expectancy and danger.

Charlie Soulson was twenty-four years old and had only just graduated to police constable in the Cheshire Constabulary after his statutory training period as a police cadet. He had reported for duty at the police station at Hyde, a small town on the outskirts of Manchester, six days earlier. Ready for a long stint on foot patrol on the damp pavements of that great northern industrial city, he was more than surprised to find himself out on the edge of the moors, guarding a short stretch of road against the invasion of the media parasites and horror-seeking ghouls.

Down by the canvas wall, some 300 yards away, he saw a policeman stagger out from the shelter and fall to his knees, retching as he knelt in the bog. A senior officer came out and stood behind him, waiting for him to finish, then helped him to

10

his feet. The two men, one helping the other, climbed towards the road, slowly, turning and slipping on the wetness of the ground.

'What's going on?' said Soulson's colleague, now joining him at the side of the road.

The young policeman didn't answer as he watched the two men. Behind him he could hear the newsmen reacting, catching their sudden excitement as they shouted amongst themselves. The senior officer hailed the two policemen on the road, waved them down.

'You stay here,' said Soulson with an authority not expected of a policeman who had only joined the Force six days earlier. 'I'll help them. Keep that lot where they are.' He gestured towards the crowd, then stepped off the road and slid down the banking towards the two men. At six foot four, with the surprising agility of most big men, he covered the ground safely and in little time.

'You'd better get down there,' said the senior officer, an inspector, to Soulson when he reached them. 'Make sure no-one gets in. Not unless they've got a warrant card.'

'Yes, sir,' replied Soulson. He looked at the young officer who was being helped. His face, with white-flecked sick over his cheeks and chin, was twisted in pain and horror. He recognized him: a young copper from the same station in Hyde who had been with the Force only a few weeks longer than Soulson.

'I hope you've got a strong stomach, son,' said the inspector. 'I'd keep outside the search area. Yes, you do that. Stay outside.'

'Yes, sir.'

Soulson passed them and walked down the slope to the canvas-shielded area. He reached the spot where he had first seen the two officers; there was an entrance into the search area where other policemen and volunteers were working. There were lights in the area, illuminating the men, whose attention was concentrated on a small area to the left of the sealed section. Most of them were standing, but two were on their knees, on tarpaulins, carefully scraping away at the turf.

'Stuck a long pole in the ground,' he heard an officer say nearby.

'And. . . ?' asked another.

'Must've gone right through the body. Bloody smell that came up. Straight from the ground, like a bloody explosion.'

'What smell?'

'Decomposition. What do you expect? Body's been rotting there for two years.'

'Bastards. Fucking scum.'

11

The scene hypnotized Soulson: the quiet intense concentration of the men kneeling on the tarpaulins, the others peering over their shoulders. He moved past the two officers who had been talking and looked down at the two men scraping away at the earth with their hands. One of them had a small trowel.

That's when he saw the body.

The young child, still half covered in earth and water, lay in a twisted position. The upper part of the torso and head were turned to the left, the lower limbs facing downward. The body was fully clothed, but torn in a manner which signified sexual activity and abuse.

It was at that moment of horror that the policeman he was to become was born. It was a memory that would never be lost to him.

It wasn't disgust or fear or terror that filled Charlie Soulson.

It was anger. That such abject violence could happen in a world he inhabited, only a few miles from the place he lived. He felt the rage, felt the desire to destroy those who had committed such atrocities.

'I told you to stay by the entrance,' snapped the voice from behind.

Soulson turned and saw the inspector who had ordered him down. 'Sorry, sir.'

'We're coppers. Not tourists. Not out for a day's sightseeing. This—,' the inspector gestured to the sealed area, '—is our office. Where we do our job. In dirty places like this. To do that job, we have to be professionals. Do you understand that?'

'Yes, sir,' replied Soulson quietly.

'Being a professional means doing as you're told. Being a cog in the machinery. Fitting in. Do that, and you'll learn how to do your job well. The worst thing in the world is an undisciplined copper. OK?'

'It won't happen again.'

The inspector looked into the young policeman's green eyes and saw that his words had been understood. He saw the steel of Soulson's gaze, saw the quiet determination in the craggy, surprisingly deeply lined young face that stared back at him. He'd be all right. Someone to rely on when you stood next to each other in the thin blue line. 'You go and watch that entrance. There's some regional crime boys on their way down. Apart from them, don't let anyone in without my say so.'

Soulson left the group and returned to his post. He guarded it as he had been instructed, and never looked back at the grisly scene as the officers slowly cleared the earth round the child's corpse.

His resolve was complete. He would never fail in his duty as a policeman again.

It was nearly midnight when Soulson parked his motorbike, an old 1930 Brough Superior SS 100, in the back yard at the little terraced house in Bold Street, Altrincham. A two up and two down with a flagged courtyard at the back which also accommodated the outside toilet, it was the type of house that one day would find favour with so-called 'yuppies'. But now it was an honest house, a working house, not bought for profit and gain, but as a home where a working-class family could bring up their children in comfort and shelter.

Mary, Soulson's twenty-two-year-old wife, his childhood sweetheart, was waiting for him in the hallway as he let himself in. As he turned to her, in the dim light of the hall, she saw the lines that ran deep into his forehead, the marks of worry that told her he was dejected. His eyes, sunken and hollow in his big face, confirmed her fears. This was more than just a long, hard day at work.

'Hello, love,' she said, wrapping her arms round his vast frame. She felt his tenseness as she held him, stiff and unbending.

'Hello,' he answered, flat and not really there.

'Are you going to put your arms round me, or do I have to call a policeman?'

'I'm sorry.' He wrapped his arms round her in turn. She was little, no more than five foot three, but a lioness to him. He was always amazed that such strength could come from such a small frame. He was still unused to this need for closeness; his relationship with his parents had never been based on touch and warmth, rather on discipline and duty. As he held her, as he felt her holding him, he started to sense the comfort he yearned, the release from the anguish and anger that had filled him all those hours earlier.

They stood, clinging together, for what seemed like five minutes. Neither needed to speak.

'I haven't eaten, you know,' he said eventually.

'It won't take long to warm the oven.' She still didn't move, waited for him to break the bond. She felt him give her a last hug, then slowly, unwillingly, she released him and stepped back, took his big hand in hers. 'Come on. In the kitchen with you.'

She led him into the small kitchen at the back, bare except for a rickety wooden table with three equally unstable chairs, a New World gas cooker and oven, a free-standing larder cupboard and an open china Belfast sink on a metal frame. It wasn't much, but as Mary proudly told everyone, 'It's ours and it's clean.'

Soulson sat on one of the chairs and watched her busily uncover the meal she had already prepared, light the oven and slip the plate into it. Then she poured out two mugs of tea, put them on the table and joined him.

'Won't be long,' she said. 'They've not sacked you, have they?'

'No. What for?'

'It's got to be something very important if it's worrying you that much.'

'Been a long day.'

'Did you eat your lunch?'

'Of course,' he lied. In the excitement of going to the moors, he had forgotten to eat. He would have to hide the sandwiches that were still in his greatcoat pocket before she found them.

They sat in silence for a while, him nursing the mug of tea but not drinking from it. Mary watched and knew he was still in some distant place. It wasn't like him; they always shared everything.

'Tessa had a tummy gripe all morning,' she said. Tessa was their nine-month-old daughter. 'But she's all right now. Went to sleep like a lamb.'

He nodded, more out of habit than agreement.

'Are you going to tell me what's going on?' she insisted.

'Just been a bad day.'

'I thought when you're married, you're meant to share the good and the bad.'

'Some things're better not being talked about.'

'What things?'

'It's to do with work. Does it matter?' His words came out wrong and he regretted them instantly. Even if he was affected by what he saw, he had no desire to upset her.

'Yes, it matters. Between us, everything matters.'

'I saw the other side of being a copper today. The ugly side. It's not what they prepare you for at cadet college.'

'What was it?'

'I saw an accident.' He decided to continue lying. 'It shook me up. The state of the fellow who was driving. I'm a copper, not a bloody doctor.'

'I can always tell when you're lying.'

'Why should I lie?'

'So's not to upset me.' She reached behind her and picked up a copy of that evening's edition of the *Manchester Evening News*. She

14

spread the broadsheet on the table so that the headline was clearly visible. 'It's not to do with this, is it?'

He looked down at the picture that filled the front page. It was of the canvas-sheeted area where he had stood guard, even more macabre because of the black and white picture that had been enlarged to fill the page, the evil somehow magnified by the grainy texture.

'Well?' she pushed.

'Yes. This.' He tapped the picture. 'It's to do with this.'

'Tell me.'

'No.'

'I want to know.'

'Why, Mary? Ugliness. It's not for you. What'll it serve?'

'I'm not a ghoul. You know that. And it probably will upset me. But I want to share it. Your hurt. I do, Charles.'

'I think you're daft. But I know you when your mind's made up.'

Then he told her of what had happened out there on the moors, of the horror he had seen as the detectives had clawed away at the twisted child's body, of the clothes riding up round the waist, of the blood that had run and dried with the soil, of the excreta that ran from the bloodied anus, of the frozen terror in the dead child's face when he had seen them lift the body out and on to a plastic sheet. The flesh, decomposing on the bones, hung like seaweed and flapped so uselessly as they moved the corpse. Some of the police had vomited openly, but Soulson had kept his emotions in check. Anger was his staff, determination his strength. He had watched the forensic men begin their search, whilst the coroner's men started their examination before taking the body away. Then, having spent five hours at his solitary post, he had been replaced and sent back to the station from where he found his way home. The last terrible act, before he left the scene, was to be confronted by the excited media pack, each after his own story, some even prepared to bribe him to tell them what he had witnessed. But he had smiled at them, a trait that would come in useful in the future of this young policeman.

By the time he had driven home, he was an experienced officer. He knew he could cope with his duties. They could never be any worse than those he had just faced.

Mary sat quietly and watched him, never interrupted, let him finish and get it out of his system.

'It could've been Tessa,' he said finally. 'That's what I kept thinking. It could've been her. And I decided then that what I do will make a difference. Do you see that, Mary? No point in

15

having this gift of life . . . if at the end of it you don't make a difference?'

''Course I see that.'

'I'm glad I'm a copper. It's what I want to do. And there's only one way to do it. The proper way. With no compromises.'

Then he started to cry, the sobs rolling out of him and shaking his large frame. She came round the table and held him, as she had done before, and let him wash the emotion from his soul. He cried for a long time. Then he quietened.

She made him a fresh cup of tea and watched him drink it. Then she turned off the oven, put his uneaten food in the larder, put her arms round him and led him to bed.

He slept fitfully that night. He had his back to her, and she wrapped herself around him, as much as his size would allow, and stayed awake in case he needed her.

He didn't wake when the front door opened and closed quietly downstairs. She was relieved. If he knew Jimmy had only just come in, he would have been impossible to control. There'd been enough in his day.

As she lay there, she heard Jimmy let himself into the room next door, heard the creak of the bed, and then the silence.

At the foot of their bed, Tessa gurgled in her sleep.

It was a long night for Mary Soulson.

'Jimmy gone?' Soulson asked as he came down to breakfast in the kitchen. It was nearly eleven and he'd finally slept, a deep sleep to hide the nightmares of what had been.

'At this time? They'll be having school dinner soon,' Mary replied, laying down his plate of eggs and bacon. The mug of tea was already on the table and Soulson picked it up and drank from it. She smiled. He always finished his tea before he started on the meal. 'What time are you going in?'

'I've got the day off. They've jumped my shift because of the long hours yesterday.' He leant across the table and tickled Tessa's cheek as she lay in the pram. 'Has he been behaving himself?'

'Jimmy? 'Course he has. Now his big brother's a policeman, he doesn't want to get into any more trouble, does he?'

'We'll see.' Soulson's younger brother, a fifteen-year-old bundle of nervous energy, had a history of truancy and a gift for antagonizing authority at any opportunity. 'That's what you get when you let the brakes off. The Swinging Sixties. More like the Sinking Sixties.'

After they had finished their morning meal, they walked in a nearby park, he pushing the pram while Mary clung to his arm. It was when she was proudest of him. He, so fine and tall, her husband and her man, out walking with his family. It was the dream that had become the reality.

'Anything wrong with my sandwiches, love?' she asked.

''Course no—' he suddenly remembered what he had left in his greatcoat pocket. 'Sorry. Just . . . with everything that was going on yesterday, I never got round to eating them.' He didn't need to say any more. She laughed and shook her head.

They were on their way back from the shops, she'd needed some milk and Farley's rusks, when Roy Armitage pulled up in his old Morris Minor Traveller. Armitage was slightly older and had been in the police force for three years. He had recently been promoted to a plainclothes officer on the newly-formed Regional Crime Squad. He had known Soulson at school and had always liked the younger lad. As Soulson had grown and developed into the biggest and strongest boy in the school, with a tremendous reputation both on the field and in the classroom, so Armitage had encouraged him, finally suggesting, many years later, to the jobless Soulson that he apply to join the police. It was a way of paying Soulson back; the younger man had supported him when he started to go out with a Chinese girl, Linda Tai. Prejudice was more natural and open in those days, and Armitage was a natural target for such attacks. Normally easy going, he had reacted strongly once after being asked if Chinese girls' vaginas ran sideways as legend suggested. Four older boys had set on him, and Soulson had come to his rescue. The big youngster was not someone the others liked to tangle with and Armitage had been saved a considerable hiding. His relationship with Linda Tai had continued and they married as soon as Armitage left school and joined the police force. To help his younger friend, Armitage had written in to the police as one of his referees and had applied some friendly pressure on those he knew to accept him. It was a friendship created of need, but one which had matured and would last a lifetime.

'Hi, Roy,' welcomed Soulson.

'Hello,' returned Armitage. 'Mary. How's the little tyke doing?'

'Which one?' retorted Mary. 'The one in the pram or the one next to me?'

'Him? He's beyond redemption. And you?'

'I'm fine. It's good to have him home.'

'Ah! That's why I'm here.'

'No, Roy.'

17

'Duty. When it calls you've got to go.'

'What's up?' asked Soulson, putting his arm round Mary to ease her disappointment.

'I'll tell you in the car. Sorry, Mary.'

'I won't be long,' Soulson bent down and kissed his wife gently. 'I'll see you when I get back.'

The Morris Minor swung out from the kerb and pulled into the traffic. Soulson waved at Mary, but she was already wheeling the pram away.

'What's so urgent?' he asked, turning back to Armitage.

'Regional boys want to see you.'

'What for?'

'See when we get there.'

They drove through the suburbs of Sale and Stretford towards Manchester, along Princess Parkway and into Moss Side.

Moss Side, once a leafy suburb of industrial middle-class Manchester during the industrial revolution, had been taken over by the black West Indian immigrants to Britain during the 1950s. Like most of the immigrant neighbourhoods, it had soon turned into a shabby lowlife image of what it had once been. Where one family had lived in a house, there were now four. Where one person had lived in a room, three now slept in the same bed. There were few jobs; racism was a real threat that enveloped them all. So the younger ones turned to what they felt they could live on: prostitution, stealing, dealing in what couldn't be got in a high street Marks and Spencer's. And as the fifties rolled into the sixties, as people wanted to live beyond their expectations, wanted their dreams to be filled on magical mystery tours with a lungful of mary jane and a drop of acid on a sugar cube, so Moss Side became the clearing house of Manchester. The leafy avenues and proud houses that had once been the heart of a vibrant community were pulled down by those who knew how others should live. It was the time of the planner, the corporate town-haller who believed that people should live together, on top of each other, whether they wanted to or not. And the cursed planners, from the safety of their town hall offices and white semi-detached suburbs, ripped down the terraced communities and family homes and built a concrete high-rise slum. Community was lost; the whites moved out and Fort Moss Side became a ghetto community within two years. The blacks, still desperate for work and a future in the land of opportunity, were shunned and, without hope or education, left to find life within the walls of their citadel community. They didn't need to go out. The whites, hyped and hot for sixties experience,

18

came pouring in. They wanted drugs, hard and soft; they wanted sex; they wanted hidden fruits. Moss Side became the 'in' place for the 'in' scenes. The night clubs and bars and pubs remained in Manchester. That's where respectability was on display. But the dirt was in Moss Side.

'After all,' Soulson had once heard a senior officer say, 'that's why they're black. You can't separate them from the filth.' It wasn't a sentiment the young policeman agreed with; even in his early days he saw that poverty was the breeding place for crime. It was just unfortunate that most of the blacks were poor.

Soulson and Armitage said little on the journey down Princess Parkway, the main artery that linked Manchester to its southern suburbs and split Moss Side down the centre. The planner's nightmare, those hideous concrete towers, was on the west of the Parkway; the old terraced homes, now shabby and in disrepair, on the east.

Armitage turned right in the middle of Moss Side, towards the terraced houses. After 300 yards he turned right once again and pulled up outside a grey-painted house where the rendering had stopped peeling a long time ago. Soulson followed him into the house. The big man was uneasy; negroes and immigrant Moss Side were not something he was familiar with. There was no-one in the street, but Soulson knew they were being watched. This was not an area where things went unnoticed. Especially when two white men suddenly arrived and entered a building.

It was dark inside; all the curtains were ragged and drawn, and an airless smell of curry powder and stale living pervaded the place.

A white man in an overcoat came down the stairs. Soulson's instinct told him he was a senior policeman. He spoke with a thick Irish accent.

'This him?' asked Armitage.

'Yes, sir.'

'I'm Superintendent Christley,' the man went on, turning to Soulson. 'Regional Crime Squad. What you see from now on is for your eyes only. You understand?'

'Yes, sir,' answered a bewildered Soulson.

'This is highly irregular. Sometimes, that's the way we have to work. Otherwise nothing'll ever get sorted. Follow me.'

He led the two of them up the narrow stairs. There was no carpet, only linoleum, and the banister had long since collapsed and been replaced by a sheet of plywood. Upstairs a woman could be heard crying. A naked bulb hung on a long flex from the landing ceiling, its harsh light absorbed by the dark nicotine-stained wall where most of the wallpaper had long since peeled off.

Christley stopped outside the front bedroom door.

'I meant what I said about this going no further. I'm only doing it because Roy said you'd deal with it.' He looked at Soulson, who gave no reaction. 'This house is a place where whores work. Bring their clients in for a fifteen-minute special, take their ten quid, then go out and pull in another. High turnover business, eh? Low overheads.' The Irishman grinned, dirty-intentioned, and Soulson immediately disliked him. He remembered the child on the moor. This was where those acts first started, where the perverts learnt their ways. Laughing at them was no way to resolve the situation. 'Whores and getting your kicks,' Christley continued as he opened the bedroom door. 'That's what happens in a hole like this.'

Soulson looked nervously at Armitage, who winked reassuringly and signalled the young policeman to follow.

Like the rest of the house, the room was run-down and squalid. Blankets were pinned across the two small windows to shut out the light and a candle flickered in the corner. A small gas-fire was the only heating. There was a smell of incense which came from the small flowerpot in which joss-sticks had been burning.

A black man, in his mid-forties, lay on the small single bed. He had no clothes on apart from a grubby pair of Y-fronts. Soulson could tell from his position, with one leg bent under the other, and from his open eyes staring at nothing in particular, that he was dead.

In the corner, next to the hissing gas-fire, a young boy was crouched in a defensive posture. He also was wearing no clothes.

This was not real.

What was Jimmy doing here, in this awful place?

'That's your brother, isn't it?' Christley said.

'Yes, sir.' Soulson replied numbly.

'Roy says he's only fifteen.'

'That's right.' He didn't know what to say. *What was Jimmy doing . . . ?*

'He should be at school.'

He nodded, suddenly remembered Mary. School dinners. That's what she'd said. This would destroy her.

'Are you all right?'

'I'm all right.' Soulson knew he wasn't, that he still hadn't collected himself. He moved past Christley and looked down at his brother. Jimmy glared back, then turned his head away.

'What're you . . . ?' Soulson asked.

'Waste of time,' Christley said behind him. 'He's so popped up he doesn't even know where he is.'

Soulson knelt in front of Jimmy and looked into his eyes. Nothing. There was no-one in. He took Jimmy's hands and pulled at them. Jimmy resisted, but Soulson straightened them and looked. There were no needle marks. At least he wasn't taking heroin. He stood up and turned to Christley.

'What's all this about?' His voice reflected his tense frustration.

'Don't have a go at me, copper. I'm on your side.' Christley waited for Soulson to bring himself under control. He understood the strain the young policeman was under. 'I guess you know nothing about any of this.'

''Course I don't.'

'He's a bit on the wild side. Eh?'

'Yes.'

'Ever seen a bloke OD before?'

'OD?'

'Overdose. Take too many drugs and you're floating permanently. Like he is.' Christley led Soulson over to the bed. 'See his arms. Pincushions. And there, between his legs. Same thing. That's because heavy users, like this one, can't find any space on their arms to inject a vein. So they stick it between their legs. Disgusting, isn't it? What humans do to themselves.' Christley turned back to Soulson. 'You really had no idea?'

'No.'

'Like you saw, there's no needle marks on him. He's not got that far yet. Just pills and stuff.'

'What's . . . he under the influence of now?'

'LSD. That's what the girl said.'

'What girl?' Soulson remembered hearing someone crying as he climbed the stairs.

'Upstairs. My sergeant's looking after her. A working girl. She says he—' Christley indicated the corpse '—picked her up, brought her back here. Personally, I don't believe that. I think she lives here. Works out of here. Anyway, one of the neighbours heard all this commotion and called the local cop shop. I was there, nothing to do, so I said I'd come down. My sergeant and Roy were with me. We found those two as you see them. The girl was in here, too. Naked, like them. And she was screaming the place down. I think she'd come down from her own trip and found him dead. That's what set her off.'

'What were they doing naked?'

21

'What do you think? Playing happy families?' Christley was irritated with Soulson's naivety. 'Look, according to the girl, your brother was here when she came in with this one. I tend to believe that. I mean, he really is high. God knows how much he's taken.'

'How long will that last?'

'Hours. Anyway, she said he was already high when they got here. Just crouching there, like he is now.' Christley reached into his overcoat pocket and took out a large envelope. He opened it and let Soulson look inside. It was a hypodermic and needle. 'We found this on the floor.' He sealed the envelope and slid it back into his pocket. 'I'll bet the girl helped him shoot up. Which is why she's so frightened. Your brother, and the girl verifies it, was in no state to do anything.'

'But he's still taking drugs.'

'So bloody what. Bloody fashionable, that's all. Till you see them like this. Look, son, you say he's only fifteen. He's got a life ahead of him. He's not part of this lot. They're scum, black scum. Bring their filthy ways into this country, and their stupid music, and expect us to look after them. I don't feel any pity for him. He's got what he deserved. Kill the bloody lot of them. That's what I believe. If we don't fight these people now, then one day we'll have a crime problem that'll be out of control, and no amount of policing will solve that.'

'They're not all like that.' Soulson cursed himself as he retaliated; whatever his feelings he quickly reminded himself that Christley had helped him.

'Bleeding sambos. 'Course they are.' Christley showed his irritation. 'Okay, you just get your boy out.'

'Just walk him out?'

'More likely carry him out. Roy'll give you a hand.'

'Why?'

'Because we look after our own,' came the exasperated reply. 'Remember that. Fight fire with fire, but always look after your own.'

Soulson glanced at Armitage, who nodded. He crossed over to Jimmy.

'Won't someone report it? That he was here?'

'Who? There's only me and the sergeant upstairs. When you've gone, we'll call the cop shop and get them round.'

'What about the girl?'

'She'll keep her mouth shut. In her business, she knows when to do as she's told. And the neighbours won't say anything. Last thing

22

they want to do is draw attention to themselves. Half of them are illegal immigrants. Look, you just get him out. And make sure you never open your mouth to anyone.'

'Come on, Charlie,' said Armitage from behind him.

Soulson helped Armitage put the clothes on Jimmy; it was a curious sensation, dressing him in his school uniform in this awful room. Christley opened the door for them when they had finished. 'Keep him out of trouble. I've seen what happens to kids who want this sort of excitement. They never win, you know.'

'Thank you, sir,' said Soulson.

The Irishman grinned. 'Just remember. A favour owed. I might need that back one day. Go on, get off.'

Christley closed the door on them and went back to the dark business he was left to deal with, and as he did so, Soulson sensed the day would come when the favour would rebound on him.

They half dragged Jimmy down the stairs. The fifteen-year-old was enjoying the tussle, laughing loudly as the two men supported him, living in some private fantasy of his own, enjoying the private party that was exploding in his mind. They could hear the girl upstairs, her sobs now having turned to a wail as the drugs she had taken wore off and she came to terms with the terrible predicament she was in.

'Doesn't anyone else live here?' Soulson asked as they opened the front door.

'Nobody lives here. It's whoever's passing through at the time. As soon as that guy OD'd, they'd've scarpered out of this rat-hole.'

It had started drizzling and the clear sky was replaced by grey overcast. Manchester weather. Drizzletown. They pushed Jimmy into the car and drove off; Soulson saw curtains move as hidden watchers followed the action. 'Thanks Roy,' he said.

'That's what mates are for. Didn't you know?'

'Never dreamt it. I knew he was a tearaway, but nothing like this.'

'What're you going to do?'

'God knows.'

'He'll need help. From you and Mary.'

'Some people are just bad.'

'Jimmy's not bad. Just reckless. They all are these days.'

'No. I never thought about it before. I mean, he lives with us. I was there when he was born. But I don't really know him. Thought I did. But this—' Soulson shook his head. The vision of the mutilated child from the night before still filled his thoughts.

23

'There's bad people in the world. Just plain bad. Evil. I don't think anything changes them. Just the way they are.'

'What's brought this on?'

Soulson told Armitage about what he had seen, about the grisly scenes behind the canvas wall. When he finished, they had sat in silence, waiting for the lights to change at Barlow Moor Road.

'I've seen worse, you know.' Armitage broke the long silence. 'But you can't stop believing in good. Otherwise there'd be nothing to protect, would there? I mean, Mary's good. She's worth protecting, isn't she?'

'I didn't say there wasn't good. Just that bad's . . . look, I don't know if I can go on living with Jimmy. Not when I know he's been involved in this lot.'

'Send him back to your parents.'

'They couldn't cope. They're farmers. Country people. They don't understand drugs. Booze, yes, not this. Anyway, Dad's nearly sixty.'

'You can't throw him out, Charlie.'

'Can't keep him, either. Not after this lot. Damn it, Roy, he could've been the one who used that needle.'

'Christley said he didn't.'

'But Christley wasn't there.'

They continued the rest of the drive in silence. The drizzle had turned to heavy rain and the whole city was shrouded in grey. Industrial city with grey smoke and grey rain and grey pavements. Armitage parked outside Soulson's front door in Bold Street.

'I'd better warn Mary,' said Soulson as he opened the door. 'I don't know how she's going to take it.' He left Armitage in the car and crossed to the front door.

Armitage watched him disappear into the house, then come out a few moments later.

'She's out,' said Soulson. 'Let's get him in before she comes back.'

The two men hauled Jimmy from the car and took him into the house. The boy was more aware of his condition and seemed almost able to stand, but they still needed to support him as they helped him up the stairs. Jimmy was surprised to be in his own home, even more surprised to see his brother there.

'What're you doing, Charles?' he slurred, then started to giggle.

Soulson ignored him and, with Armitage's help, got him into the small back bedroom and laid him on the bed. Jimmy continued chortling, still locked within his own hallucinations. 'You're going to have to stay with him,' said Armitage.

'He'll be all right up here.'

'LSD's a hallucinatory drug. He could think he's a bloody eagle and try and fly out of the window. Last thing you want to do is be scraping him off the pavement when Mary comes home.'

'I'll sit with him.'

'Shouldn't be too long. He's starting to come round.'

'I'm sorry about all this, Roy.'

'It happens.'

'He's only bloody fifteen.'

'Doesn't mean a thing. Wait until you get a bit more experience as a copper under your belt.' Armitage shook his head dolefully. 'Kids are different these days.'

'Not that different. He's only nine years younger than me.'

'Big difference these days. What's the new phrase? The generation gap. Listen, I've seen kids of twelve and thirteen out on the streets in the middle of the night. Whoring. Boys and girls. We've pulled them in, taken them home. Parents couldn't give a shit. Just send them to bed, curse us for waking them up, and slam the door in our face. Nobody's interested any more. Just take what they can get. Help themselves to whatever's going.'

'But I care about what happens to Jimmy.'

'Then why was he out in Moss Side?' Armitage stung Soulson, watched him recoil at his own shortcomings. 'It's not all your fault, Charlie. These kids. They just . . . expect too much. And we can't give it to them. They watch the telly, read the magazines, see a life there that they want to live. If a pop star's driving round in a gold-painted Roller, half pissed and taking drugs, then they want the same. They think that's what life's all about. They're only kids, for Christ's sake. They don't know any better.' Armitage went to the door. 'I've got to get back. Give my love to Mary.'

'Yes. I said it before, but . . .'

'No need to say it twice. See you.'

Soulson stayed with Jimmy for more than an hour before Mary got back. The boy seemed to have settled down and Soulson had undressed him. After searching for any needle marks between his legs and feeling relief that there were none, he tucked him under the blankets to let him sleep. Jimmy never woke up, just snored softly, unaware of what was going on.

'What's up?' Mary asked Soulson as she started to unpack her shopping in the kitchen.

Soulson came round the table and pulled out a chair for her. 'You'd better sit down.'

She listened in silence as he told her what had happened. She showed no emotion when he finished.

'You all right?' he asked, concerned about her.

She nodded, then, with relief, told him about the late nights Jimmy kept, about his reputation in the town as a jack-the-lad.

'Why didn't you tell me?' he asked.

'My fault. Thought he'd grow out of it. Anyway, you're not the most patient of men. I didn't want you both falling out. Not in our home.' She watched him, and when she got no reaction, she continued, 'Is he all right now?'

'He's asleep.'

'What're you going to do?'

He noticed she'd said '*you*', not '*we*'. She was leaving it up to him. She'd always been too soft with Jimmy, treated him like her own child. 'I don't know.'

'You'll have to talk to him. Before you make any decision.'

'Won't be easy.'

'Why not? He's your brother.'

'He's also everything I'm against.'

'Charles. He's just . . . mixed up. It's not easy for him. Living here. With his elder brother. He feels like a lodger. And he's always looked up to you. Always seen you as somewhere . . . you know . . . up there. Strong. Knowing what you want. He needs your help. Specially now. He really does.'

Someone knocked on the front door.

'God, who's that?' said Soulson rising from the table and going to answer it. He returned with Armitage. 'Roy's come to see us,' he told Mary.

'Hello. Do you want a tea?' she asked.

'No,' replied Armitage. 'Not got long.' He turned to Soulson. 'I need a minute.'

'If it's about Jimmy,' said Soulson, pulling up a chair for his colleague, 'I've told Mary.'

'No thanks. I've really got to get back. Is he all right?'

'Fast asleep.'

Jimmy kept still at the top of the stairs. He wanted to hear what Armitage said; the loud knock on the front door had wakened him.

'Well, things've got worse,' continued Armitage. 'Christley sent me down to see you.' He collected himself before he spoke. It wasn't easy in front of friends. 'The girl. She's changed her story.'

26

'What's she said?' questioned Soulson, aware of Armitage's reticence.

'That this bloke . . . and Jimmy . . . forced her into the place. Says they raped her. Then held her down and injected her with heroin.'

'I don't believe that.'

'Neither do we. She's lying to save her own skin. She also says . . . that the bloke who died didn't overdose himself. That they were all messing around, and Jimmy wanted to see how much more heroin this fellow could take. She says, even though the bloke was half unconscious, that Jimmy injected even more into him. Almost half a syringe.'

'She's accusing Jimmy of murdering him.'

'Christley's run a fingerprint check on the syringe. There's only two strong fingerprints. One's the girl's and the other's the dead man's.'

'Which clears Jimmy.'

'Maybe. Could be the girl did it.' Armitage tapped his forehead with his finger. 'She's not playing a full house, anyway. We reckon she's passing the buck. It was the only hypodermic in the place. In that room, anyway. We found all sorts of things in the rest of the house.'

'Want me to get him up?'

'No, let him sleep it off. I'm just warning you it could get nastier.'

'How did they explain him not being there?'

'Christley said he was being taken away and he bolted.'

'So they're looking for him?'

'Looking for someone. Bloody mess. I mean, we should've reported it, got the ambulance out earlier.'

'You all in trouble?'

'Nothing Christley says we can't get out of. He's told them we were on our way to break into another house. That the boy said he knew where there was a big drugs party going on, and that he scarpered out of the car when we stopped at the lights. Don't worry. We'll just get our hands smacked. And the girl'll change her story once Christley's spent some time with her. Look, there's no evidence to support her. She's just a tart scared out of her mind.'

'What do we do?'

'Sit tight. I've said you were the officer who helped me. Said we were together when I was called out and that you came along for the ride. Someone'll want to see you. Just to clear the air.'

'And Jimmy?'

'Keep him away from Moss Side. Just make sure he keeps going to school. All right?'

'Fine.'

'Do you know how he passed his days? Your brother?'

'No.' Soulson didn't want to hear any more, but he had to find out.

'Pimped for the girls. Well, didn't pimp and take their money. He'd run up to cars that were cruising and ask the drivers if they wanted a girl.' Armitage couldn't look Mary in the face. 'The girls paid him.'

'How?'

'Money. Drugs. Them. Whatever was going.'

'How long's this been going on?'

'Nearly two years.'

Soulson let Armitage out and came back into the room. He was carrying his greatcoat over his arm.

'Where're you going?' Mary asked him.

'I need to get out. Clear my mind.'

'You're thinking terrible thoughts.'

'What do you expect me to think?'

'He's your flesh and blood.'

'He's a criminal. I don't want him in this house any longer, Mary.'

'You can't just throw him out.'

'And I can't live with him.'

'Your mum and dad'll . . .'

'Too old. That's why he's here. Don't forget, he's always been in trouble. Since he could walk.'

'You still can't throw him out. Remember what the Lord says, Charles. To forgive. Isn't that what we believe in?'

'I'm a copper. I believe in being a copper. I took a vow last night, to me and to my God, that I would fight evil, fight the filth that killed that young child, fight it with all I have in me. Mary, I can't do that and have a criminal living in my own house. How do I face myself? How do I go out and arrest people when I know I've let him get away with it? It's the law, Mary. The same law for everybody. It's no different for him, just because his brother's a copper.'

'But he only took drugs.'

'He's a pimp.'

'He's not. He did wrong, but he didn't kill . . .'

'No. You don't know everything. I think he did.'

'But Roy said . . .'

'And Roy doesn't know.' Soulson reached into his greatcoat side

28

pocket and took out a syringe with a needle attached to it. In the glass area there was a dried substance, yellow and old in colour and texture. He held it towards her. 'They didn't find anything because I picked it up. This was hidden behind Jimmy, on the floor. He must've dropped it there.'

'It doesn't prove anything.' But she couldn't hide the panic in her voice.

'Come on, Mary. The girl could be telling the truth.' He put the syringe back in his pocket. 'I'm as guilty as him now, hiding evidence. And I can't live with it. Not if I'm to keep my vow.'

Upstairs, hidden on the landing, Jimmy Soulson turned and quietly went back into his bedroom. He needed to go back to sleep. The after-effects of the LSD, the shock news he had overheard and the fear of being discovered were too much for the fifteen-year-old. He tucked himself into bed. The ability to sleep when events were at their most dangerous was something that would serve him well in the future.

'You'll have to leave,' said Soulson to his younger brother. It was nearly six hours after Armitage had departed.

Jimmy shrugged, his natural defence, and looked out of the window. It was still raining heavily. *So what? Nothing new. The rain's always there in this bloody place. Waking up doesn't take that away.*

'Are you listening to me?' he heard his older brother shout.

'Can't miss you. They can probably hear you down Market Street.'

'Charles!' Mary warned her husband before he erupted. She turned to the boy. 'Listen to him, Jimmy. He's trying to help.'

Soulson shook his head in despair. She was doing it again. Always taking the boy's side. *Ignore it. Now's not the time to get everyone emotional.* He laughed. *Emotional. Bloody room was dripping with it.* 'Look, Jimmy,' he tried again, 'whatever happens, whatever I feel, it's going to come out one day.'

'Why? Only if you tell someone.' A sullen, resentful answer.

'Don't be daft. People know. Someone'll know you, will have recognized you. I mean, how long have you been going down there?'

The boy shrugged, refusing to answer.

'Tell him, Jimmy,' interjected Mary. 'If not for you, then for me.'

'What? So he can have another go at me?' replied Jimmy.

'No. We've gone past that, past having a go. I mean, you're in trouble now. We have to sort it out. It's too bloody late—' Soulson glanced at Mary, apologetic for swearing '—for having a go. I have to know if someone'll recognize you. That's all.'

'People know me.'

'How many?'

'I can't tell, can I? Some.'

'A lot?'

'Probably. Everyone's up on everyone else's business there. I mean . . .' Jimmy's voice tailed off.

'Go on,' his brother urged him.

'Well, it's not like buying ice cream, is it? Or having a cup of tea in Kendal's.' Kendal's was the big department store in Manchester where the local glitterati met for tea during their busy shopping schedules. 'You mess around in Moss Side and everyone knows you.'

'How'd you get into this mess?'

'I thought you said you wouldn't have a go.'

'Charles!' She sided with the boy once again.

'All right. All right. It doesn't matter,' retracted Soulson. 'But it proves my point. Somebody'll have recognized you. How long before you're shopped to some local bobby? We won't be able to stop it then.'

'All you're interested in is protecting your bloody reputation,' came back Jimmy.

'Come on,' protested Soulson, his hackles rising.

'I heard you. From upstairs. About how you took a vow—'

'Listening at keyholes now, are you?'

'—and nothing was going to get in the way. How do you think I'm so fucking—'

'Jimmy, don't!' shouted Mary.

'—bad. Yes, I bloody listen at keyholes. Because I'm fucking evil. Nothing more than a pimp. Like you said.'

'You should scrub your mouth out,' snapped Soulson.

'You'd like that. Scrub the little shit's mouth out.' Jimmy stood up. 'I'm not staying here. This isn't my home. This isn't where I belong.'

Soulson jumped up and pushed his way between the door and his younger brother. 'You go when I tell you to.'

'Big brother. Go on. Why don't you slap me around? You're so fucking good. Bloody Holy Joe. Beat me up and then go and confess to the bloody priest.'

Soulson, now incensed, reached out to shake his brother by the shoulders. As he grabbed him, Mary screamed. They both stopped,

30

frozen in their tableau of hate. Then she started to sob, crying for the two of them. Soulson let Jimmy go and tried to put his arms round her. But she pushed him away.

'I've had enough of you two. Why can't you just be brothers? Why can't you just help each other?'

'See what you've caused?' Soulson accused Jimmy.

'No. You're both as bad as—' She turned to the boy. 'You're in trouble. Don't you understand that? This isn't stealing sweets from the corner shop. This is about jail. For a long time. Can't you see that?' She swung round to her husband. 'And you. How can you not help your brother? Even if you were the Chief Constable, you'd still have to help him. Now tell him what we agreed.'

'He won't listen.'

'Tell him.'

'We think you should go and live with your Aunt Josie.' Josie was his mother's younger sister. She herself had been an outcast from the family, becoming pregnant when she was fifteen. The child had been adopted and Josie had emigrated to America when she was seventeen. She never forgave her family, especially her sister, who she felt should have supported her. It was Mary who had written to her, Mary who had rebuilt the relationship with Josie. 'She lives on her own. Always asked if you wanted to go over there. When she knew Mum and Dad couldn't look after you.'

'It's a long way,' rejoined Jimmy.

'We'll pay.'

'You haven't the money.'

'We'll find it.' Soulson had already decided he would have to sell his Brough motorbike. It was the only way.

Jimmy decided not to tell his brother he had over a thousand pounds in the mattress upstairs. Soulson would only complain bitterly that the money was the wages of sin and refuse to use it.

'We'll say you ran away.'

'Very original.'

'No-one's going to try that hard to find you. You're not that bloody popular.'

'Stop having a go at each other,' interceded Mary.

'I haven't got a passport,' shrugged Jimmy.

'That's no problem,' continued Soulson. 'Once we've got it, and you're away, things'll die down.'

'Sounds all right.'

'One condition.'

'Only one? Expected more.'

31

Soulson ignored him. '*You never come back.*'

'Who says?'

'I do. Whatever happens now, you're not my brother any longer.'

'Just erase me. Like chalk on a blackboard.'

'Whatever. I promise you one thing. If I see you back here I'll show them the evidence. Whatever it costs me, my job, everything. I swear that. *If you ever come back*. No compromise this time, Jimmy.' He spat the name like a curse.

'Who wants to live here, anyway? When?'

'Soon as we've got the passport. And I've rung Aunt Josie.'

'Right then,' said a cocky Jimmy. 'Always fancied America. All Beach Boys, Chevy Corvettes, Coca Cola. . .'

'You're not going on holiday.'

'Don't tell me. I'm not your responsibility any more.'

'You bastard.'

'What's that make you, then?'

'Oh, for God's sake, stop it!' exclaimed Mary.

'If that's what we're doing, let's get on with it,' snapped Soulson. 'I'm going out for a walk.' He stormed out of the room and they heard the front door slam after him.

'You've been silly,' she said.

The boy's tone suddenly softened. 'I know. But he just goes on too much.'

'He means well.'

'Does he?' It was obvious he didn't agree with her. 'It doesn't matter, anyway. Not now. I'm sorry, Mary.'

'You don't have to say that to me. You can always avoid it, you know.'

'Oh, yes?'

'Yes. By not getting into trouble in the first place.' She watched him shuffling from foot to foot. She smiled and shook her head in mock despair. He was still only a child. 'He didn't know you're out most nights. I had to tell him.'

'You know I can't sleep. Too bloody up-tight.'

'Why'd you do it?'

'Isn't enough at school. I want more.'

'Oh, Jimmy. Baby.' She put her arms round him.

'I really am sorry.' He felt the tears well up inside, but he controlled himself. He didn't want to upset Mary by letting her see him crying. 'But he'll never understand it. Up there, on his bloody . . . pedestal. I could never compete, could I?'

32

'He didn't want you to.'

'I had no choice. Not with Mister Perfect.'

She pulled away from him and smiled. 'It'll be all right, one day. You'll both come together. When you're older. Then America won't seem so far away.'

'What am I going to . . . I don't want to go, Mary.'

'Only for a while. You're confused, that's all. That's why you behave like you do. You've got to learn to live with yourself.'

'On my own. Apart from you, I've always been on . . .'

'I didn't mean that. Not on your own, like that. I mean, inside yourself. You have to share the rest of your life with you. Do you understand? If you don't like yourself, then you'll never be happy. You'll never cope. You've got to like yourself to live with yourself. Then you can live with others.'

And she hugged him again. Her little Soulson. Charles as he once had been when they were sweethearts in their teens. The son she so desperately wanted.

To Mary, family was family. And a family's place was at home.

Mary had jumped at the chance of setting up her own home with Charles. Bold Street was her fortress against those who would harm her. Now it was threatened. She felt the fear well up inside her once again; that awful terror she had felt when her sister had placed the pillow over her face, while she pinched her hard on her arms and stomach. Her sister had threatened her life to try to stop Mary telling their parents about her many boyfriends and the way she would visit them after the family had gone to bed. Mary realized now that her sister had only set out to scare her, but when she was that young the threat had been real. She had never mentioned it to Charles. Her parents, both elderly, had died when she was in her late teens, and Mary had lived with an uncle until she was old enough to leave home and marry Soulson. She had not seen her sister for years, and had no desire to find out what had become of her. Those moments had been the most frightening of Mary's life. Now the panic was back, after all these years, after she had finally felt safe in her own home.

All this Jimmy didn't understand, but he believed what she said. He always had done. To him, she was the only one who ever cared, the only one who ever mattered.

Jimmy left for Florida and Aunt Josie eight days later. During that week Soulson went to church every night to pray for Jimmy's soul. Mary accompanied him twice. She prayed that they would all be

33

together again one day. On both occasions she noted that he never attempted to go into the confessional. It was many months before he could bring himself to do that.

Jimmy never went to the farm in north Lancashire to see his parents before he left; it was something Soulson had insisted on. Nor did the police come looking for him. The girl changed her story and the coroner's verdict was death by misadventure.

Mary wrote once a month and kept Jimmy informed about life in Manchester. She said she was pleased the police had taken the matter no further and that she hoped things would soon return to normal, that Charles would learn to forgive and forget and Jimmy would eventually return. She told him not to reply as Charles might discover the letters, and that would make matters worse.

Twenty-six months later, during childbirth and after two miscarriages, Mary died in the South Manchester Hospital of Withington. She died alone, as Soulson was walking the beat and no-one could get him to the hospital in time. The child, a boy, was stillborn.

Soulson was devastated. The young man of iron commitment withdrew from all he knew and locked himself into the small home that had been his refuge with Mary. The distraught policeman took the phone off the hook, drew all the curtains, unscrewed the brass doorknocker that he and Mary had unearthed on a market stall, and made the darkness the womb where he could hide with Tessa and try to hold on to what he knew he had lost for ever. But it was all in his mind; he couldn't hide the pain. Apart from leaving the house for the funeral and a few trips to buy food, his only contact with the outside world was with Roy Armitage and his wife Linda. In the two weeks that the unshaven Soulson wandered from room to room in the darkened house, trying desperately to hold on to the memories of all that had been, Armitage and Linda were allowed in only twice.

'It's when Tessa cries, I feel the despair most,' Soulson had rambled to Armitage. Those were his worst moments; the child crying as he tried to comfort her, knowing she missed her mother, but not yet able to comprehend why she was wasn't there.

It was the nearest Soulson ever came to leaving the police force. Nothing seemed important any more. There was no-one to share the dream with. It was during the Armitages' second visit that he told the older police officer of his intention to resign. Armitage reminded him how important the job had been to Mary and how he would be letting her down. In the end, after much persuasion, he got Soulson to agree to give it time before taking any such action. Three days later, a bearded Soulson finally reported back for duty. Due to the shortage of good police officers, nothing was said about his taking extra compassionate leave without permission and not reporting in after the funeral. During those last few days, Armitage became the brother Soulson had lost; he poured out his heart to him, opened up as he had only ever done with Mary. It was a relationship that would endure; built of trust as the years progressed.

His superiors forced him to shave off his beard; it was against regulations. But he kept the moustache. It would always serve as a reminder of those awful days just after Mary died. His commitment to his job was total and he was ever zealous in his duties. The law was the law and he crusaded to uphold it. This commitment did not go unnoticed and his endeavour was soon rewarded by promotion. Charles Soulson's rapid rise through the ranks was no surprise to those who knew him. He believed he owed it all to Armitage. After all, it was his friend who had first got him into the Force, then helped protect Jimmy and finally talked him out of resigning when Mary had died. It was a debt he would never forget. It was no wonder that Armitage followed Soulson up the promotion ladder.

Nobody wrote and told Jimmy any of this. To Soulson, he had simply ceased to exist.

After a year of no letters, Jimmy decided that Mary must have been discovered and forbidden to write to him.

Aunt Josie died and bequeathed him her small house in Fort Lauderdale. He'd turned seventeen and left school, starting his first job in a restaurant as a short-order cook. He was fired for stealing steaks from the freezer three weeks later. During the next year he drifted from job to job, parking cars and washing dishes in a restless attempt to find direction. Finally, he had sold Aunt Josie's house.

The day Jimmy left Fort Lauderdale, Charles Soulson was promoted to sergeant in the Regional Crime Squad. He went home and celebrated his good fortune with his four-year-old daughter Tessa.

He watched her giggling at him over the small kitchen table as she ate the meal he had prepared. Beans on toast. He smiled back at her.

Then the loss that he always felt came over him.

She looked just like Mary.

He kept smiling, but the tears ran inside him. He prayed she was well. For a moment he thought about Jimmy, then shook the memory from his mind and concentrated on Tessa.

Three thousand miles away, his younger brother stood by the side of State Road 84 with sixteen thousand dollars stashed in his back pocket and thumbed a ride west out of Florida.

PRESENT TIMES

2

THE BEGINNING OF THE TRAIL

Ciudad de Mexico
Distrito Federal
Mexico

IT IS THE BIGGEST CITY IN THE WORLD. IT ALSO STINKS. LOCALS SAY
Mexico City is where seventeen million people eat tortillas and then
fart at the same time.

Marshall came out on to the street and into the bright sunlight.
He screwed his eyes up after the darkness of the small hotel lobby
and felt the smell churn his stomach. Temperatures were higher than
normal and the city's fragrance at its most bitter.

He looked at his watch. He was too early. That would annoy
Ronane. He always complained that Marshall arrived too early. He
decided to walk down the narrow road, out on to the Reforma and
catch a *collectivo*, one of the army of privately owned Volkswagen
taxis that cruised the city. As he walked he occasionally looked back,
making sure no-one was following.

The narrow street outside the Hotel Splendido was crowded, and
people pushed past Marshall as they rushed by. Mexican machismo
at its worst. It was the way the people were. Everything was about

pride, about being seen to be manly. Arguments erupted constantly as pedestrians collided, each one refusing to give way to the other. Machismo is a way of life and no-one escapes it in Mexico.

It may be the biggest city in the world, but Mexico City is also the most congested. Marshall hated the place. He seemed to have spent most of his life in hot, stench-filled towns, holed up in dark, grubby, small-roomed hotels that had once been someone's dream come true and had now sunk into a sordid reminder of what might have been. Cheap meals, cheap booze, cheap businessmen in cheap suits, and whores who talked expensive but fucked cheap.

He turned to his right and went with the general flow. He tripped over a beggar sitting on the pavement with his tin cup. The man cursed as the cup clattered and the money rolled amongst the crowd. Before Marshall and the beggar could retrieve it, some of the passers-by had picked up the few coins and disappeared into the swirl of passing bodies. Marshall shrugged at the unfortunate recipient of his clumsiness and was met with a further torrent of Spanish abuse. It was a language he spoke well, but he decided to play the bumbling tourist. He pulled his wallet out of his hip pocket, held on to it tightly as the city was well known for its gangs of pickpockets and muggers, and took out 5000 pesos in notes, worth no more than two US dollars. He handed them to the beggar who reached out and took the money, the stream of abuse still continuing. Then he picked up the tin cup and disappeared into the crowd, no doubt heading for the nearest bar. Marshall grinned and walked towards the Reforma. This time he studiously avoided the beggars who were littered along the pavements. A few of them smiled pitifully, then swore at him. Bloody gringo.

The Paseo de la Reforma is a wide, elegant boulevard that cuts through the city. Always crushed with honking, frustrated traffic, it is the main artery that runs east to west. The cars, an extension of the drivers in them, jostled and jousted with one another. Even in a traffic jam Mexican machismo ruled supreme.

It took Marshall ten minutes to reach the Reforma; ten minutes being jostled in the fast-moving crowd. He joined the wide boulevard where the tall statue of the Aztec emperor, Cuauhtemoc, is in turn dwarfed by the soaring skyscrapers that line the Reforma.

The traffic, trapped in its own abundance, meant he would have to walk the few blocks southwards to the Avenida Revolucion. He looked at his watch. Four o'clock. If he walked he would be late. He crossed the Reforma, dodging between the frustrated, unmoving traffic, and set off down one of the side streets.

Damn you, Ronane. There's got to be a simpler way of getting a meet. He slipped his hand into his pocket and felt for the small plastic packet. It was there, nestled into the corner. He increased his already brisk pace, the sweat now glistening on his forehead. For all his fitness, his breath was now short in the 7000-foot altitude of the city. That was the cross such a big man had to carry. Heat and six foot three of middle-aged flesh are not natural partners. At least he hadn't got his Smith and Wesson Model 15 Combat Masterpiece six-shot revolver strapped to his shoulder. A 4-inch-barrelled 38 special, it was the best close-quarter gun he knew. Most of his contemporaries preferred automatics, but Marshall knew if you hadn't hit your target with the first two shots, then he'd get you before you'd snapped off the third. Anyway, he hated carrying it in this humid heat. His armpits poured like Niagara Falls and the last thing he wanted was the pistol's mechanism affected by the damp. He'd left the gun in the hotel safe; his instinct told him he wouldn't need it on this trip.

A newspaper boy, with a pile of newspapers nearly four feet high balanced on the handlebars of his bicycle, dodged through the traffic in the opposite direction. He could've done with one of those. Then he grinned. It was a long time since he'd ridden a bike. A very long time. But he didn't go any further into the memory of his youth. He had to get to the scribe before four-fifteen.

He was four minutes late.

The scribe was still there.

An old man in his seventies, with a silver-coloured typewriter in front of him that was almost as old as he was, sat at a wooden table on the street corner. There was a queue of three people waiting their turn and Marshall joined them.

In a country where illiteracy is high, professional letter-writers pound away on their typewriters for those who need to communicate by the written word. It is an old profession; the scribes are an essential part of the community. But, because they sit in one place, day after day, and because they are a constant value in a world of perpetual movement, they are also used for a variety of other reasons. For Marshall it was not to have a letter typed, but to receive a message. The scribes were trusted, their honour and secrecy an essential part of their profession.

The old man, with steel-framed glasses, silver-streaked hair brushed back and wearing a collar and tie under his brown suit, looked up at a glistening Marshall when he had dealt with the others.

41

'It's a hot day. For a tourist,' the old man said.

'It is,' replied the big man. He envied the old man, envied his ability to remain cool in this oppressive heat.

'What do you wish me to communicate?'

'I'm a stranger in this town.' Marshall repeated the words exactly as Ronane had told him. 'I am looking for a man who reads letters. I don't know where I can find him.'

'What sort of man would want to read such a letter?' The old man's eyes, sunken behind his glasses, gave nothing away.

'A small man. With a big hat.'

The old man nodded, then reached for a sheet of paper, ratcheted it into the ancient typewriter and started to type. 'You were wrong,' he said as he typed. 'This is not a town. A city. An old city. Unlike elsewhere, the city was not named after the country, but the country after the city. It is something we are proud of. Us who live in the city. Ciudad de Mexico. Since 1325. Before the Spanish.' He finished typing and pulled the sheet of paper out. He held it towards Marshall. 'You will find the small man with the big hat here. Near the Bulevar Xola.'

Marshall took the sheet and looked at the address. It was not far from where they were. He put the paper into his top pocket and took out a wad of notes. He handed 10,000 pesos to the old man. 'Is that enough?'

The scribe nodded and took the money. He didn't feel the need to tell Marshall that he had already been paid for his services.

Marshall pushed through the small queue that had formed behind him and walked away. When he turned at the street corner and looked back, the old man was already typing for the next client. To him, the message passer, the writer, the one-man office bureau, the big American was already forgotten. Just another face in a busy world. Marshall scanned the rest of the crowd. Still no-one following. No-one obvious, anyway.

He crossed the road and headed west, towards the Bulevar Xola. It took him another fifteen minutes to reach his destination, an apartment house on a crowded block which had long seen better days. There was a row of buttons by the entrance and he pressed the last on the right.

'Yes,' crackled the voice from the intercom.

'Texas,' Marshall replied with the correct password. The door-release buzzed and he slipped into the darkened hallway. Satisfied there was no-one else there, he climbed the wide stairs to the second floor and knocked on the door.

Ronane opened it.

'You're late,' he said.

Marshall shrugged and walked into the room. Ronane was a short man, no more than five feet four; a thin man with a thick black moustache which quivered like a mouse's whiskers every time he spoke. To all appearances he was a Mexican; to those who knew him he was American blue blood from Bangor, Maine, a descendant of one of the first pilgrims to land in North America. It had always been his greatest asset, the ability to merge into any environment he happened to find himself in.

'Is he here?' asked Marshall.

'We're all here,' snapped Ronane impatiently. 'Got the stuff?'

Marshall patted his pocket. 'And I wasn't followed,' he added.

Ronane ignored the comment. He'd worked with Marshall for a long time and they had developed a healthy respect for each other. Ronane was the thinker while Marshall followed his instinct. Chalk and cheese, but it was a relationship built on trust of each other and belief in their ability. There was a closeness between them, a grudging respect that over the years had turned to a grudging affection.

A man and woman waited for them in the next room, a smaller, darker room. The man sat at a table, the woman stood by the window.

The man, a Mexican, was fat to the point of obesity. A balloon man, a series of rounded shapes that somehow stuck together.

The woman by the window was ugly, probably the ugliest woman he had ever seen. Whereas most people do have two separate halves to their face, the woman had two totally different sections. Her left cheek was bloated, her right one flat. Her eyes came from different parents and even her nostrils were flared on one side and flat on the other. The face, white in pallor, was crowned with short black hair, coarse and thick and shaped like a roof thatch. A grey woollen suit clung to her shapeless bulky body, the skirt came down to her knees and the calves and ankles looked powerful. She smoked a cigarette and Marshall saw the thick stubby fingers and powerful hand that held it. She kept clenching her fists, almost as though she was grasping the air in front of her. A black handbag was slung over her shoulder. Marshall sensed there was a weapon in it. He presumed she was the fat man's minder.

'Give me the *muestra*,' demanded the man at the the table, referring to the sample.

Marshall looked at Ronane, who nodded. He put his hand in his pocket and drew out the clear plastic pouch. He put it on the table.

The woman moved away from the window and looked over the fat man's shoulder. He unhooked the seal and put his finger into the packet, into the white substance, then brought his finger out and licked it. He nodded. Then he lifted the small flattened mass out of the packet and put it on the table. It was cocaine, cream-coloured and tightly textured. He wet his finger once more and dabbed it on the flattened pile, watched it foam into a powder before he licked it again.

'Anything we get has to be of that quality,' said Ronane.

'Of course,' confirmed the man.

'And better quality control than you just licking it?'

The fat man laughed. 'We will run chemical tests on this. We'll match it.' He took a small sharp knife with a retractable blade from his pocket and diced some of the cocaine. When he had enough, he fashioned two thin lines from the pile and then put his knife away. Behind him the woman had taken a ten-dollar bill from her handbag and rolled it into a tight thin tube. She handed it to him. He looked up at Ronane. 'You don't mind, do you?'

'Just leave enough for the analysis.'

'Of course. Business is business.' Then he bent down, put the dollar tube to his nose, and snorted the first row. When he had finished, he handed the tube to the woman, who leant over his shoulder and copied his action with the second row. She stood up, unwrapped the note and put the bill back in her purse. This time the metallic glint of a gun handle was visible. The fat man put the remainder of the cocaine into the plastic bag and pocketed it. 'We'll need three days for the shipment to come through,' he said.

'The cash'll be there. Once I've checked the quality.'

'We've never let you down before.'

Ronane ignored the comment. In this game, someone always let you down. 'Usual method. I get the shipment, check it through with your guys, then make payment through a separate place.'

'The police are watching us. No brown paper bags.'

Ronane laughed. 'Don't worry. We'll launder it through.'

'How?'

'We'll tell you when you're ready with the shipment.' He gestured towards Marshall. 'My friend here will make the payments.'

The fat man rose from the table and walked towards the door, the woman following him. 'In three days. We'll wait for you to contact the scribe. Tell him how we complete the transaction. And no tricks. We don't want you blown up by our friends.' He laughed and left with the woman, the door closing softly behind them.

'We're handling this all wrong,' said Ronane, once he was certain they were on their own.

'I agree. Only we should tell that to the boys upstairs.' Marshall walked round to the table and blew the remains of the cocaine away.

'What you do that for?'

'Felt like it. Why not tell them?'

'Because no-one listens.'

'So let's do it our way.'

'You're a crazy man. Always were. You go your own road on this one and they'll blow you away.'

'That a warning?'

'Yeah. Friendly one.'

'What did he mean anyway? About us being blown up by his friends?'

'These guys are as crazy as you.'

Marshall laughed. 'Fuck you, Ronane. We're dealing with guys who're making money while we're pussyfooting around. It's time to hit them. Hard. Get to the source. Let's squeeze them, hey? Make their fucking eyes water.'

'How do you suggest we do that?'

'There's ways.'

'This is business. We play it by the book.'

'Make this a big payment.'

'Why?'

'Gets everyone more excited.'

Ronane said nothing for a while. Then he turned and went to the door. 'Stay at the hotel. I'll contact you as soon as I've got it arranged.'

'Go for it, Ronane. Excite them. Then we'll get what we're due.'

'Fuck off, big man.'

'Why? You still chasing a pension?'

Ronane stuck two fingers up at Marshall and left the apartment.

Marshall came out into the street ten minutes later. He'd looked down from the window and checked that Ronane wasn't being followed. There was no-one after him either and he headed for the nearest bar. It was time to blow the tension from his mind.

The easiest way was a whore.

He hated his weakness. But he had no choice; it was the way he was. Always had been. Sex was his release and he needed it whenever danger crawled over his horizon.

Even though it was against his principles, he wished he'd kept some of that cocaine.

3

HOME GROUND

St Mary's Church
Manchester
England

THE OLD WOMAN IN THE FADED HEADSCARF WATCHED THE UNIFORMED policeman slowly pace up and down outside the confessional. The movement irritated her; it diverted her from her prayer. But she wondered who was in the confessional who could be so important that he warranted a police guard.

The constable, a junior officer, stopped pacing and sat on a nearby pew. He was nervous in church; it was a spooky place that was best left alone to those who had a need for whatever it had to offer. He shut his eyes and imagined himself driving the new Ford Escort GTi he had set his heart on.

The man in the confessional box had handed his coat to the constable before entering. He loved this church, known locally as the Little Gem. It was hidden in the heart of the city, a small church, without the glory and pomp of its bigger sisters. He felt it was where he could commune with his God without the ever-present trappings of his religion.

46

Soulson heard the priest enter the other side of the dark box, saw his face pressed against the metal grill that separated them.

'Are you ready to confess?' asked the priest.

'Bless me, Father, for I have sinned.' Soulson paused, suddenly frightened of what he felt inside. He knew he was about to go over the edge.

The priest sensed his hesitation. 'Yes, my son?'

'It is one month since my last confession. Since then I have missed Mass twice.'

'Why?'

'Duty, Father. I'll use my best endeavours to ensure it doesn't happen again.'

'Is that all?'

'I have also been guilty of the sin of pride. I have allowed those who are my enemies to divert me from my duty. I speak out against them . . . for my own sake. For this and all my sins that I cannot remember I am sorry and beg pardon.'

'For your penance you must say one "Our Father" and one "Hail Mary". And now make a good act of contrition.' The usual words, but the priest knew something else worried his charge. But he knew not to push, that it would come out in time.

'I am deeply troubled, Father,' Soulson said in a hushed voice after some considerable time.

The priest strained to listen. 'Go on.'

'My duty recommends that I turn against those closest to me. This . . . act of betrayal . . . forces me to sin.'

'What are these sins you have committed?'

'I . . . haven't . . . it's not happened yet.'

'Then avoid the sin. I can accept confession for what has happened, but not for what you can avoid, for that which hasn't been committed.'

'My duty . . .' Soulson paused.

'What is more important than your duty to God?'

Soulson had no answer. It was his dilemma, and he suddenly regretted telling the priest. 'There's no alternative, Father.'

'Are you certain?'

'None that I can find. Not for lack of looking.'

'Look within yourself. There's always an alternative. Always within ourselves to fight the evil that surrounds us.'

'I can't,' Soulson said helplessly. 'I want to, but I can't.'

'Then I can't help you.' The priest's words added to his hopelessness. 'In your position . . . you've got to look to yourself. Will you tell me what the problem is?'

'No, Father.'

'I'm always here. If you ever want to talk.'

'I know that.'

'Now make an act of contrition,' the priest returned to the formalities, once more secure on ground he understood.

'Oh my God, I am sorry and beg pardon for all my sins. I detest them above all things. Because they have crucified my loving saviour, Jesus Christ, and most of all . . .'

Outside the confessional, the young policeman watched the old woman light a candle and kneel to pray. He wondered who she was praying for, who had caused her the grief that made her come in here and pray for help from someone you couldn't see. Then Soulson came out of the box and towards him. He stood up quickly and held out the jacket he had been carrying. Soulson took it and slipped it on. The insignia of the Chief Constable shone out from the shoulder epaulettes.

'Thank you,' said Soulson as he walked towards the door, the young officer falling in step next to him. 'Ever been in here before?'

'No, sir,' came the reply. With all the troubles in addition to the ever-present threat of IRA attacks, the Chief Constable always had a guard when he went to pray. It was the first time the young officer had been here, having been sent up from Bootle Street Police Station.

'Don't worry,' Soulson smiled. 'It won't go against you. You know what they say, don't you?'

'What's that, sir?'

'There's no better way to face life than with one hand on the bible, and the other hand on a gun.'

'I'll remember that,' lied the young policeman.

They emerged into the grey drizzle of Manchester, the clouds above trying to break up as the sun forced its way through. Soulson's black, unmarked Jaguar was parked at the pavement. Next to it was a pile of rubbish, the result of a dustmen's strike that was crippling the city. A tramp poked around in the refuse.

'Thank you, son,' said Soulson to the constable, then walked towards the car. Paul Job, his plainclothes driver, climbed out of the driver's seat and came round to open the rear passenger door. Soulson slid into the back and Job, after closing the door, climbed into the driver's seat, started the engine and pulled away from the kerb.

'We were young and fresh like that once,' Soulson said to Roy

48

Armitage, who had waited in the back of the car while he was in the church.

'For our sins. I prefer it the way it is now,' replied Armitage. His chief superintendent's uniform backed up his statement. He had forgone the chance to become one of the six Assistant Chief Constables who controlled the various departments that constituted the Manchester Police Force. He had been in charge of the 'VO' Department, CID Operational Support Group when Soulson was promoted to Chief Constable six years earlier and had been pleased to be asked to become the new Chief's staff officer. Although this role was usually filled by a superintendent, Armitage had wanted to work closely with his old friend and ignored the fact that it could be deemed by many as a demotion. He had held the post for four years, two more than usual, and then stayed on in a new role as Staff Co-ordinator. He was the man people had to pass if they wanted to get to the Chief Constable. But he was liked, and as no-one saw Armitage as a threat to their own futures, he was treated as the old and trusted friend he had become.

'You've not sent it?' Soulson suddenly changed tack.

'No. You told me to wait.'

'Then don't send it.'

'You've changed your mind?'

'Never made it up in the first place.' Soulson knew his response was defensive. He sighed. Damn the priest. 'What's happening at the Town Hall?'

'Usual circus. All after your blood.'

Soulson laughed. 'Christians nil, lions one. That's what they think. We'll give them a run for their money.'

'We're late. Meeting was scheduled for three.'

Soulson ignored the chiding reminder. 'Press there?'

'Television, the lot.'

'She'll enjoy that. Miss Louise Spencer. Just because she's on her own turf.' Soulson shook his head. He was tired; the whole thing was getting to him. 'Don't worry, Roy. We've been here before.' It was said more to reassure himself than it was for Armitage.

'I'm just a simple bobby. Just do as I'm told.'

'That'll be the day.' Soulson laughed and nudged Armitage. He knew Armitage was the only one he could trust these days. And Paul Job, his driver. Job had been a serving paratrooper seconded to the SAS during the Iraq Gulf War. When he returned, after serving with distinction, the lack of interest from an ungrateful nation had disillusioned him and he left the army to join the police force. He was a welcome recruit at a time when terrorism was at its height and the criminal was better armed and better trained than many policemen.

'Place'll burn down soon,' Soulson heard Job say. 'At this rate the IRA won't need any bombs.' Job picked up his mike and asked the police operator to report a street fire to the Fire Department. The bag people and drifters of life watched the fire burn as they tried to salvage useful items from the other rubbish heaps along the road.

Soulson looked out at the pile of rubbish burning on the pavement, looked at those desperately sifting through other people's throwaways. The whole thing saddened him. Manchester was full of scenes like this. Burning piles of rubbish, rats out in the open, a pungent smell of decay on the streets.

'It's time they got this strike sorted out,' said Armitage. 'It's not about wages. It's about politics. Out to make names for themselves.'

'You attacking our left-wing friends again, Roy?' smiled Soulson.

'It gets to me, all this filth in the street. You know my views, you've heard them enough times before.'

'It goes with the stripes. Hammer authority and appear to side with the working classes. That's the left-wing politician's creed. Sod the law and keep in power. This strike would be over if the politicians would talk to the dustmen. But they didn't. On the one hand they support the unions who're on strike, on the other they say they can't afford the increase in salaries. Blame it on Westminster, just pass the buck down the line. Just like they are with us, Roy. Demand the police be effective, yet pull back on resources with which to police. There was a time when a bobby went out and caught the crooks. Now all a bobby does is fill in report forms to keep the politicians happy.'

'She'll be waiting for you, Chief.'

The dilemma he had faced in the confessional reared its head again. Damn it, it was the last thing he wanted. He had to clear his head. This meeting was important. He didn't need reminding that Louise Spencer was waiting for him.

'Front or back entrance, Chief?' asked Paul Job, breaking into his thoughts.

'Front, Paul.' He knew the press would be waiting for him. Their questions would spark him up, prepare him for the meeting he was about to attend. Anyway, he didn't have anything to hide. 'Let's give them what they came for.'

The Jaguar pulled up outside Manchester Town Hall, a large, red-bricked Gothic Victorian building that dwarfed Albert Square.

50

On the left of the steps was a group of refuse pickets, their banners held high as they chanted their class slogans.

'Someone should tell them Lenin's about as fashionable as Hitler,' commented Job as he swung into the kerb. 'This rent-a-mob better keep their bloody hands off the Jag.'

Soulson saw a few of the usual professional agitators at work. It all seemed so Victorian; so out of place in a modern world. But that was Manchester. An old city based on old ideals.

As soon as the demonstrators saw the Jaguar, the frenzy of the chant increased. It wasn't every day they got to abuse a Chief Constable and get away with it. The flow of abuse made some of the genuine protesters shuffle uncomfortably and not join in the chants. The police shepherding the protesters attempted to calm the situation. The media, at the top of the steps, were attracted by the commotion and rushed down towards the Chief Constable.

Soulson was the first out, with Armitage following, and he took the wide steps that led up to the Town Hall two at a time. Job stayed with the car, this was not a place to leave it on its own.

The questions they threw at him were the usual ones, and he fielded them with the non-committal humour that had become his trademark. They knew he was a controversial man, who also knew when to keep his mouth shut. They followed him down the corridor towards the big committee room where the meeting had already started. When he reached the door, with the sign that proclaimed *MEETING IN PROGRESS. MANCHESTER POLICE COMMITTEE*, he turned and faced the cameras and microphones.

'Come on, you know I can't say anything,' smiled Soulson. 'You're all just trying to get me into trouble again, aren't you?'

'Who with, Charlie?' shouted one of the reporters.

'You tell me. You know I like to keep out of trouble.'

He turned and entered the committee room as the laughter erupted behind him. Armitage followed him through and closed the door.

They were sitting at the large conference table that filled the room. Seven of them. Two Conservative councillors, one Liberal Democrat and three Labour. Louise Spencer, the Chair, as she liked to be called, sat at the head of the table. She was a short dumpy woman, surprisingly matronly for someone still in her late twenties.

'You're late. This meeting was meant to start twenty minutes ago.' Spencer's voice was shrill trying to be authoritative.

'My apologies to the committee. But until someone cleans up

51

these streets, we're going to have a lot of traffic jams. My men can cope with the traffic, but not with the rubbish that causes it.' As he finished speaking he sat at his allotted place to the left of the Chair. Armitage slipped into an empty chair behind him.

'Does everything have to be a political statement?'

'He's right,' sneered one of the Conservatives. 'Your policies over this strike are causing chaos.'

'All we're trying to do is put right what your lot fucked up in the first place.' She'd risen to the bait.

Soulson grinned. It didn't take much to get this lot raging against each other. As the insults flew he looked across the table at one of the Labour councillors, a woman in her mid-thirties, scrubbed plain face topping a straight-hipped body with extremely large breasts. He knew that because he could see the left one in plain view. Attached to it was a baby guzzling away while the arguments and counter-abuses flew across the table.

'Never was a strike in our time,' scored the Tory.

'Well, we all know what the fascist laws you introduced on strikes are, don't we?' riposted Spencer.

'Have you seen the television pictures of the rats on those rubbish piles?' came in the Liberal Democrat.

'Pictures set up by the television crews.'

'Rubbish! I've seen them myself. That big. Horrible things. It's time you settled the strike.' The Tory struck back, not keen on the Liberal Democrat muscling in on his glory.

'I will not allow this council to turn working man against working man. It's time you lot understood that.' She swung round on Soulson as the breast-feeding mother stuck her tongue out at him. He smiled sweetly before turning to Spencer. 'You really know how to get them going, don't you?' she snapped.

'I simply wanted to give a reason for my lateness,' he stated, almost too sweet. He saw the flash of anger in her eyes.

'You know why we're here. For an explanation. What are you doing about the gang warfare? About what's going on out there? In our streets. Around our homes.'

'Yes, seven killings in five weeks,' said the breast-feeding councillor. 'What are you doing?'

'My men are—' started Soulson.

'Not your men,' snapped Spencer. 'Not Soulson's private army. Our police force.' She tapped her chest.

'The city's police force. Seven thousand of them.'

'The same city that elected us to run it.'

'And we're suffering for that. High rates, bankruptcy, strikes,' the Tory councillor joined in.

Spencer turned on him. 'Will you all stick to the point?' She refocused on Soulson. 'What are you doing about it?'

'This police force is short of resources with which to police this city. My . . . the men can only do so much. With all the cutbacks being imposed—,' he ignored the second Labour councillor who was now miming playing a violin '—everyone is stretched. We have to police a five-hundred-square-mile conurbation. That's two and a half million people. This country's biggest provincial police force. We can't cover everything.'

'When twelve people get killed you should be bloody covering it.' Spencer finally scored her point.

'Twelve members of Manchester's gangs. Criminals. Drug dealers.'

'Except next time it could be an innocent member of the public.'

'I know that. But I really don't have the men. Last week I had eleven senior officers tied up in four separate committee meetings. Your committees. One of them was about clothing allowances. It took all week and at the end of it, it was agreed that you'd have another meeting in two weeks time. Three of my officers are now tied up getting information for that. Either you want this city policed properly, or you want us spending all our time wasting time. We're in the middle of a drug war. This city is already being called the drug capital of Europe. Europe, not just Britain.'

'We're not wasting time, just controlling costs. That's no excuse for you not doing your job.'

'I object to your criticism of this city's police force.'

'I said *you* weren't doing your job.'

'He's the best Chief Constable Manchester's ever had,' interjected the Tory.

'So I keep reading in the papers. Full of headlines, isn't he? You know why? Because it hides the truth. The truth about the *best* Chief Constable the city's ever had.'

The door opened and Paul Job entered. Soulson leant back and Job crossed the room, bent over and spoke quietly to his boss.

'The press seem to have plenty of theories. Yesterday they named the Quality Street Gang . . .' Spencer stopped. 'Can we continue this meeting?' she said pointedly.

Soulson nodded to Job, then turned to the others.

'Thank you,' Spencer continued. 'I want to know who the Quality Street Gang are.'

'That's just another press scare. The QSG ran Manchester twenty years ago.' Soulson referred to the gang that had controlled the protection and robbery rackets during the 1960s and 1970s. 'This is out of their league.' He stood up. 'I'm afraid I have to go.'

'Not until we have an answer for the press. Not until we show them that we're doing something.' Spencer hated his arrogance.

'Another body's been found. In a rubbish pile. Chinese, this time.'

'What's that mean?' asked the breast-feeder, pulling her baby away from her naked breast as if not wanting the child to hear this awful news. A few drops of milk squirted onto her dress and the baby sucked air noisily.

Soulson knew it would cry any minute. That would ginger Spencer up. 'That it could be spreading to Chinatown – and to the Triads,' he explained, as if to children. It wasn't something that needed explaining.

'We haven't finished,' snapped Spencer.

The baby started to cry.

'This is more important,' replied Soulson.

'Send him.' Spencer pointed to Armitage.

Soulson nodded and sat down. 'I'll catch you up,' he said to Armitage. 'Take a squad car.'

Armitage nodded and left the room.

'The police finance committee agree that you need more re-sources. But that's got to be paid for . . . by savings, by looking at everything.' Spencer smiled sweetly and Soulson knew she was laying the ground for another one of her attacks. 'What car do you have, Chief Constable?'

'A Jaguar, you know that.'

'A luxury car.'

'No different to any other Chief Constable.'

'You've asked for a new one.'

'My car is eight years old. With very high mileage.' He tried not to rise to the bait, could see what was coming.

'At a time of cutbacks, should we really be buying a new luxury car?'

The Liberal Democrat cut in, astonished at what she was saying. 'Come off it. A Chief Constable can't ride round on a moped.'

Spencer ignored him. 'What do you think, Chief Constable?'

'I agree. I'll keep the car I've got,' Soulson replied.

'No, a smaller one,' came in the breast-feeder. 'Be cheaper to run.'

'I agree with the finance committee,' added Spencer. 'We should buy a cheaper car.'

'Let's have a vote,' said the breast-feeder.

'There's no need for a vote.' Soulson stood up. He needed to get out before he lost his temper. 'You can allocate me less money for a new car. But you can't make me change what I've already got. I'm keeping the car. Now, if you'll excuse me.' He turned and walked to the door.

'We'll see. We'll see.' Spencer was suddenly shrill. Her prey was moving out of range. 'And I don't want you speaking to the press about this meeting. Do you understand that? Do you?'

Soulson shrugged, opened the door and walked out. The waiting press surrounded him, but he said nothing, was sure he would say the wrong things if he opened his mouth. He left the Town Hall with Paul Job leading the way.

The pickets started to taunt him, 'Jesus Cop' they chanted as he descended the steps and climbed into the car.

'Bloody heathens,' swore Job.

The police Jaguar swung out from the kerb, out of Albert Square, and headed for the west side of the city.

4

HOME IS WHERE THE HEART IS

**Hotel Splendido
Ciudad de Mexico
Distrito Federal**

MARSHALL HATED THE VIOLENCE THAT ALWAYS ERUPTED WITHIN HIM when he faced danger. Hated what it made him, the animal who needed to inflict pain to satisfy his own ineptitude.

His eyes were closed, but the scene with the two whores remained in his mind. He saw the blonde one, with peroxide hair and black roots, saw her slumped in the corner, sobbing for what he had made her do. The other one watched him with eyes wide open, waiting for him to move over the bed, turn her over and hurt her like he had her friend. Her legs had been painfully thin, matchsticks he could snap with his size. She had taken it all, staring up at him with those big 'seen it all before' frightened eyes and attempting to smile at his ugly fury.

The more he hurt them, the more he hated them for putting up with his excesses, all for a few pesos. They weren't the animals. He was the real beast. He could see them going out of there, straight to the nearest cantina and blowing his money on some pimp, a glassful of Mexican beer and another shot of heroin. Mexican machismo. The women were worse than the men. Take the pain and curse you at the same time. *Mala mujer*, the bad woman.

He had finally exploded into the blonde one. As he rolled off her, spent and exhausted, he threw their clothes at them and ordered them out of the room. When they had gone, paid with a few American dollars, he rushed into the bathroom and cleaned his teeth to rid himself of their taste and memory. He showered, cleansing his body before returning to the bedroom where he wiped up the blood.

He lay on the bed and resented whatever it was within him that drove him to the sordid satisfaction he dragged out of whores' bodies.

Where is she now? Who is she with? He choked up, no tears, just waves of emotion for what might have been, for what had been distanced for ever, for what he would never become.

He opened his eyes and looked at the rumpled bed. There was nowhere he could shield himself from the memory of what he had just committed. Damn it, after all these years he still didn't like himself.

He tried to think about Ronane, about the task in front of him. He used that to take his mind off the nightmare he had just lived through. But his thoughts came in disconnected bursts.

The woman. The ugly one with the fingers. He wondered what she was like in bed. He'd fucked enough lowlife hookers in his life, ugly ones, fat ones. But never anybody as ugly as her. What was it that attracted him to rough, dirty women? They all looked diseased, as though they'd spent half their lives in some unwashed bed with men dipping into them one after another. He suddenly laughed at himself, at the futility of it all.

There was a knock on the door.

He swung his legs off the bed, straightened the sheets the best he could, took his gun from the bedside drawer and crossed to the door. He stood away from it, in case someone fired through it. 'Yes?'

'Ronane.'

He recognized the voice and knew there was no-one else there. The code was simple. 'Ronane' meant all's well. 'Hi. It's Ronane here,' was the signal that he was accompanied and there was danger. He unlatched the door and let the little man in.

'All set,' said Ronane as his moustache quivered.

'How're we going to do it?'

'Easy. You're going to lose with a fistful of aces.'

5

OPEN SEASON

The Arches under the Railway Tracks
Knott Mill
Manchester

THE ARCHES UNDER THE VICTORIAN RAILWAY VIADUCT, GRIMY AND brick-black, had been cordoned off by the police.

Most of the arches had been turned into garages and storage areas. The backs had been walled off and the entrances were mainly curved double doors. Police now swarmed round this normally quiet area, their interest directed towards a pile of rubbish that overflowed the refuse area that was used by the commercial inhabitants of the arches.

Armitage saw the black Jaguar approach through the waiting crowd and he walked towards his chief.

'Steven,' he called to another senior officer nearby, 'come with me.'

Chief Superintendent Steven White, Head of Manchester's CID Operational Support Group, fell in beside Armitage. A trendy dresser, in his early forties, White was a man who believed in living a fine and fashionable life. He was also a good policeman, with a nose for clues that made him an outstanding detective. 'Bloody mess,' he swore. 'Specially now the rats have been at him. Why chop the feet off?'

'Nowhere to run. Nowhere to hide,' came the cryptic reply. 'Isn't that how the song goes?'

They reached the police line as Soulson came through the uniformed barrier. 'Chinese, eh?' he commented as his two subordinates fell in beside him. 'What's that tell you, Steven?'

'We haven't identified him,' responded White. 'It doesn't mean the Triads are involved.'

'I'm not the press, Steven. What do you really think?'

'I wouldn't be surprised if it was them. I mean, I'm amazed they've kept out of it this long.'

'So who's going to take on the Triads?'

'There's only the blacks.'

'Wouldn't they want to work with the Chinese?'

'They don't trust them. Maybe do a few deals. But nothing serious. Just because they're both immigrant based, that doesn't mean anything. Only to us, the indigenous species.' White realized his cynicism was wasted. 'The blacks feel safe in Moss Side. The Chinese don't worry them. If it came to a war, Dragon City's more vulnerable, here in the middle of Manchester.'

Manchester has the largest Chinese population in Europe and its centre had been turned into a sprawling Chinatown. It is also one of only four Dragon Cities in the world outside China, a result of a gift of a ceremonial dragon from the Chinese mainland. The other three are San Francisco, Vancouver and Hong Kong. Packed with a wide variety of restaurants and shops, it was only natural that the criminal element followed, and the city centre became a base for the Triad gangs. Traditionally they dealt in prostitution, gambling, extortion and small drugs. The mainstream of the drug trade to Europeans was not their normal business as they dealt primarily with the Chinese population. Unlike Moss Side, Dragon City was a cultural and entertainment centre enjoyed by the whole Manchester population. If there was a gang war, then innocent bystanders could easily get hurt. The difference was that no tourists ever visited Moss Side.

Armitage led Soulson to the pile of rubbish where the police were clustered. Officers stood back as their Chief Constable came up to the scene.

It was a brutal tableau.

The victim, a man, was naked. He blended into the rubbish into which he'd been thrown, piles of rotting food and the excreta of an urban society. The pallor of his skin and the stench of the decaying corpse signified he'd been there for some time. There was no visible mark of death on his upper torso or head: no bullet or knife wound, no crushed bone the result of a deadly blunt instrument. To the experienced observer these would have been the areas of a normal killing.

In this case, the blood that had flowed from his groin had mixed with the refuse it lay on, had congealed into blackened rivulets that ran under the man's twisted body. There was a mound of blackened blood where his penis was, and the sight of a gaping fleshy wound. That explained the frozen mask of pain and horror on his face. The rest of the damage was done by rats gnawing at the open flesh before the body was found. They had half eaten the man's intestines and stomach, had burrowed into him through the hole that had been ripped in his groin.

The victim's feet had also been cut off, still in their shoes, and placed side by side as a macabre joke.

Soulson didn't inspect the body for long; the pathologist's report would tell him everything he needed to know.

He turned from the scene. As he looked up he saw Tessa. She was standing next to a young plainclothes policewoman he recognized from the Intelligence Unit in Stretford.

'You shouldn't be here,' he said, moving over to her.

'Why not?' His uniformed daughter reacted sharply. 'I'm a police-woman, aren't I?'

'You are,' he replied quickly, not wanting to make an issue of it in such a public place. He turned to her companion and spoke to her to change the subject. 'You're with the Intelligence Unit, aren't you?'

'Yes, sir,' the woman replied. She was attractive, a petite twenty-nine-year-old with wavy black hair and green eyes that made you want to tell her all your secrets. 'Jill Couples. Detective. Sir.'

He remembered her now; she'd been one of the exchange police officers who'd been sent to America for further training. They'd all trooped in to his office one day for his customary meeting with them. She'd been bright and asked searching questions. She was also attractive and that made it easy to be remembered. 'You went to Washington, didn't you?' he remarked.

'Yes.'

'When was that?' He desperately wanted to talk to Tessa, but he avoided it. At least this way he would be seen as involved with his police force and shown to be aware of them as individuals.

'Three years ago, sir.'

'Good. Pity we didn't continue the programme.'

'Budgets, they said.'

'Yes, they did.' He nodded and swung round to White. 'Let's get that . . . thing covered up.' Soulson took Armitage by the arm and led him away as White went back to the group. 'Now what? How the hell do we get at this thing? My hands are tied behind my back; the bloody Police Authority's cutting the ground away from under us. Where now, Roy? Even the informants have dried up on us. They're more scared of this lot than they are of us.'

'We could cross the line, Chief.'

'No. That's not my way. Even if it was my idea in the first place.' After the visit to St Mary's, Soulson had decided to hold back on his plan. The priest was right. Do things under God's Law.

Armitage didn't respond. He couldn't. He didn't agree with his Chief. There were other ways.

'Can't wait for ever. Something's got to give,' snapped Soulson and went back to Tessa. 'When're you off duty?'

'Not till midnight,' she replied, her eyes full of concern for him. 'Don't worry about me. I can handle it.'

'I wish I could. See you at home, chuck.'

He left the arches, pushed his way through the waiting press crews, made no comment and was driven away in the Jaguar they were trying to take away from him.

Paul Job watched his chief in the rearview mirror. He saw Soulson shut his eyes and lean back.

No, thought the driver, *things were definitely not going Charlie Soulson's way.*

6

A BUSTED FLUSH

Hotel Alameda
Ciudad de Mexico
Distrito Federal

MARSHALL KNEW IT WAS GOING TO BE A BIG GAME AS SOON AS HE walked in. But then that's how Ronane wanted it, always the touch of drama.

There were five other players, Marshall was the sixth. Two Americans, one Brazilian, one Frenchman, one Mexican and the woman with the stubby fingers. Apart from her, they were either professionals or high-roller gamblers. Marshall sensed it was going to be an exciting night. They were waiting for him in a fourth-floor suite of the Hotel Alameda, the wide windows overlooking Alameda Park.

Marshall crossed the suite to the Brazilian who stood looking out of the window. 'Some view, huh?' he said.

'We have better in Brazil,' came the reply.

'Are we here to play, or admire the fucking view?' said the other American. His accent and his string necktie gave him away as a Texan. He was a tall man, more than two inches taller than

Marshall. He was also very wiry and there was a hardness about him that few would match. His eyes, a cynical light blue, had seen it all before. Instinctively Marshall knew he was a dangerous opponent.

'What do you think?' the Brazilian asked Marshall.

'I still think it's a nice view,' came the reply.

The Brazilian laughed and moved to the table, Marshall following him. The others were already seated at the round table with the green baize top. Marshall pulled up his chair and sat opposite the woman. He noted her handbag was still slung over her shoulder. He looked at his watch. Ronane would be making the pick-up now. A million dollars of cocaine with a street value of nearly six million. They'd have done that once Marshall and the woman were in the hotel. They didn't need to wait. Marshall was both the banker and the hostage. Her people would be watching the streets outside for him.

It was a crazy way of moving money round, he thought. But that was how it had become ever since the BCCI, the Bank of Credit and Commerce International, had been closed down almost overnight by the western financial agencies. The bank had spread its $20 billion empire through more than sixty countries as a money-laundering outlet for the likes of Saddam Hussein, Ferdinand Marcos and the Colombian drug barons. It had rendered services to clients that included arms deals, extortion, espionage and funds for the Iran Contras, the IRA, Islamic Jihad and any other terrorist organization. The closure of the 'black network', as it was known, forced the drug tsars into finding new ways of laundering their secret currency. It made life easier for the international drug enforcement agencies, who could now see the enemy a lot more clearly because they had to raise their heads above the parapets.

The dealer, a Mexican, unwrapped a new deck of cards and showed them to the players. 'Five stud. No limit. And if you don't have the cash to put on the table, you lose the hand. No IOUs, no holding the game up while you go get some more. Any questions?'

'Deal the fucking cards,' said the Texan, pulling a wad of American bills from his pocket and putting them on the table.

Marshall estimated the pile of dollars at over one hundred thousand. That was only for starters; he knew the Texan had a great deal more in his money belt. Just like he did.

'OK,' said the dealer. 'Let's play poker.'

As the cards were dealt, Marshall remembered the lesson he had learnt a long time ago, when he had crossed America with a few thousand dollars, playing in towns across the country, determined to increase his pile by winning at poker. 'If you haven't worked out who the sucker at the table is in the first half-hour, you're it.' He'd certainly been that. He'd been cleaned out before he got halfway across. He'd certainly been a sucker then. Young and inexperienced maybe, but still a sucker.

Only this time he wasn't here to win.

He had to lose. To the ugly woman across the table.

He was about to launder nearly a million dollars across to her.

He realized there was between three and five million dollars cash in this room. But that's why the guards at the door and out in the hall were armed. This was probably the safest room in Mexico City, even safer than the banks.

His orders were simple. Lose to the woman, only play when she's in a game with you. Make sure no-one else wins a big game against you.

He lit a cigarette as he saw her fold against the Frenchman. She wasn't getting good hands, but then they all had a long way to go.

He didn't get his first chance until twenty minutes later. She beat him with a king high; it was her hole card. He'd got an ace face down, but let her take $40,000 off him.

She looked at him as she pulled in her winnings. He ignored the sneer in her eyes, the taunting expression of a woman putting two fingers up at a man. Her hands gave her away, once more seeming to grasp at air. If this was a real game, he'd take her to the cleaners. Her hands would always give away her intentions; he could read the cards she held just by her nervous reactions.

He played a few more hands, luck was running with him, and took over $15,000 from the rest of the table.

She beat him with a pair of sixes twenty minutes later. Another thirty thousand gone.

Three deals later he drew a straight, the nine running to the king. She had no more than ace high showing, maybe a pair with her hole card. There was twenty thousand in the pot and she upped it ten. He came back with another ten and they went on in this manner until there was eighty thousand piled high in the middle of the table.

'And twenty,' she betted.

He considered carefully, knew he'd beaten her but that wasn't what he was there for. He looked round the table and saw the greed in the other players' eyes. This was a hand they'd love to be in.

He shook his head and folded his cards.

'No nerve, eh gringo?' she sneered.

He didn't react. He suddenly despised her, but he didn't react.

It went on like that for the next six hours, into the early morning. He was down six hundred thousand. The Texan was up two hundred thousand, the Frenchman a hundred grand, the Brazilian and the Mexican losing. Marshall had lost most of it to the woman. It had not been easy, she was a bad player. It was his own skills that made her look good. And she had continued to deride him after each big win, make him look foolish to the others.

If there was one thing he hated, it was someone taking away his dignity. He decided to speed it towards a satisfactory conclusion and get out of there.

The woman suddenly asked to be dealt out of the next hand and she left the room. She returned four deals later.

'Sorry,' she said, sitting down at her place. 'Had a call to make.' She looked at Marshall as she spoke; he knew she was telling him she'd reported back that all was going well. He half smiled at her as the dealer turned the cards.

His first card in the hole was the jack of diamonds. The ace of diamonds was face up.

The woman had a king showing. He caught her eye, caught the imperceptible nod. She must have another king in the hole.

'Five grand.' He opened the betting.

Three of them went with him; the woman, the Texan and the Frenchman.

His next card was the queen of diamonds. Three to a straight, or a flush. She had a ten.

The others went along with his ten thousand bet. Then she upped it another ten. He went with it and was surprised to see the other two chip in. They must've paired, and the Texan showed a queen. But she was favourite with a pair of kings.

There was a hundred thousand sitting in the middle. Marshall sensed the electricity in the room, the sudden swell of anticipation. They all knew this could be the big hand of the night. He hoped she'd take it easy, otherwise one of the others could draw three of a kind. That'd kill her pair.

He was dealt the ten of diamonds. Four to a straight or a flush.

She got another ten; was now showing a pair of tens with a king. He saw the flash of triumph in her eyes. Easy, bitch. They could still hit you.

The others didn't pair up. She was still favourite.

'Twenty thousand,' she said.

He went with her and upped it another twenty.

The Frenchman folded.

'I feel lucky,' drawled the Texan and went with the forty.

She matched the forty.

There was now two hundred and twenty thousand on the table.

The dealer turned each card over and called them as he dealt.

The Texan drew a queen. Marshall knew he had three of a kind.

The woman drew a second king. If he'd read her signals correctly, she was sitting on a full house, three kings on two tens. He was relieved. She'd beaten the Texan and avoided Marshall's money going to him. He hoped he hadn't misunderstood her.

The odds on a full house in a deck of fifty-two cards is 693 to 1.

The odds on a Royal Flush, the highest poker hand possible, is over 600,000 to 1. And the woman was already sitting on three kings.

The dealer dumped the fourth king in front of Marshall.

It was the king of diamonds.

He'd never had a Royal Flush before.

'Fifty thousand,' she said breathlessly.

'And fifty,' said Marshall. He couldn't look at her. He couldn't believe he was about to lose on a Royal Flush.

The Texan paused. He thought he'd got the woman beat, didn't believe she had the third king. The other two tens were already out. But he was wary about Marshall. He could have a straight, a flush, and maybe, just maybe, a Royal.

'And a hundred,' he suddenly bluffed and started to peel off the thousand-dollar notes.

Four hundred and eighty thousand in the middle.

'And a hundred,' came in the woman. She couldn't believe her luck. Not only was she taking Marshall's payoff, but also creaming the Texan for some extra pocket money.

Marshall watched her peel the notes with her thick fingers, like sausages, and throw them on the table. He'd up it to his limit, then call it quits. Ronane couldn't complain about how he laundered the cash.

'What about you, gringo?' she leered. 'You man, or mouse?'

He ignored her and made a great play about whether to continue betting or not.

'Big man, small cock,' she prodded him again. 'You going to stack?' she pushed him on.

'And a hundred thousand,' he said.

'Shit,' swore the Texan and slammed his cards over.

Just two of them left.

'Two hundred thousand,' she bet. She was getting greedy. 'Eh, mouseman?' She felt safe. The Texan was out and she knew Marshall had passed his limit. She'd been paid in full.

'And two.'

She looked at the big man. Why was he . . . ? Maybe there was more to come. She nodded, then upped it another hundred thousand. If that's how he wanted to play it, it was fine with her.

'See you,' said Marshall.

Her eyes blinked; he wasn't meant to see her. Just fold. She'd just walked into a charging bison. 'Full house. Kings on tens.'

Marshall flicked the jack of diamonds over. 'Royal Flush. My pot.'

Nobody said anything.

Then Marshall reached over and took the winnings. There was nearly a million and a half dollars. As he piled the money, he stared straight at her. Her breath was coming out in sharp jabs, her eyes blocked with disbelief. He grinned.

Then he flipped ten thousand to the dealer and stood up.

'Thanks for the game, boys.'

The others protested, but they would have done the same. The evening was over. Marshall ignored the woman as he counted his winnings, then turned to the hotel man who sat in the background. 'Receipt it for me and put it in your overnight safe.'

He waited while the hotel man cashed up for him, agreed the final amount, took a written receipt and walked out of the room.

He didn't waste time in the street; he knew they'd come looking for him. The receipt in his pocket was his lifeline. They'd want that before they killed him.

It was after five in the morning. Traffic was building up in the streets and he managed to flag down a *collectivo*. He told the driver to take him back to the hotel. His room was at the end of the hall, on the third floor. A small fire escape ran outside and it could come in useful. He'd chosen the room specifically so that he could protect himself if the need arose.

There was no-one watching for him at the hotel entrance. He paid off the *collectivo*, tipped him an extra ten dollars, then entered the hotel and climbed the staircase to the third floor. No lifts; there was no way he wanted the doors sliding open on an armed welcome committee.

Still no-one waiting for him.

He let himself carefully into his room, once more making sure that he was still unwatched.

67

Then he rang Ronane.

'How'd it go?' asked the sleepy, uninterested voice at the other end.

'Didn't.'

'Shit. What happened?' Ronane wasn't uninterested any more. He listened while Marshall told him what had taken place. 'Why?' he asked when Marshall had finished.

'Just think it's time we flushed them out.'

'Not your decision.'

'You'd better get moving. They could be heading your way.'

'I'm ready.' Ronane had already slipped into his clothes while Marshall had been recounting the events of the poker game.

'Did you make the pick-up?'

'Yeah. That's safe. You protected?'

'As General Custer. I know now how he felt.'

Ronane laughed. 'I hope you don't expect a happy ending. Just watch your back. Till I get hold of you.'

The phone clicked off and Marshall slowly replaced the handset. He walked to the door and looked through the peephole down the corridor. Nothing obvious. He crossed to the bed and pulled the sheets off, then dragged the mattress across to the door, doubled it up and leant it against the frame. That would stop most of the heavy iron if they opened up on him. But he doubted it. They'd want that receipt above anything, even the woman's revenge.

Nothing happened for nearly an hour.

Then there was a knock on the door followed by a whispered 'Ronane'.

'Who's that?' Marshall asked, keeping to the side of the door in case someone opened fire, his Smith 15 cradled loosely in his left hand. He regretted not having a more powerful handgun instead of his snubby close-quarters weapon.

'Ronane,' came back the hushed password once again.

Marshall waited a few moments more, then leant forward and peered through the peephole. It was Ronane, fish-eyed and alone. Marshall unlatched the door and half opened it. Ronane didn't move, so Marshall pulled the mattress clear and opened it wider.

That's when he saw the ugly woman step forward from the left, an Uzi submachine-gun in her hand, pointed at Ronane's belly. The fat man, the human balloon from their previous meeting, stood to Ronane's right. He carried no weapon.

'Leave it,' commanded Ronane. 'They just want the receipt.'

'And you agreed?' Marshall shook his head disbelievingly.

'You gotta trust people you do business with, big man,' said the drawl from the window behind him.

Marshall turned and saw the tall Texan from the poker game. So he'd been part of it. He hadn't even lost any money, just played with what was theirs anyway.

The woman pushed Ronane into the room, then followed with the balloon man, who closed the door behind them. The Texan slipped through the half-open window and into the room. He also carried an Uzi in his hand.

'Don't even think about it,' snapped the Texan. 'Unless you really wanna pop off.'

'Why?' was Marshall's sarcastic reply. 'You going to let us go?'

'Sure. Hell, I woulda done the same. Ain't natural, losing on a Royal Flush.' He paused, then laughed. 'Even if it was a crooked deal.'

'Says who?'

'Says the dealer who we keep happy with his candy habit.'

Marshall looked at Ronane, who shrugged.

'Just give them what's theirs,' Ronane said.

Marshall resigned himself to defeat and reached into his pocket, slowly so as not to startle them. He took out the receipt and held it up. The woman came forward and took it from him. Marshall could see from her eyes that if it was up to her, he was a dead man.

She spat in his face.

She took his dignity away again.

He kept his demeanour. This was not something worth dying for.

She stepped back and looked at the receipt, then, satisfied with its authenticity, nodded to the Texan. The fat man reached over and took the receipt from her.

Marshall felt the wet stickiness of her saliva running down his nose and on to his lips. He didn't move to wipe it off, he wouldn't give her the satisfaction.

She lifted the Uzi towards him, held it at genital level. He knew he was going to die; her eyes told him that. Black eyes, unfathomably deep in their hatred.

'No,' said the Texan.

'He cheated us,' she replied, not taking her eyes off Marshall.

'Let's not draw any attention to us. We still have to go and cash that receipt.'

'The Yanqui is right,' said the fat man, leaning forward and taking her arm. 'We have what we came for. There will be other times.'

She considered, then laughed and rammed the short-stubbed barrel into him, hard, so that he felt the sear of pain and sickness before he fell to his knees in front of her.

Then, as he knelt there, fighting back the vomit, she turned and left the room, the fat man following. He didn't see Ronane go and close the door after them; his mind was on the pain. It eased gradually and he finally looked up. The Texan was still there, his Uzi held steadily on Ronane.

'Get up, big man,' he commanded Marshall.

Marshall struggled to his feet and moved towards the metal-framed bed where the Texan signalled him to go. He lowered himself on to the frame where Ronane was already sitting. The Texan emptied the shells from Marshall's Model 15 and threw the empty gun on to the floor. 'Nice piece,' he remarked. 'I like the Rogers grips. Easier to handle when you got sweaty palms.' The shells went into his pocket. 'You fellas are crazy,' he went on, his machine-gun aimed lazily at them. 'But then, I won't keep you too long. Just until we've cashed that receipt. You're lucky we didn't ask for the stuff back.' He smiled. 'But then, what the hell are the DEA gonna do with it? Sell it on the streets?'

Marshall and Ronane were surprised, but didn't look at one another. The bastards had known they were US Drug Enforcement Administration agents all the time. And they'd played them along. Why? Why do that?

''Cos we like sport, fellas,' smirked the Texan, answering their unasked question. 'If you were wondering why we strung you guys along. Time you got yourselves rattled. You ever hear of the Gurkhas?'

No reaction from the two prisoners.

'Sure you have,' continued the Texan. 'Fighting men. From the north of India. Little place called Nepal. These guys were mercenaries for the British. You know what they did during the Second War? They'd get down into a German camp, with maybe ten or fifteen soldiers asleep, and they'd knock out the guard, and maybe six of the others. Just sneak in and cut their throats. Big knife they used. Bad-looking thing. Curved. Called it a kookri. Sorta had a religious thing to it. Then they'd sneak out again. And when those little Nazis woke up for reveille, guess what? Half their companions were lying there with a big smile from ear to ear. Can you imagine what that did to them, to their confidence? Be a long time before they slept easy again.' He moved back, away from them. 'Maybe now you know why we let you fellas in on the game. Don't you just wonder what we really know? Hey? Isn't this a terrible world. Just nothing safe, is there?'

'There's always some bastard ready to sell his soul,' snapped Marshall.

'Ain't there just.' The Texan came closer to Marshall. 'Where you from, big man?'

'Casablanca.'

The Texan grinned. 'You got some funny accent for an Arab. Part Texas, ain't it?'

'San Antonio.'

'How about that? From Abilene myself.' He grinned. 'Don't run to your computer when you get back to Washington. I ain't lived in Texas for a long while. Changed my identity so many times, even I don't know who I am. Not been across the border for years. And don't intend to. Just a happy foot soldier, that's me.' He turned to Ronane. 'You smell like an easterner.'

'I'm from the east coast,' said a proper Ronane.

'Well, we all got our problems. At least you don't smell Mexican. Real dogshit stink. Hey, you know what we call a Mexican in Texas if he's gonna marry into the family?'

Marshall looked at Ronane, then shook his head.

'A Spaniard,' continued the Texan. He laughed when he saw Marshall grin. At least one of them had a sense of humour. 'By the way, she ain't Mexican.' He referred to the ugly woman who had just left them. He went and sat down on the only chair in the room, a metal affair with a plastic seat. 'She's one of the families.'

Marshall caught Ronane's hushed gasp. The families were the top of the Colombian drug pyramid. He also realized the Texan wasn't going to say any more; it was nothing more than a throwaway scrap for them to feast on.

'Crap,' prodded Marshall.

'If you wanna believe that,' came the cool reply.

'I know all the Medellins,' jumped in Ronane. 'She's not one of them.'

'Who said she's Medellin?' jibed the Texan.

Marshall's eyes narrowed and he turned to Ronane. His partner gave little away. They both knew the importance of what the Texan had said.

Medellin is the second largest city in Colombia. In the 1980s the cartel made up of powerful local families organized the production and distribution of cocaine onto the streets of America and finally into the rest of the western world. The DEA and other agencies had supported the Colombian government in a twenty-two-month counter-attack that had resulted in the imprisonment of Medellin chief Pablo Escobar Gaviria, albeit in a luxury prison, on a two-and-a-half-acre compound which would please the most demanding of five-star hotel guests. The battle with the government had been long and hard, resulting in the assassinations of government ministers, army and police commanders, as well as taking its toll on the drug barons of Medellin themselves. The irony was that Escobar and those of the Medellin cartel who followed him into the five-star prison continued to run their business, reputed to be worth some $3 billion a year, without any further fear of being hunted down by government troops. Their prison had also become their office, high-walled and security-protected by the very troops who had been their greatest threat, now their greatest protection. Escobar even escaped from this palatial prison when he was bored with his entrapment; he simply got up and walked out of the front door.

During the period that the Medellins had fought their running battles with the authorities, a far more sinister network had emerged. Another cartel, this time from Colombia's third largest city and sugar-cane area, Cali, took advantage of the Medellins' predicament and formed themselves into a more insidious and sinister supplier of what had become the great yuppie drug of the eighties. The confederacy of crime families of the Cauca Valley, the Calis, insulated themselves with political influence which they had subtly cultivated over many years. They were *los caballeros*, gentlemen, compared to the Medellins' *los hampones*, thugs and hoodlums. The Head of the DEA in New York, Robert Bryden, was reported as saying, 'The Cali gangs will kill you if they have to, but they'd prefer to use their lawyers.' Such niceties did not extend into the streets where their trade flourished. They became far more ruthless and organized than the Medellins had ever been. Now responsible for over seventy per cent of the North American cocaine market, the Calis were concentrating their efforts in the lucrative growth areas of Europe and Japan.

In the tradition of the great Mediterranean trading dynasties, including the Sicilian Mafiosi, the Calis have a patriarchal structure that demands absolute loyalty and discipline, yet encourages those in its structure to run their own networks in a style that suits the individuals. It is only when that loyalty is breached, when discipline to the family is ignored, that the patriarchs inflict the most terrible vengeance on their own subordinates. The Calis, unlike the Medellins, are discreet, organized and ruthlessly efficient. Their network is based on a series of pyramidal cells, each responsible to the one above. These overseas branches, as they are known, organize the logistics of importing, warehousing and distributing cocaine to wholesale buyers, and are responsible for the laundering of the cash into legitimate banks and other financial institutions. The cells are directly responsible to their head office in Cali.

To be a Cali *Caleno*, a cell boss, is to hold a position of great honour and power.

To be a member of the Cali family is to be exalted, to be untouchable.

Cali family members, bloodstock, rarely went into the field.

'She sure as hell ain't Cali,' said Marshall. Then he remembered the fat man. 'Unless the guy with her was El Gordo.'

This time it was Ronane who jerked in surprise. Jordo Santacruz Londono Don Chepe, nicknamed the Fat One, El Gordo, was the architect of the world trafficking networks which had put the Cali cartel at the top of the cocaine tree. He was indicted in New York in 1980 for drug-trafficking conspiracy, but jumped bail and fled the country. Santacruz's legend was such that every so often he would appear in the middle of a drug deal, exchange pleasantries, shake a few hands, and disappear as quickly as he had come. The dream of every DEA man was to be at one such meeting and to arrest Santacruz in the act of dealing.

The Texan laughed. 'Don't give yourself illusions, boys. No, that wasn't the Fat One. You may be DEA, but you ain't that important. But you're getting close. She's Santacruz blood. She just decided to come out and learn the family business. Close up.' He looked at Marshall. 'You're lucky she didn't blow your balls away. She's mean enough to do that. And woulda done if she was Medellin. Different in the Cali cells. No point in unnecessary violence. But . . . for a moment there . . . yeah, I think she woulda done it. What the hell? You guys gonna get blown up anyway.'

Marshall avoided any further comments as well as Ronane's questioning gaze. His instinct had been right all along. If Ronane had gone with him, instead of aiding the Cali people, they would now have scored a major hit against the drug barons. They could've squeezed the family by taking the girl in, even killing her if necessary. That would've flushed them out. But now they were suckered into a corner. The bastards had known who they were all the time.

Ronane turned his attention to the Texan and tried to open him up further. But the Texan knew what was best for him and refused to say any more. He already regretted what little he had told them.

73

Twenty minutes later the phone rang and the Texan answered it. When he had listened to the few words that were spoken, he put the receiver back and walked to the door. 'Looks like everyone's happy, fellas,' he said before opening it. 'Now you just have yourselves a good Fourth.' Then he slipped out of the door and was gone. The two men stood in silence; they knew they'd lost the round.

'I forgot. It's the Fourth of fucking July,' Marshall said eventually.

'I rang Betty before I went to bed. Wished her and the kids a happy Fourth,' answered a matter-of-fact Ronane.

'Good. We won't want to forget that, will we?'

'Ease off. The instructions were to play it by the book.'

'Fuck the book! It's easy when you're sitting in Washington, out on Army Navy.' 700 Army Navy Drive is the DEA Headquarters. 'Out here it's down to our instincts. Hell, Ronane, we could've had us a Santacruz.'

'Small fry.'

'How do you know? We're chasing pennies in the gutter and these guys are waving dollar bills. She could've been used to put pressure on someone.'

'Who?'

'Don't play me by the book. I don't know who. But you don't know how high up she could reach. It was worth the risk.'

'We didn't know who she was.'

'But we knew my instinct was to have a go.'

'Too late now.'

'Yeah. Always is too fucking late.' Marshall heaved himself off the bed, crossed to the window and closed it. 'You'd better ring Washington.'

'Office'll be shut. Public . . .'

'. . . Holiday. Fourth of July. Hell, Ronane, I bet the Calis don't take a day off. Christmas or fucking otherwise.' Marshall slumped back on to the bed. 'Was a time when we just battled on. Before the yuppies and university grads came on the team. We were streetwise then. Didn't just play it by the book.'

'You're wrong.' Ronane stood up. 'That's an old-timer's viewpoint. They're still good men.'

'Career men.'

'No. You're good, Marshall. But you're nothing special. Not in the scheme of things. So quit sounding off. Don't take it out on us. Take it out on the congressmen and lawmakers who handcuff us every time we want to do something different. Remember Guatemala. They're the ones you should screw.' In a recent episode, the DEA had tried

74

to send a small team of agents, including Ronane, to Guatemala to help the authorities fight drug-dealers. It had taken six months and as many congressional meetings before the agents could be despatched. By then the damage had been done and the network they had gone to fight had become impregnable. Ronane went to the door. 'You'd better get some sleep. And block the door. She might change her mind. And it won't be because you're so damn pretty.'

'Up yours, Ronane.' The words bounced back off the closed door.

He had turned back into the room when Ronane opened the door again.

'Now what?' barked Marshall.

'That's the second time someone's talked about being blown up.'

'It registered. I'll tell you if I come up with anything.'

'Goodnight, Marshall.' Ronane slammed the door behind him.

Marshall set his defences once again, then spread the sheet and blanket under the doubled-up mattress, curled himself under its protection, and went to sleep on the floor. His gun, now fully loaded with new shells, lay next to his hand.

In Washington, nearly 2,000 miles to the north-east, the city awoke to celebrate the Fourth of July.

In Mexico City, with the oppressive heat that comes with morning, Marshall slept the sleep of a child and dreamt of a place where the rain fell continuously and it was always, always, cool to your face.

7

WIDENING THE FIELD

Manchester Royal Hospital
Manchester

THE SURGEONS WERE OPERATING ON THE YOUNG CONSTABLE WHEN
Soulson arrived at Manchester Royal. The press were already outside
but he was met at the entrance by Armitage and they pushed
their way into the hospital with no comment. He knew the Police
Committee would accuse him of hogging the publicity at the expense
of the injured officer. There was little he could do about that; he
always spent time with bobbies who were injured. He joined Gordon
Daley, Assistant Chief Constable of the Uniform Operations Branch,
and Phil Murray, Superintendent of 'A' Division, which covered the
city centre.

'It's a miracle he isn't dead,' said Daley as he drank from a
hot mug of tea the receptionist had given him. 'Bloody miracle.
With what happened to him. Sliced right through his—'

'Take me through it,' said Soulson. 'Without the anatomical
details, please.'

'He was walking his beat on Portland Street, watching the Fri-

76

day night crowds, when he heard someone shouting for help,' said Armitage, cutting in before Daley said more which could irritate Soulson.

'What time?'

'Just after eleven. He called in on his shoulder radio to Bootle Street Station. Said he required immediate assistance.'

'Was it a man or woman shouting for help?'

'He didn't say. Just that he needed immediate assistance and that he was going down the small lane behind Nicholas Street. That's where the noise was coming from. He said there were no street lights.'

'When we investigated later, we found all the lamps had been smashed,' added Murray.

'The shouts continued, and he kept talking on the radio to his controller. We've got a tape.'

'Have you heard it yet?' asked Soulson.

'No. They've got it at Stretford. But I know the gist of it. He just said it was dark, then he said he saw two men struggling with a third. He yelled "Someone's being mugged," into the radio and that he was going in. I suppose he started running towards them and that's when he ran into the wire.'

'It was stretched between a lamppost and a road sign on the opposite pavement,' came in Daley. 'A piano wire with razor blades soldered on to it. He must've been going full pelt when he ran into it.' Daley stopped suddenly, not wanting to go on and feel Soulson's wrath again.

'Go on,' Soulson encouraged Daley.

'It sliced through his jaw, split his bottom lip then into his throat, cutting through his larynx. If his chin hadn't taken the impact first, he'd be dead now.'

'When did support get there?'

'Two, three minutes later. There was no-one around. And no-one saw anyone running away.'

'What do the doctors say?'

'That he'll probably make it. But he'll be on critical for a long time.'

'He came round once when they got him here. Grabbed a nurse's pad and pencil and wrote something,' said Armitage. 'Three blacks.'

'That's all?' Soulson was irritated by his own impatience. 'Don't answer it. It took enough guts for him to write that.'

'Not like the blacks to come into Chinatown. Not to mug one of their own.'

'You saying it's a set-up?'

77

'Got to be,' said Murray. 'With that wire stretched across like that.'

Twenty minutes later, after the police had searched the area, all they could report was that nobody in Chinatown remembered seeing anything; nobody had a word to say.

'They're turning their efforts on to us,' Armitage commented when he was finally alone with Soulson in a small office the hospital had put aside for them. 'Either yobbos messing around . . . or could be a warning, Chief. Mind your own business, or we'll start cutting you up.'

'Not the blacks. Not here in Chinatown. They're not going to bring the fight out of their domain.' Neither man spoke for a while. Eventually Soulson said, 'You know the Chinese community. I'd like to speak to someone. At the top.'

'They'll want to handle things their own way.' Armitage knew Soulson was talking about the Triads. 'It's in their nature.'

'It's not in their nature to attack *us*. Maybe we should work this thing out together.'

'That's dangerous. You've got enough enemies. If anyone gets hold of that . . .' Armitage shrugged. 'I'll do it. That way—'

'No,' interrupted Soulson. 'I need to hear for myself.'

'They may not want to see you.'

'Then again they might. We could be on the same side here.'

'We're talking heavy villainy. These people will not want to—'

'Just do your best. Arrange a meeting.'

'Yes, Chief.'

Louise Spencer, the Chair of Manchester Police Authority, arrived ten minutes later. 'Thought you'd be the first here,' she said, when the hospital official had left them alone in the small room.

Soulson didn't answer. Politicians found it difficult to understand that not everyone had an ulterior motive for their actions.

'What happened?' Spencer continued.

'We're not sure,' he replied testily. 'The officer's still on the critical list.' Soulson stood up and crossed to the door. 'Excuse me, but there're things I need to do.' He left the room with Armitage following. 'Some people . . . ,' he said, once in the corridor, '. . . make you wonder, eh? Listen, you get going on what I asked you. I'll go along and find out what's happening. Tell Paul Job where you are.'

It was after nine in the morning, ten hours after the attack, that the young policeman came off the critical list. With the use of microsurgery for which the hospital is famous, the surgeons had

78

healed his deep cut. They told Soulson the young man would never speak naturally again, that he might be able to use an electronic voice box for communication. They'd saved his life, but his days as a policeman were over.

Soulson spent half an hour with the young officer's wife; sat and listened to her talk about her husband's hopes and ambitions. 'He wanted to be like you,' she said. 'Looked up to you. Wanted to be a Chief Constable one day.' He nodded sympathetically; there was really nothing he could add. Nothing made any difference now, the young officer's career had been wound up for him. He admired the wife as she spoke; there were few tears and no remorse. She was of good northern character and she would get on with what would be a most difficult task. She reminded him of Mary and he felt a great warmth for her. He wanted to put his arm round her and comfort her, but knew that wasn't appropriate. Eventually he left her and rejoined Armitage outside the ward to which the young policeman had now been moved.

'What time did Spencer leave?' he asked Armitage.

'Just after one this morning. She asked to be kept in touch.'

'Sod her,' he cursed, uncharacteristically.

'He's a brave young copper,' continued Armitage. He held up a large pad of paper. 'As soon as he came round, he grabbed one of the nurses' pens and made as if he wanted to write. They gave him a pad. He put this lot down. Not very detailed, but tells us what happened.'

Soulson took the pad and read it; spidery and weak in its form, sketchy in its content. 'Blacks,' he said, when he had finished. 'How can he be sure?'

'He's sure. Otherwise he wouldn't have put it down.'

'What the hell are they doing here? This isn't their turf.'

'Like I said. A message. For us.'

'And for the Chinese. Otherwise they wouldn't have come into their patch.' Soulson handed the pad back to Armitage. 'Did you get in touch with anybody?'

'I asked a few people. Nothing's come back yet.'

'Tell them about this. That'll get them going.'

'OK. You going home now?'

'Just to catch up with a little sleep. You'd better do the same. But I'd like to see the bobby.'

'No point, Chief. They sedated him and he won't know anything.'

After Soulson had checked with the surgeon on the young policeman's condition and said a final few words of comfort to his wife, he was driven home by Paul Job. It was a silent journey, Job knew when not to interrupt his Chief's brooding thoughts. It took nearly an hour in the morning traffic and Soulson told his driver to stay in the guest-room in case something erupted and they needed to get quickly on the move once again. It didn't matter to Job; he was long since divorced and with the exception of the odd visits to his two teenage sons, devoted himself to his duties and his charge.

It was a simple house; the sort an estate agent's details would describe as a detached, three-bedroomed, two-storeyed house with easily maintained garden in the town of Wilmslow, the heart of the stockbroker belt. He had bought it because he believed it was the type of house Mary would have wanted Tessa to be brought up in. Tessa, who still lived with him, had made it into a home since she was a teenager. But now that she had a full-time career, she had fallen into the same habit as her father and used it as a functional base from which to operate. The result was a house which appeared to have stopped in time, full of a young girl's teenage memorabilia, photographs and awards from Soulson's developing career, and furniture that always seemed to have been there.

Soulson was asleep as soon as his head hit the pillow; it was a gift that he enjoyed. Whatever the problems, they disappeared as soon as he went to bed.

The phone rang three hours later.

It was Armitage. 'They've agreed to a meet,' he said. There was no point in saying anything else. Even a Chief Constable's phone might be bugged. 'Where will you be at seven?'

'In Stretford.' Soulson planned to be at police headquarters by then.

'OK, Chief. I'll treat you to dinner tonight.'

'How's the lad?'

'Hospital says he's doing well.'

Soulson put the phone down and slipped out of bed. He put his robe round his shoulders and went to wake Paul Job.

'Tea'll be ready in a minute, Chief,' he heard Job shout from the kitchen. Soulson grinned. He never surprised his driver. He'd have been out of bed as soon as that phone rang. He knew Soulson stayed awake once he'd come out of a sleep. Soulson went into the bathroom and showered. Afterwards, as he dried himself, he smelt the bacon cooking. He speeded up. He suddenly felt very hungry.

It was nearly three when they got to the Stretford HQ and Soulson climbed the stairs to the eleventh floor of the modern building as was his usual habit.

'Anything that needs immediate attention?' he asked Valerie, his secretary.

'Press, Louise Spencer, Home Office about information from last night's accident,' she replied.

'Not what I'd call important,' he said drily. He saw her smile; she was used to his dismissive attitude to that which others took to be important. 'I need Roy and no interruptions,' he continued.

'And a tea?'

'And a tea,' he smiled as he entered his office.

The tea and Armitage arrived at the same time. It always amazed him, her ability to know the moment he had entered the building and get the kettle on in time for him before he had settled at his desk.

'OK,' he stared firmly at Armitage when Valerie had closed the door on them. 'Tell me why the Chinese are involved?'

'I really don't know, Chief.'

'You may not know, but you'll have some ideas. These are your friends, Roy. You married into them. You'll know more than most.'

Armitage didn't react immediately. In all the years they had known each other, this was only the second time one of them had crossed the line that separated family from duty. When he finally spoke, it was considered and deliberate. 'I'm still an outsider. When it comes to stuff like this.'

'Come on, Roy. Outsider or not, there's things you pick up that we don't.'

'I can only give a view.'

'Anything . . . that you think will help.'

'The Chinese have no idea why they're coming under attack.'

'Is it the blacks?'

'They're in there somewhere. But the Chinese don't believe they're behind it. They don't think they've got the intelligence, or the ability.' Armitage shrugged. 'But I don't think that's right. The Chinese have a natural disdain . . . a mistrust of everybody. Even us whites. To them, we're all barbarians.'

'Even you?'

Armitage smiled. 'Yes, even me. Even with a Chinese wife and three kids. Even me.'

'I never knew.'

'Listen, no regrets. Given the chance, I'd marry Linda all over again. But there is a difference. Even after all this time.'

'Tell me what you know.'

'Not much. I can just give you history. But it's a starting point. What do you know about the Triads, Chief?'

'Not that much. Just that they're there. Three main gangs. And they live off the Chinese community.'

'The Sui Fong, the 14K and the Wo Sing Wo. They're the three gangs. Stretch all the way back to Hong Kong and then into China. And it's getting worse. With 1997 coming and Hong Kong leaving British jurisdiction, there's going to be a rush for those characters to get over here. Manchester's one place they're definitely going to be heading for.'

'That's all we need. Damn secret societies.'

'How much of a history do you want?'

'I know up to Glasgow.' Soulson referred to the 1987 incident in that city when forty-six-year old restaurateur Cheng Pic Wai, John Cheng to his Glaswegian friends, was attacked by four men wielding the long, traditional knives of the Triads as customers ate their evening meal. Cheng, an expert in martial arts and a Master in the ancient Chinese art of self-defence, Sing Gung, avoided being decapitated by his violators, and was lucky to live through such a violent onslaught. One of the men continuously smashed at his legs with an iron bar, but Cheng battled to ignore the pain, even though his legs were pulped, in an attempt to stay on his feet and defend himself. His strength of mind overcame the pain, but could not avoid the knife slashes that resulted in five tendons being sliced in his upper and lower arms, an artery being severed and his flesh being opened to the bone in many places. He lived because of his mental and physical strength and his religious belief in his ability to defend himself through the martial arts at which he was an expert. Although a Home Office Commission had stated in 1985 that 'there are no Triads operating in the UK', John Cheng was willing to co-operate with the Strathclyde Police.

'Cheng's evidence . . .' said Armitage '. . . and the ensuing investigation, which included finding a sliver of metal from one of the traditional Triad knife blades in his wrist bone, proved that Triads were well and truly established within the British criminal culture. That opened doors to us where we found Triad Sui Fong organizations in Southampton, Nottingham, Sheffield, and here in Manchester.'

'Was it all one organization, or a series of individual Triads?'

'In the end, it's all the same. They traced it back to Hong Kong and a Sui Fong chopman, Golo Ming, eventually broke the cardinal rule of the Triads by giving answers to the Glasgow police.

That resulted in the conviction of two members of the team that had been sent to chop John Cheng. It was the breakthrough we needed, and . . .' Armitage smiled ruefully '. . . the Home Office revised its view that "there are no Triads operating in the UK".'

'They never change. Even over this drug thing. Sorry, go on.'

'The police authorities throughout the country applied their efforts to dig out more information on the Triads. Wasn't easy. In view of the natural secrecy of the Chinese communities. They discovered the insidious nature of the three main Triads. Gambling, extortion, prostitution, even video piracy. It's an organized criminal community that reaches into every part of Chinese life throughout the UK.'

'I know that. What about drugs?'

'The biggest earner was heroin. They controlled the flow of the stuff into Britain. It came in through Liverpool and the London docks. The growth of Manchester as a drug centre only a few miles from Liverpool and at the centre of the road and rail systems to the rest of the country just happened.'

'So why has everyone held back on them?'

'You know that as well as I do, Chief. The Triads might be part of the criminal sector, but their main targets are their own communities. In our society, if it's not the whites getting hurt, only some Chinese, who gives a damn?'

'Don't get too personal,' warned Soulson.

'What the eye doesn't see, the heart doesn't grieve. Come on, Chief. The only reason we're getting this involved with the Triads is because they've crossed the line. Because they're having a go at the blacks and some of the ordinary public could get hurt.'

'Unfair.'

'If the Moss Side gangs weren't passing drugs outside their own lot . . . it's only because they're pushing their shit into our kids that we're taking them on.'

'Let's not go into that right now.' Soulson steered the conversation back to where he wanted it. 'Are the Triads about to expand their ambitions?'

'I don't think so,' replied Armitage. 'It's not something they want. Not unless someone forces them into it.'

'Why? I don't see the point.'

'There's a fear that . . . ' Armitage pulled back suddenly.

'Come on, Roy. You're only one side here.'

'. . . that someone's after their heroin distribution.'

'Don't see that. Most of the world's heroin comes out of South-East Asia. They control both the manufacture and the distribution.'

Soulson clucked to himself. He hated it when he sounded as if he was talking about selling lollipops or chocolate bars.

'Manufacture, yes. But everyone else is in on the distribution. Even the Nigerians have got into it in a big way. They're natural traders. It's just another product to them. Latest reports show they handle thirty per cent of the world's supply.'

'That much?' Soulson was genuinely surprised.

'That much. Shotgun couriers. They stuff the heroin, in small plastic bags, into the couriers . . . make them swallow it, then send ten people on every plane and ship into Europe. So we catch three per trip. There's still seven of the bastards getting through. And so what if they go to jail. Their families are looked after back home, until they've served their sentences and go back to Nigeria.'

'What's that got to do with the Triads? Or Moss Side?'

'I don't know, Chief. But this whole thing is about drugs. That much I'm sure about. And it goes back to someone who's prepared to take on big organizations, like the Triads. The blacks in Moss Side wouldn't be doing that. Not unless they had someone behind them who made them feel confident enough to come into Chinatown and take this lot on.'

Soulson sat quietly for a moment. The enormity of what he was being told frightened him; this was not something a local police force, unarmed and under-resourced, was equipped to fight against. 'Who're we meeting later on?' he asked finally.

'Lau Lap Wong.'

'Never heard of him.'

'Freddy the Duck.'

'So that's his name.' Soulson knew Freddy the Duck, Freddy Wong, one of Manchester's best-known restaurateurs. His restaurant was renowned for its Peking Duck; even the Chinese ate at Freddy's because the quality of his food reminded them of home. Soulson and Freddy had met many times over the years, even been on the same charity fund-raising committees. 'Is he involved with the Triads?'

'Not directly. But one of his partners could be.'

'What the hell's "*could be*"?'

'Henry Lip. Runs an import-export business. I think he's a 426.'

'426?'

'They use numbers like we use titles. Highest is a 489. That's a Shan Chu, a leader. Deputies and Incense Masters are 438s. Then come Red Poles, they're 426s.'

'Like Henry Lip?'

'Yes. Goes all the way down till you get to the foot soldiers, the Sze Kau. They're just 49s.'

'All start with 4.'

'Just the way they do it. Like we call people Mister.'

'You knew all this and you kept it to yourself?'

'It's all in the files, for anyone who needs to know.'

Soulson decided not to expand the subject. He knew Armitage was a good and honest police officer and that his duty always came first. But every bobby had a conflict of interest somewhere in his life, where the line was there to be crossed. With Armitage it was family and there were no points to be gained by pushing him over that line. 'I'd like to see anything we've got on the Triads before the meeting,' he finished. 'Just to bring me up to date.'

They then covered all the other incidents that had occurred in the last few weeks. There was nothing new to add, but it helped them both put their minds in order. Valerie came in with another pot of tea for them both and copies of the day's papers.

'I've checked with the hospital,' she said, as she left the office. 'He's still doing well.'

The papers all carried the attack on their front pages. 'Cowardly', 'Horrific', 'Vicious' were the words used in the headlines. Soulson smiled when he saw the headline in one of the tabloids that referred to the attackers as 'Yellow Bellied Scum'. He hoped the Chinese wouldn't take that personally. The local paper, the *Manchester Evening News*, displayed a picture of the grief-stricken wife being comforted by the Chair of the Police Authority, Ms Louise Spencer. He cursed loudly and threw the paper at Armitage. 'The things they do for votes,' he snapped.

Armitage left him ten minutes later and went to get the report on the Triads. Not wanting to be alone, his sense of frustration eating away at him, Soulson walked round the large headquarters building on one of his general, unannounced tours. The atmosphere was subdued; it always was when one of their own came under attack. He joked and encouraged and touched shoulders and squeezed arms as he toured the departments. They enjoyed his reassurance and felt pleased that he had taken the time to see them.

When he returned to the office, he saw a confidential package on Valerie's desk. 'Delivered by Hand' was written across the top.

'What's this?' he asked, picking up the package.

'From the Town Hall,' Valerie replied. 'We've X-rayed it. No bomb.' It was a precaution they took automatically. The police were a natural target for the IRA and other terrorist factions.

He sat at his desk and opened the package.

'Compliments from the Chair of the Police Authority' proclaimed the card.

There were six brochures inside. Of middle-market cars. One was for a Rover 215, a small four-door four-seater. He felt the shame and anger flush over him and he hurled the package into the waste-paper basket. *To hell with them. A young bobby's nearly killed and they send him a pile of brochures about his next car. You couldn't fight these people out in the open. They made their own rules and played them within the law. But their actions were as insidious as anything the Triads or the blacks . . .* he stopped himself. *Control. Smile at the bastards. What the politicians did wasn't that important. Nobody got killed, nobody got decapitated. And why just blame the Chinese or the blacks. The whites, his own race, were as heavily into villainy as anyone else.* If he wasn't careful, this whole thing would become racist. He had to think himself into beating these people. *Being under-resourced didn't mean you couldn't win.*

He rang Armitage and decided to form his own task force, at this stage no more than a think-tank to explore all the information they already had. 'I want six on it,' he told Armitage. 'One senior officer, probably Steven White. Two sergeants, one uniform and one detective. Both with experience in Moss Side and in Chinatown. One from the Criminal Intelligence Unit and two bobbies from the beat. One black and one Chinese.'

'They'll want a report at the Police Authority,' replied Armitage. 'You know they expect a—'

'This is on a need to know basis only. Find the people, use Steven White. But this is top secret. I mean that, Roy. Get Valerie to take minutes of any meetings. But she keeps the only copy we make. If we fight back, then we do it on our terms.'

'What about the other?'

'Leave it.' Soulson knew what his subordinate meant. 'Let's get information first. Use the Intelligence Unit. I want all options open.'

With Armitage off the phone, he settled down to read the report on the Triads. There wasn't much he hadn't already been told; it dealt with the history and development of the organization.

The origins of the Triads date back to within a few decades of the death of Christ. Their growth was spasmodic and uneventful until 1674, when the Chafing Dynasty's second emperor was supported by a monastery of Siu Lam Buddhist monks, martial arts experts, who helped defeat an insurrection in Fukien. In his gratitude, he presented the abbot with an imperial seal, a great honour in its time. This attracted the envy of other courtiers who set about discrediting the abbot by informing the emperor that the Siu Lam monks were plotting an uprising against him. As a result, the monastery was burnt to the ground and over one hundred monks were killed, either burnt to death or put to the sword. Five escaped, and after a treacherous journey to the safety of other monasteries, they formed the Hung Man, or family as it became known. The five monks involved five monasteries which eventually grew into five secret societies, determined to exact their revenge on the dynasty that had so cruelly destroyed the Siu Lam monastery. Robin Hood in their approach to the community, by the early 1900s the original five secret societies had turned to crime, lived by a 36-point charter which resulted in death if the codes were broken, and were more reminiscent of the Mafia than of the monasteries which had inspired them. Through sailors visiting foreign ports, the Triad families soon spread their net of influence to most Chinese communities throughout the world. The violent, ritualistic and uncompromising rules of the homeland soon became the language of the Chinese communities in Britain, North America and Europe. Their great moment came during the Boxer revolution in China, that most famous war when the Chinese peasants fought the barbarous Americans, Europeans and Japanese who had carved up China between themselves. But they were no match for the mechanized and sophisticated military muscle of the Western powers who crushed the revolution. Most major cities were taken over by foreign troops and a most terrible revenge was exacted on the Boxers; whole regions were wiped out, rape and murder being the devices that brought about relative order. The final result was that the Hsin Chung, a Triad based in Hunan, supported Sun Yat-sen in a final revolution that toppled the Chafing Dynasty and established the Chinese Republic in 1911.

With no real role to play in a future political world, the Triads were used by the Western powers to create insurgence in China. In return they were protected in Hong Kong and by Chang Kai-shek's new Nationalist government, their base for the world expansion. The common enemy was now the communists, and the Triads used this fear in Western governments to work their way into Western cities. The gangs became richer and bigger, and they naturally kept their sphere of influence within the Chinese communities. It wasn't until 1977, after an armed battle between Chinese men armed with traditional swords and long knives in Queensway, West London, that the authorities realized the strength of the Triad gangs. Only this time it didn't just involve the

87

Chinese. This war was about heroin, pure No. 4 grade, and was part of
a world-wide attempt to distribute this most vicious drug into the United
States through Europe. Gang war erupted and the British police, itself
ripped apart by a series of disciplinary actions, was too slow to react.
By the time it did, the networks were in place, and Britain and Holland
became the major stepping-stones into that most lucrative of markets,
America and its ripe-for-drugs cities. Although British police forces
worked with the American Drug Enforcement Administration, their
main effort was within their own areas of responsibility. But in those
areas the Triads controlled and traded within their own communities.

Soulson put the report down. Unofficially, as Armitage had said
before, what the eye didn't see, the heart didn't care about.

Until now.

Until people were getting killed on the streets of Manchester.
And that did affect Charles Soulson. Especially when they were
also attempting to kill off his policemen.

He put down the report as Valerie came in. It had gone six and
she was off home. He asked her to tell Armitage and Paul Job to
be ready for him by six forty-five. When she had gone, he went to
the window and looked out. The mounds of rubbish ran along the
pavement, like ragged soldiers on duty. He shook his head. Nothing
was going right. Maybe tonight it would start to change. He went
back, poured himself another tea from the thermos Valerie had left,
and concentrated on the report.

As Soulson read, three miles to the south-east, at the Northenden
Road General Store which also doubled as a post office, John Winters
was closing the front door after a hard day's business.

It was a small shop, with the post office taking up little more
than a counter space. The shop filled the ground floor and steps,
through the door at the rear, led up to the first-floor flat where
Winters lived with his wife Gayle. As was her custom, she had
left him fifteen minutes before closing time to go up and prepare
supper.

In his late fifties, now soft and fat after a lifetime of working
in food shops, Winters didn't take much notice of the black youth
who was examining the windows of the store. It was something he
was used to, being next to a major bus stop. As he pulled the
blind down on the door and swung the plastic sign from 'OPEN'
to 'CLOSED', his mind was already taking in the smells and taste of
the steak and kidney pie Gayle was preparing and he didn't notice

the other two youths, both black and no more than twenty, join the window-shopper.

Winters pushed the door shut. Before he could latch it, there was a knock on the glass. Still warm with the anticipation of his meal, he half-opened the door and looked out, taking no precautions, expecting no danger.

'Need some fags, sport,' the window-shopper smiled.

'We're closed,' Winters responded, now seeing the other youths filling the doorway behind the first one. He sensed danger, but in a flabby kind of 'it isn't happening to me' way.

'Just one packet,' pleaded the youth. 'Come on, just one packet.'

John Winters sighed, opened the door and beckoned the youth in. 'You'll cost me my licence,' he said. 'But just you on your own,' he added, trying to take command of the situation.

'They want some fags as well,' said the youth, pushing past Winters and coming into the heart of the shop. The other two filed past the shopkeeper.

Leaving the door open, Winters walked round to the back of the counter. 'What cigarettes did . . . ' He stopped sharply as one of the youths turned and kicked the door shut behind him. 'You don't need to shut the door,' he said, suddenly alarmed.

'You've got something that doesn't belong to you,' said the first youth.

'Look, there's no need for all this.'

'All what?' was the reply as the youth pulled a thick metal bar from under his coat. 'You don't mean this, do you?'

Winters backed away from the counter, then leant forward and hit the till. The drawer clanged out, it was full of small change and notes. 'Take what you want.' He signalled to the shelves around him. 'Cash, cigarettes . . . just help yourself.'

'We don't want pocket money, sport.' The youth turned to one of his companions. 'Show him what we've got.' The second youth pulled a sawn-off shotgun from under his jacket. The leader turned back to Winters. 'Like I said, you've got something that doesn't belong to you.'

'I don't keep extra cash here. Not from the Post Office. It gets banked when . . . ' he tailed off into silence as the leader started to laugh.

'Your wife, sport,' said the leader, suddenly harsh, the laughter wiped off the slate. 'You want us to get her down here?' He leant forward as he saw the panic in the shopkeeper's eyes. 'You heard about us black boys? Big . . . black boys. Make your wife really happy. Only you may not like watching her enjoy herself. You really want that, sport?'

'Tell me what you want.' Winters feared the worst.

'I already did.' He watched Winters' fear. 'The laundry. I want the fucking Chinese laundry.'

Winters shut his eyes. It was the last thing he expected. They weren't just after cigarettes. 'What do you mean?' he tried to fend them off.

'We know everything.'

'Come on, Stash. Someone's going to—' The second youth was stopped by his leader's vicious look.

'Anything else you want to tell him? Like my fucking address?' The leader cursed and swung back to Winters. 'Get it. Or I'll blow your fucking head off.'

Winters decided not to object any further. He scuttled round the counter and over to a small safe behind the post office counter, pulling his key chain from his belt as he did so. He knelt, with the leader of the youths behind him and unlocked the safe. Once he had swung the door open, he reached in and took out a large red metal box. He turned, stood up and handed it to the one called Stash.

'Open it,' ordered Stash. Winters opened the box and displayed its contents to the youth. The box was full of large red envelopes. Winters opened one and Stash could clearly see cash, notes of every denomination. 'How much?' he asked.

'About thirty thousand,' replied Winters.

'No second boxes?'

'That's everything.'

Stash tossed the box to the second youth. 'You two empty them. And don't take no tips.' He waited until they had completed the task. 'Put them envelopes back in the box and leave it on the counter.' He signalled Winters back to the counter. 'Give me your takings for the day, sport. That big money's for the big boys. What's left is for us.'

Winters leant forward and put his hand in the till. As he did so, Stash took a six-inch nail from his back pocket and drove it into Winters' right hand, through the skin and flesh, pinning it to the bottom of the till. Before Winters could react, the youth smashed the iron bar on to the nail, driving it right through his hand and through the base of the money drawer.

'Forget my name, sport,' he heard Stash say. 'Otherwise next time I'll be back and fucking nail more than your stealing hand to the fucking till.' The pain suddenly hit Winters and he started to scream, then passed out. The youths turned and ran from the shop. The car waiting round the corner drew up to the kerb and the youths left for Moss Side. Passers-by saw them, but noticed nothing out of the ordinary.

Gayle Winters came down five minutes later. She'd been watching television and the sound had obliterated her husband's screams.

She didn't scream when she saw him lying there unconscious, his hand pinned to the cash till. She looked round the shop, and once convinced that all was clear crossed to the counter. The sight of her husband in that condition sickened her, but she knew she must act soon if she was to save his life. She reached for the phone.

That's when she saw the safe was open and the box was missing. She found the box on the counter top and opened it, gasping when she saw the empty red envelopes. Family comes before all to the Chinese. Which is why Gayle Winters then rang her brother and told him of the empty red envelopes before she dialled the emergency services for the police and ambulance. Once she'd done that, Gayle Winters, who had left Hong Kong thirty-two years earlier to live in England and marry a 'barbarian' she had fallen in love with, finally turned to the task of comforting her husband and attempting to save his life.

To Gayle her husband was still an outsider. Sad but true. Now that she had completed her duty, she knelt and cradled his head and cried for his pain and his injuries.

Gayle Winters, whose brother was a Red Pole in the 14K, had followed the 30th Ancient Oath of the Triads. 'I must not support or give sustenance to outsiders against the interests of my own sworn brothers. If I do not honour this code, I shall be killed by thunderbolts and myriad swords.'

As the police and ambulance services sirened their way towards the little post office, Freddy Wong's Cantonese Duck Restaurant was packed with office workers enjoying an early meal before going home. The queue stretched up the stairs from the large basement dining area and there was the usual frantic and chatty atmosphere that pervades all successful Chinese restaurants.

Paul Job had parked the car near the entrance. Soulson felt there was little point in concealing his visit to the restaurant. He entered the gaudy-entranced building in Nicholas Street with Armitage. There had been the usual comments and throw-aways from the more forward of those who recognized him, and he smiled and acknowledged them as he always did.

Freddy Wong met him; a warm welcome with hand outstretched as he came to meet his honoured guest. He was a dapper man in a grey pin-striped suit, behind thin gold-rimmed glasses, about fifty-five years old and with the practised and ever-present smile of those who make their living meeting the public. His smile showed why Freddy the Duck was easily recognizable; his top row of teeth were made of gold.

'It's busy downstairs,' Freddy Wong said, turning to lead the two policemen up the narrow stairs that wound round the narrow four-man lift. 'I reserved a small dining-room we have.'

'I didn't know you had rooms up here,' commented Soulson as they climbed the stairs.

'For functions. Christmas parties, private dinners. We own the whole building. We also have offices we rent to others.'

They entered a small room on the second floor. Designed to seat a small party of up to twenty, the room had been cleared and there was a small table for four placed in the middle. On the side, on hot plates, was a buffet of Chinese delicacies and other foods from the menu. A waiter stood by the buffet.

'My colleague will be here soon,' said Freddy Wong. 'Would you like a drink, Charles?'

'Orange juice, if you have some?'

'Of course. I know what you like.' He turned to Armitage. 'Roy?'

'That'll do me, too,' replied Armitage.

Freddy Wong nodded at the waiter who poured the drinks.

'I see there's no rubbish outside,' remarked Soulson, taking his drink.

'Why put off the customers?' joked Freddy Wong. 'We, as usual, look after our own problems. If the politicians and unions want to play games . . .' The restaurateur shrugged.

'I thought the unions said they wouldn't touch anybody's rubbish if it was cleared away while they were on strike.'

'What they say and what they do . . . two different things. When this strike's over, they'll remember how big a Christmas bonus we give them. It helps them forget their principles very quickly. And quite painlessly.'

The door opened and Henry Lip walked in. Shorter than Freddy the Duck, he was dressed in a similar suit, but was fatter and had no need for glasses. Soulson was surprised by his youth, he couldn't have been more than thirty. The introductions were made; the waiter helped them with their choices for the meal, then left the four men to their private conversation.

'Well, Charles,' opened Freddy Wong. 'What can we do for you?'

'I rather hoped it was what we could do for each other.' Soulson quietly cursed his response; he sounded like a second-hand car salesman. He saw the look that passed between the two Chinese. He decided to jam his foot in the door and shoulder it. 'Your people are coming under attack from outside. This is no inter-Triad gang war that you can hide from the authorities. Not when policemen are being dragged in and nearly killed . . . on your territory. Whatever your feelings, whatever your secret ancient codes, in this thing we're tied together.'

It was Henry Lip who answered, smiling condescendingly towards Soulson. 'Triads, Chief Constable? In the old days . . . yes, there were such things. But not today. Not in modern Britain.'

'No such thing as "*lucky money*"?' Soulson referred to protection money, one of the main Triad sources of income.

'No such thing. Nor little red packets that lucky money is delivered in. These are things of the movies, Chief Constable, not of real life. There is no Charlie Chan.'

'Then why are you here, Mr Lip?'

The young Chinese shrugged. 'Because my good friend, Freddy Wong, asked me to meet you. I am a businessman by profession, but a historian by affection. A student of Triad history. Freddy thought I might be able to help you. In matters of history. I know of your support of our community. We appreciate that. And I would take it as a great honour if you would address me as Henry.' He smiled pleasantly at Soulson, then leant forward and chopsticked a mouthful of crunched duck from his plate.

Soulson realized this was a man used to pressure, accustomed to power and being obeyed. He looked at Freddy Wong, saw that he was subservient to the younger man. Soulson knew he was talking to the man at the top. So he smiled pleasantly back at Henry Lip. 'If there were Triads. . .'

'If there were.'

'Exactly. Then why would you think they would now be coming under attack?'

'It would be unusual. The history of the Triads has always been one of isolation. They protected their own communities. They did not find it easy to do business with . . .' Henry Lip paused, the smile still on his lips.

'Barbarians?' rejoined Soulson.

'Outsiders.'

'Didn't the Triads deal in heroin and other criminal activities that involved those outside the Chinese community?' He realized he had crossed the line too quickly, saw the scowl of annoyance cross Henry Lip's face.

'You've been watching too much television. I quite enjoyed Mr Cook's programme.' Henry Lip referred to a January 1993 television show where a well-known reporter, Roger Cook, had infiltrated the Manchester Triad scene with hidden cameras. It had shown an undercover policeman being beaten up and, at one stage, having both legs broken while he was trying to escape. 'It was very flashy, but not the truth. Small-time gangsters made more important than they actually were, pretending to be members of a larger organization. Triads, if they were present, would not deal outside the Chinese community.'

'With respect to prostitution and gambling, protection and . . . even video piracy. But with drugs? Especially heroin. Doesn't that involve the general public? And other criminal groups?'

Henry Lip said nothing for a while. Then he pursed his lips and blew through them before speaking. 'The history of the Triads is to resolve their own problems.'

'In that history, have they ever been victims alongside those they consider their enemies?'

'You mean the police? Outsiders sometimes get drawn into these things.'

'Doesn't that change the situation?'

'The Chinese community keeps to itself.'

'Even if their natural enemy . . . the authorities . . .' Soulson deliberately didn't use the word *police*, '. . . shared the problem? Then what?'

'Triads generally consider all situations.'

'Would they cross the line?'

'Everything is possible.'

'Tell me,' Soulson deliberately paused for a moment before he continued, 'would they, if it suited them, join forces with those who had harmed them, and turn on the authority?'

There was no hesitation from Henry Lip. 'No,' he stated firmly. 'The Triads only fight authority when they have . . . had . . . something to protect. Outside their own communities, and outside their own sphere of activities, they never believed in encouraging trouble. To take on a modern police force in such an aggressive manner, thereby take on a whole country in which they are in a minority, is not something they would ever do. They're not the IRA, Mr Soulson. They want to go on living in this country.'

The door opened and a Chinese waiter came in. He crossed the room to Henry Lip, leant down and whispered in his ear. Soulson watched the fat Chinaman's face, but he gave nothing away. When the waiter had finished, he nodded and waved him away.

'I am sorry,' he said, looking directly at Soulson, 'but business calls.' Henry Lip stood up and offered Soulson his hand. 'I hope I have been of some help.'

'Is this *all* about drugs?' was Soulson's direct response. He didn't want the moment lost, just as he was making contact with the Chinaman.

'Drugs . . .' came Henry Lip's immediate and surprisingly open response, '. . . are greed. Business is greed. With such high rewards, violence is a result of greed. Those who get hurt know what they're involved in. Never forget that.'

'Even the victims?'

'Their choice. It's just business, Mr Soulson. Nothing more. Like automobile manufacturers who make cars, collect knighthoods and know that their cars will kill people because they're too fast. Just a different product in a fast-moving consumer world. In truth, if the market's there, someone will always exploit it.' Henry Lip bowed to Soulson. 'Now, if you'll excuse me.'

Ten minutes later, Soulson and Armitage were out in the street, walking towards the black Jaguar. Paul Job was by the car as they approached and he opened the back door. 'There's a report of a robbery in a Northenden post office,' he said as Soulson slid into the car.

'What happened?' Soulson knew it ran deeper than just an ordinary break-in, otherwise his driver would never have mentioned it.

'Three blacks broke into the post office as it was closing. Don't know what they took, but they smashed a man up and nailed the poor bastard's hand to the till.'

'God!' cursed Soulson. 'When?'

'Report came in about ten minutes ago.'

'How do they know they were black?' asked Armitage.

'Witnesses saw them running out of the shop.'

'All right. Let's get there,' growled Soulson.

It was another thirty minutes before they arrived. By then John Winters had been taken away in the ambulance, still alive but on the critical list. The police were interviewing his wife when the Chief Constable walked in. The officers were surprised to see their chief arrive unannounced. Nearly as surprised as Soulson and Armitage when they realized John Winters' wife was Chinese. In that moment Soulson turned to Armitage. His subordinate's look told him this was the urgent business that had resulted in Henry Lip suddenly being called away.

'Tell me about Freddy Wong,' Soulson demanded of Armitage as they sat in the car once again as it worked its way through the evening traffic towards the Stretford headquarters. 'And Henry Lip.'

There was little hesitation from Armitage this time. His links with the Chinese community came second to his responsibility as a policeman. It was something he had never questioned. As he spoke, Soulson realized that he had been wrong to doubt his subordinate's loyalty to the force and to him personally.

'Both of them live in Bowdon,' began Armitage. Bowdon was the heart of Manchester's stockbroker belt, where houses could cost as much as those in the most fashionable parts of central London. 'And very much part of the community. Heavily into charity work and very well respected.'

'More English than the English?'

'Something like that. Except that Lip lives on what was once a farm. Lots of outbuildings and barns. He's got a big staff, all Chinese. They could be bodyguards. The place could be sealed off as a small fortress. High walls, that sort of thing. Freddy Wong came out of Hong Kong when he was a kid. Henry Lip was born here, second-generation British. They're also Mao Shan.'

'Isn't that a religious order?'

'Yes. Based on martial arts. They meet and practise in Chinatown. I don't know how it works now but their Master used to be Cheng Pik Wai.'

'I've heard that name.'

'Known as John Cheng.'

'The one who was attacked in Glasgow?'

'The same. Cheng used to come down here twice a week to conduct the ceremonies. The Mao Shan is a strict order and both Freddy Wong and Henry Lip are at the top of the hierarchy.'

'Would Mao Shan have been involved in the attack?'

'No. That's not their way. Not something as crude as that. I don't think Winters is that important. Probably no more than a small-time fence, dealing in stolen goods, maybe some drug money, for the Chinese. He married Chinese, so they probably use him for petty cash. Feel they can trust him a little, some hold over his wife

96

somewhere.' Armitage laughed as he spoke. 'No sweat, Chief. They've no hold over me.'

'Didn't think they had.'

'But one of the Triad punishments for those who steal from them is to cut off the thief's hands . . . or nail them to the place where they stole from. Gruesome, but effective. The Chinese way.'

'Except his attackers were black.'

'That's right, Chief. Except they were black.'

Unlike Freddy Wong or Henry Lip, Abdul Paras had never been given to charitable causes or the search for that elusive panacea that hides under the bushes of respectability.

Abdul Paras was black Moss Side by birth and had fought his way to King Rat before he was twenty-one. Over six-foot-nine tall, but of a wiry build, he once had the unlikely dream of emigrating to America and playing basketball professionally. He was fifteen at the time and already over six-foot-five. But his sporting ambitions came to an abrupt halt when his half-sister Shaeron, a twenty-four-year-old prostitute, hurriedly passed him some powdered heroin to watch over one night. It belonged to a boyfriend of hers who was under police surveillance at the time, and he had given it to her to keep safe for him. Shaeron, highly nervous in case she got caught, passed it on to Paras on the assumption that he was only a child and therefore beyond the suspicion of the authorities. Two hours later, the child had wandered into a night club in the city centre and sold the drug on to users for nearly a thousand pounds. When the boyfriend returned for the goods, Paras said he had lost it. The boyfriend understandably reacted strongly and threatened him. In response, the fifteen-year-old swung his large fists and knocked him to the floor. The boyfriend reached into his pocket and took out a knuckleduster, different from most in that it had a dozen minute steel fish-hooks welded on to the knuckles.

Before he could put the weapon on his hand, Paras had wrenched it from him and then kicked him in the head. When the unfortunate boyfriend raised himself once again, he saw the mountainous youth above him, his legs spread apart, the knuckleduster now firmly strapped to his right hand. It was also the last thing he ever saw. Paras, with one powerful slash, ripped his face from ear to ear, the fish-hooks doing their worst until his victim blindly sank into unconsciousness.

Shaeron, downstairs in the family sitting-room, turned the television volume up and went on watching Coronation Street. She didn't know who was screaming, but wanted no part of what was going on upstairs. She stayed like that until Paras walked in, his arms and T-shirt covered in blood, and watched him cross the room and switch off the television set. 'I was watching that,' she complained.

He shrugged, then took off his clothes and stood naked in front of her. 'They need washing,' he said.

But all she saw was the size of his erection against the blood that spread across his midriff. Without knowing why, she rose from the armchair, crossed over to him and started to lick the blood from his stomach, then, with the instincts of her profession, tried to slip his hugeness into her mouth. It was too large for her, so she turned, slipped her skirt up and her skimpy knickers down, and knelt subserviently in front of him. She gasped as he forced himself into her; for all his manliness it was the first time he had ever mated himself with a woman. There were a few frantic strokes, then he ejected his youthful and desperate passion into her. When he had finished, he ordered her out of the house to go and pick up a client and keep bringing the money in. She accepted his commands; it was the way it would be from now on.

While she was out, he bundled the unconscious boyfriend into an old sheet and dragged him down to the small cellar, where he calmly strangled him. He would wait until the early hours before taking him out and dumping him in Alexandra Park.

When Shaeron returned with a client, Paras was lying on his bed, his hands folded behind his neck as he lay and watched the nicotine yellow forms on what had once been a white ceiling. The knuckleduster, now in the small, purpose-built leather pouch that he had found in the boyfriend's pocket as he had robbed the corpse, sat shapeless on his chest. Through the thin wall that separated their bedrooms, he listened to the antics of the punter sweating over Shaeron. He smiled with satisfaction. Within a week he had become a drug-pusher, a pimp, a tough guy and a stud. Life was good. He never thought about basketball again.

'Thirty fucking grand!' Paras exclaimed for the third time to the Irishman who sat opposite him. 'Thirty fucking grand!' he repeated for the fourth time, shaking his head at the incredulity of it all.

The two men were sitting in a darkened room at the back of the Club Nilus, the drinking and gambling shabeen in Moss Side which was Paras's base. It was his club, acquired in the manner of corporate takeovers that is normal in Moss Side. He had simply walked in four years earlier, on his twenty-first birthday, with his twelve disciples, all armed with baseball bats, and battered the hapless owner to the linoleum floor. When he'd taken his rightful seat in the back room, after the clientele had watched the cabaret that was the sudden change of ownership and then gone back to their drinking and gambling, the disciples had sung one glorious reggae rendering of 'Happy Birthday' to their leader. Since that day, nobody had challenged his title to the Club Nilus; it had simply become his headquarters for the distribution of drugs, extortion and women.

'I mean, what's a small-time fucking shopkeeper doing with thirty grand in his fucking till?' Paras lent forward and flipped open another bottle of Becks lager beer.

'I told you there'd be a handsome pile, didn't I?' replied the Irishman. Cohn Bourne was at the other end of the spectrum as far as the physical difference between them. Where one was tall and black, the other was short and pasty white with a shock of red matted hair. 'These Chinks have had thousands of years to get their act right. Old money!' he snorted. 'Old thieves. That fellow was just a small part of the action. There's hundreds of them round the country. Fencing stolen goods, handling protection money, gambling money, drug money. There's millions sitting in cash tills just waiting to be collected.'

'Stuffed them, didn't we?' beamed Paras. 'Stuffed the fucking Chinks.'

Bourne said nothing. To him, Paras was like all men who used violence as their sole weapon. They were battering rams to be manipulated by the likes of the Irishman. Let him enjoy his moment of success. Let him build his belief in his own invincibility. He'd need that strength when the Chinese, and anyone else who wanted to play in the game, came into Moss Side to avenge their position.

'Fancy a bird?' suggested Paras. He saw the Irishman shake his head. He was probably a poofter. He'd never liked doing business with poofters.

'I think we should keep our eyes open,' Bourne urged quietly.

'The Moss is sealed off,' replied Paras, suddenly irritated. 'Just 'cos there's roads in and out with traffic lights. This is a walled city. Like bloody Jericho. Nothing happens without us knowing. However hard they bang their drums. Anyway,' he laughed, 'bloody whites and Chinks all look the same to us. Don't they fucking just?'

'After this one, they'll know someone's after them.'

'Good. Shows we mean business.'

'They'll know it's a Moss Side gang. To the Chinese it could be any one of us. Small gangs, busting each other up to share the drug and tart money. That's all Moss Side is to them. They'll be closing ranks, getting ready to defend what's theirs. They won't worry about the protection game, or the prostitution. They'll know you've got to come out into the open for that. It's the drugs, the skag trail, they'll want to protect. Charlie's never been their game. Leave that cocaine to the South Americans. But skag . . . they've been pushing heroin for a thousand years. It's their network, their roads out of South-East Asia along which the stuff comes. They're not going to let all this go that easily. Just because of somewhere called Moss Side.'

'Except we got our friends, too. As big as them. With as much muscle.'

'They're not in place yet.'

'And your lot. Them as well.'

'We're with you. But we only move when we're ready.'

Paras slumped down in his chair, sulking like a child who had been admonished. 'What we going to do with the money?' he asked eventually. 'With drugs, once you've got rid of it they can't trace it back to you. Nicked money, marked money, that thirty grand's shit to get rid of.'

'We'll look after that end. Just as we did with the weapons.'

'What nett on the thirty grand?'

'Twelve.'

'Shit to that.'

'The weapons have to be paid for.'

'You lot get it all ways, don't you?'

Bourne shrugged. 'It's cost us money, too. We've all got to pay our way. To get where we want to go.' He suddenly wanted to get out of there. The windowless room was oppressive, the smell heavy with the bitter scent of the blacks. It turned his stomach and he wanted fresh air.

'That fucking copper got his oats, eh?' bragged Paras, bringing himself out of his mood. 'Fucking slit him from ear to ear.'

Bourne didn't say anything. As much as he hated the boys in blue, he had disagreed with the sudden attack on the police. The agreement had been to go into Chinatown and cause damage, preferably on a building or parked cars; the action had been designed to show the Chinese that they were vulnerable. It had been Paras's decision to involve the police, and he had done it without consulting Bourne. There'd been no fall-out yet, but the Irishman knew the police would now be alerted. Especially that suspicious bastard Soulson. He wasn't the sort who lets go easily. 'Where's your team now?'

he asked, wanting to change the subject before he let his annoyance show.

'They safe,' laughed Paras. 'They deep in a hole and they safe.'

'Let's hope so.' Bourne rose from his chair and crossed to the door. 'I'm going back to the hotel. See you tomorrow.'

The door closed behind the Irishman and Paras suddenly leapt to his feet, kicking the table away. He swore loudly, cursing everyone and no-one in particular. The door opened and Stash Maxwell came in. A light-coloured black with straight features, his half-caste face was a contrast to his Rastafarian dress, his hair under a baggy multi-coloured woollen hat. Only semi-educated, he knew he would never escape Moss Side without money. He was an ambitious man, and had learnt to hide behind Paras's power, to be his voice of reason and caution. It was a good partnership, yet unlike most who worked with Paras, Maxwell didn't spend his money on jewellery and cars, but banked it and invested it for a future away from Moss Side.

'You OK?' he asked, seeing Paras's rage as he continued to swear.

'Fucking Irish. All whites are the same. All look down on you. All think they're fucking better.'

'Gotta live with it. Till we get what we want.'

'Don't fucking tell me. Don't fucking tell me.'

'Got to be like that, man. They're not in it for money, like the rest of us. It's a bloody religion with them. Get them on your side and you take on the government, the police, the—'

'Yeah, Noddy and Big Ears and Mr Plod, the policeman. You know how much we getting for that robbery? Twelve fucking grand. We take the risk, and we get twelve shitty grand.'

'Live with it. All that'll have an end. With these people there is no end.' Maxwell moved the table back into the middle of the room and righted the chairs Paras had knocked over. He was a good lieutenant, a voice of reason to his leader's rage. They'd been friends a long time, since the days they'd played truant together. 'Come on, man. We need you cool. We got all the aces. And once we get those weapons, we'll lock this place up as tight as white girl's pussy. Just stay cool and we get everything we want.'

'We never waited before for anything we wanted.'

'Different this time. Just stay cool. Let them call the shots. There'll be a time when we take it. Just do like you doing. Be their best friend. OK?'

Paras nodded and sat back on his chair. Then he slammed his vast fist on the table. 'Twelve fucking grand. Fucking peanuts. I just hope those dickheads keep out of trouble.'

Two miles away, the dickheads Paras referred to were tucked away under the railway arches of Knott Mill, not far from where the mutilated Chinaman had been found a few days earlier. They'd kept out of Moss Side, away from their usual haunts, as instructed by Maxwell after they left the small post office. They knew they hadn't been recognized when they bundled the guy in the post office, but if that's the way it had to be, then they were used to following orders.

What they hadn't told Maxwell was that they'd taken nearly a thousand pounds from the proceeds and pocketed it for themselves. Frightened that they might be found with the money by Paras, they had headed back into Manchester, to a couple of white prossies they knew who lived in a city centre flat, and blown the money on booze, cocaine and the girls' bodies. Now, nine hours after the robbery, they had been walking the two miles towards Moss Side, when they saw a police car cruising near Deansgate. To keep clear of the police, and to take cover from the heavy rain that had now started to fall, they ducked under the railway arches and broke into one of the many garage lock-ups under the railway lines.

The police car never saw them, or the grey Ford Escort that had been following the two men ever since they left the prostitutes.

'Fucking nailed his hand right through the till,' laughed the older of the two blacks as he sat on a pile of sacking in the corner of the garage, nursing a last, half-drunk bottle of Martell Five Star Brandy.

'Gotta score,' said his companion, now edgy for some more drugs as he started to come down.

'Wait. Give it twenty minutes and we get back into the Moss and start scratching.' It was the term the blacks used for searching for drugs. 'You want some dagga?'

The younger man nodded and waited as the other pulled out a bag of cannabis. 'Here,' he said, holding it out in the darkness.

The younger man took the bag, and in the dark expertly pulled out the weed, rolled and softened it in his right hand, drew a cigarette paper out from the bag, spread it and rolled a reefer that looked as good as anything that came out of a cigarette packet. Then he passed the bag back to his friend and lit the roach.

'Fucking great night,' said the younger man. 'Those tarts were fucking A.'

'The blonde. She fancied the language, didn't she? Do this, do that.'

'Did more than just talk filth with that big mouth of hers, eh?'

The men laughed together. *Yeah, life was great.*

The double doors crashed open and a grey Ford Escort burst into the lock-up. The two men struggled to their feet, half-dazed by the blinding headlights and the influence of drugs and drink. Before they could fully collect their wits, four men had scrambled out of the car and now surrounded them. In the glare of the headlights, the older black saw that their attackers were small men armed with long steel knives. One of them, wearing a wide-brimmed hat, suddenly reminded him of Harrison Ford as Indiana Jones. That's when he realized it wasn't a knife in the man's hands, but a machete. As he turned towards his companion, he felt the man behind him suddenly move, push past him. The older man cowered, hunched his shoulders to protect himself as he stared wide-eyed at his partner. But his younger friend didn't return the look. There was a swish and the machete scraped over his head. Where there had been eyes and ears, there was now nothing. But the mouth kept moving, the lips seemed to go on talking. Then the remains of what had been his partner slid to the floor.

No point fighting. Maybe they'd let him live. Just keep talking. The older man straightened up and faced his oppressors. He stood taller than them.

One of the men had an axe in his hand and he stepped towards the wall and ran the sharpened head along the corrugated-iron sides. The sound was magnified in the small contained space, a portent of what was to come. As the older man's eyes finally focused in the harshness of the headlights, he saw that they were Chinese. He knew in that instant he was about to die.

'Here, kitty, kitty. Come on, pussy, pussy, pussy,' said the man as he dragged the axe chillingly along the corrugated wall.

The black stood his ground. Death was there and he felt a sense of calm. He suddenly grinned. No point in dying like a jungle bunny. They'd expect him to jump up and down and roll his eyes and start screaming.

'Now you can see what it's like on the other foot, you bastard,' said the Chinaman with the hat and the machete.

'He won't be needing shoes when we've finished,' joined in the man who scraped the axe along the wall, remembering his friend who had been found with his feet hacked off a few nights earlier.

Outside, on Deansgate, the police patrol car cruised along looking for any drunks and revellers who would keep them occupied on what had been, for once, a very quiet night.

The rain fell more heavily and the rubbish stacks by the side

of the road were swollen with the water and burst. The rubbish
started to flow into the gutters and on to the road.

Detective Jill Couples had only called into the Intelligence Unit
to leave her overnight report before going home when the phone
rang.

It was the Drug Division. 'Two bodies. Black. Pretty hacked
about in a lock-up in Knott Mill,' said the tired voice.

'Thanks,' she acknowledged, asked for the address, then hung
up. She was tired, having spent the previous night in an unmarked
car watching an acid house party being raided, then following one
of the organizers. It had been a long vigil; the suspect had visited
three different houses, in different parts of the city, before finally
going home.

There was no-one else in the department, so she decided to call in
at Knott Mill on her way home. It was something they always tried
to do in the unit; get to the scene of the crime while it was still fresh
and before the other departments had taken their chunks out of it.
She left a note on her inspector's desk, got her battered Fiesta out
of the car park and drove to Knott Mill.

The area had been cordoned off and she parked near the line
of flashing patrol cars and made her way on foot to the lock-up.
It wasn't something she enjoyed, this view of the battered side of
life. She'd hated scraping bodies off the street when she'd been in
uniform, and had never become accustomed to the sights of violence
that were a natural part of her life.

The mutilation of the two bodies was as she expected, yet it still
shocked her senses. She started to retch and turned away quickly,
straight into Soulson and Armitage. She tried to stand to attention,
but the natural reaction to the bloody scene defeated her and she
pushed past Soulson and spewed the bile from her empty stomach
against the wall. After a few minutes, the retching subsided and she
leant against the brickwork and started to bring herself under control.

'Never easy,' said Soulson's voice behind her. 'Never get used to it.'

'Sorry, sir,' she apologized. She felt the bile rise again as she spoke.

'Don't be silly,' he replied, concern in his voice. 'Feeling better
now?'

She nodded.

'Detective Couples, isn't it?' Soulson continued.

She nodded again.

'I remember you from before. You know Tessa.'

Another nod.

He realized she was still fighting the nausea and decided to take her mind off what distressed her. 'Intelligence Unit. You're part of a good team there. Excellent work. It's that sort of research that makes us win against these people. What're you concentrating on?'

'Drugs,' she replied quietly.

'What're your specific duties?'

She took a few deep breaths before she spoke. 'Information gathering,' she said eventually. 'Then try and link together, you know, see if there are any common points between unrelated events. I'm covering the Moss Side and Chinese problems.'

'Things seem to be moving slowly.'

'There's not a lot to go at, sir. I mean, I spent last night on surveillance at an acid party. We got a tip that the Chinese were moving in on that market. Which, as you know, is run by the blacks.'

'What happened?'

'Nothing. Yet I could've arrested the dealer I was tailing. I saw him pass tablets three times. But my orders were clear. Only observe. Watch for Chinese, or anything unusual. If passing drugs isn't unusual, then I don't know what is.' She suddenly realized she had gone too far. 'I know that's the way things are going, sir. I've spent time on the American methods.'

Soulson looked across to Armitage. His subordinate's eyes gave nothing away. 'What methods?' he asked Jill.

'General tactics. How they combat drugs.'

'They have an intelligence unit, don't they? The DEA.'

'Wouldn't let us near it. But I speak to a DEA man in London.'

'Who?'

'Chap in their London embassy. John Pentanzi. He covers Europe.'

'Met him?'

'No, sir. Only on the phone.'

'And what do you think of their methods?'

'Different.'

'Why?'

'Because they fight fire with fire,' she answered cautiously, not wanting to criticize openly.

'And we don't?'

'I didn't say that, sir.'

'If you've got a point of view, stand by it.'

'I think it's more difficult for us.'

'How?'

'The politicians. The way we have to tread carefully all the time.

105

Don't upset anyone, anyone the politicians can use to slap down the force. I mean, you wonder if we'll ever be allowed to really take on the crooks. I know your hands are tied, sir . . . but it's bloody difficult to get on and do a decent job.'

'Goes with the stripes,' replied Soulson, slapping three fingers against his upper arm as if signifying a sergeant's stripes. 'We all have to work within the system.'

'Then we haven't got a cat in hell's chance of winning.'

Soulson grinned. 'We'll come through. You feeling better now?'

'Yes, sir. I'm sorry about that.'

'Don't be. Like I said, it's not something you get used to.'

'Thank you, sir.' She returned to the floodlit scene under the arch. The two senior officers watched her.

'She's right, you know,' said Armitage.

'So you keep telling me.'

'Time to take the initiative. Otherwise this sort of thing'll just get worse.'

'Damn it, Roy. We're playing into their hands. If the politicians find out, they'll . . .' He stopped, then grinned. 'Never worried me before. But it is immoral. Goes against everything I ever stood for.'

'We won't win by playing by the rules, Chief.' Armitage nodded towards Jill Couples. 'She's right about that. And if it goes on much longer, they'll be asking for your stripes. Permanently.'

Soulson took a deep breath before he answered. 'OK, Roy. I don't think we've anywhere else to go.' He didn't need to tell Armitage to be careful; he knew the risks they were taking. 'Lord, I can't wait any longer,' he muttered softly, remembering his confessional with the priest and how he had dissuaded himself from taking the matter further.

'What?'

'Nothing.'

Armitage knew when not to push. 'We'll use the girl. It's an obvious way in.'

'Is she trustworthy?'

'As anyone.'

'She's a friend of Tessa's.'

'Could work in our favour. From what I've just seen, she's got fire in her belly and is good at her job. And got the best cover for going over there. Seeing if the American methods have changed since her last trip. Don't worry, I'll run a thorough check on her before I take it any further.'

'All right. But hide her expenses. I don't want the politicians digging this one out.'

'I'm a past master at that.'

Soulson suddenly pulled back. 'One more try. One more go at shutting the bastards down before we go outside our lines of responsibility.'

'Whatever you say, Chief. But, for what it's worth, I think we'll find ourselves back at this point again. In the meantime, I'll make sure the girl's ready if we need her.'

'She's carrying a big responsibility for someone so young.'

'Yeah. And my bleeding pension. I hope she appreciates that.'

8

RENEGADE ACTION

**Drug Enforcement Administration
700 Army Navy Drive
Arlington
Virginia**

'WHY'S HE GONE TO EL PASO?'

'He's been with it a long time. Nobody knows it better than him.'

'Damn it, Ronane . . .' cursed the Deputy Assistant Administrator of the DEA's Operations Division. He reached into his desk drawer and took out a packet of Camels and flipped a cigarette out, '. . . he's the cause of this mess. He could've blown our Mexican operation out of the water.'

'Except they already knew who we were.' Ronane stuck to his guns, not wanting Marshall recalled.

'He's a maverick. We don't need him working on what is essentially a team game. No room for individual action.'

'He's one of our best.'

'He's unorthodox.'

'That's why he's one of the best. If it hadn't been for him, we'd've been suckered because they knew we were DEA.'

'You telling me he knew something?'

'No. But I think he had an instinct, some sort of sixth sense, that something was wrong. Which is why I need him to finish this assignment. Hell, we wouldn't have found out about the Cali girl either.' Ronane changed the subject. 'You'd better watch out for those smoke alarms.'

The administrator was about to light the Camel; he angrily shook his head, then crushed the unlit cigarette into the ashtray in front of him. The DEA building was a cigarette-free work area and the smoke alarms were highly sensitive and could be triggered off by the occasional secret smoker. 'We've got enough stress in this place without having our nerves destroyed by not smoking.' He sighed before he continued. 'He's old-style, Ronane. It worked out this time. But when it goes wrong on these characters, it usually has a big fall-out area. A lot of people could get hurt.'

'He's a good man.'

'Maybe it's time to bring him in. After all these years. Personal advancement. Career expansion. Here at headquarters.'

'Where are you going to put him? In Equal Employment Opportunities?'

'Don't get feisty.'

'He's a pro. He's where he's good. In the field. And that's where I need him.'

'OK.' The administrator held up his hands in mock surrender, then shrugged his shoulders. 'It's your section. But take this from an old pro. When he goes wrong, it'll be in a big way. And it won't just be his pension that's on the line. When that happens, Equal Opportunities might just suddenly look very attractive.' He leant back in his chair. He knew Ronane was right, that Marshall was an exceptional agent. It was just his way of going about things that upset the administrator. 'You're both lucky it wasn't another Leyenda.'

'That crossed our minds.' Ronane had been involved with Operation Leyenda. It had been a successful investigation which, in August 1990, led to the conviction of four defendants on charges relating to the kidnapping, torture and brutal murder of DEA Special Agent Enrique Camarena and the murder of two American tourists in Guadalajara, Mexico, some five years earlier. The investigation had also revealed a multi-billion dollar cocaine-trafficking organization in Mexico and a further indictment of twenty-two high-ranking Mexican government officials, including the Director of the Mexican Judicial

Police. The investigation had opened up the vital artery that Mexico had become in the drug routes that led out of Colombia.

'Why let you guys out alive?' The administrator changed tack.

Ronane shrugged, then recounted the story of the Gurkhas the Texan had told them.

'You believe that shit?' the administrator asked.

'No. But I don't see any other reason.'

'Maybe they just didn't want too much heat. They know we don't like our guys being knocked off.'

'Never stopped them before.'

'No. Except something really big could be brewing. And maybe they just want us putting out fires somewhere else.'

Westbound, US 290
South of Interstate 10
The Road to El Paso
Texas

Happy birthday.

Forty-three today and Marshall was bored.

He trundled the 1988 Ford Granada, 'my old man car' he called it, along the straight-line, single-lane highway that disappeared into the vast blue horizon that is Texas.

He'd set out in the early hours of the morning from his home in San Antonio, set out on a drive that would take him more than twelve hours to cover the 580 miles that stretched along Interstate 10 between San Antonio and El Paso. He enjoyed driving, enjoyed the solace of the Texan countryside that he had made his home. Normally he would have flown but he wanted time to himself. The fiasco in Mexico City had drained him; he hated it when everything went wrong.

He'd got bored after eight hours, two fuel stops and 450 miles of the twin highway that was Interstate 10. When he reached the small town of Brogado, he'd swung south on to the US 290 loop that linked back with I 10 twenty miles farther on. The road was a wide, shallow loop; as far as the eye was concerned it ran in a straight line. Clear of the highway patrols, he accelerated and pushed the car up to ninety. He enjoyed the speed, the feeling of racing along the narrower road with the fields and brush that ran alongside. In the distance he saw a single-wing crop-duster working the fields, up and down with small

110

tight turns at the end of its run as it looped back to spray the next section of the area. It was like mowing a lawn, he thought. He wondered if the field was striped from the air.

Nine miles farther on he came across a road construction sign and he slowed down as the road narrowed into one lane. There were no workmen, just a peeled back section on one half where new tarmac would soon be laid. The road was divided in half by red and white-striped plastic bollards, circular in design like oil drums and spaced some twenty yards apart. He eased the Granada into the left-hand lane, which was now split by a temporary white continuous line, and slowed to the 35 mph limit. The striped bollards disappeared into the horizon.

The boredom increased.

Forty-three years old and not a single birthday card. All he'd found in the mailbox was a bill from the Great Western Boot and Saddle Company and a note from Ronane telling him where to meet in El Paso.

The red-and-white bollards reminded him of candles, waiting to be lit.

Happy Birthday, Marshall.

He wondered if they'd remembered.

He wondered if they knew he was alive.

He wondered if they cared.

Most of all, he wanted her to remember.

'Happy Birthday to you,' he started to sing, loud and untuned.

He swung the car over the line of bollards, on to the untarmacked section, around a bollard and then back on to the main road again.

'Happy Birthday to you.'

He swung back across again, the car digging in as it was violently turned between the bollards. 'Happy Birthday dear Marshall of the DEA.'

He was now slaloming, as a skier would, between the red and white road dividers, swinging between the unmade half and the tarmacked section.

'Happy Birthday to you.'

He started to laugh, his boredom momentarily relieved. He'd passed eight bollards now and he started to count them – nine, ten, eleven, twelve . . .

He was slaloming round the thirty-sixth bollard when he heard the siren and the big highway patrol car filled his rear-view mirror, its red light dancing across his windscreen.

Damn and blast.

He flicked his indicator out and pulled into the right, on the untarmacked section. He waited for the patrolman to get out and come over to the car. He saw the officer had already unclipped his side holster. Marshall kept his hand on the steering wheel. No point in startling the man.

'Out of the car,' said the officer, a gruff Texan of medium build and height. 'And take your time.' He leant forward and pulled the driver's door wide open.

Marshall slid out of the seat and stood up. He saw his reflection in the patrolman's dark shades, then turned, without being ordered to, and spread himself over the car bonnet.

'You done this before?' said the officer.

'Only to others,' replied Marshall, feeling himself being expertly frisked. The sun was beating down on his head and he wished he'd worn a hat. It must've been over 100 degrees. Dry and too damn hot. He felt the policeman step away, satisfied that he was unarmed. His Model 15 was stored in the glove compartment.

'What do you mean, to others? You a law enforcement officer?'

'No. DEA.'

'Turn round. Easy.'

Marshall straightened up and turned round. He still kept his hands high.

'Show me your ID,' ordered the patrolman, holding his hand out.

Marshall carefully reached into his waistband and took out his gold badge. He held it up so that the officer could identify it clearly.

'What the hell were you doing?' said the patrolman, now satisfied that Marshall was who he said he was. As he spoke he clipped his holster shut and moved closer to Marshall.

'Blowing out candles.'

'What?'

'It's my birthday today. I'm forty-three. I was just dodging forty-three of those things. Like on a cake. To celebrate.'

'Jesus. You don't act forty-three. More like three.'

'Sorry. But the road was clear. And the idea just grabbed me.'

The patrolman shook his head. 'Crazy. You drug people sure are crazy.'

Marshall laughed. 'Got to be to do the job.'

'Where you going?'

'El Paso.'

'You're off the route. You need to be on I 10.'

'Driven on it from San Antonio. I wanted to get off it. For a change of scenery.'

'Takes all sorts I guess. OK, you'd better get on your way.'

'Thanks.'

'And take it easy.'

Marshall grinned and climbed into the car. He shut the door.

'Hey!' shouted the policeman.

'Yeah?'

'How many of those things did you duck?'

'Thirty-six.'

'Seven to go, huh?'

'That's right.'

'Lonely way for a guy to spend his birthday. Out here, dodging them.' He indicated the bollards.

'There you go.'

'Hell. You can finish the last seven. But you knock one over, or do eight, and I'll throw the book at you.'

'Thanks. Have a good one.'

'You too. And happy birthday. Make sure you don't come back for your forty-fourth.'

Marshall laughed and pulled away.

The patrolman had cheered him up.

Seven bollards, 140 miles, and three hours later Marshall drove into El Paso. It was five in the afternoon and over 106 degrees in the streets.

Ronane was waiting for him at the Westin Paso de Norte Hotel, near the downtown area and opposite the El Paso bus station.

'Why drive?' was the first thing he asked.

'Made a change,' replied Marshall. 'What's up?'

'Nothing yet. We're at the intelligence unit tomorrow. Want something to eat?'

'Yeah. But I need a shower.'

'OK. See you in the lobby at six-thirty. Casual.'

Ronane, his usual dapper self in a light-grey suit, pink shirt and no tie, was waiting for him when Marshall came down.

'I thought it was casual,' said Marshall in a denim shirt, dark-blue Dockers and ostrich-skin tan Tony Llama boots.

'Washington casual.'

'Christ, we look like a couple of New York hit men in disguise. Out of sorts.' Marshall laughed. They were an incongruous pair; he towered over his small companion.

113

'You want me to go change?'

'No. If they expected DEA men, the last thing they'd expect was an odd couple like us. Where're we going?'

'Kettle Restaurant. Near the border. Steak joint.'

They walked the six blocks to the border crossing.

Magoffinsville, then Franklin, and now El Paso. A settlement that had grown from the days of the Wild West when it was the key all-weather crossing point from East Coast to California and the Pacific. Texas border town and the real Wild West. The Apaches attacked the town, and in 1861, twelve years after those heading west for the Gold Rush had passed through, the army set up a major post, Fort Bliss. Twenty years later the town's population finally exploded when the Southern Pacific railroad tracks were laid from California, and were soon joined by the Santa Fe railroad. El Paso, cattle-drive centre and staging-post into California and Mexico, attracted the wild boys like Billy the Kid, Bat Masterson, Wyatt Earp, Pat Garrett and John Wesley Hardin. Most of them moved on, but Hardin, reputed to be the fastest gun of them all and the taker of forty-four lives, was killed in 1895 and is now buried in Concordia Cemetery, near downtown. Even after that things never quietened down. As well as booming with the industries of agribusiness, manufacturing and the refining and processing of copper ore, oil and gas, El Paso also became a centre for soldiers of fortune, a jumping-off point for those who crossed into Mexico and followed the revolutions of Pancho Villa and whoever else was seeking power at the time. Many of these soldiers fought for the American army in Fort Bliss as well as supporting the Mexicans.

During this time, across the meandering Rio Grande, that great river that is the border between the two countries, the Mexican city of Juarez grew at the same pace as El Paso. In essence they are one city and the inhabitants cross freely over the two border posts that straddle the river, both one way, one into Mexico, the other back into the United States. It is this freedom of movement, albeit through guarded customs posts, that created El Paso's largest untapped market, the flow of cocaine that originated in Colombia and other South American countries and was distributed via Mexico into the lucrative North American markets.

The hustlers were already out in the streets as Marshall and Ronane walked towards the border. Two young women standing by an old rusty Dodge Charger were dealing openly with passers-by; a Hispanic man sat at the wheel, watching for any trouble. The two DEA men didn't need telling that the Charger's engine would be finely tuned and its massive horsepower ready to roar away in the face of any sudden trouble. They crossed the road, towards one of the many boot stores that proliferate in El Paso, the centre of the western boot trade. Marshall stopped and looked in one of the shop windows. Ronane waited patiently for him, his partner's penchant for western wear was well known.

The Kettle Restaurant is a Texas steak house pure and simple. It is near the bridge where the one-way traffic runs from Mexico into the United States. The other bridges spanning the Rio Grande don't bother the authorities as their traffic crosses into Mexico and no drugs pass from the USA into that country. The two men took a place by the window so they could see the customs post as they ate.

The checkpoint straddled the wide four-lane Santa Fe bridge. Segmented into four drive-through channels, a line of stationary traffic stretched back over the bridge into Mexico. The customs and immigration officers questioned the driver of each car as it arrived at the barrier. Occasionally a vehicle would be ordered into a customs bay and would then be searched. Nothing they saw was unusual; it was part of the everyday life at the border post. To the side of the bridge, along a wire, caged-in pavement, pedestrians crossed the bridge into and out of the United States.

'Leaky as a fucking sieve,' commented Marshall. He knew the area well and had served four years undercover in El Paso. He also knew very little came through the border posts, that the drug runners had more sophisticated methods at their disposal.

'Wad'ya want?' asked the waiter, his pad ready in his hand.

'Got some iced water?' asked Ronane.

'I get some for ya. You wanna eat?'

'Prime rib and steak house fries,' snapped Marshall, ordering the large unskinned French fries for which Texas is famous.

'Same for me,' added Ronane.

'And a Pearl Lite.'

'You still want iced water?' the waiter asked Ronane. 'Only we got rationing in this town.'

'No water,' replied the small DEA man.

The waiter shuffled away as the two men watched him.

'What happened to good old-fashioned service?' commented Ronane.

'This is a tough town. Anyway, that's what they believe.'

'Is it?'

'No. No more than most. Just act the way they think you expect them to.'

115

They ignored business while they waited for the meal to arrive. Ronane waxed on about his hobby, fishing. It suited him to relax away from the heat of the battle, just to sit in a small boat and wait to catch a fish. 'You ever heard of bone fishing?' he asked Marshall.

The big man shook his head.

'That's the best,' continued Ronane. 'Down in Florida, near the Keys, in the shadows. You get out there, in a small boat, no engine, just a long pole. And you wait for a bone fish. When they come, you see their little tails sticking up, while they grub round for some food. You take the pole and you just ease yourself along towards it. Like a punt. Don't ripple the water, nothing, otherwise he's off.' He snapped his fingers. 'Just like that. Then, when you're about twenty feet away, you take your rod, small shrimp on the end, and you lower the bait slowly near the bone fish. Real gentle. And you wait. Till he comes and snaps up that shrimp. And then you got a fight. He runs, fastest thing you've ever seen, a hundred, two hundred feet away from you. You just let it reel out. Then he changes direction, comes running at you, so damn fast you got to just keep reeling, don't let that line go slack or he'll snap it. Then he's under your boat and heading out the other way, another hundred yards, just flashing away. And you're reeling out again. Then he changes direction and does it all over again. Fantastic. Can take half an hour to bring him in. That's after taking an hour to get him to take the shrimp.'

'I thought you went fishing to relax?'

Ronane laughed. 'Like busting pushers, huh?'

'Sounds tougher.'

They enjoyed the meal when it came, then, satisfied that they wouldn't be disturbed, Ronane turned to more serious matters.

'There's a big cache of money coming through. They reckon about ten million.'

'Coming out? I thought it usually went in.'

'Things've changed. Ever since BCCI. I don't know why the money's going out, but whoever wants paying off, wants it pretty quick. Without the bank's black network, this is the only way to get it so fast.'

'Colombian money going overseas. Where? Stateside?'

'We think Europe. All we know is that it's Cali money. So it's something big and something damned important. There's also one thousand kilos of pure cocaine with it. Not hydrochloride, but the pure stuff. They're not processing it in any of the usual places like Southern California. That's why we think it's for Europe.'

116

Marshall whistled softly. That was $24 million on the street. The whole thing was a $35 million deal. He knew the European market was the one the Colombians were after. It didn't take much to work out why. In North America, cocaine sold for $24,000 a kilo. In Britain for £26,000. At today's exchange rate, that meant they were getting more than $45,000 for their kilo. He realized, if Ronane was right, this was a lot more than a $35 million deal. 'How did we find out?' he asked eventually.

'Mix of things. Intelligence unit, feeder information out of Colombia and Mexico . . . and a courier that we happened to fall over.'

'Yeah.' Marshall was more than aware of the importance of luck in this most dangerous of games.

'El Paso sector of Border Patrol picked up about thirty runners coming across under a railway bridge not far from the centre of town. Did you know they make over six hundred alien apprehensions just here in El Paso every day?'

'I knew.'

'I forgot. This was your patch. Anyway, they threw them in the cage, ready to go back into Mexico next morning, when this guy had a fit. I mean, he was really sick. When they pulled him to a doctor, they found he was reacting to an overdose. So they stuck him in hospital, pumped him out and managed to pull him through. When they told him they were going to send him back to Mexico, he panicked and asked to see the border patrol. He said he was scared to go back, that there was a death warrant out on him.'

'Mexican?'

'Yeah. He mentioned Rodriguez-Orejuela.'

'Now it gets interesting.' Miguel Angel Rodriguez-Orejuela was a top Cali operator.

'The border police didn't know about Rodriguez-Orejuela. But, just before they sent him back, they contacted us to see if we knew anything.'

'Bless the border patrol.'

'Yeah. We took it from there. Got him into Fort Bliss, then wrapped his clothes round a drowned alien they found floating in the Rio Grande and returned the corpse to the Mexican authorities. For good measure we cut the throat on the corpse just so it looked like he'd been murdered.' It was an old trick and they both knew it didn't always fool the opposition. But the Mexicans don't keep dental records to match and there was a good chance the man's death would be reported back to the Calis.

'What's his name?'

117

'Ramon Cortez.' Ronane laughed. 'Him and six million others.' It was one of the many false names popularized by the aliens who came across the border. 'He says he's a part of a ring that operates out of Piedras Negras.' Piedras Negras was a Mexican border town 400 miles to the south-east which was another route for the drugs trail. 'He was exported up here for a big shipment that's due through. Only while he was up here, he managed to overhear, by chance, exactly what was going on. He's just a carrier, nothing more. The stuff he heard was not for his ears. Trouble was they found out and went after him. He got away and came straight over the border. That's when the patrol picked him up.'

'Why the OD?'

'He was running scared. Stuffed himself full of snow so that he could handle the situation. Guess he just took too much. He tells us there's a cargo coming through. One thousand kilos. Wherever it's going, it's got to be important. And they obviously want to keep this within the family. Secret, secret. Otherwise they wouldn't be after Cortez. He also heard that there was a second shipment of cash. Heard the amount mentioned. I think there was also a second cache of drugs going through. In case the first one got taken. Apparently all the guys at the meeting were pretty high up. Soldiers at the door, everything. He was there, in some warehouse, because he'd fallen asleep earlier on. The only thing he didn't hear was how they were going to do it. Except they're coming over the customs bridge out there.' Ronane pointed out of the window. 'And that it's going to take place by the end of the week.' It was Monday. Four days to go.

'Left it a bit late, haven't we?'

'Not yet. He knows the shipment wasn't in Juarez till Wednesday. They brought his team up from Piedras Negras 'cos they didn't want any locals involved. He also heard the name Rodriguez-Orejuela mentioned as the boss back home.'

'Could be a decoy?'

'He could.' He didn't need to tell Marshall that they took their chances where they could.

'I presume they're using the bridge because that's usually safe from heavy drug traffic.'

'That's what we thought.'

'Who else is on it?'

'Three special agents. That's all the administrator wanted. Low profile, but effective. Two of them are in Juarez, usual undercover stuff. Third's at Fort Bliss, working with the intelligence boys.'

'And me?'

'My wild card. Only this time you get to play the winning hand.' He saw Marshall grin at the memory of the poker game in Mexico City. 'Headquarters didn't think it funny.'

'I was right.'

'I told them that.'

'Did they agree?'

'They shrugged.'

'Am I working alone?'

'Yeah. Radio contact, that's all.'

'OK.' Marshall was pleased. If anyone could churn things up, he could. 'I need to get into Fort Bliss.'

'Fine.'

'Tonight.'

Ronane looked at his watch. 'We'll get back to the hotel and I'll call them.'

They returned to the hotel and after Ronane had made his calls, Marshall hired a car and drove the two of them to the army base.

The DEA Intelligence Centre, one of its most secret departments, used to be based next to Interstate 10 which runs into El Paso. But, in the accountable age that is American democracy, the unit's address was listed in the local Yellow Pages. As a result, this most classified and sensitive of establishments was regularly under the surveillance of criminals as well as the gawking tourists. The unit was rapidly moved behind the barricades and security of Fort Bliss. The vacant lot that now overgrows where the intelligence unit once stood is dwarfed by a massive sign that tells passers-by to 'GIVE US THE DOPE ON DRUG DEALERS' and 'GET PAID BY CRIME STOPPERS. CALL 543–6000.' The unit's new home, Fort Bliss, the centre for air defence activity in the US Army, covers over one million acres and houses over 20,000 troops. Although open to the public, with its high-wire barrier and security gates the fort is vast enough to hide the Intelligence Centre.

After presenting their cards, Marshall and Ronane drove into the army installation and made their way towards the unit. The intelligence team Ronane had asked to see was already present and they settled into a small meeting room with their visitors. Most of the team knew Marshall and, after a brief welcome, they explained what they had done.

'We started with Miguel Angel Rodriguez-Orejuela,' explained Spender, the leader of the group. 'We don't have that much on him, except that he took over day-to-day operations in 1984 when his elder brother, Gilberto, was captured in Spain. There was nothing new. He stays in Colombia, runs the whole distribution network from there. He is mainly responsible for smuggling multi-ton quantities of cocaine into Canada and Europe through the transhipment countries of Panama and Mexico. After his brother's incarceration, he just strapped himself in and got on with the job. Spends wildly, enjoys all the extravagances of living. He also owns a soccer team in Colombia. We even ran that through the computers, to see if there was any link with Europe. There was. The team, without Rodriguez-Orejuela, visited Europe last year. Exchange games, you know, friendly competition. They played against teams in England, Germany, France and Ireland. All good teams, top division stuff. Except in Ireland. They just did exhibition matches there, against small-time opposition. The tour was whistle-stop; one night in a town and move on. Except for Ireland. They spent two weeks there. Only played three matches. The rest was a vacation.'

'Who was with the team?' asked Marshall. He didn't need reminding of the time in 1990 when DEA agents scoured football matches in Bologna, Italy, in an attempt to trap Medellin and Cali leaders who supported the Colombian teams.

'No-one high up. But all Colombians.'

'Where'd they play? North or South Ireland?'

'Both. Dublin and Belfast. We tried, but we don't have any record of who they met, where they stayed, or anything.'

'Ireland doesn't have a serious drug problem. Not in Belfast, anyway. It's something the loyalist and republican paramilitary groups keep under control.'

'Not what our people say in London.'

'All the reports from the British authorities say there's no serious drugs in Belfast.'

'Doesn't mean the paramilitaries aren't getting involved. Higher yield and better returns than robbing a bank. And you don't always get shot back at.'

'They also blow things up,' said Ronane quietly to Marshall.

'Meaning?' asked Spender.

Ronane told them about their work in Mexico City; went over ground he knew had already been logged in the computers. But nobody had mentioned the two remarks about blowing things up. It was a tiny morsel, but something the intelligence unit devoured. Spender despatched one of his team to enter the information they had just received and to start preparing a report on terrorist activities in Ireland.

'Anything else?' asked Marshall.

'Nothing concrete. Except he says one of the guys present at the meeting had a foreign accent. Spoke good English, but foreign.'

'Did you test him?'

'Yeah.' The test was simple. The DEA officers simply ran tapes of people speaking in different dialects until the interviewee recognized one. 'He wasn't foreign. He picked an Englishman.'

'English?'

'That was the nearest. Wasn't quite like it, but close. So we ran some English dialects. Including Scottish. Nearest was from northern England. Liverpool. That's all we picked up. This guy Cortez . . . I guess you want to see him?'

Marshall nodded.

'He's small potatoes. But it stacks up that he's from Piedras Negras. All he's told us about their operations there we already knew. We've grilled him so many times that I doubt he could've kept the same story going over and over. No slip-ups, nothing suspicious.'

'Unless he was deliberately misled.'

'I don't think so. They don't know he came to us. And he nearly died of an overdose.'

'But he didn't.'

'You always were a suspicious bastard.'

'Got like that working with you.'

Spender snorted good-humouredly. 'Crap, Marshall. You're the one going to blow up one day. An unguided missile. That's all you are. Anyway, I think our boy Cortez is clean. I saw the hospital records. Nobody can come that close to an OD on purpose.'

Twenty minutes later, with no further information of interest, Marshall and Ronane were let into the small bedroom that was Cortez's barred prison. A frightened Mexican, he was glad to tell his story once again. The two men listened without interrupting. There was nothing new to what they had already been told.

'This foreigner, the Englishman; you sure he was part of it?'

'Si. He speak good English. I didn't know they spoke so good, like the Yanquis.'

Marshall didn't bother telling him that English originated in England. It was a common belief among the less educated that the language was founded in the United States.

'Do you think he sounded a bit like this, like I'm talking to

121

you now. I mean you couldn't see him and he was one of a group of people all talking to each other at the same time,' he said to the Mexican in a strange dialect.

'Si. It was like that.' The Mexican obviously had trouble understanding the strange accent.

'Like I'm sounding now, is that how the foreigner sounded when he was talking to all the others? You've got to be sure that's what he sounded like.'

'Si. Just like you are.'

'And what did he say to the others when he was talking in this strange tongue?'

'That he would be ready. That everything was ready when the shipment arrived.'

After they had grilled him for another hour, they left him to his solitude and returned to the meeting room. They had nothing new to report, and everything the computer had produced on Ireland and its paramilitary groups was already common knowledge to Marshall. The intelligence officers agreed to contact the DEA London office and get a check run on where the football team had stayed in Ireland. They said their goodbyes and were soon on the road back to the Westin.

'What was the accent you ran over the Mex?' asked Ronane as soon as they left Fort Bliss.

'Northern Irish.'

'How'd you know?'

'It's when he said Liverpool. Most of those guys come from Ireland originally. It's in their blood and in their accent. It was a long shot.'

'I'll pass that on to Washington.'

Marshall, tired after his long drive, excused himself and went to his bed. As he undressed, he looked out of the window, down on the bus station. In the ten minutes that he watched he saw three separate deals being conducted. You could always find it if you knew what you were looking for.

It was a low moment for him; they always were. To be able to look out on a city street and see drugs so freely dealt. It made him wonder about his job, about whether he made any difference to what was really going on down there.

Then he remembered where he had come from.

He climbed into bed, closed his eyes and tried to sleep. For once it didn't work, it never did when he remembered the past. He lay on his back, his arms crossed behind his head in the softness of the pillow as he stared out of the window at the clearness of the Texan sky and the hunched silhouette of the Franklin Mountains.

Vietnam.

That's where it began.

1970.

Saigon.

The draft had caught up with him in Los Angeles. He was broke and in need of food, clothes, rent and new shoe leather when the card came. It was a way out of his predicament and he headed for the recruitment office. He had moonlighted from his apartment and avoided paying the rent that was long overdue. He grinned as he remembered the obese Polish landlord who pestered him at every moment for the rent. He wondered what had happened to the old man. It was the only debt he had never repaid. Except one, but that was in the days before Los Angeles.

He'd been a willing student at Boot Camp and enjoyed the punishing schedule the rookies were pushed through. Then one morning he was a PFC and ready for the war that was still being waged all those miles away in South East Asia.

'Wanna join the military police?' asked his sergeant one day. The older man had been impressed with the big raw rookie and felt he had more to offer the army than simply ending up in a ditch with a sniper's bullet in his head.

'Yes,' he replied instinctively. Wouldn't that be a turnout for the books, he thought.

He arrived in Saigon on 29 January 1970.

Two days later, he was patrolling the streets of the city in his spanking new, knife-creased uniform. Marshall was guarding the perimeter of the American embassy, a building of reinforced construction surrounded by a thick high wall, when a bomb went off in a nearby street. Two military policemen were killed when they stumbled across the bombers. Two further MPs in a jeep responded to the call, but were cut down in the hail of fire that met them. Marshall was lucky. He reached for his pistol and opened fire, missing his targets in the panic of his first action. They scattered rifle shot at him, but were surprised by a marine on a roof who opened up with an M60 light machine-gun. Marshall took cover and waited for support. It soon arrived and six hours later the whole Vietcong team had been killed.

Throughout the next few days, whilst the VC bombarded the city with both 122mm rockets and suicide squads, Marshall came to see the horrors of war close to. He saw children die, families blown up and made homeless, and soldiers dying as they fought an enemy they rarely saw.

When the offensive was over, Marshall, in just that short time, was a hardened veteran. He learnt to watch his back, to be always prepared, and to trust no-one except himself. It was a lesson that would last him all his life.

The most terrible of all the scenes he witnessed was when a small boy, no more than twelve, walked towards a group of soldiers outside a bar. Marshall watched from across the street, watched the boy reach out and beg from the soldiers. They ignored him. It was a common scene in the streets of Saigon. But the boy persevered and pushed into the centre of the group. The soldiers started laughing at his persistence and one of them reached into his pocket to give the boy some coins. He never succeeded, because the boy, booby trapped with high explosives, simply blew up and wiped out four of the soldiers. It was his first experience of the power of drugs. The boy, a heroin addict, had been promised some drugs if he would walk up to the group. He was told to carry a parcel tucked in the waistband of his pyjamas which carried a microphone. The VC who sent him in told him to get amongst the soldiers so that he could overhear what they were talking about. The boy, desperate for his fix, never questioned the VC's motives.

When Marshall returned to the States two years later he was a buck sergeant. The boy was now a man and returned to a land which ignored its heroes and treated the Vietnam veterans as a nightmare they wanted to forget.

He left the army, was discharged in Washington DC, and applied to join the capital's Metropolitan Police. The choice they gave him was simple. Either get out on the streets or join the White House police. He opted for the White House. After two years of Vietnam, the last thing he wanted to do was battle on the streets of Washington. He elected to watch the squirrels on the famous lawn and check the IDs of those who visited this place of government.

But the boredom got to Marshall. He wasn't a man to let life idle by and four years later he joined the Bureau of Narcotics and Dangerous Drugs. The authorities, realizing the growth of drug use and supply was now a major problem, soon merged the various drug-busting organizations into the Drug Enforcement Administration. Marshall suddenly found himself an important cog in the new organization and he put his vast experience to good use. He was a successful undercover agent, a man who was often sent in to the most dangerous of situations. It was a life he enjoyed; and in his loneliness he found he was a man with a vocation. Danger never worried him; he was a born survivor in a world which was difficult to survive in.

The only time he feared his vulnerability was when he was seconded for a short period to the FBI Training and Weapons Centre in Quantico, Virginia. Quantico was used by the DEA for their weapons and unarmed combat drills.

It was the first and only time he fell in love. He was forty and a confirmed bachelor. He found it difficult to relate to women and most of his time was spent with prostitutes. He was used to them from his youth. The rougher they were, the easier it was for him. Nothing asked, nothing given. Sex exchanged for the hard dollar. The more time he spent with them, the more he came to resent them. He didn't know why, except they highlighted his loneliness and his weaknesses. Death, drugs, war and women who gave him release in the confines of their sweat-ridden beds where their bottoms bounced to the vagaries of the hundreds of men who climbed on top of them. Those four were the substances of his life, all he had ever known and he never had the time to differentiate between them.

She was fourteen years younger and a police officer being trained in weapon use. She attracted him like no other woman had, in an elegant sort of way. He had somehow sensed her vulnerability. He spent extra time with her on the shooting range. She hated the weapons she was expected to use and he coaxed her through her distaste for what he knew could one day save her life. She began to rely on him and he enjoyed that. He suddenly felt wanted, felt he had reached into another human being. They became companions and he would take her to restaurants and listen while she poured out her heart to him. Recently divorced, she seemed to jump from relationship to relationship. But they were all short lived; she couldn't form the deep bonds that were needed for a truly loving involvement. He would later come to realize that she trusted no-one, but lived in a false world of emotion that somehow misguided men into thinking she cared. But when they had been dragged into this web of emotion, when they reached out to take her soul and mate it with theirs, she would pull back and not know how to give in return. It frustrated her lovers, had frustrated her husband and now frustrated Marshall.

They became lovers and he found a gentleness in himself he never knew existed. But with all her experience in the wrapping and togetherness of the bed sheets, he was never convinced she returned the love that he felt. His frustration with her modern values, where

125

sex was something that as naturally followed an evening out as a cup of coffee followed an evening meal, forced him into rows sparked by what he saw as her callousness. The worst was when he realized she made him feel old; that the age gap wasn't just in their physical being but also in their spiritual difference. For a man used to giving nothing, he now gave all and became obsessed with the belief that she gave little in return. He'd question her for hours about her previous lovers, probing and digging till he left her exhausted and angry at having to defend her past. But then, apart from his childhood, the only women he had known were those to whom sex was something they did for a living. His obsession was intermingled with a passion neither of them had felt before and it drove them deeper into an emotion that culminated in a wild sexual whirlpool that left them with a high from which they would crash down as his jealousy erupted as soon as he'd climaxed. Then the frustration would explode into more frantic and soul-searching love-making that always seemed to reach a higher peak than they had ever reached before. Their passion was out of control, and neither wanted it any other way.

It was, simply, love at its best and worst.

The arguments grew more bitter and eighteen weeks later, when she left Washington to return to her home base, Marshall was devastated. She ended it at Dulles Airport where he had driven her to catch her plane and he never, in spite of phone calls to an answerphone she never responded to, heard from her again. That night he had called an escort agency, been visited by two hookers and sat in the corner of the room and cried for what he had lost as the women completed their squalid act on the bed he had shared with her and in which he would later sleep alone.

He saw her face now, saw her clearly in his mind as he stared at the hotel ceiling. *Where are you, girl? Who's looking down into your eyes right now and watching those little fluttering gasps that I still remember every day of my life.*

Damn it. This is not the time for it. He reminded himself that he was about to enter danger, that he needed all his strength and reserves for the battles that were about to come. He forced his mind away from her and into the present.

Ramon Cortez, the prisoner in Fort Bliss, had mentioned that he had hung round La Posada del Indio Topless Bar in Juarez. That is where he would start tomorrow.

Then he finally turned over and went to sleep. But he held the pillow to his stomach, as he always did, imagined she was still tucked into him. His last thought was the smell of her hair and the shape of her neck and shoulders as she slept with him.

The unguided missile was about to find a target.

Marshall stayed in his hotel room till after twelve, then set out for Juarez. He crossed the Santa Fe bridge on foot and hailed one of the yellow Mexican taxis once he had crossed the border. The shops he wanted were only a few blocks further down, along the Avenida Juarez, but he was playing the Texan tourist out for the day so he allowed himself to be driven around the city by the driver who knew a sucker when he saw one. Ten minutes later, on a journey that should only have taken two, Marshall paid off the driver, slapped a big tip on him, and went into the shops in what the Mexicans ambitiously call a mall.

Border towns are a haggler's heaven and Marshall started at the Casa Openheim, where he rooted amongst the silverware till he found a cowboy belt buckle that he liked. That passed twenty minutes before he was on the street again and into the next shop.

Juarez is a faded, peeling town. Whereas El Paso is clean and wealthy and American, its border sister is a sleazy, scrabble-a-living, dirty sort of place. The inhabitants live off the tourists and Marshall was soon being offered girls, postcards, earthenware pots and trips to donkey shows and whatever else was his fancy. He spent nearly two hours cruising the shops on the Avenida Juarez and the Avenida Lincoln before he turned down the Avenida de las Americas and ensconced himself in the Shangri-La Restaurant. He'd never trusted Mexican cooking and he felt safer in this place that had served some of the best Cantonese food on the American continent for more than twenty-five years. The meal took an hour and he was soon back on the streets.

He knew he was being watched. That was normal in Juarez. He didn't think he'd been recognized; after all it was twelve years since he'd last been here. And with his big Stetson, cowboy shirt, crisp tailored jeans and cowboy boots, he looked the perfect Texan on a wild time out as he hid behind his Serengeti Driver shades. He crossed towards the Ignacio Mejia where La Posada del Indio Topless Bar was situated. A paper seller sitting on a wooden box followed him with his eyes. Another hustler, thought Marshall, as he walked down to the bar.

The club had a purple tiled front, the small high windows were barred and the double wooden doors were solid and hung loosely on their hinges. He entered the dark bar; the music they were blasting out deafened him after the comparative quiet of the streets. The doors closed behind him on their springs as he walked up to a table near the bar.

The topless, yet shapeless waitress who came to serve him would have been better covered up. But he leered at her as he was expected to and ordered a beer. As she walked away, he took his hat off and put it on the table. The girl at the bar, a black-haired Mexican hooker, tried to catch his eye. He grinned at her, then beckoned her over.

'Wanna drink, little woman?' he drawled at her. *Watch it, Marshall, you're going over the top*. Before she could answer, he pushed the other chair out. 'Sit down, honey. Tell me where I get a good time in this town.'

The girl smiled and sat down. 'I'm Julietta.'

'Hi, Julietta. Call me Mike.'

'Hi, Mike.'

'What you drinking?'

'Champagne?'

'Come on, honey, I ain't paying for no lemonade. You want a beer?'

'Sure.' Maybe this one wasn't as stupid as she looked.

He flirted with her for the next half hour, downed two more beers and got another hooker to join them. This one was Rosa, a peroxided blonde in an even shorter skirt who also tried to get him to buy her a fancy lemonade.

An hour passed before he leant across and asked if they could get any stuff.

'Stuff?' asked Rosa.

'Yeah. Candy. You know?'

'You want drugs?' she asked quietly.

'Yeah. Then we can all have a real good time.'

She smiled at him, then looked towards the end of the bar. There was an older man leaning against the counter, a half-empty beer glass in his hand. He was wiry, but tall, of Mexican origin with pony-tailed black hair. Marshall could see he was a hard man, quickly identified the angular bulge in the back pocket of his jeans that signified either a cosh or a small revolver.

'The man?' Marshall asked Rosa.

'Si. You want I get him?'

'Sure.'

As she crossed the bar to the pusher, Marshall leant back in his chair and put his arm round Julietta. He kissed her on the back of her neck and gave her breast a tight squeeze. She giggled and laughed encouragement at him, then took his hand and moved it back to her waist. From the corner of his eye he saw Rosa talk to the pusher, then watched them both come back towards the table. The man was partially crippled; he was supported by what looked like a Denver Boot, a parking tyre clamp strapped to the lower half of his left leg. It was metal, red and octagonal. When he got close Marshall realized it was a road sign, the word ALTO! still stamped on it, that had been remodelled as a support to the callipers. *Welcome to the Third World.*

The man slid into the chair left vacant by Rosa, who stood behind him as they watched Marshall nuzzle Julietta.

'You want see me?' interrupted the man.

Marshall looked up from his endeavours and blinked as he pretended to focus on the pusher. 'You the man?' he asked eventually.

'Carlos,' replied the pusher. 'What you want?'

'The girls and I want some fun.'

'What they do is not my business.'

'Shit. I know that. But we want to have some real fun.'

'You must ask them.'

Marshall leant conspiratorially across the table, dragging Julietta with him. 'We want some candy. Blow our minds.'

'Why d'you think I can help you?'

'Fuck it,' said Marshall leaning back again, his arm still around the girl. 'Either help or piss off. Take your choice.'

'I must know who you are,' replied Carlos calmly.

'I'm a cop,' giggled Marshall. 'Out to bust the lot of you.'

'Maybe you are.'

'Come on, fella. I just want some fun. Tell you what. I'll give the girl some money, you give it to her in the toilet, and nobody knows nothing.'

Carlos considered. 'I cannot help you, señor. But . . . maybe I know people who can.'

'Maybe you do.'

'Si. Is possible. What shall I tell them you like?'

'Just some candy. Enough for us three.'

'Will take time.'

'Ain't got much of that. With what I'm drinking, my meat might just lose its interest in these two little ladies.' *Easy Marshall, don't go over the top with this Texan tourist crap.*

'Not so long,' replied Carlos. 'Three hundred dollars. They will ask for that much.'

'Too much. One hundred.'

'No.' Carlos rose to go. He knew when he had a sucker on the line.

'One fifty,' replied the sucker.

'Two hundred.'

'OK.'

'Give the money to the girl.'

'How do I know she'll be back with it?'

'You don't. But that's how you say you do it.'

Marshall shrugged, took out his wallet and passed two hundred dollar bills to Rosa, making sure that they all saw the big wad of notes tucked in the leather. He saw Rosa's eyes flare up; there was a high roller in town. 'You better come back, girl. Otherwise your little friend here's going to get short changed.'

Rosa gave him a warm grin, then turned and followed the pusher to the back of the bar.

Marshall turned to Julietta and nuzzled her once again. 'Where we going, honey?'

'We have place. Down street. Big bed for us.'

'Hell, honey, we don't need a big bed for what I got planned.'

He continued to nuzzle and fondle the girl while he waited. Rosa and Carlos had disappeared into the rear of the bar. The place was full now; a mixture of tourists, idlers, workmen going home and cheap-scented, cheap-clothed hookers. Most stood around the bar, few people seemed to take seats. Through it all, through the floating smoke and the bustle of the crowd, naked breasts of a variety of shapes and sizes jiggled their way around the bar as the waitresses served the drinks. The evening was normal at La Posada del Indio Topless Bar.

Five minutes later Rosa returned to the table, the pusher still in tow, and slid into her seat. She grinned and nodded at Marshall.

'You like Juarez?' asked Carlos, leaning over the table.

'Helluva place,' lied Marshall. 'You wanna drink?'

'Si. OK,' replied Carlos, twisting his strangely callipered leg as he sat on the stool that was still vacant.

'And no champagne,' laughed Marshall.

Carlos turned to a nearby waitress and ordered a beer. 'The women are nice, eh?' he leered at Marshall.

'These two beauties sure are. You from these parts?'

'Si. From Juarez.'

'San Antonio myself. Texas through and through.'

'You never been here before?'

'No. Been to El Paso a few times. But never crossed the border here. Only ever crossed the border once. When I did some work down in Piedras Negras.' He watched, but saw no flicker of alarm in the Mexican's eyes. 'You know where that is?' he continued.

'Si. It's a small town,' came the dismissive reply.

'You been there?'

'Why? Is not important. No big tourists. No big money.'

'You do anything else apart from this?'

The Mexican shrugged, not wanting to commit himself. 'What you do?'

'Chemicals.'

'What that?'

'Industrial chemicals. Cleaning things out, that sorta thing. I sell.'

'You salesman?'

'Yeah. And a damn good one.'

'You make lot of money?'

'More than most. I got a good territory. All of Texas, Arizona, right across to the Carolinas and Florida. Hard work, easy pickings and good money.'

'Is good.'

'You handle these girls?'

Carlos smiled and shook his head.

'How much they want?' Marshall continued.

'Ask her,' said Carlos, turning to Rosa.

'Twenty dollars.'

'For two?' queried Marshall.

'For one. Forty dollars for two.'

'OK,' smiled the big man. 'Forty bucks for the two. Make it a big night and you could be millionaires,' he joked; it was lost on the other three.

'You go now?' joined in Julietta.

'When the man's had his beer, honey.' Marshall saw the waitress approaching the table. 'When the man's had his beer.' He saw the man who had been standing near Carlos earlier on watching them and knew instinctively that they were a team. He drew some notes out and paid for the beer. 'This a big tourist trap, huh?' he asked Carlos as the Mexican gulped his beer.

'Lot of tourists. Si,' replied the white froth-lipped pusher.

'Lot of business for you here. With the tourists.'

'Why you ask so much?' came the guarded answer.

'Maybe I wanna make some more money.'

'How?'

'You tell me. That stuff you hand out, ain't you guys always

131

looking for new distribution networks?'

'You talk dangerous.'

'Listen, I go all over the southern states. And I'm legit . . . you understand th—'

'Si.'

'I could move stuff all over for you.'

'Why?'

'I like making money.'

Carlos grinned. 'You are amateur. And I am not . . . a supplier. I cannot help you. I have enough trouble making my own money.' Carlos stood up and held the glass towards Marshall, then tipped it and drank the remains. He put the glass on the table, turned and merged into the crowd as he returned to the bar. Marshall saw the other man, also Mexican and with a puffy bully's face, join Carlos at the bar.

'We go now?' urged Rosa. She wanted this trick out of the way so she could get back to the crowd. It was busy and she expected a hectic night.

Marshall didn't want to leave, but neither did he want to create suspicion. Hell, he'd be back on the street in half an hour. Play drunk, be impotent and pay the girls off.

They left the bar and walked to a shabby little store just around the corner. There were stone steps without a balustrade at the side and Rosa led Marshall and Julietta to the top of the store. The first floor was a living area with a metalled balcony that ran all round the front. There were three doors, each leading into a separate room. The windows were curtained and drawn. As Rosa opened a door, he saw the movement in the street. Carlos ducked into the shadows. Marshall grinned; they were taking the bait.

It was a small room, one bed on a metal frame and a thin mattress and sheet. The rest of the room was as functional, two wooden chairs, a washbasin and a door leading to a cupboard or toilet.

The two girls started to work fast. While Julietta began undressing him, Rosa unceremoniously took off her clothes. It wasn't a good body, even with his usual choice in women. She had bruises on her thighs and stomach; he was repulsed by women with pale skin and bruises.

'You got the money?' asked a naked Rosa, holding her hand out.

'Sure, honey.' He pulled away from Julietta's attentions. He'd been here before. One undresses the punter and excites him, the other lies back and gets laid. That way, the punter shoots off his rocks on one instead of two and everyone wipes up and goes about their business. He reached into his wallet and dug out forty dollars. They had disappeared into Rosa's bag before he'd even let go. Eager, he thought. He moved away from Julietta and slipped his coat by the side of the bed. He didn't want them to know he was armed. 'Your clothes. Off, honey,' he ordered Julietta. Then he started to peel off his shirt. The girls looked at each other, this was going to take longer than they planned.

He signalled them on to the bed; they lay there, naked and bored and waiting patiently for the next move. 'Start without me, girls. I wanna watch. Then we'll take some candy and really have some fun.'

The girls looked at each other, then Rosa leaned over and feigned kissing Julietta's breasts. Marshall watched them, not excited by their lack-lustre performance. 'Come on, honey,' he urged. 'Show her what's what.'

It didn't make much difference. Rosa moved her hand between her companion's legs, into the warmth and softness of her mound, and Julietta moaned as she was expected to. Shit, thought Marshall, they're not even good enough to be film extras. He crossed over to the bed, his desire to hurt their dismissal of him as a man building within him. Through their careless and apathetic performance he felt they were laughing at him. He suddenly forgot why he was here, hated them for their shallow indifference to his manhood. He leant on the bed as Rosa looked up. She smiled at him, trying to be warm, but he saw only her mockery. He lashed at her with his hand, caught her on the side of her head and snapped it back. Julietta froze, startled by his sudden aggression. Then Rosa screamed and as her shriek filled the room, the door burst open.

Marshall cursed; he'd been carried away by his own emotion. He rolled over the bed, towards his coat and slapped his hand into the pocket where he felt the metal of the Smith 15. But before he drew it, he heard Carlos laughing.

He left the gun there, his hand still round the butt, and focused on the door. Two of them; Carlos and his companion from the bar. 'Hi there,' Marshall said, grinning. 'You change your mind about doing business?'

'Si. We want business.'

'What sort, fella?'

Carlos pulled a metal cosh from his back pocket. Marshall was relieved, at least he didn't carry a shooter. Behind him, his companion held up a knife; a long thin knife that would poke right

133

through a man, enter the stomach and come out of his back. He held it high so Marshall could see. As they stood watching each other, the girls moved to the other side of the bed, away from Marshall, and started dressing. Marshall looked at Rosa, saw her whimpering and the new lump on her face told him there'd be another bruise to join the others. He regretted lashing out at the woman. It had been unnecessary.

'Business with your wallet, señor,' tormented Carlos.

They were thieves. Nothing more. Small time pushers and thieves. He cursed himself. He should've realized that earlier.

The girls were near the door now, hurrying into their clothes. The second man pushed the door open and shoved them out. They cursed him and the man laughed.

'We do not want to hurt you, señor,' said Carlos. 'Just your money.'

'Sure,' replied Marshall. He stood up slowly, the coat still over his hand. When he was fully upright, he stepped back and drew the small revolver from his coat pocket. He grinned as he pointed it at Carlos, grinned even more when he saw the fear in the Mexican's face.

'Listen, fellas,' he said, amiable as ever. 'Why don't you set yourselves down on the end of the bed. Slow.' He watched them move warily towards the bed. 'And drop those,' he added, still smiling and friendly.

The two Mexicans dropped their weapons and did as they were ordered. Marshall moved round in front of them.

'So, you wanna do business?' he smiled at them.

'We would not hurt you, señor,' whimpered Carlos.

'Yeah. I believe you,' was his sarcastic reply. 'That's a real friendly knife you got.'

Carlos shrugged, expansive and warm. He shifted his leg, the home-made leg iron was causing him problems. 'Only to scare you.'

'Sure.' Marshall wasn't worried about the girls getting support; they'd be down the road by now looking for new customers. 'I really meant what I said earlier.'

'About what?'

'Distributing. I mean, I want to make some real money.'

'Is not so easy.'

'Why not? You get the stuff. You can get it for me.'

'I only deal in small . . . ' Carlos rubbed his fingers together. 'I buy a little, I sell a little. To keep alive.'

'I know. Wife and six papooses to feed. Come on, who do

we have to see?'

'Is not possible.'

Marshall leant forward and rammed Carlos in the nose with his gun, making him squeal as the blood spurted. 'I really want to do this thing,' he reiterated. He already knew it was a waste of time. Carlos was small potatoes; he'd pick up a small supply from a local dealer. Probably just enough to pay for his own habit. He looked at the Mexican, now holding his nose, his eyes resentful and fearful at the same time. Marshall stepped back, picked up his shirt and slipped it on, the Smith 15 always in his hand pointed at the two. 'Been a bad night,' he sighed. 'Didn't even get my rocks off. Say, you owe me forty dollars.'

'I have not the money.'

'You want me to bust your nose this time?'

Carlos shook his head, then took his hands away from his red smeared face and reached into the side of his calliper. Marshall had relaxed, he was only playing a game now, his revolver loosely held in his hand.

He forgot the prime rule.

Never take your eye off the ball. He'd forgotten they still wanted his wallet and all those juicy hundred dollar bills that lay folded in it.

Carlos unclipped the ALTO! road sign that was strapped to his leg-iron and flicked it, as a kid would a frisbee, straight at Marshall's head. Only this was no plastic soft edged toy, but a spinning sheet of sharpened metal that could slice his neck to the bone with the ease of a knife cutting through butter.

The door opened behind him, straight into his back and sent him sprawling. The ALTO! sign spun into Rosa's face, cutting her from ear to chin, cutting her so fast and deep that the blood didn't appear for several slow-motion seconds. There was just a big lop-sided smile on a face that wasn't where its mouth was.

The gun was knocked from Marshall's hand as he fell. Rosa was screaming as he hit the floor. Her accomplices ignored her as they reached for their weapons.

Marshall knew he'd never get to the gun in time, so he slewed his body to the right, reaching for the knife that lay on the floor. But the other man was there first, his fingers grabbing round the blade as he tried to scoop it up. Marshall kept his momentum going, wrapped his big hand round the Mexican's and squeezed, knocking it into the metal leg of the bed at the same time. The Mexican fought back, but was no match for the big Texan. The grunts of exertion turned to shrieks of pain as the sharp blade cut deep into the soft flesh of his palm.

Carlos hit Marshall on the shoulder with his cosh, but Marshall squeezed his accomplice's arm whilst twisting his body so that he could lash out with his feet at his attacker.

But it was Rosa who saved him. She staggered forward and tripped over Carlos as he raised his cosh once again. The two of them fell forward, tangled in a slow-motion corkscrew as they collapsed to the floor. Marshall released his hand and pulled himself away, towards his gun. He felt the comfort of its butt in his palm and he rolled over, away from the frantic scenes behind him, and stood up. He aimed the revolver at the three scrabbling figures, but there was little need. He quickly picked up his coat, stepped over the Mexicans, smacked Carlos over the head with the butt of his revolver for good measure, and went out onto the balcony. The yelling continued behind him and he rapidly descended the steps on to the street and crossed to a dark corner. Moments later the first of the crowd arrived, attracted by the cacophony of pain and anger that came from the apartment. Marshall watched people run up the stairs, waited until a crowd of onlookers had built up and joined them at the rear. A policeman arrived soon afterwards and then the usual array of patrol cars and ambulances.

There was no sign of Julietta, so Marshall moved away and towards the Avenida Juarez.

He stepped back in the dark of a doorway when he saw her.

It wasn't Julietta, but the woman in the grey suit whom he had last seen in Mexico City. He was sure she hadn't spotted him as she briskly marched past to see what the excitement was, her black handbag swinging over her shoulder, her multi-ringed masculine fingers clutching at the air in that agitated manner that he remembered.

So the Calis were in town.

He waited for her to turn the corner before he headed towards the border and back to the organized insanity that was El Paso and the good old US of A.

Two days later they were still kicking their heels.

Marshall and Ronane spent most of their time watching the border crossing from a small window in the Ropa Usada building that was the first structure on Santa Fe as you entered the United States. It was a bright red building, three storeys high, which gave an excellent view of the border point and the traffic that ran down

136

the bridge to it.

The whole operation was on a strictly need-to-know basis and a few customs officials had already been briefed. The intelligence unit had created a file of photographs of potential smugglers which had included a substantial list of those involved in drugs in the Piedras Negras area. In addition to the customs officers, there was a team of six DEA operatives mixing with the throng of tourists and workers who crossed the bridge on foot in the special, caged-in walkway that traversed the border. Ronane, in charge of the surveillance, had decided, after consulting Washington, that there was little need for any excessive customs search of vehicles. 'Let's not warn them off,' he had told Marshall.

The two men sat with a third DEA man in the small room and watched the customs post. They all had powerful Nikon binoculars and were scanning the activity taking place no more than fifty yards from their vantage point.

'Dead as Luco Brasi in *The Godfather*,' said the DEA man.

'He sleeps with the fish,' joked Marshall, recalling the words that were used in the film to inform all that the assassin Brasi was dead. He watched Ronane as he spoke, saw the tension in the little man. It was his show and he dreaded the surveillance fouling up. Especially after Mexico City. 'They've not gone through yet,' he said in an effort to support Ronane.

Ronane didn't reply, just continued to keep watch.

'Who says?' interjected the DEA man, a newcomer who knew all the answers. 'Washington's crazy. We need more manpower. And more customs involvement.'

The two older men said nothing. They were used to new kids who knew all the answers. Give them a few years, a few wasted stakeouts backed with the nightmares of the victims as they screamed for their next shot. Give them that and they'd sit patiently waiting, hour after hour, day after day, seemingly for ever, to reel in a small fish in a pond that was now growing into an ocean.

'I'm going out again,' said Ronane, putting his glasses down and going to the back of the room. Marshall sensed his impatience, but said nothing. Ronane pulled some clothes from the pile of disguises on the table and decided to go out as an army corporal on his R and R. It was something they did often when they were on a hit and their wardrobe was considerable. Ronane checked his radio, nodded and left the room to mingle with the pedestrians downstairs.

'Jumpy, isn't he?' said the DEA man.

'So would you be.' He added the word arsehole silently, then regretted it. The kid was only being young, his heart was in the right place; otherwise he wouldn't be in this crazy job. He suddenly wanted to justify his annoyance. 'He's wearing the stripes on this one. If it goes right, then they'll pick up the tab in Washington. If it goes wrong, then it'll be his fault.'

'I guess so.'

It was another five minutes before the kid spoke. 'Christ, you're right. She really is ugly.'

Marshall moved nearer to his colleague and focused his glasses to where the kid was pointing.

'On the walkway, halfway down. Walking towards customs. Dressed like an old woman. But walking young.'

'Where?'

'Next to the family. Three kids and a dad in a red Hawaii shirt. Got it?'

'Yeah.' He recognized the Cali woman. *How the hell did . . . ?*

'Her hands. Covered in rings,' the kid answered, knowing that Marshall would be wondering.

'Good,' said an impressed Marshall. Maybe these kids weren't as bad as he thought. He moved away from the window and picked up the radio. 'Ace of Hearts crossing bridge,' he said, hoping Ronane was on the street and with his earpiece in place. 'Disguise.'

The answer was almost immediate. 'Watching brief.'

That was it. The order was radio silence, until one of the team saw something that needed action.

Marshall returned to the window and watched the Cali woman through his binoculars.

She shuffled down towards the border crossing. He zoomed in on her and focused on her face. As ugly as he remembered. She was wearing a black dress, long as an old woman's, with a red shawl that she wrapped round her head. He saw she still carried the large black handbag. Her weapon, probably the Uzi she'd used against him, would be hidden there.

'She the one spat in your face?' asked the kid.

So Ronane had put that in the report. There wasn't anything Washington didn't know. 'Yeah,' he growled, remembering the shame he'd felt. 'You stay watching her,' he added, getting back to the business at hand. 'I'm going to scan.'

He started to pan across the vehicles, watching for anything that was unusual, anything suspicious.

Nothing.

He checked the woman again. She just continued to shuffle down.

He knew it was wrong. His instincts told him that. He scanned the vehicles again, then the moving line of pedestrians.

To his left, at the second customs bay, a battered grey Chevrolet Impala was signalled into the search area. There were three young Mexicans on board; wild-looking characters who had that no-good look about them. They had been honking while they waited in line, impatient to move on through the border. They certainly knew how to draw attention to themselves and the annoyed official was about to show them who was in charge. Marshall kept his attention on them; no reason except they were the only game in town. The customs officer, not one of those who knew what was going on, signalled them all to step out of the Impala. The men stood back, letting the officer search the interior of the car. They laughed at him as he searched, nudged each other with the joke of it all. Satisfied that there was no contraband there, he signalled one of them to open the boot. The Mexican who had been driving stepped forward and unlocked the compartment, stepped back as it sprung up. There were a couple of cases in there and the customs man leant forward and opened them. Clothes, nothing important. Then he started to go through the contents of the case.

Another customs officer, one of the surveillance team, had now approached the group. His radio would pick up what was going on. Marshall identified the official, checked his list and then tuned into channel 12.

'Let's see your IDs,' ordered the second customs man in Spanish.

Marshall watched them laughing as they reached for their cards.

'Where you people going?' continued the waiting official.

'To America,' joked one of the Mexicans. 'To the Land of the Free.'

'OK, OK. Let's keep it under control. Where are you going?'

'To El Paso. Then we wanna see Texas. We're on vacation.' The Mexican passed over his ID.

'You all from Piedras Negras?' asked the official. Marshall picked up the change in his tone.

'Si. Si,' came the laughing reply. 'You know Piedras Negras, señor?'

'I've heard of it. Why don't you men just come over this way?' The customs man signalled them away from the car towards the personnel search zone at the back.

'Hey man, we're on vacation.'

'Come on, fellas. Let's get in the back.' As he spoke, he waved a couple of officials over to join him. Other DEA men were also moving towards the group.

'What's this?' shouted the official searching the car. He held up a clear plastic bag which looked like it was full of marijuana. Marshall saw sudden activity towards the Impala. The team were moving in.

'Leave it, Ronane,' he said into his second radio. He didn't know why he said it. But it was all too easy.

'They've got them,' shouted the kid, his attention now on the group. The Mexicans were now shouting loudly, generally creating a furore.

'Do as you're told,' ordered Marshall. 'Watch the woman.'

'But they've . . . '

'Say again,' came Ronane's voice on the radio.

'Watch the fucking woman,' Marshall boomed, and the kid swung his attention back to his target. He'd heard of Marshall and his black temper.

'Say again,' repeated Ronane, more urgent this time.

'Don't hit.' Marshall spoke into the radio.

'The trunk floor's been lifted,' said the searching officer's voice over the first radio. 'It's a false compartment.'

'What's she doing?' Marshall asked the kid.

'Marshall, you there?' snapped Ronane.

'Yeah,' replied the kid. 'She's still coming towards us.'

'Can she see what's going on down there?'

'Yeah. It's in her line.'

'Marshall, we're going in,' concluded Ronane.

'Don't,' came Marshall's reply.

'Why not?'

'Stay loose.'

'There's some stuff here. Bagful of white stuff,' crackled the customs officer's voice.

'Leave them to it, Ronane. They can handle it.'

'Why?'

'Why not?'

There was silence for a moment, then Ronane's voice came over clearly. 'Hold back. Watching brief.'

Then there was silence.

Marshall turned his attention back to the customs post. The searching officer was holding up a bag of cocaine. It was all too simple. He watched further bags being dragged out. The customs officers had now drawn their weapons and the three Mexicans were being handcuffed. 'What's she doing?' he asked the kid.

140

'Slowed down. But still moving towards the border.'

'Don't lose her.' Marshall started to scan the crowd once again, then the vehicles.

'IRISH TEXAN IMPORT COMPANY' said the black lettering on the side of the light-green, twelve-wheeler refrigerated truck.

'Check the green truck,' he warned Ronane.

'I got it,' came the answer thirty seconds later.

Marshall kept his glasses trained on the truck. One driver, Anglo Saxon, just waiting patiently for his turn to get through the border. Over the radio he heard Ronane instruct a customs man to question the trucker and to determine what his cargo was. Marshall turned his attention to the woman. She'd reached the border and was showing her ID. A moment later she was waved through.

'Get down there and keep an eye on her,' said Marshall.

'Now?' asked the kid.

'No, tomorrow. Get out of here.'

The kid put down his glasses and left the room grumbling. Marshall continued to watch the truck.

'There's a mountain of stuff here,' crackled the customs man on the second radio.

Marshall switched his attention to the Impala. His experience told him there were nearly fifty kilos. A good haul, but 900 short if Ramon Cortez was to be believed.

The truck edged forward and was waved into a search area. Marshall watched the driver closely; he seemed unperturbed by the action. The customs officer instructed the driver out of the cab. The trucker, a large, athletic man, shrugged and climbed down. Marshall switched channels on his second radio until he picked up the dialogue between the two.

'Big stack of beef,' said the trucker.

'From Mexico?' asked the customs man.

'Hell no. That's from Texas. I gotta get it across to Corpus Christi where they'll ship it across to Europe.'

'Where in Europe?'

'I don't know. Hell, I just got to get it to Corpus Christi.'

'Why you been in Mexico?'

'Having some fun. Didn't want to leave that load behind. Didn't want some bad guy hijacking it.'

'They could've taken it in Juarez.'

'No way. I was watching it out'a this gal's window. Humping away with one eye looking out for my truck. I'm loaded, man. I'd'a blasted anybody got near that truck.'

141

'How'd you get over the border without showing your manifesto?'

'Like I always do. They know me. Hell, I like me some of that Mexican ass before a long trip. What's this for, anyhow? I come through here three, four times a month. You customs guys know me.'

'I don't know you.'

'It's what I always do.' The trucker started to sulk.

'Let's look at your load.'

'Sure.' The trucker turned and led the officer to the rear of the rig. He reached into his pocket, took out a selection of keys and unlocked the padlock on the back with one of them. Then he slid the bolts and swung one of the big doors open. 'You wanna climb up?' he asked.

The customs man pulled himself up and into the back of the truck. The driver followed him, turned to see if they were being watched, then pulled the door shut.

'What the . . . ?' he heard Ronane shout over the first radio.

'It's refrigerated,' came an answer. 'Maybe they gotta keep the door shut.'

'Keep close,' Ronane ordered. 'Keep watching.'

Nothing came over the second radio except for a crackling hiss. The sealed truck had blocked out the signal. Two minutes later the door swung open and the driver jumped down. He looked round, then, satisfied that he wasn't observed, he turned and closed the door. Then he walked rapidly towards the cab, climbed in and started the engine.

'Go, go, go,' he heard Ronane yell over the radio.

Marshall rammed the radio into his side pocket and ran from the room, out into the blinding sunlight. He jumped down the stairs of the Ropa Usada building and on to the pavement. As he ran, he unclipped his sidearm ready for use.

The truck had already reversed out of the customs bay and was picking up speed towards the barriers. A customs officer jumped out in front and reached for his gun.

The driver never braked, just floored the accelerator and smashed his gleaming radiator into the unfortunate officer, smashed him to pulp and ran him into the gritty tarmac of the hot road.

Someone opened fire, but it had little effect as the vast vehicle hurtled up to and through the barrier, snapping it as a rhinoceros would a twig.

Marshall moved down Santa Fe, away from the border. He wished he'd got something more than his handgun. As he backed down the pavement, watching the truck crash through the barrier some hundred yards away, a roar of gunfire following it as pedestrians scattered for safety, he heard the repeater gunfire of an Uzi machine-gun.

He swung round and saw the woman across the road, the Uzi held to her hip as she sprayed lead at anyone trying to stop the truck.

'No,' he shouted at the kid as he saw him run towards the woman, reaching for his sidearm as he did. No-one heard him over the din of the machine gun, but everyone saw the kid tumble and fall as the bullets stripped worms of flesh from his body on to the street where he finally died.

'Smart-ass fucking kid,' shouted Marshall, the Smith 15 now in his hand as he dived for cover behind a parked car. Poor kid. All that talent. All that terrible waste. That was all he thought before she sprayed the Uzi towards him, kept him trapped as the truck rushed onwards down Santa Fe. Marshall looked back at the customs post and saw that people were still scattering for cover. That's when he realized there were gunmen in the back of the truck who had opened fire at the authorities.

'Marshall, you OK?' Ronane's voice spluttered over the radio.

He didn't wait to answer. The truck slowed, and as it passed the woman, she leapt up on to the running-board. He realized they were escaping into El Paso, into some warehouse not far from here, where the cocaine, probably buried in the frozen carcases of some of the animals, would be transferred into smaller vehicles and then distributed towards their destination.

As he broke cover and started to run towards the slow-moving truck, he heard an explosion from the border. Someone was throwing grenades and it wasn't his own people. The Calis had prepared for every eventuality. They were turning it into a war zone and the DEA and Customs only had a few pea-shooters.

In your hands, Marshall.

'Go for it, Marshall,' screamed Ronane over the radio. He'd seen the big man running for the truck.

Fuck you, Ronane. Why's it always me? As he cursed Ronane he jumped on to the running-board, hung on to the big rear-view mirror, and pointed his pistol at the driver's head. 'Stop this rig, shithead,' he shouted.

The driver jerked his head back, clearing the way for the woman to shoot Marshall from the other side.

Bang.

It was louder than the word.

The bullet exploded out of the Smith 15 and popped into the driver's head, just above the left temple, and the look of surprise on his face was strange because the man was already dead.

Marshall threw himself backwards as the Uzi clattered out its death sound, but his luck held and the bullets whizzed harmlessly past. He leant forward and grabbed the steering wheel and yanked it to the left. As the truck careered into a line of parked cars and over the pavement, Marshall jumped off, slid over a crushed car and fell to the pavement. As he lay there, he watched the rig, all twelve wheels of it slow-motion into a roll, then crash on to its side and slither along the pavement, pushing and scrunching parked cars as it did so. There were the awful sounds of some sort of metallic dinosaur in its death throes, then an empty silence.

Just dust and stillness as it was all over.

Marshall tried to stand up, but his leg was twisted under him and he had to roll over. As he turned on to his back he saw the woman running towards him, the Uzi still in her hand. He reached for the Smith 15, but it wasn't there, had fallen from his hand as he rolled from the truck.

'I should've killed you in Mexico City,' she screamed at him. She drew level, her Uzi now pointed at his head. 'This time, there'll—'

Then she toppled on to him, her mouth frozen with hate. It was only as she rolled on to her side that he saw the gaping wound in the back of her head. As she finally rolled on to her back, her face towards him, Marshall saw the point of a bullet lodged in the cornea of her left eye. Her brain had slowed the flight and stopped the bullet, fired from some distance away, coming right through her head.

''Bout time you stepped in,' he said to Ronane, who approached with a smoking Coonan Magnum in his hand. 'At that distance, it had to be a lucky shot.'

'Yeah, aren't you the lucky one. Shit, Marshall. I would like to have captured her.'

'Why? She's as ugly dead as alive.' Marshall put his hand up and Ronane pulled him to his feet. He saw the Smith 15 lying there and he picked it up and holstered it.

'She'd've been a good catch for the department. Fucking family, for Christ's sake.'

'She took the kid out.'

'I saw. What the hell was he doing down here?'

'I sent him. To follow the woman.'

'Damn it, Marshall. He was surveillance only. It was his first assignment.'

'Yeah, well . . . He was doing a man's job. Shut your mouth, Ronane. He was a good kid.'

And Marshall turned and walked away into El Paso and towards the Westin Paso de Norte Hotel.

They could clear up the mess.

Ronane could write his report.

He just wanted to be alone to think about her.

Wherever she was.

That way he didn't have to think about this damn job and the games he had to play.

That way he didn't have to think about that poor, damned, dead kid who wasn't around to be smart-assed any more.

Drug Enforcement Administration
700 Army Navy Drive
Arlington
Virginia

In Washington the Deputy Assistant Administrator cursed and slammed the phone down.

'Fuck Marshall! Fuck them all!' He reached in the desk drawer, took the packet of opened Camels and took out a cigarette.

'Smoke alarms,' warned his special assistant, Peter Smith, in charge of the Office of Intelligence.

'Tough.' The administrator lit the cigarette, inhaled deeply, then on second thoughts leant forward and blew the smoke into the open drawer and closed it. He had three more puffs, followed the same procedure, slamming the drawer shut each time, then put the Camel out in the ashtray. He kept his hand cupped over the ashtray while he fanned the smoke thin. 'Stupid way for a grown man to behave,' he said, daring his assistant to comment.

'I could do with one, too,' said Smith. 'Why not go down to the smoke hole?'

'Good idea.'

The administrator picked up his Camels and the two men left the office. They took the lift down to the ground floor, walked past the security desk and out into the late afternoon sunlight. A group of DEA workers were all smoking as they sat on the benches outside the

145

main entrance. The smokers, a minority, took their habit seriously and wore it as a badge of honour. They regularly took breaks for smoking time and enjoyed congregating outside the entrance as a permanent reminder to those inside who disapproved of their ways, that freedom still included the right to smoke.

The two men sat on a bench some distance away from the other social lepers and lit up.

'I get more stress from having to come down here and smoke than I get from all the shit I handle upstairs.' The administrator took a deep draw at his Camel, then blew the smoke out slowly and watched it drift into the warm air. 'Fuck Marshall,' he said eventually.

'He was right.'

'Except he didn't know there was a second shipment.'

'Why not?'

'That was on a need-to-know basis.'

'I would've thought the guys in the field needed to know.'

'Breakdown of communications. Hope he doesn't find out.'

'He's still one of the best.'

'For how long. He was forty-three a few days ago.'

'You want to pull him out of the field?'

'I've got nowhere to put him. He's a fucking maverick.'

'Like hell. He's an animal. His idea of a seven-course meal is a hot dog and a six-pack.' Smith didn't say it as a joke, but it made the administrator smile. 'Put him back in Intelligence.'

'No. Ronane's the best brain there. That's what makes them such a good team. Ronane's brain and Marshall's instincts. Why don't you take him?'

'Nope.'

'Why not? If he's so fucking good.'

''Cos he's best where he is. He's a pro. It's all he can do and he does it well.'

'He's going to be too old soon.'

'Worry about that when it happens.'

'That's the problem. When Marshall goes wrong, it'll be in a big way. It'll be the biggest fuck-up this Agency's ever known.'

'Is this why you called me over?'

'No.' The administrator ground his cigarette out with his foot, then lit another one. 'Just need to get him off my chest. I want to know what this thing was all about. Why were they busting through the customs post in that rig? What the hell was so important about it?'

146

'Big important load. They were ready for trouble. That truck was reinforced to the extent it could've driven through concrete. If it hadn't been for Marshall, they would've slipped down one of those El Paso roads and into a hidey-hole before the police could get to them. The cocaine was in the beef carcases. Hell, it's been done so many times before. Fish, beef, sheep. Those boys like using that stuff.'

'But no money,' stated the administrator.

'Not a smell of a dollar, let alone ten million.'

'What about the Irish Texan Import Company?'

'Nothing. Shell company. Customs people say they've seen the truck go over the border plenty of times. Even searched it. Just carcases.'

'Probably the same beef on board all the time. The Piedras Negras boys?'

'Suckered into taking drugs across the border. They were told it was a safe job.'

'So where now?' queried the administrator.

'We think the money, and the second shipment, was bound for Europe. Maybe even Ireland, like Ronane says. That would open up a new avenue into England and then across to the continent.'

'But no proof.'

'No. Except for the soccer teams.'

The administrator paused for a while. None of it made sense. Why take the risk of getting so much out in such a short time? Who needed cocaine so desperately? 'Anything on those teams?'

'London bureau's still checking.' Smith had been on the DEA exercise covering the Italian World Cup games in 1990. The result was a success in that several Cali bodyguards and family members were identified. 'I think the soccer lead's pretty important.'

'How big was the second shipment?'

'Another thousand kilos.'

'This was an important transaction to the Calis. They could afford another thousand. Hell, they've still got to get the stuff through.'

'Then why get one of their family killed?'

'The woman? Maybe they just wanted us to believe she was Cali.'

'Could be. Unless they're into equal opportunities. She could've been their Griselda.' Smith referred to Griselda Blanco de Trujillo, who had been the Godmother of the Medellin cartel, having started life as a pickpocket. She had climbed the ladder of success by marrying four men, each one a higher Medellin boss than the

147

last, and had the misfortune, or fortune, of becoming a widow four times over. Above all, it was Blanco's ruthless methods that led to the bloody battles between the Colombian authorities and the Medellin cartel in the 1980s when ministers, judges and generals were killed by the traffickers. 'Anyway, even if she was, they'll need someone new to take over her role. In retrospect, I think the rest of the shipment probably got through.' Smith realized a car could have driven through easily after the exciting events at El Paso. The surveillance team would have been satisfied they'd caught the main shipment, especially if they believed they'd killed a member of the family. 'Could be,' he repeated. 'What do you want me to do?' he asked.

'Keep pressure on Ireland. London may need some help on that.'

'No sweat.'

'And send Marshall to Quantico.'

'Why?'

'He's been out for a long time.'

'How long in Quantico?'

'Until we've got something for him. I think they made some stupid mistakes. They were wrong in Mexico City. They should've stuck to the game plan. Maybe then we would've found out more.' He didn't ask his assistant's advice; he knew the man disagreed with him, that Marshall had uncovered the fact that the Calis knew they were DEA men. 'I also think Ronane's tired. He needs to get out from the field for a while. Time he got his career advanced.'

Smith threw his cigarette away. He felt sorry for Ronane and Marshall.

They both deserved better.

Eastbound Carriageway
Interstate 10
The Road from El Paso
Texas

The red Ford LTD never wavered from the 65 mph speed limit.

Four hundred yards behind, the green Pontiac Firebird did exactly the same.

Inside each car there was a husband, wife and two children. The only difference was that the children in the LTD were two girls whilst those in the Pontiac were a boy and a girl.

148

The cars had been waiting patiently to cross the border from Juarez into El Paso when the incident with the truck erupted. They waited an hour before the road was cleared enough for traffic to be let through.

Nice families not worth a second glance.

The highway patrolman, parked at the side of the road, saw the cars keep to the speed limit as they drove eastbound on Interstate 10, and wished he was home with his own wife and children. But then he had no suspicion that two such cars, not out to break the law, with such normal families on board, each carried 500 pounds of cocaine in special compartments in their doors.

Nor did he know that the blue Ford Mustang that followed them, once again adhering to the speed limit, carried $10 million worth of uncut diamonds in a suitcase on the back seat.

As the patrolman watched, the three cars trundled their way to the East Coast and towards the destination that eagerly awaited them.

9

POINT OF NO RETURN

The White Tower
Charlotte Street
London

CHARLIE SOULSON HAD ALREADY TAKEN HIS SEAT IN THE FASHIONABLE
Greek restaurant when John Pentanzi arrived. The two men had
never met before and the maître d' showed Pentanzi to the table
in the corner.

'Popular place,' said Pentanzi as the two men shook hands.

'Excellent food,' replied Soulson as he sat down again. 'My
favourite London watering hole.' He didn't allow his surprise at
Pentanzi being black to show.

'I just wondered why we didn't meet at the American embassy.
Or at New Scotland Yard. If this is, as you said on the phone, on
official business.'

Soulson shrugged. 'I rarely get the chance to have a good meal
when I come up to London. I'm usually whisked from meeting to
meeting, then slapped back on the shuttle to Manchester. I just
thought I'd . . .' he laughed '. . . mix business with pleasure. I hope
it doesn't embarrass you.'

'What? Being seen with the Jesus Cop? No.'

Soulson warmed immediately to the American. Not many people had the temerity or gall to use Soulson's public nickname as openly as Pentanzi had done. 'Would you like some wine?'

Pentanzi grinned and pushed his glass forward, watched as Soulson poured from the bottle. 'Only if it's been blessed,' he tested.

'I refuse to be drawn,' smiled Soulson.

'I'm sorry. My wife left me and took up religion. I guess I never forgave her for that.'

The waiter arrived and the two men ordered, Soulson helping the DEA man through the menu.

'So what's the official business?' said Pentanzi when the waiter had gone.

'Can we keep this between ourselves?'

'Not easy. I mean, as Head of the London Bureau of the DEA, one of my briefs is not to get involved with your internal problems. Eating in a public place like this isn't going to make that easier.'

'I thought that would ease suspicion. As far as anyone is concerned, I wanted to meet you and find out, personally, face to face, about your views on the British drug problem.'

'We're here to advise, when asked, and to monitor. And to pass on any information that we think will be of assistance.'

'Unless you're directly asked to be involved.'

'Sure. By your Home Office.'

'Not by a maverick policeman like me.'

'You said it. Hell, you do draw a lot of media attention to yourself. We can't afford to be compromised.'

'Nor intend to be.' Soulson watched the American, who said nothing. He decided to press on. 'You've been talking to one of my staff. A detective in the Intelligence Unit.'

'Jill Couples. Bright girl. Went to the States on a training course.'

'She learnt a lot.'

'We get a lot of calls from junior staff all over England. You'd be surprised who rings for advice.'

'Off the record.'

Pentanzi stonewalled. 'Like I said, we're here to advise and monitor.'

'When asked.'

'I hope the girl's not in trouble.'

'No. I need help.' He took a deep breath before continuing. 'You know my problems in Manchester.'

'Yeah. They haven't gone unnoticed.' Pentanzi gave a wry smile.

151

'Makes a change to have a city outside the USA become the drug capital of the world.'

'Why Manchester?'

'You know that as well as I do. Market forces. $24,000 a kilo in America and £26,000 a kilo over here. A better return on capital employed. That's cocaine.'

'But why Manchester? Why not London, or Birmingham?'

'Because, as your business community says, you've got the best road, rail and air network in the country.'

'Got to be more than that.'

'I'm not here to be compromised.'

'Like I said, I'm here for help.'

The American paused, sucked his lips through his teeth, then finally spoke. 'You've got a bad police system.'

'In Manchester?'

'All over. You people don't hit hard enough.'

'Guns?'

'That's only part of it. Sure, you can't use pea-shooters against howitzers. But it's the way you do things.'

'It'll change.'

Pentanzi was surprised by Soulson's remark. It wasn't what he expected from such a senior police official; most Chief Constables were proud of the fact that their officers didn't bear arms to carry out their duties. 'Is that the new official line?' he asked.

Soulson shook his head. 'No. Just a pragmatic line.'

'Because of drugs?'

'No. The IRA. In the end it'll be terrorism that'll force police to wear arms. At some stage they're going to start shooting at bobbies. When that happens there won't be a choice.'

'Maybe that's why they don't shoot policemen.'

'Might just be. Anyway, your view is that we don't hit hard enough, as far as narcotics are concerned.'

'You just don't go in to win. You guys play buy and bust.'

'What's that?'

'Putting squads in to buy drugs, then arresting the pushers. Anyone can do that. Hell, even we do. When our arrest figures are down, we stick a few agents into towns to mop up the street dealers. Looks impressive, but it's fuck all.'

'If we changed tactics, would you support us?'

'What can we do?'

'It's important that we win. It helps us all.'

'Some of our people like the Colombians putting their resources

152

over here. It means they aren't trying so hard in our backyard.'

'Cynical view.'

'Cynical world.'

They said nothing as the waiter approached and served them their meze starter. When their dishes were laid out on the table, Pentanzi smiled and applied himself joyfully to the task at hand. Soulson watched him, then chose and ate sparingly as was his habit. Neither spoke until plates were scraped clean.

'If I go on like this, I'm going to die of a heart attack before I get back to the States.'

'You like your food,' stated Soulson.

'Sure do. That's why this assignment's so great. I get to eat in places like this all over Europe.'

'I hope it all means more than good meals.' Soulson regretted his words as he said them; it was his impatience that caused it.

Pentanzi didn't reply immediately. He felt no sudden anger at the taunt. He leant back in the chair. 'Why did you become a policeman?' he asked Soulson.

'I wanted to make a difference.'

'Got to be a reason.'

'I have my reasons.' Soulson remembered the shallow graves and the small bodies all those years ago on Saddleworth Moor. He shut out the memory that always came back to haunt him.

'Let me tell you about making a difference. You heard of Haight-Ashbury?'

'San Francisco.'

'Yeah. Centre of the hippy world. In the sixties, before the DEA was formed, I worked for US Customs, undercover.' Pentanzi laughed. 'Shit, I was Black American, twenty-three and out in the world for the first time. We were amateurs then. No training, nothing. Just told to get in there and dig up what we could. I lived rough, my mattress was the nearest floorboard. Mixed with all the junkies and the gays. Queers, that's what they were then. The great drug culture. Flower power, man.' Pentanzi mockingly waved two fingers in a Peace sign.

'We had it here.'

'Not like Haight-Ashbury. There was nowhere like Haight-Ashbury. I had a room in this old brownstone. There was a woman lived upstairs. About thirty. Long blonde hair and long hippy beads. Asked me to come up and see her. So I go up there. The apartment was filthy and had this awful smell. I mean, like shit smell. And pot. The place had all the staleness of smoked weed. And she was pretty blotted out.

153

High, real high. In the corner of the room there was like a blocked-off area, with chairs and tables, you know, making barriers. And there was an old carpet draped over it, like a shelter. There was a lot of yelping going on in there. Puppies. I thought the woman kept dogs up there. No wonder the place stank. While she was in the kitchen, I went to look at the pups. I pulled the carpet back. They weren't dogs. They were babies. Two little babies. Twins. Her twins. Boy and a girl, no more than six months old. And they were crawling round in their own shit. No diapers, nothing. She used to feed them on biscuits and put their milk in a bowl. Like you'd feed an animal. That, Mr Jesus Cop, was the drug culture she was so proud of. The great drug experiment. So don't talk to me about making a difference. I fight drugs because I hate them. And everyone at the DEA has got a similar story. Because I enjoy my food, that doesn't make me cheap.'

'I'm sorry.'

'It's forgotten. So what can I do for you? Without going round the houses.'

'I'm thinking of changing the rules of combat. Doing things your way.'

'Difficult. Not something your tradition of fair play encourages.'

'We didn't get an empire by fair play. That's how we lost it.'

Pentanzi laughed. 'So tell me your plans.'

'As long as you understand they are only thoughts. Not plans to be acted on. Yet, anyway. Let's say I'm looking for a consultant. Someone who understands the rules you play by.'

When he finished, Pentanzi refused to comment and spoke instead of the food the waiter now put before them. When they were on their own again, Pentanzi opened up on the subject once more. 'Dangerous game you're playing.'

'No choice.'

'There's always a choice.'

'Not when things are out of control.'

'You understand that when you talk to me, you could be talking to the whole United States Administration.'

Soulson noted the American had said *could be*. 'Which is why I wanted it to remain between the two of us.'

'Who've you got in mind? To help you out on this little caper.'

'Nobody yet,' Soulson lied.

'You want me to suggest someone?'

'No. I just want your views. And information that will help me deal with the problem.'

'We've done things like that. Private action. If it rebounds, then it blows up in your face.'

'You don't think I should do it?'

'Didn't say that. Just said that private action can blow up in your face.'

'Can it work?'

'Yeah. It can work. You decided to go ahead?'

'Not yet.'

'How can I help?'

'Your people must have information on the Manchester scene.'

'I told you. We're here to liaise and advise . . . when asked to.'

'What do you know about Manchester?'

'Just rumour. That Manchester's a way in for the Colombians. They've been trying to set up in Europe for years, now that we're slowly regaining control in North America. They also get a better return on their narcotics. You people don't just pay more for your cars and VCRs. Your coke costs more, too. And let's not forget the heroin and where that comes from. Your city is a distribution centre for both the Colombians and the Asians. It ain't just the South Americans. You got a big Chinese population.'

'That's going to get worse by 1997 when Hong Kong reverts back to China.'

'Did you know there are nearly half a million Triad members in Hong Kong?'

'As many as that?'

'Damn right. All trying to get out by '97. Triads are running gangs that're as dangerous as the Colombians. That's nothing new. In the States, the Triads are using the Vietnamese gangs. Be lucky you haven't got them yet. Or the Jamaicans.'

'We've got the Yardies,' commented Soulson, referring to the Jamaican-based gangs who controlled much of the London heroin. 'Only leaves the Mafia,' he continued sarcastically.

'Hey, at times I wish we still had them. Ever since John Gotti got taken out of circulation, the Cosa Nostra have been running round like headless chickens.' Gotti, known as the Teflon Don until he was jailed, when he became the Velcro Don, was the last of the flamboyant Godfathers of New York. 'They're second division now. Too many years of easy living made them soft. Yeah, they were a lot easier to deal with. Had their own standards. These new creeps have none. But, coming back to your problem, our sources tell us Manchester's the new hot centre for narcotics. That's where the battle lines are being drawn.'

155

'You said it's rumour,' persisted Soulson.

'It's what your people in London say. Got their bloody heads buried in the sand. I'm telling you, Manchester is the pitcher's mound for a whole new ball game.'

'Will the DEA help?'

'No. Officially or unofficially. They don't want to get involved in a political fracas with your Home Office. Listen, we believe in fighting the suppliers and the dealers, not each other.' Pentanzi paused for a moment. 'I'll get you whatever names I can. And any other information I think will help. That is, if you decide to go ahead with it.'

'Thank you.'

'But that's personal. My risk. Not the DEA's.'

'Why?'

'Because we're hasslin' the same crowd. Your enemy is my enemy. We'll have to work out a method of communication.'

'I appreciate that.' Soulson guessed that Pentanzi would only help within Washington's guidelines. That meant he would probably report back on this meeting. The policeman felt the flush of panic; it had been a stupid decision to arrange it.

'You've been looking at this thing from the inside. All you see are the petty crooks. Small penny-ante stuff. If you want to kill it, you've got to widen your horizons. This isn't just a local problem. This whole thing is global. *Time* magazine cover stuff. Start looking outside. Look where it comes from. That's what the DEA's about.'

'I understand that.' The panic eased; he realized it was unlikely the DEA would inform the British of Soulson's concerns. Like all organizations, they preferred keeping their cards face down. 'We know most of the routes into Britain, anyway.'

'Into Europe, you mean. Don't forget, your immigration and customs posts are open to the continent. Hell, that's a damn big hole to pour drugs through. You got cannabis coming out of Morocco into Spain, new Eastern European transit routes out of the old communist bloc into Germany, the heroin trail from Turkey along the Balkan and Greek routes, and all that South American cocaine and heroin from Asia into Holland. There's even cannabis from the West Indies being shipped through Sweden and Denmark. And that's just some of what we know about. These guys are pushing all the time for new routes into the continent.' He grinned suddenly. 'And, boy, do they have some cute tricks. The other day I heard this South American woman was coming through customs carrying a new-born baby in her arms, all wrapped up. They pulled her in for questioning, found the baby was dead, had been dead for days, and was stuffed with cocaine. That's the world we live in.'

'Which is why I need help.'

Pentanzi considered for a moment before answering. 'I'll get you what I can. Do you know of any Irish connection?'

The question surprised Soulson. 'What sort of Irish connection?'

'I just wondered.' This time Pentanzi lied. 'We just want to know if that's the way the stuff comes into this country.'

'No. We only know of the coloureds and the Chinese.' He immediately regretted using the word coloured, knew the word black was what they preferred. They! Guilt now joined the regret and Soulson silently cursed his stupidity.

'Ain't heard that for a long time,' commented Pentanzi, a wry grin spreading across his face. 'Always preferred it, you know. Black. Too damn harsh a word. Anyway, if your people pick up anything on the Irish, tell me. It's only a possibility, but an avenue worth following.'

'All right.' Soulson knew he had gone far enough. 'Anything you get for us will be welcomed. And . . . if I decide to go ahead with this . . . private action . . . then I'll come back to you.'

'Fine.' Pentanzi sensed the policeman was lying, that he was further down the track than he was prepared to admit. He attacked his meal once again with gusto. 'You're right about one thing. The food here is really great.'

The two men settled down to enjoy their meal.

There was nothing else to be said. They both understood that they would be there to help each other if the need arose in the future. The Irish link worried Soulson. Damn. Manchester was getting like the United Nations.

He decided to add that new fact to the letter. It was something that could have a bearing.

The Town of Wilmslow
Stockbroker Belt
Cheshire
England

'The Irish and blacks just don't mix,' said Armitage. 'Unless they happen to meet in a pub.'

'Well, that's what he said.' Soulson shrugged. It was early evening and he had just arrived back from London. Job and Armitage had met him off the shuttle and driven him straight home. Tessa was out for the evening; a short note informed him she was on a date and not to wait up for her. Paul Job had been despatched to the kitchen to prepare a snack for the three of them while Soulson and Armitage retired to the living-room. 'I don't think it was an idle question. Almost like he knew something.'

'I'll see what the Intelligence Unit's got. But I would've heard something by now.'

'Get them to look in that direction. But low key. Let's not scare anyone off.'

'How do we know Pentanzi won't go straight to his superiors?'

'We don't.'

'They'll see through it.'

'Possibly. That's the risk. Listen, Roy, I don't care if it gets to the President of the United States. As long as they decide to help. Our methods are no good on their own. Pentanzi was right when he said we had to widen our horizons. We have to use the methods they employ. Fire with fire. Wasn't that what Christley said?'

'Yes.' Armitage remembered the scene in Moss Side all those years ago when they had been young coppers.

'We can't beat this drug problem until we centralize and co-ordinate our efforts. It's no good each individual police force dealing with their own problems. And while we're fighting the petty thieves, the customs people are on their own trying to stop drugs coming into the country. It's not on, Roy. It's a shambles. It has to be one effort, one national drug squad.'

'Let's hope they don't find out,' warned Armitage.

'The Yanks aren't going to say anything. They'll be pleased to get more information out of us than they normally do. They always moan we aren't forthcoming enough. And they're right. I bet they know more about our drug problems than we do.'

'Like this Irish connection?'

'Every report I see says the Provos and the Loyalists aren't into narcotics. I don't believe that. At the end of the day they're terrorists. They're into protection and extortion and most things that make money. Why not drugs? They'll make more money out of that than the rest put together.'

Armitage shrugged. 'Does that mean you're ready to send the letter?'

'Not yet.' He saw Armitage turn away. Soulson realized how difficult it must be for him, all this vacillating. 'I want to give it one more go before we jump over the cliff.'

158

'It's your decision.'

'I know. The one thing Pentanzi and I agreed on was that we've got to fight them on their terms. Let's do that. But on our own, without outside help.'

'Sounds like you've come up with something.'

'It's worth a try. When we get back, I want you to get me all the information we've got on Moss Side. The gangs, the leaders, the full drugs operation.'

'And then?'

'Let's make our presence felt. I want to move fast, Roy. Within a few days. It's time they knew they weren't outside the law. Anything else happen today?'

'Spencer wanted to know why you'd gone to London.'

'Like being at bloody school.'

'I told her you'd gone for a smoke in the toilets.'

Soulson grinned. 'Very funny. What did you say?'

'Like you said. That you were meeting a DEA man from the American embassy.'

'How'd she take that?'

'*Mr Soulson's not hoping for a job, is he?*' Armitage mimicked in a high voice. 'I didn't tell her you were wearing your best interview suit. Then she said you should've attended the clothing allowance committee meeting.'

'Why? Doesn't she like what I wear?'

Armitage decided to change the subject. He could see Soulson was getting agitated with frustration. 'That young bobby whose neck was cut, he came out today. They say he's going to be fine.'

'Apart from his voice.'

'At least he's alive.'

'Anything on the other attacks?'

'Still nothing. The Chinese are saying nothing and Moss Side's as clamped up as ever.'

'What I've got planned might shake up a few of them.'

'Hope so. I think we've covered everything. Good news is the binmen's strike is over.'

'Today?'

'Yes. They settled for everything the union wanted.'

'Bloody left-wingers. What a waste of time. I suppose they'll want to win a battle somewhere. To prove how good they really are. It'll be the car.'

'The AA road test should sort that out.'

'When?'

'Tomorrow. Late afternoon. She'll get the report in a couple of days.'

'Good. As long as the car performs as you promise.'

'It will. I've put my best driver on to it.'

Police Driving Test Circuit
Openshaw
Manchester

It was a new car, spanking new, polished and gleaming just as it had been delivered from the showroom. A black Rover 216Si. The type of car that a salesman would be proud to drive and that the majority of the left-wing Police Committee wanted Soulson to use. A 1400cc, four-cylinder, eight-valve transverse engine with a five-speed manual transmission. There were three sandbags in the car, two strapped in the back, one in the passenger seat. Each bag weighed over 160 pounds and represented a person. There was a smaller sandbag in the boot.

Chief Inspector Desmond Mailer of the Motorway Unit, wearing a crash helmet and a set of white overalls over his police uniform, climbed in and switched on the engine. He let it run for a moment to warm up, so that it would perform to the best of its design capabilities, then slipped it into gear and pulled away from the parking bay.

He'd been told to play it by the book and that was what he intended to do. He started gently, driving her as any Sunday driver would, coaxing her through the gears, testing her within the tolerances of the handbook. The evening sun glinted off the skid pan, a mixture of oil and water, that covered the area by the side of the track.

By the small brick building at the side, three instructors, also in white overalls and carrying their crash helmets under their arms, waited their turn in the demonstration. They stood beside three cars: two plain-wrapper jobs and a fully marked patrol car. The unmarked cars were a Mini 1000 and a Jaguar XJS, the patrol car a 24-valve Rover Vitesse powered by a 2.7-litre engine. Next to them stood an engineer, his clipboard and stopwatch in his hand. The men's attention was firmly fixed on their Chief Inspector as he put the small Rover through its paces.

After ten minutes, when Mailer was satisfied that the engine had been properly warmed, he slipped into third gear and eased the accelerator to the deck. The engine screamed as it revved into the red at nearly 6000 rpm and at its top speed in third of 75 mph. Mailer held her on the track for another ten minutes before he heeled and toed her into second and max-revved her at 46 mph for another ten minutes. She stood her ground well; the temperature gauge barely moved from its centre position.

Then he flicked her through the gears into fifth and, at her top speed of 103 mph, drove her round the track for another fifteen minutes. It was as Mailer flicked her down through the gears into second that he saw the first belch of smoke from the exhaust in his rear-view mirror. He smiled to himself. She'd lasted longer than he'd expected. Maybe the Brits didn't make such bad cars after all.

He held her in second for another ten minutes, then flicked her up through the gears into top and kept her at 101. The temperature gauge was rising positively towards the red. Ten minutes later he slammed the brakes on violently, felt the car break into a skid and turned into it. He rammed the accelerator to the floor, skipped into third and hurtled away from the skid. He repeated the manoeuvre thirty times before he pushed her back to top speed and held her for the customary ten minutes. Then he repeated the exercise with the skid, brakes and violent acceleration before bringing her in to park beside the three instructors who stood waiting for him. He leant forward and pulled the bonnet lever.

Mailer felt sorry for the car as he climbed out and took off his helmet. He liked cars; they were like women who responded well if you looked after them. He didn't enjoy raping her; it went against all his instincts. He stood back as the engineer pulled the bonnet up and checked the oil, water, hydraulics and general condition of the engine. As he scrutinized each item, he made notes on his pad.

'You take her on the skid pan, Willie. Fifteen minutes, no more,' he told the nearest of the three men, then turned and walked into the brick building. As he sat in the inspector's rest room, a cup of coffee in his hand, he watched Willie through the window, saw him put her through her paces on the skid pan. The car seemed to handle well, but the smoke was now constant through the tailpipe. The brakes were also squealing and he knew their heat would soon be producing more smoke.

After the skid pan, another instructor took her out on the track and ran her for nearly an hour as Mailer had done. When he returned he reported that the brakes were beginning to fade and that the temperature gauge was very near the red.

After further scrutiny and a fresh tank of petrol, Mailer took

161

over and drove her on to the track. This time she was followed by the two unmarked cars. He pulled away and the two cars kept in close formation. The Mini was closest and, after two circuits at maximum speed, it tried to force the Rover off the road. The slowness of Mailer's car made it an easy target for the nimble Mini and within two further circuits it had overtaken Mailer and slid to a stop in front of him. To escape the attempted terrorist attack, Mailer clicked into reverse, spun the wheel and drove off in the opposite direction. Two laps later the Mini had overtaken him again and forced him to stop.

The exercise was repeated with the Jaguar XJS and the marked patrol car. The Jaguar took three laps to force the small Rover to a stop, but that was due to its bulk and lack of agility. The patrol car equalled the Mini in its attempts.

'No car for an ambush,' said Mailer to his men when they had returned to the building. It was dark now and the circuit was lit by floodlights. He sat with the engineer as they went through the report. While they worked, the three instructors took turns as they put the Rover through its paces on the track.

Fast.

Slow.

Brake hard.

Skid.

Turn.

Stand her on her head.

Two hours later, with smoke pouring from the exhaust and the brakes worn and snatched into a squealing shadow of their recent newness, she was parked by the building for the last time.

The engineer did his final report.

'I think it's pretty fair,' commented Willie to no-one in particular. 'Hell, we haven't run her through mud, water, metal spikes or any of the other tests we put our patrol cars through.'

Then, when the engineer had finished his final report, the five men went home.

They left the Rover where she had come to a stop. Covered in dust and oil, the smell of burning material clinging to her body, she was a sorry sight. Hard to believe she had only 400 miles on her clock and had three days earlier commanded pride of place in the showroom window of a large Manchester car dealership.

But that was before the police came and bought her as the latest addition to their fleet. Her only future now would be in a used-car sales-lot.

St Mary's Church
Manchester

It was early morning and the commuters hadn't started to clog the roads yet. The rubbish still lay spilled across the pavements and streets. The strike was over but the debris would take weeks to clear.

Soulson had been driven in early to avoid the rush hour. It was going to be a long day and he wanted some peace before the phones started ringing. If there was one thing he was certain of, today was the day the phones would never stop ringing.

Paul Job parked the Jaguar on the double yellow line and walked into the church with his chief. As was his habit, when there wasn't time to inform Bootle Street that a bobby was needed, Job stood at the rear, protecting Soulson's back while the big man prayed.

The church was empty and Soulson took a pew halfway down to the altar. He knelt and prayed for forgiveness, for Tessa, for his friends, and for those who were about to embark on this most dangerous of days.

Then he thought of what he had set in motion. He thought of that most secret plan that he knew was wrong but was his only solution.

He thought of his family, those beyond where he could reach except in his thoughts. He thought of Jimmy. Brother lost. *Damn you, Jimmy. For what you've made me.*

Then her face came smiling through.

Mary. Mary mine.

He knew she could see him, knew that he'd never been unfaithful to her since those distant days of her death and that sad little funeral. It had never entered his mind to be carnal with another woman. He wondered if she'd forgive what he was about to embark on. Whether the good points he'd scored with his fidelity would count when she understood the full horror of what he had planned.

If you believed in God, as he did, then he knew Mary was aware of his plan. He remembered his confessional with the priest and was suddenly embarrassed. He didn't know why he'd gone to him. To absolve his actions? To ask forgiveness before the crime was committed?

He thought of his stillborn son, the brother Tessa never had. Would he have been a policeman, following in his father's footsteps?

163

It's only dreams, Charlie Soulson. That's what old men and sinners are made of.

He shook his head clear. This was not a day to have a muddled mind. Today was the first warning shot.

Armageddon in Moss Side was a long way off. The Angel of Death was yet to come.

Sedgeley Park Police Training College
Prestwich
North Manchester

There were forty vehicles in the convoy.

More than 200 police officers were taking part in the operation. They had all arrived in small groups at the eleven-acre college the evening before, and overnighted in the Halls of Residence. They'd been thoroughly briefed in the training rooms and were now ready and eager, in the early hours of the morning, to get on with their individual responsibilities. It had been a hastily conceived plan, but nevertheless well organized, with little left to chance.

The convoy left Sedgeley Park at 7 a.m., swung on to the motorway that circled Manchester, and drove south at high speed. Motorcycle outriders and selected motorway police vehicles had cleared the outside lane of the three lane highway and the convoy covered the ten mile trip to Moss Side within fifteen minutes.

They came off the motorway and drove down Princess Parkway into the centre of Moss Side.

Soulson arrived at Stretford ten minutes before the convoy left Prestwich. He went straight to the modern communications centre that had recently been built next to the police headquarters and made his way up to the Major Incident Room. The room, reminiscent to him of the wartime RAF operations rooms when fighters were scrambled to shoot down the German bombers, was a hive of activity. There was a central table, policed by officers on radio telephones, a large map covering Manchester and Moss Side on one wall, a bank of computer and communications monitors built into a second wall, and a raised dais at which senior officers sat so they could monitor and supervise the operation as it progressed.

The hum of activity died as he walked in and he smiled at the people in the room before waving them back to their duties.

He crossed over to the dais and stood behind his Assistant Chief Constable, 'V' Department, the Head of Criminal Investigation.

'They're about to leave, Chief,' said the ACC.

'Any last minute hiccups?' asked Soulson.

'No, sir. I spoke to Steven ten minutes ago. No problems at all.' Chief Superintendent Steven White, Head of the CID Operations Group, was in charge on the ground.

'Mind if I stay down here?'

'Of course not,' joked the ACC. 'It'll save on phone calls to your office.'

Soulson watched as the operation swung into action. The man by the two maps had a row of magnetic coloured markers and he now placed them on the board. As the radio crackled with more information, so the row of magnetic markers was moved across the map. It was a simple system, but one that enabled those watching to monitor the action visually as it happened.

'OK,' the ACC called when the markers were about to leave the motorway and drive down Princess Parkway. 'Let's tell the community leaders.'

Officers on the left of the table picked up their phones, dialled and started to speak into them. They were all members of 'R' Department, the section which dealt with community relations. They were warning local leaders in Moss Side of what they were about to do. They were the ones people would turn to and it was important that they had a life-line to the police. Their influence would matter greatly in the next few hours.

'Left that a little late, haven't you?' remarked Soulson.

'No, Chief. I don't want anyone being warned. Community leaders or not, their loyalty doesn't lie with us.'

Soulson accepted what his ACC said. These were his people and he had to trust their judgement. He knew a second team of officers was now on its way to the area with explanatory printed letters which would be pushed through household letter-boxes explaining what was going on. Most of the Moss Side community were against drugs and they would be pleased to see action being taken to stamp out this awful situation in the midst of where they lived.

Five minutes later the convoy split as planned and hit thirty separate addresses in Moss Side; houses which had been secretly filmed and infiltrated by undercover officers over the last few months. Soulson watched the row of markers spread across the Moss Side map.

The first arrest report came in ten minutes later.

'Just broke down the door into a council house in Gooch Close,' said one of the officers at the desk. 'Eight members of the gang in there and they've found some heroin. Also a crossbow with some bolts, machetes and some baseball bats.'

There was a small cheer from the dais. The Gooch Close gang was one of the two worst drug gangs in Moss Side.

'Call for you,' said one of the superintendents. He held out the phone to Soulson.

It was Armitage, upstairs on the eleventh floor handling the difficult calls. 'Spencer's been on for you,' he told Soulson. 'I said you were in an operational situation and couldn't be disturbed.'

'Keep it that way,' replied Soulson.

'She's jumping up and down. Said she should've been told about the raid instead of receiving a short memo on her desk after it had started.'

Soulson could imagine the anger in her face. He'd told the uniformed motorcycle courier to deliver the short note to the Town Hall at exactly seven twenty. Spencer was well known for getting to the Town Hall early. 'Make sure she keeps away. If she rings back, tell her this is an executive operation and out of her jurisdiction. At this time.'

'She's already had some of the community leaders on to her.'

'I bet she has.'

Within the next hour thirty arrests had been made. Three policemen were hurt, one critically after a raid on a shabeen which resulted in the officer being attacked by an escaping gang member with a knuckleduster with fish-hooks soldered to it.

There had been a special cheer when the two shabeens on Moss Lane East had been broken into. They were part of the Front, a row of shops where all manner of drugs were easily obtained. Once likened to a supermarket checkout counter, police officers had spent years watching cars pull up at the kerb, hand money over and drive off with a fistful of drugs. One of the shabeens that cornered the Front was the Club Nilus. The officers were particularly pleased with the stealth with which they'd achieved their objectives. The usual Moss Side early-warning system had failed to pick up their approach until it was too late. The sentries, posted along the long open walkways of the high-rise flats, had been negligent in their duties. They, like their leaders, believed in their own invincibility and couldn't foresee a police snatch squad bursting into what was now considered a no-go area. It would shake them. The drug-dealers would know that the police were bringing the battle zone into their own territory.

In addition to the arrests there were also considerable finds of heroin, some cocaine, a mishmash of small drugs and a wide variety of weapons, including shotguns and pistols. The most surprising find was a carton of Semtex explosives. It wasn't something that was expected in Moss Side. In the Irish community, but not Moss Side.

The explosives find worried Soulson. As the Major Incident Room congratulated themselves on a job well done, he was silent, recalling what the American, Pentanzi, had said.

Maybe the Irish were involved after all.

Abdul Paras was on the run.

It had been a late night. Paras had stayed in the shabeen until it closed at four, then played a few rounds of brag with his lieutenants before going to bed. He'd lost over £2,000 in fifteen minutes. He sent one of the sentries out to fetch Shaeron from her terraced house, then retired to the bedroom with a sore head and an even sorer disposition. When Shaeron arrived fifteen minutes later, having been woken from a deep sleep after an unusually heavy night with fourteen punters, she found Paras had already masturbated. He'd been impatient and not even bothered taking his trousers off; had simply rolled them down to his ankles and proceeded to satisfy his erection. She saw him as he lay there, his belly and groin wet and sticky in the aftermath of his pleasure.

'You could've waited,' she said as she lay down beside him.

'Just shut up and get into bed, will you?' he snarled at her.

Then they went to sleep.

The noise that woke him two hours later didn't alarm him at first. Some of his men lived in the small rooms below and ensured that no-one could come up the stairs and ambush him. And the card game was probably still in play on the ground floor. He heard some shouting from downstairs, then someone running up the stairs.

'Shut your fucking noise,' he screamed at whoever had woken him, waking Shaeron suddenly as he did. She sat up in the bed.

'What's up?' she snapped at him.

Someone continued to run up the stairs, on to the landing below, and then up the second flight towards Paras's attic-floor bedroom.

Paras sensed danger, pushed Shaeron off the bed and rolled on to the floor. His trousers, still wrapped round his ankles, tripped him and he fell forward. As he hit the floor, the door was pushed open sharply and a policeman, a middle-aged uniformed sergeant from the local station, burst into the room.

'You Abdul Paras?' asked the sergeant, a truncheon in his hand as he circled the fallen drug leader. The room was dark, the morning sun blotted out by the curtains.

'No!' shouted Paras, trying to pick himself off the floor.

'Get up. Come on.'

'Give us a chance. Shit, give us a fucking chance.'

'And watch your language.' The sergeant turned to Shaeron and told her to get dressed. For a short moment his eyes were off the man on the floor.

It was all the time Paras needed. He pulled himself up, yanking at his trousers as he did so. His hand, now shielded from the policeman, found the knuckleduster in his pocket and he slipped it on. Then, as the policeman turned towards him once again, he swung at the sergeant's face.

The policeman screamed and brought his hand to his face, to protect himself from the deadly onslaught. To no avail. Paras attacked again and again until the man fell unconscious to the floor.

Shaeron, as was usual in these times of crisis, turned her head away and stared out of the window at a Moss Side which was being rudely awakened to the day. As she heard the frantic blows being rained down behind her, she saw the slow-moving line of commuter traffic in the street below and she wondered if any of her punters were passing by and remembering their efforts from the night before.

Then the noise stopped and she turned round. She ignored the policeman on the floor, just watched Paras pull his trousers up.

'Say you had a client up here and he fucking got away,' snapped Paras. He pushed past her, opened the window and stepped out on to the wide ledge.

Then he was gone from her. She knew the ledge led round the building to the scaffolding at the back. It had been put up years before as an escape route in case of ambush, but had only been used previously by errant husbands dodging their wives. She crossed to the window and closed it as a second policeman burst into the room. She saw him stop sharply at the scene of carnage, then turn towards the bed and start retching.

Behind the unfortunate man, the room was suddenly full of more blue uniforms and peaked caps and pointed helmets and everyone was shouting at her.

She sat on the end of the bed and waited for the hysteria to die. She wondered if he'd got away.

The raid and its aftermath cheered up Cohn Bourne. The Irishman

168

knew this could be the catalyst that brought Moss Side into line.

He sat opposite Paras and Stash Maxwell. The two had arrived unexpectedly at his flat in Didsbury, the heart of Manchester University's student residential area. Bourne had been fast asleep when the urgent knocking on the front door brought him awake sharply. At first he thought it was the police and he had refused to answer it, but the banging persisted and then he recognized Paras's muffled cursing through the thick reinforced door.

'That's good news,' he said when Paras had told him of the police raid. He sat opposite the two men in his towelling robe, a cup of coffee steaming in front of him.

'What's so fucking good about that?' retaliated an angry Paras. He was annoyed that Bourne had made him wait while he made himself a coffee.

'Just what we've been waiting for. Now's the time to organize.'

'The pigs have arrested half the ganglords.'

'Perfect. While their men are running round headless, you can go in and get them on your side. Forget all this separate gangs stuff. Get them into one unit, one big force that can take on the police. And the Chinese.'

'Nobody's going to agree to that. Not in Moss Side.'

'He's right, Abdul,' interrupted Maxwell. 'They're all going to be wondering what to do next. Even the Jamaican shit like the Yardies. Apart from you, all the ganglords are locked away. They won't be out for at least twenty-four hours.'

'You've got the weapons,' continued Bourne. 'Organize a meet, get the lieutenants together, show them how strong they can become, and you'll be the only ganglord left in Moss Side.' Bourne laughed harshly. 'When the others find out, they'll probably ask to stay under police protection.'

The two men watched the idea ferment in Paras. Even for a man who lived by a simple code of brutality and violence, he quickly realized the advantage he found himself in. He nodded his agreement, a big grin spreading across his face.

'I can get the meet sorted,' broke in Maxwell, not one to let an opportunity pass. He knew how the ganglord could suddenly change his mind.

'Yeah. Yeah, Jedie. Get it done,' agreed Paras.

'I'll see you later.'

'Where you going to meet?' asked Bourne. 'Shabeen's not safe. Cops'll be watching.'

'How about Shaeron's?'

'No,' came in Paras. 'That'll be staked out, too.'

'Come back here,' said Bourne. 'Only make sure you're not followed.'

'I could do with a drink,' Paras said when Maxwell had gone.

'Haven't got anything,' lied the Irishman. He wanted Paras with a clear head, not wound up with strong emotions generated by alcohol. 'How about some coffee?'

'Yeah.'

Bourne walked through into the kitchen and switched the kettle back on. He was glad Stash Maxwell wasn't the ganglord. That boy had brains and cunning. This one, the big thick nigger, was easier to handle. Just direct the violence and sit back and pick up the rewards.

'Jedie knows what he's doing,' said Paras as he came into the kitchen, startling Bourne.

''Course he does. You put together a good team. That's all down to you.'

'Fucking pigs. I'll pay them back. Coming in here and trying to stuff us. Them and the fucking Chinks for starting this shit.'

The idea was formed in Bourne's head before he even thought about it. 'Let's do that.'

'I'll get the bastards.'

'Sooner than you think.'

'Eh?'

'Good idea, Abdul. We can run it to them.' He turned and led Paras into the living-room to explain the idea to him. He also wanted him out of the small kitchen. He hated the bitter smell of the bastards and the stink would linger for days in the small room.

Christ, it was bad enough having him hole up here for the next few days.

He sighed and remembered the Maze Prison, the dirty demonstrations in the H Blocks. All that shit smeared over the cell walls. Hell, it was hard believing in an idea when all you saw was the arse end of life. But that's the way it was.

Then he remembered the policeman. Manchester Blue. It was time he started to earn his corn. His superiors would like that one. He needed to activate Manchester Blue.

He sat down and patiently explained his idea to Paras.

They held the meeting in the conference room on the eleventh floor. Soulson had gone up in the lifts with the rest of the senior officers from the Major Incident Room.

Chief Superintendent Steven White and his deputy, the ACCs

170

'X' Department, Uniform Operations Branch, and 'Y' Department, Discipline and Complaints, and the Chief Superintendents of Community Relations and Press were waiting for him in the conference room.

'Don't get up,' said Soulson as he walked in and took his place at the head of the long table. He looked round at his subordinates and saw the smugness of success on their faces. Then he laughed and punched his fist into the air. 'Well done, well bloody done. I'm proud of you all.'

The men round the table joined in with him, turned to each other and congratulated themselves. Soulson let them enjoy their moment of triumph, sat back and waited for the celebrations to come to a natural conclusion.

'That's only the first step,' he said, when quiet had returned to the meeting. 'Things'll get tougher now. Next time they'll expect us. But at least they know we've got teeth.'

'And we don't just bark. We bite,' said White.

Soulson joined in the laughter, then continued. 'What's the final count, Steven?'

'Thirty arrests. Five of them ganglords. We missed two. Leader of the Peppertea Mob and a character called Abdul Paras. Paras is the less important of the two. Small-time stuff, concentrates his efforts on a shabeen called the Club Nilus. We raided his place but there were no finds. Weapons or drugs. We were surprised the place was that clean. We know it's a drug base.'

'Any ideas?' asked the ACC 'V', White's immediate superior in the Criminal Investigation Department and the man who had controlled the Major Incident Room during the raid.

'No, sir.'

'Could they have been warned?'

'I don't think so. It was pretty watertight.'

'I agree,' said the Chief Superintendent of Press. 'My press department's been on to me complaining the first they knew about it was when the media rang asking what the hell was going on.'

'Let's hear the rest of the report,' Soulson brought the meeting back to order.

'All those arrested were found with drugs or weapons on them,' went on White. 'Some pretty strong cases against them. Two of the bobbies hurt are out of hospital. One got his face scratched by a girlfriend of someone we arrested, and the other got hit on the shoulder with a baseball bat by a ganglord resisting arrest. The third bobby's still on the critical list. He's a sergeant from Platt

171

Lane and he's been blinded in one eye and had most of his cheek scraped down to the bone. It was some sort of knuckleduster with spikes on it. He didn't see much. It all happened too quick.'

'Can he identify the assailant?' asked ACC 'V'.

'No. The room was curtained off. Too dark. He was looking for Paras, but there's no positive ID.'

'Bloody hell,' said ACC 'X'.

'The plastic boys are doing the best they can, but it'll be a while before he's off the critical. Lost a lot of blood.'

'His family?' asked Soulson.

'Wife and two grown-up kids. I'm getting all the details for you, sir.'

'Good.' Soulson decided he would visit the officer as soon as the meeting was over.

White ran through the rest of the report, including a message of congratulations from the Chinese community on a job well done, but there was little to add to what they already knew. Soulson turned to the Chief Superintendent of Community Relations. 'Any flack yet?'

'No, sir,' came the reply. 'Most of the community leaders were a bit upset we hadn't contacted them earlier, but they accepted the reasons. And the press coverage has been good. *Manchester Evening News* have given it front page and everyone's calling it a success. Because it's drugs, they're all on our side. Except for some of the local politicians.'

'Bloody Lefties,' said ACC 'X'.

'You know we're not supposed to be political,' quipped Soulson, and the team round the table, his men, laughed. 'Well, just stonewall as long as possible. Then pass them on to me. Anything else been going on out there I should know about?'

'Good news, Chief,' said ACC 'X'. 'We've had a load of phone calls from Moss Side residents. Praising us. Thanking us. Saying it's about time we took control of the situation.'

'When?'

'All in the last hour. We've even had people go in to the police stations and say well done.'

'Good. Make sure we pass that on to the men.'

'There's one bone of contention, Chief,' said Armitage.

'What's that?'

'Some of the officers, both in the field and in here, think we should go after the Chinese as well.' Armitage trod warily; he knew Soulson didn't want anything to diminish what they had achieved. But he had been pushed to bring the matter up with the Chief Constable. 'There's one opium den we know of, and two or

172

three places where heroin could be stored. We know some of the pushers.'

'But you can't guarantee we'll find anything?' Soulson replied abruptly.

'No, sir. Not like Moss Side.'

'I want this to be a hundred per center. If there's no guarantees, we don't touch it.'

'The feeling was that we shouldn't just appear to be hitting the blacks, but all the drug boys.'

'Now's not the time.' Soulson shot a warning glance at Armitage. 'Unless you've got any further points.'

'No, Chief.' Armitage knew there was little point in pursuing the discussion.

'Right then. I'm going on to the hospital. Thank you, gentlemen. Well done.'

'What about the Major Incident Room?' asked ACC 'Y'. 'Can we close it down?'

'Yes. We won't be needing that for a while.'

It was a remark that would haunt him for a long time to come.

The first Jill Couples heard of the raid was on the car radio as she came in to Stretford. The news excited her and she raced to her small office. By the time she arrived everyone was talking about the bold raid on the Moss. Small excited groups were congregating in the canteens and corridors; there was a general sense of elation that the police had finally hit back. As the arrests increased, so did the euphoria amongst members of a Force who had recently been constant victims of criticism and violence.

Having scoured the building for more information, Jill finally arrived at her desk half an hour late. The other three officers she shared the room with were out, so she opened the files she had been working on the night before and spread them over the two desks they all shared. She was disappointed that she hadn't been involved in the operation, especially as she had spent the last few days hurriedly preparing information on Moss Side. The information, she now realized, had been for the raid. She decided to shrug off the hurt she felt that they hadn't told her what the information was needed for. Hers was not to question why.

The information she spread out on the desk was for a different matter. Armitage had asked her to prepare a report on the latest American methods. It was a confidential report; he had instructed her to make only verbal reports to him. She had already had two meetings with him in the last week. His main concern had been about Quantico and her time there. He asked about the instructors and their various training methods. At first she thought she was under investigation, but soon realized he was genuinely interested in the DEA and FBI methods. The questioning had opened up old wounds and she tried to ignore the emotion that welled inside her. She had answered all his questions as factually as possible; her instinct told her he hadn't sensed anything untoward in her manner.

She pushed the past out of her thoughts and tried to concentrate on the information before her. She started to read a DEA report on Colombian drug-traffickers and specific covert operations in Miami. It was hard work; her mind was still full of the disappointment of the raid and the memories of Quantico.

Twenty minutes later she went to the canteen and sat alone as she sipped a coffee. The results of the raid were now filtering through and she overheard officers at the next table discussing the fact that weapons had been used by the police when they hit Moss Side. She wondered if that was how it was going to be now. Guns and methods imported from America. Maybe that's why she was doing this specific report for Armitage.

It suddenly dawned on her that she might be preparing the groundwork for a new type of police force, one which took the battle to the enemy instead of waiting for events to unfold.

A subdued Jill Couples returned to her office and set about completing the report for Chief Superintendent Armitage.

Nine in the evening on a dark clear night and all's well.

Greenhayes Lane Police Station, Moss Side, was the first to be hit.

It wasn't the first time that the Moss Side police station had come under attack. It had been almost razed to the ground by fire attacks during the inner-city riots which had rocked the major conurbations in the 1980s and almost brought the government down. Since then the police station had been reinforced by steel roller-shutters and fireproof doors and was close enough to the community to know when trouble was brewing.

Whatever Soulson and his men believed, the officers of Greenhayes Lane knew better. The successful operation against the drug gangs put them at jeopardy. If there was to be retaliation it would be in their manor. The men and women of Greenhayes Lane cursed Soulson. It was all right jumping all over Moss Side, but *they* didn't have to pick up the pieces. Then they shrugged their shoulders, cursed once more, and got on with policing the streets. It was a dirty job, but it was their job.

'Watch your backs,' the desk sergeant warned his teams as they went out in pairs. 'Just be careful and remember all the shit out there helps pay the mortgage.'

Things were quiet in the streets until the sun went down. The only excitement was the flow of pleasure seekers from the suburbs driving through Princess Parkway on their way into Manchester for a good night out.

The first group of Paras's men, six of them, stole four cars from a nearby road and drove towards the Parkway. Two cars parked at the southern end, near the YMCA, and waited for the others to drive northwards for three-quarters of a mile and pull up next to the Skol lager brewery that straddled the boundary between Manchester and Moss Side. They swung the cars across the two carriageways, blocking both north and south routes, and climbed out. The honks of protest from following drivers soon stopped when they saw the men light Molotov cocktails, flaming rags stuffed into milk bottles full of petrol, and toss them through the windows of the stolen cars.

Down the road, taking their signal from the explosions near the brewery, the second team drove across the southern carriageways and blocked them, lit their Molotov cocktails and set the second pair of cars ablaze. All six men then vanished into the darkness of the side streets, their mission accomplished.

Princess Parkway, the main artery into Moss Side, was now successfully sealed off. By the time the police had resolved that issue, the rest of Paras's and Bourne's mayhem would be well under way.

The meeting they'd called earlier, at the Moss Side People's Centre in St Mary's Road, had been well attended. As one of only two ganglords not under arrest, the foot-soldiers of Moss Side's various gangs knew they could be in danger if they ignored Paras' summons. That was confirmed when he appeared with the second ganglord in tow, dragged in by two of his henchmen. The unfortunate man was unconscious, his reddened face, scarred across the cheek and nose, a testimony to Paras's reputation with his famed knuckleduster.

'We got hit bad this morning,' opened Paras, once his rival had been dragged out of the crowded room that was being used as their meeting place. 'The rozzers think they've stuffed us. All your ganglords are behind bars. They'll be watched so closely now they won't be able to fart without being done for creating a disturbance. Even fucking GBH.' He laughed loudly at his own joke, then glared at the room. Some people joined in the laughter, then others followed. They knew his reputation. It was a serious time, but a laugh could just save their lives. Most of them were armed with knives and machetes. But they couldn't help notice the three foot-soldiers from Paras's gang who had followed them in with shotguns held loosely in the crooks of their arms. Nor did they miss the two men who protected Paras, two foot-soldiers with Uzi machine-guns slung across their chests. Yes, if that was what the man wanted, then it was a time to laugh.

'The only way we fight back is by organizing. No more of this small gang shit. We got to be organized. One mob. One big gang. As big as the fucking police. And anyone else who wants to take us on. Like a fucking army. On our own turf. Here. Moss Side. Where nothing moves without us knowing about it, or letting it. You all understand me?' He looked round the room. He saw he'd caught their attention, knew they understood. 'Only we do it together.' He remembered what Bourne had told him. Appeal to their greed. Well, he was doing that. 'Birds, a good time, and all the money you fucking need. Do it my way and you'll have it all. On a fucking plate.' He was pleased with himself. That should appeal to their greed. But his real strength was their fear. And the Uzis and shotguns and his knuckleduster paid testimony to that. They were going to follow him because they were frightened of him. Whatever he said they would agree with. 'I'm not wasting any more fucking time. If we got to have one big gang, then we got to have one lord. And I don't have to tell you who that's going to be. Understand?' He leered at the room, they nodded assent. 'All right. The Nilus Gang. That's what we are now. And if any of you got any other ideas . . .' he looked threateningly round the room '. . . just remember what's been happening to the Chinese.' He stopped and let the shiver of knowledge run round the room. 'Yeah. That was us. I just want you to know how mean we can really be. Now, we got plans to hit back at the pigs. Our way. To show we haven't lost our balls. Is there any of you bastards who don't want in?' Nobody responded. The machine guns made them his subjects. 'OK. But I'm warning you. If one of you lets me down, then you're dead meat.' He liked the words. Movie words, but words they understood. He turned to Stash Maxwell, who was standing behind him, and beckoned him forward. 'You all know Jedie. He's going to tell you the plan. Split you into teams. Tell you who the bosses are. Do like he says. We haven't got much time. So just do as he says.'

Paras left Maxwell to explain Bourne's plan; the detail bored him

176

and he had other things to attend to. But first he needed Shaeron; she was his relief. She would calm him before the evil of the night ahead roused him into the violence that he relished so much.

While Paras stayed with Shaeron, Maxwell worked with the new group. The plan was the Irishman's, but that was of no concern to them. He knew they trusted him, he was one of their own. As he spoke, he made sure his audience were always aware of the weapons his people now carried. He saw the excitement in their eyes and knew that they wanted to share in the new order that was being offered. Their first task was to scour the town for ankle length black leather coats and Doc Martin boots. From now on, they would wear a uniform and would be recognized for the power they were about to become.

'How about something to keep our heads warm?' a wag yelled from the middle of the room.

'Black berets. And no jewellery. You got dreadlocks, you stuff them under your hats.'

There was a roar of disapproval from the room. They all wore their wealth on their bodies; in chains and medallions and bracelets and rings.

'When you on duty, no jewellery,' he reiterated. 'Off duty, that's your business. But when you on our time, you do things our way. No jewellery, no markings. Just the uniform.' He remembered Bourne's words. Dress them so you frighten the opposition and make them feel like a team. He looked towards the Yardies gang, those with international links through their Jamaican contacts with America and the West Indies. There seemed little opposition there; Maxwell didn't need to tell them that they were in a small minority which could easily be taken out by the rest of the Moss Side gangs.

Sealing off Princess Parkway had been the first tactic in the strategy. Within minutes the roads that paralleled the Parkway to the east and west had also been blocked off in an identical manner.

The desk sergeant at Greenhayes Lane Police Station was signing off duty when the call came through from the emergency services about the burning cars on the Parkway. His instincts warned him that trouble was about to erupt and he ordered the shutters to be put up on all the windows and across the entrance before he called his area chief inspector at home. Both men were experienced police officers in the district and there was little discussion before they triggered off a riot alert. Once the sergeant had hung up on his inspector, who was now busily ringing Stretford HQ before returning to Greenhayes Lane, he put out a radio call to all his officers on the street and ordered them to return immediately to the police station. The burnt cars could flame a while longer while they waited for reinforcements. Then, as he anxiously waited for his men to return safely, he used the phone once more and told his wife that he loved her and not to wait dinner on him. As an afterthought he mentioned it could be a long night.

The radio call to his men on their beats was picked up by Maxwell on a radio scanner. He grinned as he listened to the sergeant's troubled tones. They had the cops on the run now; he could smell the pigs running for cover. He picked up the CB radio that connected him to his team leaders, switched to channel eight and barked his coded message into it.

'Smack the lane now,' said Maxwell, triggering off the second phase of the attack.

His signal sparked off five teams of four men each who were waiting in the darkened streets around the police station.

Two of the teams, armed with machetes and baseball bats hidden under their new ankle-length leather coats, scoured the area for returning policemen. Their first target was a police Metro with a single uniformed driver. As the car hurried towards the police station, the leader of the team pulled a milk bottle from under his coat, a bottle filled with napalm liquid, lit the rag that was jammed into the neck, and threw it at the passing car. The bottle exploded as it shattered across the Metro roof and the napalm, a syrupy spreading liquid, enveloped the car in a flaming orange ball. The driver jammed the brakes on and slid to a stop. By the time he had forced the door open, the napalm was burning and droplets of the liquid stuck to him as he hurled himself through the flames on to the street. Some of the flames stuck to him, burning pinpoint holes through his uniform and into his skin. But he didn't wait to pat the flames out; the sight of the charging, leather-coated blacks waving their machetes and baseball bats had him frantically running towards the sanctuary of the police station. He reached it just before they did, and thanks to the vigilance of the officer on duty at the door, dived through the entrance as the door was slammed safely behind him.

Within two minutes four napalm-filled Molotov cocktails had been ignited against the front and side of the building. The desk sergeant got on the radio and ordered all other officers to disregard his previous instructions and to leave the area immediately. Then he picked up the phone and called Stretford. He reported he had a riot on his hands and it was time for the tactical squad groups to be moved in.

All the officers returning to Greenhayes Lane, whether on foot or in mobiles, heard the order and made their way out of Moss Side. Two beat officers flagged down a passing car and were driven to safety. Two others, near the Alexandra Park area, took off their jackets, ties and helmets, threw them in the bushes, rolled their sleeves up and made their way south out of the area. They were fortunate not to be recognized and found a haven in a friend's house in Levenshulme. The remaining three mobiles, all Metros, left Moss Side immediately for the safety of adjoining police stations.

Policewoman Margaret Selnec was not so fortunate. She was off duty, still in uniform and waiting for a bus to take her to the home she shared with her boyfriend in the neighbouring suburb of Wythenshawe. She was in no hurry to get home; her boyfriend was working late and she'd spent some considerable time in a late night corner shop buying food for supper before walking leisurely to the bus stop, stopping to talk to various shopkeepers and residents whom she knew. She was well liked amongst the community, and was mostly remembered for once entering a burning house before the fire service arrived and saving two babies who were trapped in there. It was a familiar story in Moss Side; the mother had gone off to a pub with her boyfriend and left the children in their cots. The bravery of her actions had earned Margaret Selnec considerable respect in a closed community and she enjoyed having the trust and confidence, albeit relatively little by normal standards, of those she policed and protected.

The three men, all dressed in long black leather coats and black berets, who saw her waiting at the bus stop gave no thought to such matters. To them she was only a uniform to be hunted down and destroyed. They surrounded her as she stood in the queue, forcing others waiting for their buses to walk away from the darkened spot. She knew she was in trouble; all five foot six of her knew that these men meant her harm. She tried to reason with them as they jostled her, laughing lewdly as they pulled the shopping bag from her hand and spilt its contents over the pavement. She tried to push past but they hemmed her in, then grabbed her and dragged her into an alley. She fought now, furious and tigerish, but to no avail as they ripped her tunic from her, poked and tore at her naked breasts, animal and jeering as they forced her to the dirt of the unmade path. They went no further than that, even though their thoughts were excited and carnal.

179

'Finish it,' said one of them. 'Otherwise we in trouble if we late.'

One of his companions pulled out the machete he carried under his coat, and held it high above her. Margaret Selnec's fear suddenly vanished as she saw it, that sharp glint of metal that was held high over her. She knew she was about to die. She closed her eyes and started to pray. For a moment she wondered what her life would have been like if she had lived for a future. One wild, fatal slash and the men were gone. Her body would not be discovered until the early hours of the morning. By then the worst would be over and she would be just another casualty of a night that would be long remembered.

The next wave came on mountain bikes, those 24-geared trail bicycles which are considered trendy in the streets of London amongst those who like to be seen exercising their yuppie muscles in a stylish and chic manner. Only there was nothing fashionable about these bikes; they were chosen for their speed and manoeuvrability down the alleyways and back streets where cars couldn't follow and pursuers couldn't keep pace on foot.

There were over forty of them, each ridden by an armed, black-clothed gang member. They waited, in small groups of three or four, for the first police cars to enter Moss Side from the city centre. They knew they were coming; they wouldn't leave their colleagues alone to face the wrath of what was happening in Moss Side.

The first two cars, Rover patrol cars with blue lights flashing, entered the area from Alexandra Road South. The alert signal from Stretford had been simple: get in there and find out what happened; back-up is on its way. What the radio operator hadn't passed on, because he didn't know, was that the flare-up wasn't a small incident but the start of a full-scale riot. The mountain bikers, on seeing the two vehicles, rode out from the shadows and pedalled up to full speed as the cars passed. The first Molotov cocktail, thrown by the lead biker, shattered across the roof of the first car and exploded into flames. A second followed and hit the car's radiator, discharging its deadly inflammable liquid into the engine before it ignited. Within seconds, as the car careered across the road and crashed into a line of parked cars on the opposite side, the front section blew up, sending the bonnet and chunks of the engine skywards before they crashed down on the pavement. The firewall saved the two policemen and they scrambled from the flaming car to the safety of the street. Behind them, the second police car skidded to a frantic stop, its sudden change of pace confusing the third biker who missed as he threw his napalm bomb. It hit the road and roaring flame seared across it. The two policemen in the second car climbed out to help their colleagues. One of them, in a rage of anger, started to run after the third biker, who now rode after his two colleagues into the safety of the dark alleyway. The policeman, his adrenalin flowing, gave chase and almost caught the bomber, who had fumbled his gear change in the panic of escaping and was now pedalling furiously in the lowest gear, which propelled him forward at no more than two miles an hour. The policeman was almost on him when the lead biker swung round and opened fire with an Uzi submachine-gun. He missed the policeman, who dived to the pavement, but hit the biker, who was killed instantly. The two remaining bikers disappeared into the darkness and quiet descended on the scene.

The chasing policeman rejoined his colleagues, ignoring the dead biker, and they hurriedly drove out of Moss Side in the remaining car.

The first Soulson heard of the incidents was when Armitage burst into his office as he was preparing to go home and told him of the shootings and attack on Greenhayes Lane.

'I want armed policemen out,' Soulson ordered immediately.

'We need Home Office approval,' warned Armitage.

'Just give them weapons and whatever other protective equipment they need,' snapped back Soulson. 'The Home Office can wait. This is an emergency. And I want full Tactical Aid Group support. If we've a riot on our hands, then I want it handled with everything we've got. Including armoured personnel carriers.'

'I'll get the Major Incident Room operational again.'

The two men looked at each other, suddenly reminded of their triumphant meeting only a few hours earlier. Soulson remembered his last words when he'd called the meeting to a close. He should've known better than to pat himself on the back. He nodded to Armitage, who turned and left the room.

His secretary's voice crackled over the intercom. 'Head of the Police Authority on the line.'

He took a deep breath. It was time to face the problems as they came. 'Put the cow on,' he commanded. Then he added, 'Sorry.' This wasn't a time to turn his staff against him.

Emotion and a bad temper were not going to win the day.

'Range Rovers are moving in now,' Stash Maxwell said into the CB radio, channel seven. The Moss Side People's Centre was operations headquarters and Maxwell had not left the building

181

since the meeting when he and Paras had set out to unite the local gangs.

'So far so good, *maan*,' crackled back the disguised West Indian voice.

Maxwell grinned. Bourne still sounded Irish to those who knew the real thing. But they both realized that all the CB channels were probably monitored by the police. 'Everything going to plan so far,' he replied.

'Where's the big *maan*?' Bourne suddenly sounded Scottish.

'He in touch,' replied Maxwell. The big man was Paras, still locked away with Shaeron in her flat. Maxwell kept him informed, but knew Paras was waiting for the planned action to come to an end so he could return for the big finale. It was getting like a bloody stage show.

'And the coppers?'

'Still out of the area. They won't come in for at least another twenty minutes. And we'll be done by then.'

'Greenhayes?'

'Barricaded for the night. Ain't nothing getting in or out of there for a long time.'

'Well done. Call me if anything changes.' Bourne crackled off and Maxwell switched to channel eleven. 'OK, rovers,' he ordered into the microphone. 'Get yourselves on the road.'

There were four vehicles in the operation, all Range Rovers. The four-wheel drive vehicles had been stolen earlier in the day from the rich suburban towns of Wilmslow and Knutsford. They were driven to garages in Moss Side and a team of black mechanics had gone to work on the luxury transports.

The Range Rovers triggered off by Maxwell's radio message had been transformed into war wagons. Bourne's experience in Northern Ireland was being used to the full; he knew that the police would bring everything they had to bear on the situation. The reputation of the city's Tactical Aid Group was well known; they were one of the toughest riot squads in Britain, specially trained for incidents on this scale. Bourne had insisted that wire-mesh frames be welded together so that they could be used as a defence against any attacks by the police. The frames were designed to be wrapped round all the windows of the vehicles, and included flaps that protected the wheels from being punctured. The bumpers, front and rear, had been replaced with steel girders as battering rams. On top of each vehicle there was a red flashing light and a siren and loudspeaker had also been fitted. 'We want them to know when we're on the

182

streets,' Bourne had said to Maxwell. 'We want them to know they're our streets.'

The four vehicles, each with three fully-armed occupants including the driver, formatted on the west side of Princess Parkway.

'Anything out there?' asked the lead driver over his CB.

Four mountain-bike teams, posted at various entry points into Moss Side, replied that there was no police activity visible yet. But a TV news crew had arrived to the south and was filming one of the burning cars.

'Hit the Parkway,' ordered the lead driver, now aware that the news crew would be recording their actions at a distance.

They drove the Range Rovers on to the now traffic-free Princess Parkway. They could see the vehicles still burning at each end of the long road. There were people on the street, milling around, attracted by the commotion of the explosions and the uncertainty of what was happening.

'Get out of the shops. Get out of the flats above the shops. Get off the streets,' the leader blared over his loudspeaker. 'Come on, do it now or you fuckin' get hurt.' As he spoke, his microphone held next to his mouth, he steered his vehicle on to the pavement, herding pedestrians on to the street and clearing the area. When the pavement was clear, and the row of shops emptied of the occupants who lived above them, the first vehicle rammed into the shop windows, smashing through the metal guards that were designed to stop looting. But the guards were useless against the steel battering rams and crumpled like tissue in front of them. The other vehicles joined in, like bulls on a rampage, and within minutes all the shop fronts had been smashed in.

'It's my party and I'll cry if I want to,' blared the song over the loudspeakers as the lead driver switched on his tape-player. That had been Maxwell's idea. He knew it was something people would always remember.

Then they torched the row of shops and the piles of rubbish that were strewn along the pavement; simply threw in the small incendiary bombs that Bourne had supplied, fired a round of shots from the rifles and handguns into the air, Beirut style, and drove south down the Parkway so that the film crew could clearly see the war wagons before they disappeared into the darkness from which they had come.

The news crew, on a portable phone, contacted their studio and passed on a report of what they had filmed. It was in this fashion, through the local news producer to the switchboard operator at police

183

headquarters to the Head of Press and Publicity Unit to the Assistant Chief Constable of 'R' Department, that Soulson and the others in the Major Incident Room finally realized what was happening. There was a stunned silence in the room while the ACC 'R' relayed the report from the news crew.

Soulson finally broke the silence. 'Well, at least we know where we stand.' It was time to alert the Home Secretary to the seriousness of the situation. But first he had to get his men in before they lost total control of Moss Side. He turned to ACC 'X', Head of the Uniform Operations Branch. 'How long before we've got the TAG ready?'

ACC 'X' was not a happy man. Although the Tactical Aid Group team was meant to be in a constant state of readiness, financial cutbacks had meant that training had been reduced to a minimum. The TAG had not been in a real heat operation for many years. A collection of the best policemen from all areas of the Greater Manchester Force, it took time to gather the teams and their riot gear together. Police shields, batons, transport, weapons, riot clothing. Too much to get together for an immediate response. He shook his head, knowing he was defeated before he spoke. 'Not easy. It'll take time. With the cutbacks we've had—'

'I don't want to hear the excuses,' snarled Soulson. 'How long?'

'Two to three hours.'

'Too long.'

'It's already in motion. As soon as Roy called me, I called the divisions. But it'll—'

'How many can I get in straightaway?'

'You can't, Chief. They're trained teams. The quickest is going to be two hours.'

'We need people in there.' Soulson turned to Armitage. 'How're Greenhayes holding out?'

'Under control. They're locked in and no-one's made any serious attempts to invade the station. Or any of the other Moss Side stations. As far as we know, every bobby's accounted for.' Armitage didn't know yet that Margaret Selnec hadn't made it home.

'I can't wait two hours. We're talking guns. And armoured cars, if that TV crew's to be believed.'

'I've asked for them to bring me a video copy here as soon as the team gets back to the studios,' interrupted ACC 'R'.

'I'll speed it up,' said ACC 'X'. 'Maybe an hour and a half. But we have to wait till then, Chief. If that news report's anything to go by. Otherwise we're going to get more of our own people hurt and it'll take us longer to bring it under control.'

'He's right,' supported Armitage.

'We've got the helicopter up. At least we'll get something from them soon.'

Soulson slumped at the top of the table. 'The city's burning and I can't do a fucking thing about it.'

The others all looked at each other. It was the first time anyone could remember the Chief swearing. Nobody said anything. They were all fiddling their violins while Manchester burned.

The war wagons had not gone to ground. They left Moss Side heading south-west, and drove towards the suburb of Chorlton-cum-Hardy. Their sirens and flashing rooftop lights were switched off, and although they made an unusual procession through the town centre, they weren't taken as a threat by those who saw them.

Sergeant Phil Daniels of Chorlton Police Station, 'E' Division, didn't pay much attention to the four Range Rovers. News of the filmed attack on the shops hadn't been made public and Sergeant Daniels, parked in his police Metro, was more interested in the antics of three drunken youths who were relieving themselves in a darkened shop doorway, to the disgust of other passers-by.

The Range Rovers had slowed to a crawl when they saw him get out of the Metro and approach the urinating drunks. They came alongside the pavement as Daniels started to castigate the youths for their behaviour. Suddenly they roared their engines and swept on to the pavement, surrounding the policeman and the drunks. Totally surprised, Daniels turned towards the vehicles and ordered the drivers to back off the pavement. But the only response was that the occupants of the war wagons climbed out of the vehicles and started pushing the policeman. Before he could react further, one of the men took out a shotgun and held it to the sergeant's head.

'Let's go, copper,' said the gunman. 'No point being a dead hero.'

That's when Sergeant Daniels realized that the other men, all in their black leather coats and similar uniforms, were armed. He decided not to argue; there seemed little point with the cold steel of a double barrel pressed against his head. The blacks jostled him into the lead Range Rover; backed the war wagons into his small Metro and smashed it with their battering rams; then with sirens screaming and lights flashing, they tore down the road, past Chorlton Police Station and back into Moss Side.

'Why you picking on me?' he asked as he was thrown around in the back seat as the Range Rover hurtled round a corner.

185

''Cos you a fucking cop,' one of the men replied, cuffing him round the head as he spoke.

It didn't matter to them that Sergeant Phil Daniels was black.

He was a uniform.

And that's what they'd been ordered to go out and get.

'They've kidnapped a police sergeant,' said ACC 'X' to those in the Major Incident Room. 'In Chorlton.'

'I'd better tell the Chief,' said Armitage.

'He's a black copper.'

'Colour doesn't come into it. He's a copper.'

'I know that. He's one of mine. I bloody promoted him.'

'All right. I'm sorry. We're all getting worked up.' Armitage reached out and touched ACC 'X' on the shoulder. 'I'm sorry, Jim. Any idea why?'

'No. He was dealing with some drunks when these Range Rovers came up and took him away. They say they were armed. Who knows? All the witnesses were pissed out of their minds.'

'Same vehicles we saw on the tape?' The video from the news crew had been delivered to the Major Incident Room over half an hour earlier.

'Have to be, don't they?'

'What the hell are they playing at? Who the hell's organizing them?'

'Takes on a different meaning, doesn't it? When they're coming out after us.'

'How long before you can get the TAG in?'

'We'll be ready in twenty minutes. Not a full force, but enough to be organized and have a presence.'

'If there's anything left by then. Christ, from that helicopter report it looks like they're burning the bloody place down.'

Louise Spencer was in full flood as Soulson sat in his office with her. He had just shown her the tape from the local news crew.

'That's what comes of your methods,' she shrieked. 'Not understanding what these people have to live through. Deprive the people and they turn against you. In bloody force.'

'The raid this morning was not about deprived people. It was about drugs and those who make a living out of it. It's about villains.'

'That's not what the community leaders say.'

'Half of them are involved.'

'Are you prepared to say that outside this office?'

'Of course not.' Soulson immediately regretted his outburst. 'But they're not solving the drug problem. Are they?'

'They're not starting riots, either.'

'I think that's unfair.'

'Then why's the Home Secretary on his way up here. And half the world's press. All out to get political brownie points.' She didn't need to add that this would make the government look bad, another nail in their coffin. 'You don't do Manchester any favours, do you?'

'Look, you've got my report. I need to get back to the Incident Room now.'

'Not much you can do from there. The city's burning and . . .'

'A few shops in Moss Side are burning. Deliberately set alight by gangsters. Organized gangsters.'

'At the moment. And how do you know? You haven't even got any police in the area.'

'The TAG teams will be moving in soon. And the fire engines will follow them, once the area's secured.'

'More violence.'

'We didn't start it.'

'What do you think the public will think when they see the TAG team go in. Riot shields, baton charges. Is that the way to police this city? That's all we need. A racist attack on our citizens.'

'Most of the people in Moss Side are decent people.'

'I wish I could believe you meant that.'

'I'm not going to react to that statement. They are decent people. Most of them don't want drugs and villainy any more than we do. But Moss Side is controlled by gangsters who make money out of terror. The people there are intimidated by violence. Not our violence, but that of the drug barons. I'm telling you, they'll be relieved to see our TAG groups in there. Like they were pleased that we took action this morning.'

'That's not what the community leaders say.'

Soulson shrugged. 'We've logged over a hundred phone calls from residents thanking us. They're all recorded.'

'I bet they won't be saying that now. Not when it's burning down round them.'

Soulson stood up. 'I need to get back to the situation. I'll keep you and the committee informed.'

'There is one other matter.'

'Yes.'

Louise Spencer took out a typed sheet of paper from her handbag and tossed it on to Soulson's desk.

He picked it up and glanced over it. 'You've got to be joking!'

'Destruction of public property.'

Soulson handed the report back to her. 'I suggest we deal with this when we get back to normal.'

'No. This is important. I don't like the committee's authority being thrown back in its face.'

'That wasn't the intention.'

'Who is Desmond Mailer? The one who signed the report?'

'Chief Inspector Desmond Mailer. Head of the Motorway Unit. He's responsible for the operation of all—'

'At this rate he won't be responsible for the dog kennels.'

'He acted under my orders.'

'And were your orders the destruction of a—' Spencer picked up the report and read from it '—Rover 216Si?'

'He was asked to test it.'

'Some test. He destroyed the car.'

'No. The car I use has to be able to escape from a terrorist attack, has to be able to be driven hard and stand up to the sort of battering that a Chief Constable's car may have to take in certain adverse conditions. This car, according to the report, isn't capable of handling such a situation.'

'We'll see.' Her anger was out of control. 'You have to be accountable. Understand? You're not above the law. Do you understand, Soulson? Not above the law.'

There was a knock on the door. Soulson walked past her and opened it.

It was Armitage. 'We need you in the Incident Room, Chief. TAG's nearly ready.'

'About time.' He swung back to Spencer. 'Was there anything else, Councillor?'

Her anger leapfrogged her senses, she was speechless at his cold dismissal of her. She picked up her handbag and stormed out of his office.

'What was all that about?' asked Armitage.

'What it's always about. Nothing. Except flexing their muscles.'

The final show of strength came two hours later. The violence had stopped as suddenly as it had started. Although the sky was red with the burnings on Princess Parkway, little else had been damaged in Moss Side.

188

The Range Rovers, with their red beacon lights now stripped off so as not to draw attention to themselves, led a procession of cars and vans down Princess Parkway, out of Moss Side and into West Didsbury, half a mile to the south. The cortege, for that's what it now was, pulled into the vast Manchester Southern Cemetery, and made its way to the centre, well away from any prying eyes from the surrounding streets.

There were twelve vehicles carrying some fifty black-leather-uniformed members of the new Nilus Gang. Most were armed and all wore balaclavas to hide their identities. The procession pulled up at a freshly dug grave where four further armed gang members waited with a young priest. He had been woken rudely in his bed in Chorlton-cum-Hardy and forced to accompany the men to the cemetery. One of the men was Stash Maxwell.

When the vehicles had parked around the grave, a coffin was taken from the last van and carried ceremoniously to the grave. One of the pallbearers was Abdul Paras.

A film crew from the local TV station set up their camera and started to video the proceedings. They were present because a call had been made to the newsdesk by Bourne informing them of a news scoop which they could film, as long as they didn't divulge the location to the authorities.

The coffin was lowered into the grave; it was the body of the dead mountain biker. The priest, frightened for his life, stepped forward and carried out the burial service. He was in no mood to argue against such unusual methods; two of the terrorists had been left behind in his house to guard his family and ensure he did as he was instructed. When the ceremony was finally over, a guard of honour surrounded the grave and raised their rifles and machine-guns.

'You filming this?' a hooded Maxwell called to the news crew.

'We're getting it all,' came the reply.

Maxwell signalled the guard of honour and they fired five rounds into the air. Then they stepped back and other members moved forward and started covering the coffin with earth.

'Get them out of here,' Paras ordered Maxwell.

Maxwell signalled three men to join him and went over to the film crew. Another gang member brought the priest with him.

'Thank you, Father. And don't worry. Your family's OK,' said Maxwell before turning to the film crew. 'And you boys as well. Just make sure you get us all the coverage you can. You'll all be escorted safely from here. But we won't release you for another twenty minutes. There's still things we need to do.'

189

One of the newsmen started to ask a question, but Maxwell hushed him. Then he went back to the graveyard while the film crew and the priest were led away.

'They gone?' asked Paras when the grave was filled in.

'Out of sight,' replied Maxwell.

'Get the cop,' said Paras as he pulled off his balaclava. 'And stop digging.'

The others followed his example and watched as Sergeant Daniels was dragged from another van. He was handcuffed with his own cuffs and led to the grave area. The foot-soldiers stepped back and let him enter their enclave. Paras stood in the middle, a giant and frightening form in the moonlight that flooded the scene.

'You fucking black and you a fucking copper,' sneered Paras.

'You're all crazy,' replied the defiant Daniels, surprised that he could speak in spite of the fear that choked him.

'No, you crazy. For turning on your brothers.'

'I've not turned on anybody. But this is wrong.'

'What's wrong, bro? What you see that's so fucking wrong?'

'Whatever you people're up to. This is no way to live.'

'Speak for yourself. You just a slave. They dress you up in a uniform, feed you, give you some little semi-detached to live in. You're still black, man. Whatever they pay you, they can't scrub your skin clean. That what you want? Think you fucking white?'

'I'm black and proud. And I'm doing something about it.'

'Like what, slave?'

'Like standing on my own feet. And not being scum.'

'You the scum, shithead,' Paras laughed. 'You dead scum.'

Paras moved forward, the knuckleduster on his hand. Daniels lurched backwards into the ring of men. He was pushed back, towards Paras. The gangleader slashed at him, hitting him across the chest, tearing the cloth and flesh of the policeman. Daniels turned away as Paras hit him again, this time across his shoulder, once again slicing the uniform into the flesh. The blow knocked Daniels to the ground and Paras stepped up behind him and kicked at him, knocking him over on to his back. Then Paras knelt down, sat astride Daniels' chest and started to beat his face and head with all the force he had. The brave policeman never screamed, closed his eyes and thought of his young wife and two children. And of his God. He would look after him when this awful thing was over and done with. Paras rained punches at him, never saw the look of peace on the dying policeman's face.

Paras stood up when it was over, his red, dripping hands a

190

testimony to what he was capable of. He looked round at the silent group. 'Anyone still not believe in what we can do against these bastards?' Nobody replied, they were his men, body and soul. 'It starts now. This is our ground. All we got left is the Chinks. And we'll do that in our own time. We the Nilus Gang. We the only gang. And if you don't want to finish up like him—' Paras pointed down at the battered corpse '—then you just do like you told.'

They left Sergeant Phil Daniels there, his face unrecognizable for those who would discover him, for his wife and colleagues to identify him.

The Nilus Gang left Manchester Southern Cemetery and drove, or rode their bikes, back to Moss Side. They left the Range Rovers behind, next to the grave, as a grisly reminder of what they could achieve.

When Manchester's Tactical Aid Group went into Moss Side, sirens blaring and riot shields at the ready, the area had returned to quiet. There was nothing for them to find, no-one to arrest, no incident to quell. The fire tenders put out the fires and everyone went home.

The next morning Princess Parkway was filled with commuter traffic driving into Manchester city centre. The drivers had all heard or watched the morning news reports. But it all seemed normal now, except for the blackened row of shops that lined the Parkway. It would be a reminder that would stay there for many months to come while the insurance companies argued about who was responsible for the mess.

Soulson and his senior officers never went to bed that night. The Chief Constable toured the area after it had been secured. Then he returned to Stretford to face the Home Secretary, the media and everyone else who was after his blood. It was after seven the next evening, with a stronger police presence on the streets of Moss Side in case of further trouble, that he finally made his way home.

It would be a while before trouble was to erupt in the city again. Only this time Soulson had insisted they leave a skeleton crew in the Major Incident Room.

Bourne waited by the Rochdale Canal. It was nearly eleven thirty and the pubs would be turning out soon. It was a good time not to be noticed.

The man he waited for arrived exactly at half past, his overcoat collar turned up against the cold.

'Good thing this strike's ended,' commented Bourne, pointing at the bags of rubbish that floated in the canal. 'This town's a mess.'

'So was last night. Your handiwork? Certainly your trademark,' replied Manchester Blue.

Bourne ignored the question. 'Surprised to hear from us? After all these years.'

'I'd almost forgotten.'

'We never forget. You owe us a favour, Manchester Blue.'

'That's not my name.'

'Of course it is. Your codename. Just like it was with Christley.'

'Depends on the favour.'

'You and Christley were a rum pair. Had a good innings, didn't you?'

'What favour?'

'Don't know yet. But we'll be calling it in. Soon.'

'What favour?' Manchester Blue persevered.

'If you've got a picture of me in the police files, lose it. That's your first payback.' Bourne turned and started to walk away.

'Why call me at home? Just because of the picture?' Manchester Blue shouted after him.

'Just letting you know we haven't forgotten. That we'll be calling in our marker.'

'If I get your picture out, we're square.' He heard Bourne laugh back at him. 'Did you have anything to do with last night?'

The question was lost in the darkness as Bourne disappeared. Manchester Blue cursed, then swung round and walked in the opposite direction. He kept his head bowed so that he wouldn't be recognized.

He knew the bastards were involved in Moss Side. How the hell could he do anything about it when they'd tied his hands behind his back and were now calling the tune?

Three days later, after weeks of deliberation, Soulson read the letter that Armitage had drafted. It covered everything, hid nothing from the person for whom it was intended.

When he had finished, he dialled Armitage's extension. 'Seems OK,' he said.

'Still time to pull back,' came the answer.

'No. We're past the point of no return. Is everything in place?'

'It will be after I come off this phone.'

'Good.'

'Only two copies. One for you and the other for him.'

'Good. Let's do it.'

He put down the phone.

One hour later Charlie Soulson went to St Mary's Church and jammed himself into the confessional. His confession was straightforward, for sins he had committed of a simple and daily nature. This time he didn't ask forgiveness for sins he was about to commit. In that, he was only prepared to be judged directly by his God and not by the cassocked intermediary who sat and listened in the darkened protection of the wooden confessional box.

10

PUT OUT TO GRASS

Drug Enforcement Administration
700 Army Navy Drive
Arlington
Virginia

THERE ARE FORTY-TWO NAMES ON THE HONOUR ROLL THAT DOMINATES the marble entrance hall.

Forty-two names of DEA agents killed in the line of duty from 1921 to the present day.

Marshall stood in front of the big board and grinned. There were a few in this building who were surprised he wasn't on the Honour Roll. With some of the crazy things he'd done, he even surprised himself that he was standing here reading the list.

Agent Charles A. Wood. March 22, 1921. Place of Death. El Paso, Texas.

Agent Stafford E. Becket. March 22, 1921. Place of Death. El Paso, Texas.

The first two to die. Just names to invoke a feeling of honour and pride. Who cared now, all these years later? Especially when

194

some of the more recent names had been friends, colleagues in this desperate war. Would anyone remember him, if this list included his name, fifty years from now? *Who the hell would be the winners, anyway?*

'Mr Marshall?' asked the voice from behind.

Marshall rounded on the security receptionist who approached him. 'Yes.'

'You can go up to Mr Ronane now, sir.'

'Thank you.'

'Could you wear your identity badge, please?'

Marshall nodded and clipped his gold shield on to his jacket pocket. He followed the security man to the lifts.

'Mr Ronane's on the eleventh floor.'

Marshall took the lift to the eleventh and walked out on to the brown carpet where a secretary was waiting for him. He followed her into Ronane's office and accepted her offer of a coffee.

'All right for some,' he said to Ronane when the door closed behind her.

'Don't start on me, Marshall,' came the gruff reply. Ronane was seated at a big desk, lost in the large leather executive chair that dwarfed the little man.

'Job for life, isn't it? Chief Co-ordinator of Public Relations.'

'I said, cut it out. I didn't ask for this job.'

'I know, but someone's got to do it.'

Ronane shook his head wearily. 'Career advancement. That's what they call it.'

Marshall sat down opposite Ronane. 'It may be a desk job, but at least you're doing something. They've got me kicking my heels. Sent me to Quantico training the rookies. Now they're sending me home for some R and R.'

'That's what you get for bucking the system.'

'Like hell. That's what you get for proving the bastards wrong.' The door opened and the secretary came in with two cups of coffee. Marshall thanked her and waited till she'd left the room. 'You know how much leave I got owing to me? Six months. Stuff I haven't taken over the years. Now I get this letter saying they want me to take it. All at once. What the hell am I going to do for six months?'

'Sit on the beach? Build sand castles?'

'Come on, Ronane. I need your help. I'll even go out on a Buy and Bust patrol.'

'Pity you haven't got family. Or someone you can share—'

'Well, I haven't,' Marshall interrupted. 'Shit, they'll be retiring

195

me next.'

'It was discussed.'

'You're kidding.'

'No.'

'What changed their minds?'

'I did. Batted hard for you, Marshall. They just don't like mavericks.'

'We're all mavericks. This isn't exactly a normal occupation, is it?'

'They understand that. But they've got a game plan. They need a team. Let's face it, you go overboard when you get that crazy instinct of yours.'

'I was right in El Paso.'

'You were wrong.'

'Who says?'

'Intelligence.'

'How?'

'It was a decoy shipment. A bigger load following. And because of what happened, it got through. We haven't been able to track it. We think it's for Europe. If we'd followed it through, we could've closed down what Intelligence says is one of the biggest Cali networks.'

'Are they sure?'

'As sure as they can be.'

'Could be through Ireland.'

'They don't think so.'

'But *they* don't know. Was all this common knowledge before we went in?'

'Yes.'

'So why didn't they tell us?'

'Breakdown in communications.'

'You mean nigger rigging. A half-arsed job.'

'Cut out that southern prejudice crap.'

'Prejudice, my arse. I hate niggers.'

'I know, you hate everybody. Chinks, Jews, faggots, priests. Even women. But mostly yourself. Come on, Marshall. I've worked with you for too long. I've seen you when you're out there, pegged out, with nowhere to go. Remember Milken? He was black. You took two slugs trying to protect him. Saved the guy's life. That's your nature. You're soft chocolate, big man. You don't hate anyone. I think you just hurt.'

Marshall was silent for a while, then leant forward and drank his coffee. 'Doesn't change things,' he said eventually. 'I need something to do.'

'Go fishing.'

'Very original, Ronane.'

'A rest could do you good.'

'Tell me about it some time.'

'I mean it. I know you don't have family, but it's where I go when things get on top of me. Just take time off and head out in the trailer for peaceful country. You live in a great town. San Antonio's a place most of us would be content to rest up in.'

'For six months?'

'Chill out, Marshall. Behave yourself and I might even come and see you.'

'Yeah?'

'Yeah. They owe me time. Kids are out of school. I always wanted to see the Alamo. You ever see it?'

'No.'

'You live in San Antonio and you've never seen it?'

Marshall shrugged. 'No. Driven past it. Like New Yorkers never go up the Empire State Building.' He laughed. 'You can show me round when you get there.'

'OK.'

'I know they got great hot dogs.'

'Yeah?'

'Right outside the Alamo. Mile-long hot dogs with stinky onions. Best I ever had.'

'First one's on me.'

'They won't leave me out there for six months, will they?'

'I don't know. Don't forget, you've blown your cover. There's people out there looking for you.'

'So what's different?' Marshall shrugged off the danger. 'It's crazy, Ronane. You give your whole life to the department, even prepared to die for it, then they switch you off and tell you to go home and don't call us, we'll call you.'

'Things move on.'

'I'd like to have one more hit. Before they put me out to pasture.'

'It's out of my hands.'

'Pontius fucking Pilate.'

'At least they sent him home to his wife and kids.'

'Just one more hit. This whole thing. I'd really like to do something . . . that made a difference.'

'Who to?'

'Just made a difference. Something that made the whole of what I've done, to get to this point in my life, somehow worthwhile.'

197

Tony Marley Quigley, at forty-three, was one of Ireland's leading entrepreneurs who had built an international business empire centred on newspapers, television and property. He was also a pillar of the establishment and made no bones of his ambition to enter politics in his native country. This was the stuff prime ministers were made of.

The trouble was that Tony Marley Quigley was also very dead.

They found him dead in his car, at two in the morning down a Boston side street, with a bullet hole in his temple. His wife, sitting next to him, in an expensive, $30,000 Paris evening creation, had also been shot dead. His business partner lay sprawled in the back seat. There'd been no shots for him, only the knife wound in the side of his neck. The trio had been returning to their hotel after a night out on the town. Quigley was a man who believed in controlling his own destiny and was well known for never being chauffeured.

When the police searched the bodies, they found all the jewellery missing and the wallets and purses stolen. The car radio, cassette-player and telephone had also been ripped out. The police naturally presumed that Quigley had lost his way and stumbled down this side street in a neighbourhood that had a reputation for violence. It was an obvious case of robbery with violence and the bodies were removed, at the request of Quigley's Dublin headquarters, to a well-known local mortician to prepare them for their return to Ireland.

After the corpses had been prepared, the bullet holes and knife wounds cosmetically repaired, they were sealed in coffins and dispatched to Logan Airport, where they were loaded on to Quigley's Gulfstream G IV private jet and flown across the Atlantic. Nobody commented on the thirty-five pieces of Louis Vuitton luggage that were also loaded. Everyone knew the Quigleys always travelled in style.

There were few customs delays in Dublin; after all they knew what the coffins contained. They were opened, given a cursory glance, then sealed and driven to a funeral parlour in the centre of Dublin. The customs men had been more aware of the cameramen who filmed Quigley's arrival and had given a good impression of being no bureaucratic barrier to the great man's sad return.

198

Once the doors had been closed in the funeral parlour, the two men on duty opened the coffins, expertly cut and stripped the three cadavers of the 400 kilos of cocaine that had been stuffed into them. The baggage accompanying the coffins was also opened and another 600 kilos was unloaded. One of the suitcases contained $10 million of US currency in large-denomination bills.

The bodies were then patched up for relatives, friends and well-wishers to pay their respects to before the burial ceremony two days later. It was, even by Irish standards, a funeral to be remembered.

By the time the Quigleys and their business partner had been lowered six feet under, the cocaine and the money had been absorbed into the Irish underground ready for the next phase in its deadly journey.

1426 Military Trail
San Antonio
Texas

The girl found the house easily.

It was as he had described it; exactly as she imagined it would be. Wooden-framed, single-storey, small windows, white-painted and set back from the road. No different from the rest of the houses that ran down Military Trail, except that there was none of the paraphernalia of living that cluttered the front lawns of the others, no littered toys or basketball hoops over the garage. This was a reclusive house, a keep-off-my-space sort of house. She sensed it as she walked past the 1988 Ford Granada that was parked in the driveway, felt the raw emotion backwash inside her as she came closer to him.

Damn you, Marshall. You were the only bastard who ever got through. She fought to control herself. She was here for a purpose, and that purpose had nothing to do with her feelings for the man. She put down her suitcase and rapped on the door.

He opened it suddenly and she saw the anger in his eyes. He must've seen the cab arrive and watched her struggling up the path with her case.

'What're you doing here?' He was cold; no more than she expected after all this time.

'Needed to see you.'

'I hoped I'd seen the last of you.'

She ignored his rudeness. 'I'm not going away.'

'I can do without this,' he said. 'Have you paid the cab off?'

'No. Didn't know if you were in.'

'Come in,' he sighed. Then he pushed past her and went down the path and paid the taxi. When he returned, she had carried the suitcase into the lobby and was in the sitting-room. The room was as functional as she'd imagined. Simple, sprawling furniture and paintings of western scenes on the wall. What surprised her were the books that lined the shelves and the tables. The room was like a library. She checked some of the titles before he returned. There was a wide and confusing variety, ranging from the lives of Marilyn Monroe and President Truman to the complete works of Stephen King and Jack Kerouac.

'How'd you know I was here?' he asked.

'I rang Washington. They said you were on leave. I still had your number, so . . . it was me who rang last night and put the phone down.'

'What're you doing here?'

'Work.'

'Didn't know the Manchester Police Force extended its activities to Texas. Why me? Can't they afford hotels on your expenses?'

'I wanted to stay with you.'

'You messed me up enough at Quantico.'

'I was wrong.'

'Nobody can be that wrong. You're just a natural born bitch.'

'You're the only one who got through to me.' Her words were soft and inviting. 'The only one I opened up to.'

'Fuck you,' swore Marshall.

Then he put his arms out and scooped Detective Jill Couples of the Manchester Police Force up in his arms and carried her through to the bedroom. She wrapped her arms round his neck and nuzzled in to him.

Some things never change, just go on from where they left off. So it was between them. They would never remember how they got undressed before their naked bodies were together in the unmade bed.

There was no expectancy, none of the delicious foreplay they normally enjoyed. There was some shyness, but it was quickly lost in the urgency and hunger they felt for each other.

He held her on top of him and kissed her, deeply with his tongue. It startled him; like the first kiss of puppy love when the stomach backflips and the world is a new place to live in. He felt her shudder and knew the spark of whatever drove her had

200

been ignited. The excitement of her kiss, wet and drowning, raced through him and he moved his legs to part her thighs; it was an easy movement for she was ready and eager for him.

Then he felt her wetness through her soft fur and he slipped easily into her, his stiffness hard and unforgiving. He heard her gasp, not with surprise but with greed and pleasure; then he arched his back so she could enjoy all he had to push into her.

God, he'd forgotten how soft and welcoming her love tunnel was; how supple her body as she writhed against him. It was hot and they melted together into one being; he was suddenly pleased he'd left the air conditioning off so that he could enjoy the afternoon breeze.

Then he tried to roll her over; tried desperately not to let himself be released from inside her as he twisted round. But it was to no avail and he slipped out of her before she had rolled on to her back.

'You never could manage that,' she chided him, mocking him with a smile that told him she loved him and shared the joy of the moment with him.

He grinned and entered her again. Then, as he held her tight in the sweat and juices of their loveplay, he pushed down on her with all his weight. In the early days he'd tried to be careful, from a fear of crushing her, but she'd soon let him know she wanted all of his weight on her, that it was part of the dominance and sharing she enjoyed. He moved gently inside her, probing each part of her, while she squeezed him with her muscles and tried to hold him in one place. It was a gentleness they always enjoyed, a moment of sharing they had once developed, a time of gradual lovemaking during which they locked their eyes together and believed they looked into one another's souls.

'I want your pain,' she said, reminding him of the hurt she'd put him through.

He shook his head, wanting to forget what had been, only wanting what she had to offer now. He gripped her tighter, as she always liked it, and moved with deeper penetration, his eyes still fastened on hers, still telling her how much he loved her. It was the only place he had ever felt he belonged.

Then he lifted himself up on his elbows.

'No,' she complained, trying to pull his weight down on her again.

He put his arms round her legs, lifted her so that her legs were now doubled back over his shoulders, straddled her and started to push harder, more violently and deeper into her.

She groaned loudly, almost a half scream, then took her hands away from his neck and put them under him so that she could feel the straining muscles of his thighs. As he pushed harder into her, she gently stroked them, running her long fingers softly up and down, squeezing them, feeling their power, remembering them as she always did when she thought of him. To her, they were like no other man's thighs, solid, rock like, with strength that was there to love her.

'I love your thighs,' she said. 'I've always loved your thighs. Hard hard thighs, like your hard hard cock. Fuck me, thigh man, fuck me like only you can.'

The crude brutality of her words smashed through his tenderness and he was suddenly immersed in the torment of his love. In his mind he saw the ugly visions of the others she had been with, imagined her in a myriad of greedy positions, crying and gasping and wanting them to fuck her with a passion that he felt he never achieved. As he moved on top of her, slow and deep and purposeful, as if each muscle that slid against and inside her was alive and electric, he saw her writhe and twist beneath the faces of those she must have been with, eager selfish men only after the pleasure of her body and mouth and whatever else they could get before they wiped up the mess and went home to their own beds. He hated the seaminess of it all, the sex without love that they pumped into her and, worst of all, that she craved so desperately.

Oh why did he love her? Why did he hurt for her? Didn't she understand?

'I love you.' She twisted against him as she said it, once again wrapping her arms round him and squeezing as hard as she could.

He grew more frantic, knowing she lied to him, visualizing her with all those others. He hated her for what she was, for the torment she put him through.

'I love you for ever.' Her words were a secret for them both, to be shared and believed in this time that was theirs to remember for ever. Her open legs suddenly broke from his grip, wrapped round him, joined at the ankles and locked him into her.

'Don't stop,' he heard her plead. 'Don't stop now.'

'I love you, Jill Bum,' he heard his voice use the name he hadn't called her for so long now. 'I've loved you for ever.'

'Don't stop. Please don't stop. Don't ever stop.'

He closed his eyes as he rammed harder into her. Bitch. Bitch. Liar. Liar. Then the hate and hurt were lost in the explosion. It came from nowhere, that sudden burst of love and lust and being alive that tears through the body and erupts into that which is your whole life and the only place you ever want to be. She shuddered with him, shared that moment of living, that moment of joy when you die in the greatest of passion, then are slowly born once again.

When he'd caught his breath, he rolled over on to his back and lay there. She moved next to him, snuggling her bottom into his thighs, half turned away from him. Her cheeks were still cold. He remembered that; they'd always been cold, even after the warmest of nights. He'd never known anyone else whose cheeks were like that.

'Why didn't you return my calls?' he said when his breath was more even. He recalled the many times he'd rung her flat and left messages of anger followed by messages of love. 'I hated talking to that damn answerphone.'

'I couldn't cope with you. You were just too obsessive.'

'It's not my fault I fell in love with you. You could've rung me.'

'Why? To have another row? I needed space.'

'You still could've rung. Just once.' He hated his obsession; he could feel its tentacles wrapping round his stomach. Space. To go out and get drunk and be fucked by whoever was buying. Damn it, he had to stop before he pushed her away again.

'I didn't want to spend the rest of my life dreaming about what might have been.'

'What do you mean?' Her answer surprised him.

'I love you, big man. But the whole thing was too much. You destroyed us both with your jealousy.'

'Just one call. Just some consideration.' He hated his silly whimpering. Why couldn't he just accept her as she was?

'You never believed in us. That we could make it. You're the only person that ever made me feel safe. You got through to me. And then you destroyed it with all your hang-ups. About being old. About not being man enough. Damn you, Marshall. Why didn't you just take the risk and keep me here, just learn to trust me? I wanted to be with you. After I left, I just didn't want to go on thinking about what could have been.'

He closed his eyes and locked himself into his thoughts. As much as he resented her, even now after all this time, he knew he was where he wanted to be. After a while she moved and he felt her lips kiss his cheek. He opened his eyes and looked up at her; those soulful eyes were warm and smiling at him.

'Where's the Kleenex box?' she said.

'What?'

'I heard Yanks always reached for the Kleenex box as soon as they'd come.'

He grinned, returned her kiss and then turned on to his side. She wrapped herself round him, her right arm under his and across his chest.

They went to sleep like that.

They didn't wake for four hours, except to turn over. He smiled when they did that. They'd always turned together, as one person; she would wrap round him, then he would wrap round her.

Marshall was a contented man.

Before she went to sleep, Jill Couples hoped he wouldn't lose his temper and throw her out when he knew the real purpose of her visit. To her, he was something special. Maybe this time there could be life beyond the dream.

She woke to see him standing above her, a steaming mug of coffee in his hand, a green towel wrapped round his waist.

It took a moment to realize where she was, then she smiled and stretched her body awake. She saw his satisfaction as he watched her naked body and she continued to stretch her joints. He put the mug on the bedside table, then knelt on the bed and lowered his head between her legs and softly pushed his tongue into her, worked it slowly with little gentle kisses until she was aroused. Then he rolled over beside her, put his arm round her shoulder and held her to him. Her head rested on his chest with her hair falling across him as she nibbled his nipple.

'Stop that,' he said lightly.

'You started it.'

'You looked very inviting. And I've wanted to taste you ever since I woke up.'

She lifted her head and kissed him on the lips, licking her juices from his mouth.

'You shouldn't start something you don't mean to finish,' she purred.

'I know. But I think we should talk first.'

She looked down at his stiffening flesh as it parted the towel. 'Are you sure?' she encouraged.

'Yes.'

'Damn you, big man.' She lifted herself from him and sat upright. 'How long have I been asleep?'

'Six hours. I've been up for two. You're jet-lagged.'

'I liked your cure.' She was still coquettish.

He took the mug and passed it over to her. He watched her sip from it.

'That's good,' she said.

'So why're you here?'

'Why do you think?'

'Not to see me.'

'I wanted to come.'

'Why?'

'Because, even after all this time, and no, I haven't been celibate, even nearly got engaged, I realized you were the only one who made me feel different. Whatever happened to me back in England, I never got over you.'

'Who was the guy you nearly married?'

'Got engaged to,' she interjected quickly. 'I'd never have married him.'

'Then why get engaged?'

'I didn't.'

'You must've cared about him.'

'For a moment. In the newness of it all. He wasn't that important.'

'How old was he?'

She paused. Then, 'Twenty-three.'

'That young.'

'Too young. It really wasn't that serious.'

'Why tell me that?'

'Because I want you to know. I want you to believe that, big man.' She rose from the bed and walked out into the sitting room. He watched her from the door as she took an envelope from her handbag. She came back and handed it to him, then climbed back into bed and continued drinking her coffee. 'I jumped at the chance of coming over. Because then I could see you again.'

He nodded, then slit the envelope open and took out the type-written sheets inside. She watched him as he read it, saw his face stiffen as he digested the contents. When he had finished, he carefully folded the sheets and put them back.

'Do you know what's in here?' he asked, tapping the envelope.

'No. I was just told to deliver it.'

'That all?'

'That I was to take it as holiday and it wasn't official police business. They paid for the trip.'

'They?'

'Same person who signed the letter. I was told it was to be kept secret. Undercover.'

'Which department are you in now?'

'Criminal Intelligence.'

'What's that?'

'It gets information on all criminal activity in the town. Links it together so we can help the CID, or drugs, or anyone else that needs support.'

'Beats vice, I suppose.' He couldn't hide the sarcasm in his voice.

'That was a long time ago. Do you have to bring it up again?'

'No.' It had always been a bone of contention between them. Ever since she told him she'd hustled punters in cars to see what the prostitutes actually went through. It had sickened him, but she somehow never saw the wrong in it. It had only happened twice, and she had insisted she never let it go all the way, but he never believed her. He took her for the amoral person he understood her to be, but accepted that he had fallen in love with someone who had different standards to himself. 'I need to make a call,' he said, getting up from the bed and going through into the sitting room. She sat there, nursing her coffee as she heard him dial a number. 'Hi, it's Marshall . . . I need to know when you're coming out on vacation . . . Can you arrange it sooner? I really could do with meeting you . . . No, not in Washington . . . Yeah, you could say it's urgent . . . OK, call me as soon as you know. But this is kind of an immediate nature . . . Bye.' He put down the phone, then disappeared into the kitchen before returning with a can of locally brewed Pearl Lite Lager. He flopped on to the bed again.

'Was that to do with my letter?' she asked.

'Yeah.' He decided not to further the matter. 'So, how do you feel?'

'Meaning?'

'Seeing me. After all this time.'

'Strange. I've thought about you so many times. And to see you now, in the flesh instead of in my head . . . ' she shrugged.

'Disappointed?'

'No. Why should I be?'

'After twenty-three-year-olds, maybe I look older.'

'Cut it out, Marshall. You were never old to me. To yourself, yes. But never to me.' She leant over and cupped his face with her hands. 'Look, I made a lot of mistakes in my time. I probably still will. But you, with your rotten face and your rotten temper, were the only one who ever got through. We didn't have that much time together, but it mattered the most in my life.'

'We yelled a lot.'

'Maybe we did.' She leant back against her pillow. 'That was the passion. I never had that before. Or since. The reason I didn't ring you was because it could never work at a distance. You were, probably still are, married to that bloody job of yours. At the end of the day, it's all that matters. And it's a dangerous job. Your scars testify to that. I couldn't take worrying about where you were in the world, who was shooting at you, not knowing if you were alive or not. Damn you, Marshall, I didn't want to ring here one day and find the phone had been disconnected, that you'd just disappeared and I'd never find out why. That's why I never rang.'

'No guarantees in life, Jill Bum.' He smiled; her words had softened him. Then he remembered the letter. 'So why come back?'

'Because they said it was important.'

'So it's just the letter.'

'No. Because you can only run so far. You've got to remember, Jimmy Marshall, that I'm a northern girl. The first time I left England was when I came to Quantico on the training course. Since then, all I've managed is a two-week package tour in Portugal.'

'Who with?'

'Stop the jealousy,' she snapped. 'Learn to control yourself. With a girlfriend. All right? Look, don't keep interrupting. This is important to me. I'm just trying to tell you that, for all you think about me, I'm only a normal girl without a lot of experience. What you'd call worldly experience. I know about the seamy side of life because I've done nothing but be a bobby since I left school. Drugs and prossies and kids being battered and scraping dead people off the road after a car accident. That's all I've ever known. It hardens you. You become cynical. I remember once being called to a house in Altrincham. There was a girl there, about my age, she'd been attacked with a kitchen knife. I never saw anything like it. The guy'd done it in a frenzy. He'd accused her of sleeping around. Which she wasn't. It was all bloody jealousy. He'd stabbed her over a hundred times. Can you imagine what it must take to stab someone over a hundred times? But the worst was going along to arrest him. He was married. Two young kids. His wife knew nothing about it. You should've seen her face when we told her. He was no monster to her. He was just her husband. I was nineteen years old. And you wonder why I'm cynical. Then I met you. Just as bloody cynical as me. Because you're also scraping people off the road. Only I fell for you. Didn't give a damn if you were old or not. I just saw someone who took the shit in life, fought it every day, and still kept going. I admired you, Marshall. They don't make them like you any more.

207

And because of your hang-ups, just because you were born a few years earlier than me, you turned my love back on me. So I ran away. I didn't want to ring. There wasn't room in my house for two bloody cynics. But I couldn't get over you. When they came to me with this chance, I decided I couldn't hide any more. And there must've been a reason, even if you don't believe in God, as to why we should be thrown together again. Everything in life has to have a reason.'

'We lead a merry dance, don't we?'

'Don't we just.'

'For what it's worth, I'm glad you're back.'

'Really, big man?'

'Yeah. Really.'

'Did you miss me? Or is this a one way thing?'

'You never left me either.'

'Because you missed me, or because you didn't want anyone else to have me?'

He laughed. 'Very astute.' But he felt the demons stir; her words sparked off the jealousy that was always just under the surface.

'Love me for me, Marshall. Come out of your own mind and see me simply as I am.' She leant forward and jerked the towel off him. 'For an old man, you've got a great body.'

'I thought you said age didn't matter?'

'It doesn't. And when you learn to accept it, things'll be a lot better between us,' she said, her annoyance reflected in the sudden harshness of her tone.

'Meaning?'

'Meaning you've suddenly gone very touchy.'

He shrugged. He didn't want her to see his demons. But they were stronger than him and the question was asked before he could stop himself. 'When your father . . . ?'

'Not again,' she sighed. 'Not after all this time.'

'I've been thinking about what . . .' he persevered.

'I don't want to go through it again.'

'Just this time.'

'You always say that. Just leave it, Jimmy.'

'I can't. Some things just don't make sense.'

'I should never have told you. For God's sake, we've discussed this so many times before.'

'It matters. Because what your father did affected the way you look at men.'

'Rubbish! And it was stepfather, not father,' she pointed out.

208

'Still family.'

'I was sixteen, Jimmy, when he moved in. He didn't marry Mum until I was seventeen. I was living on my own when he made a pass at me.'

'Did you lead him on?'

'I've told you before, no.'

'But you slept with him.'

'In the end. After he'd hassled me for months. I was confused. He'd ring me all the time, tell me how he only stayed with Mum so he could be near me. Then I broke up with a boyfriend, someone I thought I loved. I was so fucked up, and he was there to comfort me, that I let him do it. I needed someone, anyone who could make me feel good, give me my confidence back.'

'He abused you.'

'At eighteen!' she protested. 'That's not exactly below the age of consent.' She didn't tell Marshall that it had become a game with her stepfather, that she enjoyed encouraging him, seeing how far he could be pushed. It wasn't the result she had wanted, but it was years later before she realized it had been inevitable.

'Then you must've enjoyed it.'

'I didn't. I didn't. It just happened.'

'But he kept coming back for more.'

'Well, he got a taste for me, didn't he?' she taunted.

Marshall slapped her across the face and she rolled back. It wasn't a hard blow but it stung her. She sat up immediately, holding her cheek.

'You bastard! That's what he did. Slapped me around because I wouldn't go with him any more. Are you like him, Jimmy? Beat me up so that I have to sleep with you?'

He saw her eyes were furious, didn't realize that the whole thing now excited her. 'I'm sorry,' he apologized, ashamed of his sudden reaction to her taunt.

'Just like him,' she continued. 'No different. Just take what you bloody want.'

'I really am sorry.' He knew he was grovelling, but it was how she made him, a man lost of control. He held his arms out to her.

She revelled in the power, seeing him want her, watching his remorse and shame. That's why she let the twenty-one-year-olds touch and grope her when she went out with them. Her age and experience gave her a mastery over them; she loved watching the helpless desire in their faces. She felt her cheek redden and she rubbed it harder, to make it glow so that it looked as though it was worse than it was. She knew he'd hate that, knowing he'd hurt her. 'I love you,' she said. 'More than you know.' Then she leant forward and she slipped his manliness into her mouth, moved it gently with her lips and tongue as she felt him excite and grow to his full strength.

He watched her and felt the warmth spread inside him. She was love and she was his. He held his hand out and stroked her hair. It was good to have her back.

The horrors in his mind that the demons had disturbed were now purged; only by speaking of them could he now ignore them. She had calmed him and for a short time he felt he could trust her once again. When they made love, he never saw the other men in his imagination.

This time he only saw her.

Drug Enforcement Administration
700 Army Navy Drive
Arlington
Virginia

The Deputy Assistant Administrator went down for a smoke for two reasons. Firstly he wanted somewhere where he could talk with his assistant, Smith, without being heard; and secondly he was, as usual, desperate for a cigarette when a crisis loomed.

Smith watched him light up, then pace backwards and forwards, well out of earshot of the other smokers. It was a cold day and the wind whipped around their suit jackets. The assistant wished he had worn a topcoat.

'I thought Ronane could be trusted,' stated the administrator.

'We don't know that he can't. He's always followed department procedure before.'

'Then why suddenly ask to go on vacation, and when we check up where he said he's gone, they never even heard of him?'

'Maybe he changed his mind. Said he just wanted to get away with his family.'

'The rule is sacrosanct. You always tell the department where you are.'

Smith shrugged. He had no answer to that and Ronane was known to be a stickler for procedure. 'Maybe he'll ring in.'

210

'And maybe he won't. I think it's Marshall. There's something there.'

'As far as we know Marshall's still at home in San Antonio.'

'I want him covered.'

'He'll pick up a surveillance straightaway.'

'So what. If he and Ronane are up to no good, at least they'll know we're aware of it.'

'We need a strong reason for watching our own people.' The assistant trod carefully. He knew Marshall was popular and whoever was put on the job would expect a damn solid reason.

'I know that. But I want to know what's going on. Give it to someone who isn't too close to Marshall. Or Ronane. And make it clear that we don't suspect them of turning. Even I don't need to be told that Marshall hates the pushers more than anyone else in this organization. He's brave and he's dedicated. But he's also headstrong and that makes him stupid. Shit, the FBI will love this one if they ever get hold of it.' The rivalry between the two departments was well known. The FBI had always looked down on the cavalier fashion in which the DEA carried out their duties and were continually looking at ways in which they could embarrass their law-enforcement rivals.

The administrator ground out his cigarette and walked away. Smith followed him. Marshall wasn't going to like this, and being the maverick he was, meant this whole thing could take a totally unpredictable turn.

1426 Military Trail
San Antonio
Texas

They spent two days and nights in the house: days of closeness and love and flashes of jealousy and shared hamburgers, long nights interspaced with deep sleep and desperate bouts of love-making.

In their frenzied efforts they tried to wipe away the lost years. There were few disturbing thoughts in Marshall's mind; somehow he forced himself to believe she loved him and that he had hated her only to protect what he really felt.

The second morning he let her sleep and went to make himself a coffee at eight. He sat in his small den and reread the letter she had delivered. Then he dialled Ronane's home number, and after

211

it had rung out unanswered he put the phone down. He hadn't communicated with Ronane since he first opened the letter and the unanswered call told him the family were on their way. He grinned, remembering Ronane's mode of vacation transport, and decided he wouldn't arrive for another day.

He was cooking breakfast an hour later when he noticed the watcher. He was parked in an old Ford pick-up, part of a group of workmen who were digging up a gas pipe down the road. But, with all his experience, Marshall could tell that he wasn't part of the group. The guy was good, but not that good. Marshall grinned, then switched off the grill and returned to the den where he slipped his jeans and shirt on and pushed his handgun into the waistbelt. He looked into the bedroom, checked that Jill was still asleep, and left the house by the back door.

He worked his way along his neighbours' backyards, crossed behind the working gang and approached the pick-up from the driver's blind side. Once he was sure that there wasn't a back-up man, he opened the passenger door and slid into the seat, his gun in his hand and held towards the driver's waist.

'Fuck you,' said the driver as the gun prodded into his portly waistline.

'Bang, bang. You're dead,' grinned Marshall. Then he put the gun back into his waistband. 'What the hell are you doing here, Jack?'

Jack Dimple, forty-three years old and one of the department's most experienced undercover men, laughed as he replied. 'Waiting for you, dickhead. You took your time.'

'Meaning?'

'You been shuffling round that house for an hour now and you only just realized I was here. You're getting old, Marshall. Old and slow.'

'You going to tell me that you wanted to be seen.'

'Of course.'

'Come off it, Jack.'

'I'm telling you. Listen, they tell me to get down here and cover you. Outside your house. I said, nobody can cover Marshall and keep things quiet. So they told me to handle it however I wanted to. I just decided to let you see me. Makes it easi-er.'

'Who's *they*?'

'Who do you think? The KGB?'

'Why?' Marshall ignored the joke.

212

'You probably know better than me. Just told me to find out what you get up to . . . and if you meet Ronane.'

'Fucking desk jockeys.'

'Nobody thinks you've turned. They wanted me to make that clear to you.'

'Did they say anything else?'

'No. Except Ronane's gone travelling without permission and they want to know if he's coming here.'

'He's not here.'

'OK. You going to invite me in for breakfast?'

'No.'

'Hey, that's not in the spirit of things.'

'I got company. Not Ronane,' he reiterated.

'OK. I'll wait out here.'

'I'll bring you a refill later on.' Marshall tapped the coffee flask that Dimple had next to him.

He returned to the house by the front door and went into the kitchen where he finished cooking breakfast. Then he went into the bedroom with a big tray and woke Jill. They sat on the bed and ate together; he decided not to tell her about the surveillance team outside. He was convinced it was a team. Dimple had been too forthcoming. There had to be a secondary. He wasn't concerned. He had no plans to leave the house until the call came.

It was another quiet day. Still content with each other's company, they spent most of it between the bedroom and the sitting room. The warm smell of sex and their bodies wrapped them in a cone of contentment and most of their talk was of dreams to be fulfilled rather than the past of their separation. The closeness was only broken once when Marshall had gone into the kitchen for a glass of water. Jill had followed him and seen him lean to look out of the window.

'Expecting someone?' she asked.

'No. Why?'

'Every time you come in here, you strain to look out of the window. You didn't do that yesterday.'

'Your police training coming through.'

'I can't help noticing the obvious.'

'Just habit, I guess. You get used to watching your back.'

She followed him back into the sitting-room. 'You've not been jumpy for the last few days.'

'I had other things on my mind,' he joked, then turned round and kissed her, crushing her with his arms.

213

'I love that,' she said when they broke. 'You make me feel I'm at home.'

'You are.'

She stepped back, took his hand and led him to the sofa. She pulled him down to sit next to her. 'Is it the letter?'

'Is what the letter?'

'Why you're so jumpy today.'

'I'm not jumpy.'

'You are, big man. You've been different all morning.'

'Yeah, it's the letter.'

'You going to tell me?'

'Not yet.'

'Why not?'

'Ever the cop.'

'Ever the secretive narc agent.'

'Touché. OK, but as much as you need to know for now.'

'Why not all of it?'

'Because what you know might hurt you. Trust me.'

'All right.'

'I guess you know Roy Armitage.'

'Of course.'

'The letter's from him. It seems you have a major drug problem in Manchester.'

'Don't I know it.'

'He wants help.'

'What sort of help?'

'Just help.'

'How do you know Armitage?'

'We met. A long time ago.' Now was not the time for Marshall to tell her about his early life.

'Why contact you? Why the secrecy?'

'Because some people in Manchester feel it's time for more covert action.'

'That sounds illegal.'

Marshall laughed. 'It's all illegal, Jill Bum. Sometimes it's the only way to fight back.'

'Does the Chief Constable know? Charlie Soulson.'

'Just say I owe a favour.'

'The trouble's in Moss Side, you know. In the black area.'

'The letter says the Chinese are involved. That they run the heroin, the blacks concentrate on cocaine.'

'Why you, Marshall?'

214

'Because they don't know what to do. And because they know our people fight back.'

'So you're going in with all guns blazing?'

'No. They just need different tactics.'

'Is danger your kick?'

'Don't cheapen it, baby. I didn't invent drugs. This is about genocide by guys who make more money than half the governments in the world.'

'I've seen it, Marshall.'

'So has any cop. But I'm out there where I can get to the source. Not to some penny-ante drug-pusher on the street corner, but the guys who control the whole thing. Do you know how strong this stuff really is?'

'Of course.'

'I mean, really how addictive? Ever heard of Dr James Olds?'

'No.'

'He ran tests on drug usage. Had rats for his experiments. The reason he did it was because crack had just started to be used. Now you know all about crack. You burn the stuff so you inhale the cocaine smoke straight into the lungs. No slowing down like when you snort, no membranes to ease it into the bloodstream. When you get straight to the lungs, to the one area that is designed to speed things into your bloodstream, that's when cocaine gets into you fast. You know why the suppliers pushed crack on the streets? Because it created more addicts quicker. Increase fucking turnover, that's what it's about. Anyway, Dr Olds showed how rats took to cocaine, how they enjoyed the pleasure it gave them. Then someone tried a different experiment. They stretched a live electric wire across a box. Put food one side and a rat the other. The rat tried to get to the food. After a couple of shocks, it didn't try to cross the wire. It starved to death. Then they gave some rats a sniff of crack, and put cocaine the other side of the wire. This time, after just one whiff, the rats electrocuted themselves because nothing was going to stop them getting to that stuff.'

'That's horrible.'

'That's where I go to work nine to five.'

'So, big man, why do you keep looking out of the window?'

He laughed. 'Once a cop, always . . .'

'. . . a bobby.'

'There's a guy out there watching me.'

'You're joking. A drug-dealer?'

'No. DEA.'

215

'Why're they watching you?' She was suddenly concerned.

'Because they think I know something they don't.' He laughed. 'Only we're going to give him, and his secondary, the slip later on.'

'Sounds like fun.'

'Don't worry. No-one's going to shoot at us.'

'That only happens in the movies.'

'Don't believe it. Now can we turn to more serious matters?'

'I wondered when you'd get—'

Marshall leant over and kissed her. She never finished her sentence. Before long they both had other things on their minds.

The phone rang after midnight on the third night.

'Mile long and stinky onions. Ex aye,' said Ronane before the phone clicked off.

Marshall put the receiver down and grinned. Even if they were bugging the phone, that one would fox them. He knew where the mile-long hot dogs with stinky onions were. And ex aye was a reference to the Roman numerals. XI. Eleven o'clock was the time.

'Who was that?' murmured a drowsy Jill.

'A friend. We're going sightseeing tomorrow.'

Ronane returned to the 1965 Airliner Silver Trailer that was the pride of his eye. It was parked in one of the many RV Trailer camps that abound in San Antonio.

He had towed it down from Washington with the family, putting up with their complaints of him only stopping for fuel and night stops. But they were happy now; journey's end was complete and they were here to vacation. He joined the kids and started to prepare their evening cookout. It was good to be away from Washington.

He decided not to worry about the fact he'd broken the rules and not warned them that he had changed plans. He'd ring them tomorrow night and apologize. Say he'd forgotten. He smiled to himself. They weren't used to him breaking rules. But then neither was he.

As he played with the kids he didn't notice the two men observing him from the pick-up behind the next row of trailers. Once they had seen him set up camp, they drove away, not wanting to be noticed. They knew he wasn't going to move until the morning and were prepared to bide their time.

After all, Ronane was the only reason they were there.

216

Getting away from Dimple was relatively easy.

Marshall, with Jill next to him in the front, backed out of the drive and up to the pick-up. Marshall climbed out of the Granada and went to the pick-up window.

'We're going into town, Jack,' he told Dimple.

'You want me to come with you or follow you?' replied the DEA man.

'Better follow.' Marshall smiled, then leant in and whipped out the ignition key before Dimple could react.

'Oh, come on, Marshall,' grumbled Dimple as he saw the big man pocket the key.

'Easier than backing into you and jamming your fender against the front wheel. Or shooting up your tyres.'

'Shit to you.'

Marshall climbed back into the Granada and drove off with a backward wave.

'Where's the back-up?' asked Jill.

They picked him up two streets later, following in a green Chevrolet Impala.

'So let's see how you get rid of him, clever clogs.'

Marshall smiled patronizingly, then drove at a steady 40 mph towards the downtown area. When he passed a police car, he signalled the policeman to stop and they pulled into the soft shoulder. In the wing mirror, Jill saw the Chevrolet slide into a car park in front of a western boot shop. She saw Marshall talking to the policeman, then return to the car, flick into gear and move off towards San Antonio.

'Watch the birdie,' he said.

She turned her attention to the wing mirror and watched the Chevrolet. As it passed the police car the sirens started, and within a minute the Chevrolet had been pulled in.

'He'll only keep him for a minute.'

'Long enough for us to lose him.'

'You make it all so simple.'

'Just keep a look-out. There could be a third.'

'But you doubt it.'

'Yeah. I don't warrant that much attention.'

She turned and watched the DEA watcher being escorted from his car and spread over the bonnet as they turned the corner. 'What did you say to him?'

'Who? George?'

'You know him?'

217

'This is my town. These guys all know who I am. If I say I'm being followed, then they take it seriously.'

'What if he orders George to radio ahead and keep an eye on us?'

'No. It's a covert operation. Involve the police and you involve everyone. This is internal stuff, for departmental eyes only.'

They drove, by way of PanAm Expressway and Travis Street, into the centre of San Antonio. They parked in the Hilton Hotel's underground car park and climbed the stairs to River Walk. The Walk, a 40-foot-wide river, winds picturesquely through the town and is sidewalked with pavement cafés and fashionable eateries. Jill linked her arm through Marshall's and hugged him as they walked.

The Alamo surprised her. It was smaller than she expected, this fort that had once played such a vital part in Texan and American history. Set back from the big square with a big F.W.Woolworth, Wendy's 'Old Fashioned Hamburger Store' and 'Americana – Preserving what you never had', this shrine to history was dwarfed by the clutter and industry of modern consumerism. History with a hamburger in your hand and sunglasses on your forehead. He led her towards the hot dog stand.

Jill watched the queue of tourists waiting to go into the old chapel, the only remaining part of the Alamo that had once stood against the Mexican forces of Santa Anna over a hundred years earlier.

'This it?' she asked. 'The heartbeat of Texas.'

He laughed. 'A hundred and eighty-eight Texans against four thousand Mexicans. If they hadn't slowed down that army, all this would be smelly and shitty like the rest of Mexico. But you know the truth? There were hardly any Texans. Twelve English. Twelve Irish. Half a dozen Scots. Even a couple of Welshmen. The biggest force, nearly forty of them, was from Tennessee. You ever heard of Davy Crockett?'

'King of the Wild Frontier,' she sang.

'The same. He died here.'

'Really?'

'Yeah. And Jim Bowie.'

'Who was he?'

'Invented the Bowie Knife.'

'What's that?'

'Just the greatest fighting knife ever.' He shook his head. 'Don't they teach you anything in Police Academy?'

'No, we're all dumbos. Did they all die?'

'Yeah.'

She was silent for a while. 'You'd like that, wouldn't you?'

'What?'

'To be in some hopeless cause like that. To be a hero for ever.'

'Not me.'

'It's wrong.' She turned back to him.

'What is?'

'Nobody knows about you, big man. Just because you're under-cover. Nobody'll ever know you're a hero.'

'I didn't do this to sign autographs.'

'But it would be nice. For all these people lining up here to turn round and know just what you do.'

'The world's full of heroes who never got noticed. Every time a war finishes and they come down the gangplank with their kitbags over their shoulders. They don't all get medals. It's just the way it is, Jill Bum.'

'Well, you're my hero.' She leant over and kissed him. 'And you always will be.'

'Do you have to do it in public?' said Ronane from behind.

Marshall swung round. 'Still sneaking around?' he joked.

'Yeah.'

'This is Jill.'

'Hello, Jill. I'm Ronane.'

'Hello.' She smiled and immediately liked the small man. She sensed the closeness between him and Marshall. 'Nice to meet you.'

'English?'

'Yes.'

'I like the English. Civilized and cultured. What the hell do you see in this meathead?'

'I've been asking myself that.'

'You surprise me,' he said to Marshall. 'Didn't know you were human. Or had such good taste. Come on. Come and say hello to Betty and the kids. They're inside.'

The trio entered the old chapel, Ronane pushing to the front of the line brandishing the tickets he had already obtained. The interior was lined with paintings and artefacts from the great battle. The swords and pistols and reminders of a bloody struggle seemed in conflict with the hushed atmosphere of the place, made even more reverential by the signs that reminded all that '*This is a shrine so please be quiet*'. 'And have a nice day,' whispered Jill.

'What?' asked Marshall.

'Nothing,' she lied. This place mattered to him and she didn't want to spoil it.

219

'You really never been here before?' said Ronane.

'I told you.'

'So how do you know so much about it?' added Jill.

'It's part of every Texan's heritage. Maybe I just didn't want to see it with the tourists. Sort of devalued it for me.'

They found Betty and the children at the back of the chapel, and after Marshall had kissed her and hugged the young ones, he and Ronane left by the rear door to walk in the garden of remembrance.

'What the hell's that?' said Ronane, pointing up at the tall building that stood next to the Alamo. 'A skyscraper church?'

Marshall laughed. The top of the building was steepled like a church with high-arched, ornate windows. 'It's the Alamo Plaza Hotel,' he answered.

'You Texans have no sense of style.' Ronane shook his head in mock disgust at the modern Gothic design. 'Good to see you, Marshall.'

'They expected you to come here. Jack Dimple's been sitting outside my place. Still is, as far as I know.'

'No secondary?'

'I lost him.'

'So what's the urgency?'

Marshall took the letter from his back pocket and held it up. 'A blast from the past.' He handed the letter to Ronane, who opened it and read it.

'What does support mean?' he said when he had finished.

'Whatever I want it to, I guess. They're in a hole and . . .'

'Who isn't? But we're not the cavalry.'

'Touchy, aren't you?'

Ronane shrugged. 'Damn it, Marshall, let the Brits sort their own mess out. We're not exactly flavour of the month.' He handed the letter back to Marshall.

'It also mentions the Irish.'

'So?'

'Keeps coming back, doesn't it? The Irish link.'

'Helluva thin link.'

'Still ties together.'

'The letter says *maybe* they're involved.'

'It wouldn't be in there unless they had a strong hunch. It mentions they found explosives. Same materials as used in Belfast.'

'General store stuff. Hell, they'd find that stuff in Beirut and Frankfurt and anywhere else those terrorists make bombs. Still not strong enough.'

'I think that—'

'Shit, Marshall, I can feel your instinct chugging away in there.'

'Well, it's not been wrong yet. I think this could be where that Cali stuff out of El Paso was due for.'

'Ireland?'

'Yeah. Then into England. All this . . .' he waved the letter at Ronane '. . . organized riots, shootings, planned media coverage, terrorist funerals. This is not your everyday street-corner drug-dealers. This is the start of a planned campaign. Like the Colombians, they're bringing the war to us.'

'Is *us* America or Britain?'

'It's all the same.'

'No it isn't. Anything that keeps it out of our backyard suits me.'

'I'm telling you, there's a strong possibility that this is where that Cali shipment was headed for. Shit, it's probably already there.'

'Trouble is the Brits hate the IRA. You can only presume—'

'This is not about the IRA. This is about drugs. This is about what you and I get up in the morning for.'

Ronane shrugged. 'If I tell Washington about the letter, then they'll take it over. And it'll become another political football. Ronanegate.'

'I know that. But I'm on vacation. I can go.'

'Ireland?'

'No, England.'

'God help England. Haven't they got enough trouble already? What do you want me to do?'

'Tell me if there's any changes here. Keep me informed. Unless you want to come.'

'Go to hell. That's your backyard.' They walked around the rear of the mission building, both lost in their own thoughts. 'Must've been scary,' Ronane said eventually. 'Looking out and seeing the Mexican army riding over the horizon. What was all this? Farmland?'

'Yeah. The river curved right in front of the place.'

'What happened to it?'

'They moved it. So the tourists wouldn't get their feet wet.'

'What do you expect to find?'

'I don't know. Not till I get there.'

'I think you're wrong.'

'Why?'

'Because we always worked within our own jurisdiction. We bent the rules a few times, but it was always for the department. Never for ourselves, Marshall.'

'This war isn't the department's sole jurisdiction either. I've got five months to do nothing but sit on my hands. Can't do it.'

'What about Jill?'

'She can't stay here for that long.'

'She going back to England?'

'Yeah.'

'That your reason for going over there?'

'It helps. But I've got to work. It's all I know to do. Shit, Ronane, they're the only people who want me. All Washington's done is send me to purgatory.'

'You won't have the protection of the department.'

'They just want advice. Some new ideas. Who says I'm going to get into trouble?'

Ronane snorted. 'You always get into trouble.'

'Are you going to help me or not?' came the exasperated reply.

'Don't I always? OK, when I get back to Washington I'll keep my ears open. Anything that comes up on that shipment, I'll get the information to you.'

'Good.'

'That's if I've still got a job. After my disappearance I could end up as Head of the Janitor's Section.'

'What're you going to tell them?'

'That you said to come down here for a few days. And that I forgot to tell them I changed my route. I'll do that tonight.' He laughed. 'Won't be the first time I've crawled up someone's arse to get you what you wanted.'

They found their way back into the mission building, and after another half-hour decided to split up and meet later that evening for a meal. It was something Marshall looked forward to. He had already tasted the excellence of Ronane's barbecues when the little man was on one of his trailer holidays.

'I want to tell Washington that you think the shipment's going to Ireland,' said Ronane just before they separated.

'Why?'

'Because they still pay your salary. And just because you've gone independent doesn't mean they don't need all the help they can get.'

Marshall agreed and returned to River Walk where he and Jill walked hand in hand looking for a restaurant.

'I like him,' said Jill.

'He's the closest I have to family.'

'How long have you known each other?'

222

'Fifteen years. He's the best damn section head in the DEA.'

'Has he killed people?'

Marshall looked up sharply. 'That's a strange question.' Then he remembered her background, that the British police never carried firearms in the normal course of events. It was difficult to explain that guns and bullets and death were part of the American way of police life. 'Yeah. He's used a gun in the pursuance of duty. Usually self-defence.'

'He's so mild-mannered. And so close to his family.'

'They're his sanity. The place he can go when everything else gets black and ugly.'

'Where do you go, big man?'

He grinned, put his hand across the table and squeezed her hand. 'Do you think I'm too old to find somewhere to go?'

'No.'

'There's hope for me yet.' As he looked down on her, the loneliness and fear that she had created in him suddenly surfaced. What if she was just riding the emotion of the moment; what if she suddenly looked up at him and suddenly saw the older man? He remembered how he had always felt she was shallow and that her own impatience and youth would push her away from him, looking for new excitements and new youthful emotions. When she was fifty, young by today's standards, he would be sixty-four. Damn it, would she, could she, still love him then? He suddenly rubbed his arm, felt the skin still firm. It would probably be sagging by then, an old man's reptile texture. He swung away and looked at a pleasure barge going down the river, its excited passengers pointing at the passing buildings as they toured San Antonio. He shut the nightmare from his mind. Life was a lot easier when you didn't love, when you had nothing to lose.

But the fear still remained with Marshall. He clung to his youth and wanted her for ever and tried to push away the vision of her under the others. But this time they stayed and he hated himself for his weakness.

They took Betty and the children away in the car.

Then they sat Ronane in a chair in the 1965 Airliner Trailer and started to question him. One of the men held a Desert Eagle Magnum to his head to ensure he didn't try and break away.

They'd been waiting for him when he returned from the Alamo. He hadn't expected any trouble and by the time he realized the danger, the five men had surrounded the family and pushed them into the Airliner.

'We're going to take your family for a ride,' said the Texan.

Ronane recognized him immediately, remembered the last time he had seen him in Mexico City. 'Leave them alone.'

'Nobody's going to get hurt. We just want to talk. They're going sightseeing.'

Ronane looked at Betty, held her eyes as he tried to calm her. 'It'll be OK. Just do as they say.'

Betty's intense look had never wavered from his eyes as she shepherded the children out of the trailer. When the family had gone, he pushed past the Texan and looked out of the window. He watched Betty hold the children's hands as she led them towards the car that was parked there. When they had been driven off, poor Betty with a last plaintive yet brave look towards the trailer, he turned back to the Texan. 'They've nothing to do with this.'

'Insurance. We just want to make sure you concentrate your mind on what we have to discuss.'

'I want their safety guaranteed.'

'It's in your hands, Mr Ronane. Depends on what you tell us. So why not just sit down?'

Ronane knew he was in a hopeless situation. He shrugged and sat down in the chair. One of the Texan's accomplices pushed the muzzle of the Desert Eagle Magnum hard against his temple. 'Do we need all this?' Ronane appealed to the Texan. 'You're not going to blow my brains out until you get what you want.'

The Texan waved the gunman away. 'Keep him covered. Just in case.'

'So what's all this for?'

'You, and that crazy partner of yours, you owe us.'

'You mean Mexico City? I thought—'

'I mean El Paso. You cost us dear.'

'You already knew who we were.'

'Don't matter. You cost us. Made me look bad. We can't let that go. You DEA people got to understand we don't just flip on our backs and wag our tails.'

'You're not going to gain anything by dragging kids into it.'

The Texan smiled mischievously. 'Like I said, you behave and they'll be OK. So why don't we start with your big friend. Mr James Marshall. Where's he right now?'

'On vacation.'

'Where?'

'I don't know.'

'Maybe he likes historic places. Like the Alamo.' The Texan

watched Ronane closely; the little man was giving nothing away. The Texan shook his head. 'There's two ways of doing this thing. The easy way, and that saves your family. Or this way.' From his side pocket he pulled out a metal-bladed microtome. He held it close to Ronane's face so that its awful message was clearly understood. 'Look, we want this thing resolved. Hell, you come over to us and we'll even give you a witness rehabilitation programme. Ain't that a laugh? You'll get a new identity, any place you want to live, all the money in the world, a new and safe life away from all this shit. And all you got to do is sing. Tell us about the DEA. We ain't after you. We're after the big man. Do a deal, man, or else you're going to hurt everybody. Shit, Ronane, are you really going to protect Marshall and those fuckers in Washington? You really going to put your family on the front line?'

Ronane said nothing; his training told him to hang on until all possibilities had been exhausted, that the cavalry sometimes did ride over the horizon. The Texan nodded to two of the men and stepped back. They pulled Ronane from the chair and stripped him of his clothes, clipping him hard across his temple every time he resisted, kicking him in the chest and shins to force him down as they undressed him. When they had him naked, they pinned him back to the chair. The Texan came close to him again, the microtome held up for Ronane to see clearly.

'Ever see a microtome before? Sometimes they call it a dermatone. Same thing. Doctors use it. Well, plastic surgeons more than doctors.' He turned the microtome over so that Ronane could see the long twelve inch knife blade, no more than two inches wide, which was attached to a semicircular metal cylinder. The knife was sharp, sharper than any instrument Ronane had ever seen. 'Pretty little thing, isn't it? For skin grafts. Just run it along your skin, little sawing action, and it'll fillet you thinner than any slice of smoked salmon. Just slice you clean.' The Texan laughed. 'You know how they fix people who got bad burns? They slice this thin bit of skin off another part of your body, then lay it across the burn so that it'll patch up with your ordinary skin. It ain't that which hurts. It's the donor zone. 'Cos when they cut you, that's when they expose the nerve-ends. Raw ends. With no protection. Sounds bad. Just waiting in pain till that little piece of skin grows again.'

He nodded to the men who now dragged Ronane from the chair and spreadeagled him on his back on the floor. Ronane struggled, but the man with the pistol cracked him across the nose, breaking it as the blood gushed out. Ronane stopped and lay still. Whatever they did would be made worse by him fighting back. He cursed himself for retaliating and closed his eyes. The numbness in his nose slowly turned into a throbbing pain. He fought to concentrate, to bring himself under control. *Damn you, Marshall. You made this happen. Where are you?* Then he shook the bitterness from his mind. This wasn't Marshall's fault. This was just part of the bloody war they were in.

The Texan knelt in front of Ronane and hit him on the inside of his thigh with his elbow, forcing the DEA man to open his legs. Then he held the microtome to Ronane's left thigh and sawing in a to-and-fro motion, sliced away a thin layer of skin an inch wide and four inches long. When he got to the end, he ripped the skin off as roughly as he could. He saw Ronane flinch, but there was no further reaction. The Texan shrugged and turned his attention to the inside of his right thigh. He repeated the action, only this time taking a longer strip, some seven inches long.

Ronane concentrated on the searing pain that the centre of his face had become. It was a trick they had been taught in the DEA. Concentrate on an alternative pain, even if it has to be self-inflicted, and it eases any new hurt that comes.

His eyes were still clamped shut, so he didn't see the bottle of hydrogen peroxide, simple hair bleach, that the Texan now opened. He poured it over the sliced areas of Ronane's thighs, burning into the opened and unprotected nerve-ends.

Ronane screamed as the pain seared through him and he struggled to sit up. The others held him down, and one of them forced the end of a towel into his mouth as a gag. He screamed again as the second surge of pain racked him, but the gag brought on a coughing fit. Then he tried to bring himself under control once again, but the pain was too great and he started to cry.

The Texan let him sob until he eventually calmed down. 'You should've taken the chance I gave you,' he said. 'Now we can go on all night like this. Or you can talk. Your choice, Ronane.'

Ronane shook his head, then clamped his eyes shut again. The Texan signalled the others to push him down again, then once more used the microtome, this time sawing away at Ronane's left breast, cutting the nipple away as part of the four inch strip of flesh and skin he sliced off. Then he poured the peroxide over the cut area and waited for Ronane to react. It didn't take long and the DEA man's attempt to scream through the gag acknowledged the pain he was enduring. When he finally subsided, the Texan knelt down and grabbed Ronane's hair and pulled him into a sitting position.

'Next time it'll be just under your balls. A real ball breaker. Now that'll bring tears to your eyes,' said the Texan as he removed the towel. 'And if you get past that little one, how do you think your family's going to react to some of the same.'

'Go to hell!' said a defiant Ronane.

'Not in this world. Who told you the shipment was coming through?'

'Nobody.'

'Come on, you guys weren't waiting at the border post for the hell of it. Who told you?'

'A Mexican.' Ronane decided to keep the Texan talking, keep him going until help arrived. Maybe? *Where are you, Marshall?*

'What Mexican?'

'Cortez. Was part of your Piedras Negras team.' Ronane knew the DEA had moved Ramon Cortez out west and given him a false identity. The Calis would never trace him.

'Why'd he come to you?'

'Overheard some talk about the shipment. Got scared at the size of the thing. Decided he preferred us on his side.'

'Just like that?'

'No. Immigration had got their hooks into him.'

'That don't answer how you knew we were coming through at that time.'

'A hunch.'

'Whose?'

'I don't remember.'

'Marshall?'

'Why him?'

'No offence to the rest of you, but he's always heading the action. Even the Calis know his reputation.' The Texan tapped his forehead. 'They say he's loopy.'

'He's OK.'

'Yeah. But then, you're his partner. He's still a little crazy.' The Texan changed tack. 'So tell me where this Cortez is now.'

'I wouldn't know. He was given a new identity.'

'And he heard about the shipment.'

'Yes.'

'So why run to you guys?'

'Thought you'd take him out. He stumbled on a meeting about the shipment. When he heard Rodriguez-Orejuela mentioned . . .' Ronane let the Cali boss's name sink in '. . . he knew he was dead if they found him. So he shot himself full of snow and went into hiding. That's how the border patrol picked him up. When he knew he was being deported back to Mexico, he did a deal with us.'

'What else?'

'That there was a thousand kilos going through.'

'That it?'

'That's it.' Ronane, even in his deep pain, decided not to tell the Texan about the Irish connection or the shipment of money that had gone through.

'So why jump the big truck?'

'Marshall. He saw something the rest of us missed.'

'He caused some good people to die.'

'He was doing his duty.'

'Yeah, just like my people were doing theirs. Including a woman.'

'She was from Mexico. You said she was Cali.'

'That why Marshall took her out? Because he was after the family?'

Ronane realized the Texan believed it was Marshall who had killed the woman. He kept silent, there was no need to tell them that it was he himself who had pulled the trigger. 'He was just doing . . .'

'He knew he'd hurt the family.'

'That wasn't the only reason that . . .'

'Fuck you, Ronane. It was reason enough. Just 'cos she's family. Only he got one thing wrong. She wasn't just Cali. She was my family. She was my fucking wife.'

Ronane was stunned by the disclosure. *Who the hell was the Texan?* They had presumed he was just another adventurer, one of the thousands of lieutenants employed by the drug cartels. But to marry a Cali? Now that moved him up the ladder.

'I also got two kids,' continued the Texan. 'Only they got no mother. It wasn't us who made it personal. Only this time understand one thing. It's your family against your partner. Your wife and kids traded for Marshall.' The Texan held the microtome towards Ronane. 'Any which way, DEA man. Only this time it's my deck of cards. This time ain't nobody going to draw a Royal Flush.'

'Try the dolphin,' Marshall advised Jill as the waiter hovered with his pad in his hand.

'You're joking.'

'No. Best fish there is.'

'It's not a fish. And you're a cannibal.'

Marshall laughed. 'Hey, we're not talking Flipper. Over here, we call that a porpoise.'

228

'This one doesn't go Eek, Eek, and clap its fins,' joined in the smiling waiter.

'You sure?' asked an unsure Jill.

'I promise you,' said Marshall. 'It's a fish, couple of feet long.'

'All right.'

'Two dolphins. Grilled. And stuffed red potatoes. Cheese and jalapena,' Marshall told the waiter. 'And iced tea.'

'I like being taken in hand,' she said when the waiter had gone. She leant across the table and stroked his hand. She felt him stiffen. 'Stop it,' she said, gripping his hand tightly so he couldn't pull away.

'Stop what?'

'Thinking everyone's looking at us. *Look at that old feller with the young girl,*' she mimicked.

'Cut it out.'

'No. I'm here because I want to be here. I wish you'd understand that. I love you, big man. And if they are looking, that's all they see. Two people very much in love. If you can't see it in my eyes, I know they can.' She saw him grin and relax a little. 'We're OK. Just one person. Age is something you worry about when you've got pimples.'

'There speaks the voice of youth. I'll remind you of this when you're nearly fifty.'

She laughed. 'At least you accept we'll be together when I'm fifty. You think I'm stupid. I only want to be with you so that you can tell me what to expect when I get there.'

'Very funny.' He inadvertently tried to pull his hand away as the waiter came back with the iced teas, but she held it firmly as her eyes mocked him while the drinks were set on the table. 'Point taken,' he said when they were alone again. 'I meant to ask you, does anybody in Manchester know about us?'

'Like who?'

'Like those who sent you here.'

'No. Except that I met you at Quantico. That you were my trainer. Only they didn't know what you really trained me in,' she added mischievously.

'Who's they?'

'Chief Superintendent Armitage. I made a full report to him about the systems and procedures at Quantico.'

'Did you tell them I lived in England when I was a boy?'

'Yes.'

'In Manchester?'

'Yes.'

Marshall realized that was how they had stumbled across him. They knew he had taken his Aunt Josie's surname. The old fox Armitage would have been intrigued with the link in the name and traced it back. 'What was his reaction when you mentioned my name?'

'Raised eyebrows. Then he kept asking questions about you.'

'Like what?'

'Like what you looked like. Were you a good officer? How tall you were? Were you married?' She looked intently at him. 'It's the closest I came to ringing you. I mean, you were still fresh inside me. And, damn you, I couldn't believe how much I missed you.'

'Just had to pick up the phone. That simple.'

'It was a long time ago,' she said regretfully and shrugged. 'Anyway, I was surprised about how much he wanted to know about you. All personal stuff. In the end he covered it by saying he'd known you from the past.'

Marshall pulled his hand away from hers, took the letter from his inside pocket and put it on the table. 'For a policewoman, you don't seem that inquisitive about what's in this.' He tapped the letter with his forefinger. 'And why you brought it.'

'Because I knew you. I'm only a courier, and I suppose they felt they could trust me.'

'They?'

'Don't try to catch me out. I presume Armitage isn't working on his own initiative.' When Marshall didn't confirm her view, she continued, only this time a note of irritation had crept into her voice. 'This is why I didn't bring the letter up. I don't want anything to come between us. The last few days have been fantastic. I meant it when I said I'll give up everything to stay here. If you want me. I'm more interested in us than in policework, or that bloody letter. Anyway, I worked on the principle that you'll tell me whenever you're ready. Maybe, my love, I don't want to know what's in that letter. Maybe I don't want what we have to come to an end.'

'I wish life were that simple, Jill Bum.'

'It can be.'

'How?'

'Just forget the world's there. You've done your share. Enjoy what you've fought for. We could have a great life.' As she spoke, she regretted some of her words. The emotion of the moment overcame her logic. She enjoyed her work in Manchester, enjoyed her independence. As much as she loved the big man, she wasn't convinced she would be prepared to give that up for him. But the words were out; emotion was the temporary winner.

He was silent for a while, then shook his head. 'I love you. But I have to finish what I started.'

'You'll never stop.' She felt the relief within her.

'I will. When they stick me behind a desk.'

'We'll see. But, just so you know, I'm not going anywhere this time.'

'Not back to England?'

'Only if you told me you didn't want me.' She knew she was on safe ground this time.

'I'm not about to do that. But I can't just sit on my butt all day.'

'Why not? With me?'

'I've got to finish what I started.' He pushed the letter towards her. 'I think you should read it.'

She picked it up hesitatingly and opened it. As she read the letter, the waiter arrived with their meal. Marshall let her finish reading before he suggested they eat. Not much was said while they ate; he watched her digest both the meal and contents of Armitage's letter.

When the waiter had cleared the meal and served the iced teas, Jill finally brought the conversation back to the letter. 'It says your brother wants you. Who's that?'

'Your boss. Charlie Soulson.'

'Christ!' came the stunned reply.

Then Marshall told her about all those years ago, about the dark days of his youth and Mary and of the time in Moss Side that had ended with his banishment to America.

'It was a long time ago,' she said when he had finished. 'People forget.'

'Not my brother.'

'Do you really think he would hold it against you after all these years?'

'There was more than that. More than came out at the time.'

'What? That you were dealing in drugs and pimping at fifteen. Do you think that would affect you in the DEA?'

'I wish it was that simple. I think if I had gone back, and things got out because I was the Chief Constable's brother, then people could dig deeper and . . .' he paused. 'The guy who was pumped full of heroin, the one who was dead . . . Christ, I've told no-one. But it's always been in me, Jill. It never goes away.'

'What?'

231

'I was a young tearaway. Always looking for a new bloody experience. A real child of the sixties.' He leant forward and held both her hands. 'In my drugged way, looking for that ultimate experience, I stuffed the poor bastard full of heroin. Wasn't difficult, he was diced out anyway. But I injected the stuff into him. I don't know how much. I think he'd already OD'd. Then I sat there and watched him die. Didn't bother me at all. I was pretty spaced out myself. To this day I don't know whether or not I killed him.' He pulled his hands away suddenly. 'That's why I never went back. And you, my little love, are the first person I've ever told.'

'Did your brother know?'

'I don't know. I think he guessed. I know they never found the syringe I used. I think he hid it.' He watched Jill closely; there was no emotion on show. 'Sort of freaks the mind, doesn't it? You know I've killed people. In the line of duty. Part of the job. Hate to say it, but it never affects me. They deserve it. For what they do to others. But that . . . to unnecessarily take life . . . to know I'm capable of that . . . that takes some living with.'

'You don't even know if you killed him.'

'But I was prepared to.'

'You were only fifteen. And high on drugs.'

'No excuse. I still did it.'

She reached forward and took his hands. 'Why did you want to tell me?'

'Whatever there is between us has to be clean.' He squeezed her hands. 'I know there's an age difference, and I do feel old sometimes with you. I can't help that. But before you I always held back. What I've done, and I've had a lot of years to live it over and over again, made me into some sort of monster. To me. So I never let anyone through. I did things, lived the way a monster should.' He remembered the women and the way he had always abused them. 'In a twisted sort of way, it made it all easier.'

'Maybe that's what we all do,' she said, remembering her own past and her own diversions from loneliness over the years.

'Then you came along. And you mattered. You gave me a reason for not being a monster.'

'I'm sorry I went away.'

He shrugged. 'It's only what I deserved.'

'I'm back now.'

'Even knowing the truth? Of what I am?'

'Especially knowing the truth. We'll get there, big man.'

'I hope so.'

'Is going back to Manchester going to expunge it?'

'Maybe. And it also ties in with something else I've been doing,' he went on. Then he told her about Mexico City and Ronane and El Paso and his enforced vacation.

'You can't take on the whole world,' she said when he had finished.

'But I can't let go. Not till I've reached the end.'

Then they said nothing else; there was simply nothing else to be said; and they finished their iced teas and drove back to the house on Military Trail.

'He'll be ready for a refill,' said Marshall as they turned the corner and saw the pick-up still parked where they had last seen it.

'He's going to be hopping mad,' Jill replied.

'Not Jack. He's too cool for that.' Marshall pulled into the driveway and passed Jill the house keys as they climbed out of the car. 'You go on in,' he told her. 'I'll see if he wants anything else.'

'I'll put the coffee on.'

He crossed the road, a mischievous, yet apologetic smile on his face as he approached the pick-up. Dimple watched him, not moving, a stern, frozen expression on his face. Marshall waved, the grin growing wider on his face.

His instincts, because of his state of happiness, had slipped. He was only a few yards from the vehicle when his warning senses took over. He accelerated his pace and swung the door of the pick-up open.

He knew Jack Dimple was dead before he saw the DEA man was propped up in the seat and tied to the steering wheel, before he saw the blood-congealed bullet hole in the nape of his neck. He swung round as Jill, her hand on the key in the front-door lock, was about to turn it and enter the house. 'No!' he shouted, his warning booming across Military Trail. 'Run, Jill, runrunrun.' He saw her turn, startled by his yell, not knowing what was happening. 'Get behind the car!' He started to run towards her. 'Gogo,' he shouted again.

She reacted fast, spinning round and diving behind the Granada. Marshall was sprinting towards the car when the first shots rang out, automatic fire, coming from the house, spraying lead and tarmac off the road around him as he ran. He ducked and dived and managed to reach the safety of the Granada. He wrenched the driver's door open and reached for the Colt .45 automatic that was always strapped under the dashboard. Once the weapon was in his hand, he rolled

233

towards Jill, who was cowering under the rear wheel, and checked she was all right. Seeing she was unhurt, he grabbed her and pulled her away from the car, using it as cover, and ran with her, half dragging her, to the safety of the trees that were his neighbour's pride and joy. Nobody fired at them. It was as if the danger that had threatened them was no longer there.

In the distance he heard the wail of a police siren. He hoped a neighbour had heard the shots and called the police. 'Stay here,' he instructed Jill. The look on her face told him there was no chance of her disobeying him. He moved, under cover of the trees, towards the house. He saw nothing that alarmed him, no curtains moving, no shadows that shouldn't be there.

He heard a car start up the street, from behind one of the houses. The police siren was now getting closer. It was time to take a chance, just in case whoever had been in the house had taken an escape route out of the back. He showed himself as a target, still half hidden by the trees but open enough to be shot at.

There was no reaction. Still no obvious signs of ambush from the windows. He heard the car that had been started move off. He broke cover from the trees and ran towards the front door, weaving as he did in case someone opened fire. He reached the door and stepped to the side, just in case someone opened up through the wooden door. Still no reaction. He saw the car, a blue station wagon, pull into the street and turn away from him. He recognized it; it belonged to one of his elderly, widowed neighbours. But it was not being driven by its owner; only three large shapes of men huddled low so as not to be recognized.

He had no alternative, he had to check the house first. *Where the hell was that police car?*

He reached forward, turned the handle and tried to push the door open. It was bolted on the inside. Up the road, the station wagon disappeared round the corner. Marshall stepped back on to the porch, his gun held out in front of him and pointed at the house.

Nothing happened.

He knew they'd escaped from the back of the house and driven off in the station wagon. He ran to the Granada to give chase, but stopped when he saw both front tyres had been shot and punctured. He wouldn't get very far in that. He looked up the road. There was no other vehicle in sight. Nothing except for Jack Dimple's pick-up. He remembered the key in his pocket and he ran towards it.

Dimple sat there, lashed to the steering wheel in his deadly pose.

Marshall opened the door and pushed the limp body over until he could squeeze in and sit next to it. Dimple's hands were tied to the steering wheel with wire, the harsh steel had cut deep into the dead man's hands.

'Shit,' swore Marshall as he inserted the key and switched on the engine. He put the gear into D and pulled away from the kerb. The road the station wagon had disappeared down was part of a loop and would double back lower down the street.

The pick-up lurched down the road in the opposite direction to the station wagon, careering drunkenly as Marshall steered it with Dimple's hands, trying to hold the vehicle in a straight line. As he turned the corner he saw Jill come out from behind the trees, her face a blur of confusion as he passed.

At the bottom of the street, the police car swung up Military Trail towards the house and passed the pick-up. Marshall ignored it, his attention concentrated on keeping the pick-up on the road and getting to the junction before the station wagon got there. He saw it hurtling towards the junction; he felt a surge of euphoria that he'd beaten them to it. He slowed down, waited for them to reach his position. As they came closer, he slammed the accelerator down and roared out of the side road, ramming the station wagon in the side. The two vehicles skidded across the road and into the front yard of a house opposite.

The sudden impact of the pick-up stopping threw Dimple's body forward into the windscreen. The glass shattered but held, and Dimple bounced back across Marshall who was reaching for his gun. The force of the collision was so great that the wire tore through the dead man's wrists and severed them from the body. The hands, stiffened by rigor mortis, emptily gripped the steering wheel, the tendons draped uselessly over the horn button.

Marshall, trapped under Dimple's dead weight, struggled to get out of the vehicle. Out of the side window he saw one of the men in the station wagon turn towards him with a semi-automatic rifle and open fire. Marshall ducked, shielding himself with Dimple, and felt the body jerk as the bullets ripped into it. Then the firing stopped and he heard the station wagon roar and drive away. He pushed the door open and slid out from under Dimple and on to the pavement. By the time he had pulled his handgun out and was in a position to fire, the station wagon was off down the road and round the corner.

Marshall cursed and started to run back towards his house. As he reached the corner he saw one of the two policemen from the car running towards him, obviously attracted by the sound of gunfire.

'Freeze!' yelled the policeman, pointing his revolver at Marshall.

The big man stopped in his tracks and threw his Colt .45 to the ground. The policeman was jumpy and there was little point in getting shot. Marshall held his hands high as the policeman approached him.

'What the hell's going on, Marshall?' yelled the second policeman, who had recognized him.

Thank God he knew him. 'I don't know. But one of my guy's been killed. Down there in the pick-up.'

'What the . . .?' shouted the first officer, his gun still cocked and pointed at Marshall.

'Put your weapon down,' ordered the second officer. 'He's DEA.'

Marshall lowered his arms as the first officer holstered his gun. 'Get an APB out,' Marshall shouted. 'A blue Dodge station wagon. Texas and San Antonio tags. Smashed in right side. Occupants armed and dangerous. Including a semi-automatic rifle.'

The second officer sprinted to his patrol car to radio his call. Marshall picked up his handgun, waved Jill away and told the first officer to follow him into the house.

They went in through the back door.

There was nothing downstairs apart from the shattered windows through which the gunmen had fired. Marshall unbolted the front door and Jill came into the house. He put his arm round her and comforted her. He heard the policeman go upstairs to check the rest of the house.

'What was all that about?' asked a frightened Jill.

'Welcome to my world,' he replied.

'Do you really want to see it through to the end?'

He shook his head. Maybe it was time to settle down. Then he remembered Dimple. He'd had a family. Somewhere in Washington. *Maybe he was getting too old for . . .*

'You better come up here,' he heard the policeman shout from upstairs.

He took his arms away from Jill and climbed the stairs. The policeman, his face white and strained, waited for him. Marshall pushed past him and entered the bedroom.

Betty and the two children lay on their backs on the bed, the mother in the middle with a child on either side. They had been stripped of their clothes and their throats had been cut. The murderers had then linked their hands as if the young family were out on a Sunday walk. He didn't need to examine them to know they were dead.

236

'Oh, my God!' he heard Jill behind him.

He swung round and put his arm round her to shield her from this most brutal tableau. Her eyes were transfixed, wide open in shock. He led her out of the room.

When they were downstairs, he sat her in a chair. 'You're going to have to stay here,' he said. 'I need to go somewhere.'

'Where?' she asked, her mind still trying to take in the horrors of what she had just witnessed.

'Ronane. He'll be in trouble.' There was no reason to add that Ronane was probably dead. He smiled reassuringly and walked to the front door.

'Marshall,' she called after him.

He turned to face her.

'I understand now,' she continued. 'Why you've got to finish it.'

He nodded. He left the house to find Ronane.

What was left of Ronane was still alive.

They had stripped the skin from his chest, the tops of his arms, the soles of his feet, his buttocks, his cheeks, his thighs and most of his back. Then they covered him with peroxide and left him to die.

But, for all his small stature, the man was a lion.

The pain was second to his concern for his family.

That's how Marshall found him, semi-conscious, but breathing lightly and still alive. His body resembled a huge open sore and Marshall decided to leave him where he lay until the emergency medical team arrived.

'Betty,' whispered Ronane to Marshall as he knelt beside him.

'OK,' lied Marshall. 'Fight it, man, and get better for them.'

Ronane nodded and passed into unconsciousness.

The medical team arrived ten minutes later and pumped him full of pain-killers. Then they lifted him as gently as they could, wrapped him in paraffin gauze and took him to the hospital.

Jill met Marshall at the hospital where he waited in a small room for news of Ronane. 'I found this,' she said, holding out a sheet of paper.

He took the sheet and read the handwritten note.

'FORGET THE ALAMO. REMEMBER EL PASO. THE GURKHAS ARE COMING. KEEP LOOKING OVER YOUR SHOULDER, DICKHEAD.'

'Where was it?' he asked, carefully folding the sheet.

'Stuck to the kitchen table with a steak knife,' replied Jill.

'Did the police see it?'

'No. Should they have?'

'You did right. This is for the DEA.'

'It's for you, isn't it?'

He nodded and pocketed the sheet.

'What's the message?' she urged quietly.

'The Texan war cry was always "Remember the Alamo". The bastards are trying to be funny. Christ, what a mess.'

'What happened in El Paso? And why the Gurkhas?'

He told her of the Texan's story while they had waited for the poker money to be collected by the ugly woman in Mexico City. Then they sat quietly and waited for news of Ronane.

'And you really believe the answer's in Manchester?' she asked as they waited.

'That's what I think.'

'It's a big risk to take.'

'Long shot. That's what we Yanks say.'

She reached over and squeezed his hand. 'Is that why they left Ronane alive? To show you that they can do anything they want.'

'Something like that.' He didn't need to add that those in the house had seen Jill, that she could now be in equal danger.

A policeman came into the room. 'I've got someone from the DEA for you. You want to take the call in here?'

'Yeah, thanks,' replied Marshall and the officer left the room. 'I wondered when Washington was going to make its presence felt,' said Marshall as he crossed to the phone in the corner. A few moments later it rang and he picked it up.

'That you, Marshall?'

Marshall recognized the Deputy Administrator's assistant, Peter Smith. 'Yes, Pete,' he replied. Smith was a good man, a defender against the bureaucrats.

'What the hell's going on?'

'What you got?'

'The police reports are that we got one DEA man dead . . .'

'Jack Dimple.'

'Shit.'

'You had him tailing me.'

'I didn't think that was reason for killing him. I'm sorry. That was in bad taste.'

'They found Ronane and stripped his skin off him.'

Silence. Then, 'Is he going to make it?'

238

'Touch and go. They also killed his wife and kids.'

'Betty's dead?'

'Killed in my house.'

'Jesus Christ!' Silence again for a moment. 'What about the constabulary?' They both understood that someone was probably listening in on the conversation. 'They only reported we got one agent dead, you being shot at and some involvement in a serial killing. They said they'd wait till we got down.' He played to his gallery of listeners. 'Pretty damn decent of them.'

'I didn't tell them who Ronane is.'

'I think you should. That he's DEA. And that it's his family that got killed.' Smith knew that would hold the police off until he got to San Antonio. It was all DEA business now. 'Any idea who caused this mess?'

'It's all about El Paso.'

'How?'

'Maybe Ronane knows. I don't. Except that it's the same people.'

'I had another agent out there.'

'He's outside. Keeping watch on Ronane's room.'

'I'm getting a plane to jet me down there. Bringing a team with me. What about the perpetrators?'

'They got away. Stole a station wagon and ditched it down the road. Nobody got a handle on them.'

'Does Ronane know about Betty?'

'Thinks they're alive. That's what's keeping him going.'

'Ask the police to make sure he doesn't find out. What's the hospital doing?'

'They've got him in an isolation room. In a sterile unit. On some sort of air bed. He's naked; they say they can't put any dressing or anything on him. His body just needs air.'

'They say anything about his condition?'

'Just that he's losing a lot of liquid. He's on a saline drip to help balance that out. And the room's at a constant 75 degrees.'

'How'd they get him there?'

'The emergency team wrapped him in paraffin gauze. They'd never seen anyone in that condition before, but they seem to know what they're doing.'

'I hope so. I'm on my way to the airport.' There was a pause on the line. Then, 'Why did he change his plans and come down to see you?'

'You tell me. I'm just on vacation.'

'Fuck you, Marshall.'

239

Marshall put down the phone and moved back with Jill. 'Washington's sending people down. They'll want to know why you're here.'

'Because I'm your girlfriend.'

'And that's all they need to know. I want you back home. In England.'

'Now?'

'As soon as I can get you out of here. I don't want Washington knowing you're from Manchester.'

'What about us?'

'I'll follow you as soon as I know Ronane's OK. Come on, let's go.'

They found the police officer in charge of the operation and Marshall explained that he had to get Jill to the airport to catch a flight. The officer was uncertain about letting her leave, but Marshall convinced him that Jill had little to add which would be of help, apart from the fact she had been present when he was shot at. After a phone call to the Sheriff's office, it was agreed that Jill could leave, subject to her being contactable should the need arise.

He drove her home in a borrowed car, helped her pack, and continued on to the airport. They said little; it was a sad time for them and the softness of their lives had been abruptly brought to an end. She knew nothing would stop him now; that he would follow this thing through to the end, like a snake that is swallowing its prey and cannot let go even if it chokes to death. He bought her a ticket to Miami – it was the earliest flight out – where she could catch a connecting British Airways flight to Manchester.

'What do I tell Armitage?' she asked.

'That I'll see what I can do. To wait for me to contact him. And don't tell him you know what's going on.'

'I love you, Jimmy Marshall. Or is it Jimmy Soulson?'

'It'll always be Jimmy Marshall.' He put his arm round her and held her still and tight for some time. 'I love you, girl.' He sensed her distance from him, but still held her. 'What's the matter?' he said, when he finally stepped back.

'I was scared. When they were shooting. It's only just hit me how scared.'

'It'll pass.'

'It was different at Quantico.' She let out a nervous little laugh. 'I mean, the targets never shot back.'

'That's what law enforcement is like over here. It's a different world, sweetheart.'

He didn't wait to see the Boeing 727 lift off towards Miami, or

240

the tears well in her eyes as she watched the ground fall away, but drove straight back to the hospital. There was no change in Ronane and he went back into the small waiting room to wait for Smith and the DEA crew.

He leant back and shut his eyes and thought of Ronane and Jill. The only two people he loved. He felt a deep loneliness, sharper and far worse than anything he had ever felt before.

Then he started to cry, the tears just rolled down his cheeks and he was helpless to stop. The sobs racked his body and he put his arms round himself and held himself tight to shield himself from the horror of it all. He was glad no-one came in; shows of emotion were not part of Marshall's natural armoury.

That's how Smith and the DEA men found him an hour later. Nobody thought it strange that the big man had been crying and that his eyes were swollen and red. They all knew how close he had been to Ronane.

That made it all the more difficult when they told him that Ronane had died half an hour earlier. Then they shut the door on him and left him in his anguish. When he finally left the waiting room and found Smith, the sadness had been cried out of his body.

He knew what he had to do.

With or without anyone's help, Jimmy Marshall knew how he was going to follow this thing through and see it to its end.

He owed Ronane and Betty and the kids that. He was relieved that Ronane had known nothing of his family's death. That would have made his dying easier.

'If it means anything . . .' Smith had said '. . . Ronane yelled your name twice before he died. Like he was calling for you.'

Marshall said nothing. It was nothing new being aloof and alienated from those around him. Only this time he really was on his own. He had no choice but to put himself into exile.

He went home, cleaned up the house and set his final plans in motion.

11

HOME IS WHERE THE HEART ISN'T

Manchester and District
England

MARSHALL LOOKED OUT OF THE 747'S OVAL WINDOW AND SAW THE first clouds as they approached the Scottish coast.

This sceptred isle. Rubbish! This rain-sodden land he had left all those years ago. Still damp and drizzly and overcast, just as he remembered it. He shut his eyes and thought of Texas, of the endless skies and clear horizons he had left behind. It was a place a man could spread himself and feel he was part of something vast and important in the scheme of things. Not like this introverted little island that he had once called home. He recalled how frightened he had been when he first left, that reckless teenager who had hardly strayed further than the boundaries of South Manchester. How big and fearsome America had seemed to the young Jimmy Soulson packed off and told never to return. All so long ago and forgotten, all so suddenly fresh and remembered.

The big plane bumped along as it entered the rain clouds and started its descent into Manchester's Ringway Airport. The seat belt warning and 'No Smoking' lights snapped on and he stiffened. Being strapped into a seat in an enormous metal can that hurtled through the sky at 500 miles an hour wasn't something that Marshall readily accepted. He looked out of the window and saw the rain lashing the wings and the grey-black clouds obliterating any sight of land. Then he felt the rumble of the wheels unload out of the plane's belly as they set up for final approach into Ringway's Runway 24. He fixed his gaze firmly out of the window, searching for the ground. Nothing happened until he saw the runway flash underneath him and the big plane hurriedly belly-flopped on to the tarmac and roared to a shuddering stop with full blast on the reverse thrusts. He relaxed immediately. Outside the window the rain didn't ease as the 747 taxied towards the terminal.

The customs officer looked at Marshall as if he had something to hide. He hated them; they always made him feel guilty. He kept walking through the green channel, but the officer stepped forward and signalled him to the search area.

'You on the Atlanta flight, sir?' the sharp-eyed officer asked him politely.

'Yeah,' replied Marshall, returning the gaze, trying desperately not to look guilty.

'And you've nothing to declare?'

'No,' lied Marshall. The hardened-plastic 9mm Glock 17 autopistol body-taped to his stomach contradicted that. He had removed the metal firing-pin, steel slide and firing tube and put them with his camera equipment in his suitcase to camouflage them. He counted on Armitage supplying him with bullets when he got to Manchester; they were easy to get and couldn't be traced like guns. In that way the body-search metal-detector in the Atlanta departure lounge had picked nothing up as he walked through to join his flight. Nothing apart from his Zippo lighter which he had handed over to the security man before walking through the detector for the second time. 'Always does that,' he had joked.

'Do you mind if I check your case, sir?' the customs official continued.

'If you want,' replied Marshall. 'We don't tend to smuggle in our business,' he went on.

'What business is that?' queried the officer, turning Marshall's case round to be opened.

'Drugs. To help your police,' Marshall said quietly, then took out his passport and DEA identity card and held them open.

The customs man inspected them, then smiled and waved Marshall through. 'I suppose we are on the same side,' he said as the big man swung his case off the bench. 'Have a good and successful stay in Manchester.'

'Thanks. I hope the weather improves.'

'Not here,' joked the official. 'Not in the Rainy City.'

Marshall grinned and walked out of the customs area. It wasn't just the weaponry that he had been worried about. That was nothing compared to the ten kilos of best cocaine he had crammed in loose powdered form into his toiletry bag.

It was wet, cold and windy as he waited in line to catch a taxi. He wrapped his coat around him and made a decision to get some warmer clothes as soon as he had booked into the hotel. He was shivering when he finally climbed into a taxi and ordered the driver to take him to the Midland Hotel in the city centre.

'Crowne Plaza, you mean,' said the taxi-driver.

'Is that what it's called now?'

'Ever since Holiday Inn took it over.'

Corporate America on the move. He wondered if they had air-conditioning and iced water.

The drive into Manchester went through Moss Side. It wasn't as he remembered it. Where there had been small rows of terraced houses, there was now a modern estate. But there was a general shabbiness to the area; it was as though the modern homes had simply replaced the slums that he remembered. But the planners' dream had rapidly become a nightmare ghetto; the graffiti on the walls and occasional boarded up windows attested to that. As they drove down Princess Parkway, Marshall saw a group of burnt-out shops among other stores which had steel bars across the windows to protect them. In his day this had been a teeming thoroughfare with greengrocers and fishmongers displaying their wares on the pavement. It now reminded him of the tenements of New York. On a street corner he recognized a scene he had so often witnessed before. A black pusher was dealing with drugs, probably heroin from the look of the buyers. So this was what he had run from all that time ago. It was no different from being back home. He laughed suddenly. Which one was home?

'You American?' asked the taxi driver.

'Yeah.'

'Where from?'

'All over the place. The south, mostly. What's this place? Looks like there's been a riot going on.'

'Just what it was. Not so long ago.'

'Didn't think England had riots.'

'We have our share. Los Angeles don't have all the fun.'

'What happened?'

'God knows. In the morning the police raided the place for drugs and in the evening the blacks tried to burn Moss Side down. Daft, isn't it? I mean, burning down the place you bloody live in.'

'This where the blacks live?'

'Yes. Moss Side. If you go out alone in the evenings, don't come down here. They'll slit your throat for a few quid. It's like bloody Belfast. After dark, this is a no-go area.'

'I'll remember that. Why haven't the cops got this under control?'

'They've lost in this town. Bleeding useless.'

'Why?'

'Because Soulson's lost control.'

'Soulson?'

'Chief Constable. Ever since he's been here the whole place has gone to the dogs. Religious nut. First thing he did when he became Chief was close down half the night-clubs and bars. The rest of them had to close by one in the morning. All that did was send the night life underground. The crooks just took over. Drugs, heavy drinking, birds. It was still there, if you wanted it. Trouble was it was out of police control. By the time they decided to do something about it – shit – it was too late. By then the drug gangs were shooting at each other and the tarts were giving everyone else the clap.'

'Same story in a lot of places.'

'Maybe in America. This country's still bloody civilized. Except for Manchester. It's out of control because they let it. That's Charlie Soulson's legacy to Manchester. Drugs, guns and anarchy.'

He registered at the Holiday Inn Crowne Plaza ten minutes later. An old Victorian hotel, it had once been one of the great Railway Hotels that had spanned across the country and been the premier hotel in Manchester. Run down over the years, it had been bought by the Holiday Inn group and remodelled. Still classed a luxury hotel, it remained known as the Midland to Mancunians. It was not somewhere Marshall had visited when he was last in Manchester, he had only seen it from the street and wished he had the means to walk into that old marbled lobby. The Midland had represented wealth and power and influence then. All Marshall saw now was a lobby that could be found in any American hotel: a functional place for business travellers and passing tourists.

The rooms were the same. After all these years he had finally made it through the doors of the Midland. And all he found was a Holiday Inn. He was surprised at his disappointment. After all, he hadn't even wanted to come back to Manchester. He went to the window and looked out on St Peter's Square and the vast circular Library building that dominated it. It hadn't changed that much. He suddenly saw himself as he had been; out there with his coat collar turned up against the wind, watching the rich parade themselves in and out of this fine old building. How he had wanted what they had. How desperate he had been to be like them. Then he remembered why he had walked the streets. To pull clients for the girls and set up deals for the pushers who had become his friends. It had been easy then, in the heady days of the sixties when everyone was looking for a harmless thrill. It wasn't so harmless now. He wondered how he would have turned out, if he hadn't gone to America.

He unpacked. There was nothing he could do until they contacted him. The last thing he was going to do was hang around, caged up in this small room. It was time to do the town. He wanted to get a feel for the place. Anyway, it kept his mind off Jill. He was desperate to ring her. But now wasn't the time.

He went out of the hotel and walked the streets of his youth.

Greater Manchester Police Headquarters
Stretford

'Where the hell is he?'

'I don't know, Chief. The hotel said he just went out.'

'No messages?' asked a furious Soulson. He squirmed inside the Chief Constable's dress uniform that he wore. He had to make another speech tonight; another dinner in some Manchester hotel in front of a faceless audience of chartered accountants or bankers or quantity surveyors. He usually complained, but accepted it was a part of his job. In truth he enjoyed these dinners; except tonight he had his mind on other things.

'Nothing.' Armitage had rung the Midland four times in two hours. He hadn't left his name; the last thing he wanted to do was let people know the police were trying to contact Marshall. 'He probably wanted to stretch his legs.'

'His instructions were to stay put. What if he's recognized?'

'Not after all these years.'

'Not the way our luck's been running.'

'He knows his business.'

Soulson stood up. His frustration was obvious. 'No point just sitting around here. I can't just sit on my hands doing nothing.'

246

'We've waited this long, Chief. Just a few more hours. Then it starts to happen.'

'I'd like to talk to the girl.' Soulson swung round and glared at Armitage. 'Get a feel for this thing.'

'Can't do it. Look, keeping you out of it is for the best.'

'It's not easy, Roy.'

'I know that, Chief. You always did like getting in there with your men. But this time . . .'

'It's not about that. It's about Jimmy.'

'He's one of their best.'

'He's also my brother. Always did his own thing and got into hot water.'

'Going out for a walk doesn't mean—'

'People don't change. He was a troublemaker then, and he's . . . he just hides behind a badge now.'

'That's not fair.'

'You know what he was like, Roy. You were there.'

'I also know why we asked him over here.'

'For advice.'

'For help. And that's what he came for. Forget how he was. He's one of us now.'

Soulson shook his head and sat down again. 'Then let him understand that he's under our control.'

'I'll reaffirm that to him.'

'When you find him. When he decides to show his face again.'

The Midland Hotel
Manchester

Marshall was depressed by his walk through the city centre. It was no longer the Manchester of his youth. The shops and pubs he knew had long since closed down; even Lewis's department store in Piccadilly Plaza wasn't there any longer. The heart of the city had been ripped apart and replaced by a shopping mall that covered three blocks. It was a faceless concrete shoe-box that had killed off the rest of the tradition of this great northern city; it was a monolith to the planners' mediocrity.

He had returned to the Midland, dejected by the bright tinsel nothingness that surrounded him. No soul in the place. He didn't know whether that made it easier for him or not.

There were no messages, so he rang room service for a coffee and a beef sandwich. Then he took the Glock 17 that he had hidden in the safe and started to assemble it. Ten minutes later there was a knock on the door and he slipped the nearly complete pistol under the pillow. He rose to answer the door when it suddenly opened and a waiter walked in.

'Room service,' he announced brightly as he waltzed into the room. 'On the table, sir?'

'Fine.'

The waiter put the tray on the table by the bed and stood up, offering Marshall the bill to sign. Marshall reached for it but took the waiter's hand and twisted it, making him wince in pain as he was forced on to his knees.

'Next time, don't come into the room until I tell you to.' Marshall twisted harder. 'Do you understand, my little gay friend?'

'Yes,' gasped the waiter.

'I'll get rougher next time.' The big man gave one final twist then let the waiter go. He leant over and picked up the bill as the waiter scrambled to his feet. When he had signed it, he held it out. 'Go on, take it. I'm not going to hurt you any more.' When the waiter had nervously taken the bill, Marshall reached into his pocket and took out three hundred-dollar bills from his wallet. He held them out to the waiter. 'That's to look after me. Share it with someone you trust who's on duty when you're off. Just make sure you're the only two who come up when I ring down for room service. And if anyone asks questions about me, you make sure I know about it. OK?'

The waiter reached out and took the money. 'I'll make sure that happens, sir.'

Marshall had just finished assembling the autopistol when the phone rang.

'Yes?' he spoke into it.

'You're finally back.'

Marshall grinned. Even after all these years he recognized Roy Armitage's scratchy, high-pitched voice. 'When do we meet?'

'I can come over now.'

'It's too late. I'm jet-lagged,' Marshall lied, but he wanted to lay the ground rules from the start. If he was going to work with them, he had to have a free rein. He knew they wouldn't want that but it was the only way.

'It would be easier now.' Armitage was insistent.

'The lobby's pretty deserted at this time of night. You'll be recognized.'

'Then meet me in the street.'

'No. For breakfast. Up here. I'll get it ordered for eight.'

'I think we—' Armitage's voice was cut off as Marshall hung up.

Marshall rang the operator and instructed her to put through no more calls as he was going to sleep. After he had placed his alarm call and ordered breakfast, he undressed and went to bed. He slept well that night, as he always did when a crisis drew near. His last thought was of Jill and he fell asleep with a gentle smile of affection on his face.

Police Headquarters
Stretford

She had rung the hotel once. The operator told her that Mr Marshall had booked in but was not in his room.

'No message,' she'd said and hung up. They had agreed not to contact each other, but the urge to hear his voice had been too great.

She tried to concentrate on the report in front of her but it was useless. Earlier on, the ringing phone had been a welcome diversion.

'Have you heard from him?'

She had recognized Armitage's tense tone. So they didn't know where he was either. *That's my boy.* 'No, sir,' she replied.

'Well, if he's in touch . . . call me.' Armitage's hesitancy had made her realize he was concerned about Marshall. 'I'll call you as soon as he rings me,' she replied immediately as she tried to allay any suspicion he might feel about her.

'Good. Have you got anything on this disco thing yet?'

'What disco thing? I've been up here going through my reports.'

'Damn it, they should've rung the Intelligence Unit. There's been an incident in Spring Gardens. Definitely drug-related. At somewhere called the . . .' she heard him shuffle some papers round before he continued '. . . the Crazy Totem Disco. It may, or may not, have anything to do with our problem. There's been two deaths, one quite nasty. I suggest you get down there and see if there's any connection.'

'You don't think he . . .' she cut herself short.

'No, of course not.' Armitage lightened up and she heard him chuckle. 'Not yet, anyway.' He returned to his normal assertive

249

self. 'Forget you heard that. It was in bad taste. No, the incident at the club may have links with the overall problem. It gives us more information to work with.'

'I'll ring Operations, see what they've got and get down there immediately.'

The call to Operations had yielded little more than the simple facts. A white twenty-one-year-old male, Joseph Taynor, had taken some ecstasy tablets, probably a lethal drug cocktail handed out in a 'lucky bag', and died of a heart attack while he danced. His dance partner, and also his sister, nineteen-year-old Louise Taynor, had rushed out of the club and was found in a side street with her throat cut.

'That's it?' queried Jill.

'All we have at the moment. It only happened an hour ago,' came the defensive reply.

She thanked the officer in Operations and left Stretford to drive to Spring Gardens. It was now raining heavily which she knew would make it more difficult for the detectives to find any clues.

'Haven't you got a home to go to?' Chief Superintendent White of the CID Operational Support Group commented when she arrived.

'I heard what happened and thought it might help with the report I'm working on, sir.' She decided not to mention that Armitage had told her to come down.

White grinned. He had a soft spot for her and the Intelligence Unit came under his authority. 'All right, I need someone to take notes while I'm questioning witnesses. It's going to be a long night, so I hope you haven't got a boyfriend waiting for you.'

White was true to his word; it was a long night. The police had cordoned off the club, a favourite amongst the youngsters who frequented it. It was one of the many clubs that had recently sprung up in Manchester; a place where the music was loud, drink was cheap and the drumbeat of youth was vibrant.

There were also drugs, mostly ecstasy tablets, which fuelled the dance-crazy youths when the bodies were exhausted and needed a stimulant to keep them moving. Most of the clientele had been on 'E' since their mid teens, and the Taynors, as was being discovered, had been no different from the rest of their friends. It was nothing unusual in the circle they mixed with; it was estimated that 20,000 youngsters were taking over 100,000 'E' tablets a week in the north-west. It was living in the fast lane by simply popping something on the end of your tongue. Easy kicks in an easy culture.

But, as always, where there are drugs there is always greed. The distributors of 'E' were constantly looking for new ways of enlarging their income from the sale of the tablets. To satisfy the ever-increasing demand of the club ravers, the dealers were cutting the drug with LSD and amphetamines. This cocktail drug was handed out in small bags, as sweets would be, and the dancers were dipping into these 'lucky bags' for the latest mixture of stimulant and psychedelic drugs. No-one knew what they were taking; the uncertainty of it all added to the experience of the evening. To maximize their profits, the pushers cut 'E' with other substances, which included aspirin, caffeine, antihistamines, and even methadone. The results sometimes caused serious illness, coma, and occasionally death. None of this worried the dancers; it all added to the spice of the moment.

'Nobody's admitting it,' one of the detectives told White as they stood on the pavement outside the club, 'but both those kids drew out of a lucky bag.'

'You sure?' asked White.

'Nobody's denying it, either. I think that's what the autopsy's going to show. They were both smackheads.'

'Death caused by heart suffering atrial fibrillation.'

'I think so. Poor bugger's heart just couldn't cope with the increased speed. A few of those inside have seen some of their other mates suffer from the same. Some of them saw a dancer die about five months ago. He popped off in a similar way.'

'A lot of them are getting restless, Chief,' interrupted another officer. 'They want to get off home.'

'When we're bloody ready,' snapped White. 'What about the girl?'

'She always danced with her brother. Always just the two of them,' continued the first officer. 'They're from Altrincham. Both unemployed. Live with their mother. She was pissed when we got to her house.'

'Just the three of them?'

'No. Another sister and a younger bloke who's her boyfriend. They all live in a two-bedroomed terrace house. All of them unemployed.'

White shook his head in disgust. It was a story he had heard many times before. *No wonder the kids went off the rails.* 'Why did she leave the club after he died?'

'They reckon she went after the pusher. She was screaming when she pushed past the bouncers. Something about "the dirty bastard killed him".'

'Got anything on the pusher?'

'I know who handles this patch.'

'Get him in.'

251

'We could be wasting our time.'

'Why?'

'Because he was in the club while the Taynors were dancing. There's plenty of witnesses to that. It wasn't him the girl went rushing after.'

'You sure?'

'There's too many witnesses. I don't think it was him.'

'Somebody cut her fucking throat when she ran out.'

'There's a suggestion that 'E' was on sale outside the club.'

'These pushers all have their own territory. That means someone was muscling in.'

'These dancers are pretty cagey. They're scared of getting busted if they say too much. The gist of what they're telling me, in their bloody obtuse way, is that most of the "E" comes out of Moss Side. But there was another pusher in the streets last night. Not one of the regulars.'

'Except he was Chinese,' White stated flatly.

'Yes, sir. Selling cheap stuff in the street. Too good a deal for most of the kids to pass up. I think that's who supplied the Taynors.'

'Fuck it. That makes it deliberate. The girl must've gone after him.' This time nobody needed to answer the obvious. White swore once again, then spoke to the second officer. 'Get back in there, make sure we've got all their names and addresses, and check that against any identification they've got. Then let them go home.' White turned back to the first officer. 'This could be a set-up. To protect the pusher inside and deflect us away from him.'

'This is my patch. I spend too much time with these kids. I really believe that's how it was.'

White trusted the officer; he was one of his most able junior men. 'Did the Chinaman make his presence obvious?'

'That's what surprised me. He made sure everyone noticed him.'

'Any chance of identification?'

The officer shook his head. 'Nobody'd ever seen him before.'

'OK,' said White as he put his arm supportively round the young officer's shoulders. 'Keep at it. Something new might turn up.' He watched his subordinate walk back towards the club. 'When you give that report to Roy Armitage,' he said to Jill, 'tell him I think the Chinese are deliberately winding up the blacks. Still bringing the war into Moss Side.'

'He'll ask why, sir?' She didn't feel the need to hide the fact

252

that Armitage had sent her. She realized White had suspected it all along.

'That, my sweet, is what all this is about. Tell him I don't fucking know.'

The Midland Hotel
Manchester

'You look older,' said Marshall as he let Armitage into the room.

'I am older. It's been nearly thirty years, for Christ's sake.' Armitage took his overcoat off and threw it on to the bed. 'Anything else you want to have a go at?'

Marshall grinned. He had always liked the man. 'It's good to see you, Roy.' He held out his hand and the older man took it. 'In truth, you don't look any different from when I last saw you.'

'Flattery, my son, will get you everywhere.'

'Bacon and eggs OK?' Marshall said as he led Armitage to the small table that had been set out by room service.

'Sounds good.'

'I ordered tea and coffee.'

'Mine's a tea.'

Marshall poured a cup of tea for Armitage and a coffee for himself, then sat down at the table. He held up his cup as though toasting Armitage.

'Cheers,' said Armitage, clinking his cup against Marshall's.

'Long time since I've heard that.'

'Things've changed a lot since your day.'

'So I noticed last night. Where's Manchester gone?'

'The planners ripped its guts out a long time ago. The only thing they left is the rain and the cold.'

'I guess some things are beyond even them.'

The men ate in silence for a while before Armitage spoke. 'Never thought I'd see you as a law officer.'

'You and Charles never did have any faith in me.'

'Not true.'

'Come on. I was always the rotten egg. It was the same with Dad. I mean, why didn't they ever try and contact me? Not a letter, nothing.'

'You left home, remember.'

'Didn't have much choice.'

'I mean before you went to America. Walked out on your parents and disappeared into Manchester. It was only because your brother looked after you that they knew you were alive. Bloody hell, Jimmy. You were thieving all round the neighbourhood when you were thirteen. And you set fire to the next-door farmer's haystack just because he warned you off his property. You're lucky you didn't end up in Borstal there and then. They couldn't cope with you. You were just too wild for them.'

'They still alive?'

'Your mother died six years ago.'

Marshall said nothing. It was what he had half expected. He didn't want any pain; it was something he had switched off a long time ago.

'Her last thoughts were of you when she died,' Armitage continued.

'Who said?'

'Doesn't matter. I just know she asked the priest's forgiveness for leaving you when you needed her.'

'Bit bloody late then, wasn't it?'

'Grow up, Jimmy. I saw her just before she died. All she could think about was what did she call you, her little chick. She wanted you to be settled, to have a family.'

'Why?'

'Because she said you were the one who needed family. Reminded her of your grandad. He was always restless, always wanting to move on. Don't say she didn't care about you. Her little pup, always the one with a thorn in its paw. That's what she said.'

'Leave it, Roy,' Marshall snapped. 'Don't resurrect the past. We all died a long time ago. Was Charles there when she died?'

'Most of the time. He knew you were her favourite. He found that difficult to stomach. He's like your Dad. Likes everything in its proper place.'

'If he's so bloody proper, why get me over?'

'Because Manchester's out of control.'

'So I hear.' Marshall remembered the taxi driver's words.

'It's no secret. The gangs, all drug-motivated, are carving it up for themselves. It was a lot easier in the old days. Just had a few prossies and thieving to cope with. This thing goes deeper, touches everybody. From school upwards. There's nothing that drugs don't come into contact with.'

'Tell me about it.'

'What did Jill Couples tell you?'

'Not much,' he lied. 'Just outline stuff.'

Marshall toyed with the remains of his breakfast as Armitage took him through the events that dominated the Manchester crime scene. It was a story of mayhem and brutality that Marshall had heard many times before; nothing he was told shocked or surprised him. More than half an hour passed before Armitage had finished. The table was now littered with confidential police reports and press cuttings that confirmed the older man's story.

'To top it all,' he concluded, 'two youngsters, a brother and sister, got killed last night. The boy died of an overdose, we've not had the coroner's report yet. The girl had her throat cut outside the club. Witnesses remember her running after a Chinaman. I don't know if he was the killer. What I do know is that "E" drugs come from small-time pushers out of Moss Side. It's primarily a black pushers' network. If the Chinaman was being chased by the girl for peddling the stuff, then you could also presume they're trying to break into the market.'

'In this game, always presume the worst. Then nothing surprises you.'

'Ever since the formation of Abdul Paras's supergang, the war between the Chinese and blacks seemed to have died down. This thing could trigger it off again.'

'Will trigger it off again. The way you describe it, that Chink wanted to be recognized.'

Armitage shrugged. The word Chink stung. Maybe Marshall had forgotten that he was married to one.

Marshall watched him closely. There had been no reaction from Armitage when he deliberately used the word Chink. He decided not to push further. At least he determined that the older man had tremendous self-control and showed little emotion. He decided not to trust Armitage. He was Charles Soulson's man. And people who controlled their emotions that well could never be totally trusted. 'I need some 9mm bullets. Hollow-nosed.'

'You managed to get a gun into the country?' Armitage was genuinely surprised.

'It's part of my job, Roy. But I need some ammo. Couple of boxes.'

'You're not going to war.'

'I don't aim to take these people on with a truncheon in my hand.'

'This isn't Chicago.'

'You're damn right,' Marshall snorted. 'Prohibition was easy. If Mr Paras starts blasting back at the Chinese, I need protection. I want that ammo, Roy. And quick.' Marshall softened his attitude.

'I'm not a lunatic. I'm a pro. One of the best. I don't intend to go out and start popping off at people. I'm trained to be a bit more subtle than that.'

Armitage nodded. 'I'll see what I can get. What's your plan?'

'I'm going to operate on a need to know basis. And the basis is that I'm the only one who needs to know.'

'Your brother won't wear that.'

'He'll wear anything. Like you said, it's out of control. How is he?'

'He's well.'

'Am I going to see him?'

'Not a good idea.'

'And Dad?'

'Still lives on the farm. Except he doesn't work it any more. They rented out all the fields.'

'What does he think happened to me?'

'That after your aunt died, you went to sea. And we never heard from you again.'

'Convenient.'

'It seemed the right thing to do. At the time.'

'Yeah. At the time. You mentioned Mary in your letter. I didn't know she'd died. Not till then.'

'I wasn't sure. That's why I put it in. I know how close you were.'

'What happened?'

'She died in childbirth.'

'And the kid?'

'Stillborn.' The words were so soft that he thought Marshall hadn't heard. 'Stillborn,' he repeated.

'I heard you.' Marshall closed his mind to the nightmares that Mary had been through. Sister and mother and friend. She had been all to him. 'I need to see Charles.'

'Maybe when this thing's over.'

'No. Before it goes any further.'

'Come on, Jimmy. That's not a—'

'It's part of the deal, Roy.'

'He'll say no.'

'Then get him to change his mind. He started this thing. The least he can do is meet. I'll leave you to arrange the place and the time.'

'He's high profile. Easily recognized.'

'I don't care if I meet him in an upturned toilet bowl. Arrange it, Roy. Or there's no deal.' Marshall left it at that and returned to the situation at hand. 'Who's the Chinese Mr Big?'

256

'It's Triad-controlled. The names are in the documents. Freddy the Duck's probably the best contact man.'

'OK. How do I contact you?'

'Through Jill Couples. Her number's with a list of useful phone numbers I've typed out for you.'

Marshall felt his dark mood start to lift. He would be able to meet Jill under the guise of the job in hand. 'Good. Can she research stuff for me?'

'Yes. She's with the Intelligence Unit.'

'She told me.'

'She put all this stuff together.' Armitage slid the thick report across the table. 'It's very comprehensive. Mug shots, maps of the area, pretty much everything.'

'Why do you think the blacks are so aggressive in this thing?' asked Marshall as he flicked through the report. 'I thought they were more integrated here in England.'

'It's the young ones. The first lot, the immigrants, they were lazy. We called them melon suckers.' Armitage laughed. 'You'd get arrested for saying that now. They just sold drugs, stole a bit, ran a few prossies, just so they could live day by day. Never any ambition. But their kids. Different. Feel the country owes them. And they're prepared to take it. But they don't educate themselves, make a contribution. No, take the easy way. Drugs, tarts, the shabeens in Moss Side, armed robbery, it's all organized now.' Armitage suddenly pulled back, not wanting to be seen as a racist. 'I've nothing against blacks. I'm not prejudiced. Most of them work hard, strong family people. We've got some good ones in the force. But the bad ones are bad. And, unfortunately, they're bringing the prejudice out in the whites. It's not getting better. If anything it's getting worse.' He decided he'd gone on for too long. 'Trouble is, the rest of the country knows about Moss Side now. I mean, nobody cared before. Then a fourteen-year-old kid, Benji Stanley, got killed while riding his BMX. Shot by pushers. The national press rolled in here on their usual crusading bandwagon when all they're really trying to do is sell more papers, and suddenly we're the country's number one crime city.'

'You've a long way to go,' said Marshall. 'In Washington last year they had 453 murders. You know what the mayor said? "Things are improving. In 1991 we had 481."'

Armitage chuckled. 'There's always someone worse off, I suppose. Anything else?'

'No. Except how Mum died.'

257

'Cancer. She was on pretty strong medicine. I don't think there was a lot of pain.'

'Good.'

'Welcome back, Jimmy.'

Marshall laughed. 'To what? This is just another town to me. Just another job.'

'Is it really just that?'

Marshall shrugged and rose from the table. When he had let Armitage out, he poured himself another coffee and switched on the television. He settled down in front of it and started to read through the documents.

The local news announcer cut across his deliberations. He looked up at the screen. 'Last night the body of a teenage girl was found in the Spring Gardens district of Manchester. The girl had rushed out of a discothèque after her brother died from a lethal overdose of drugs. In a quiet back street, well away from the night-club revellers, nineteen-year-old Louise Taynor was brutally murdered with a knife. Passers-by saw a Chinese youth in the side street just before the teenager was killed. Police have not yet confirmed whether the two deaths are related, but one newspaper report has suggested that it is part of the intense drug war that has rocked Manchester. Chief Constable Charles Soulson and his police force have been subject to mounting criticism from politicians, media and the public in recent months. Police morale is at a low point and Mr Soulson, at a dinner last night, made a plea for more support for his officers.'

Marshall put down the papers, picked up the remote control to turn up the volume as the screen was filled with his brother, resplendent in the full uniform of a Chief Constable.

'It's the attack-the-man-in-uniform syndrome,' said Charles Soulson to the camera in a room filled with dinner-jacketed businessmen to whom he was little more than a course during the meal they were eating. 'You all feel it every time a bobby pulls you up for speeding. Yet people expect that same policeman to stand up, sometimes alone, to a mob, to a hooligan football crowd or chase a gang of muggers down a side street in the dead of night. They expect him to be prepared to give up his life for one reason only, because he wears a blue uniform. Yet how many people look at what's behind that uniform?

'The next time you pass a copper on the beat, or one sitting in a car, look to the man - or woman - who's really there. Each bobby has the same fears, same ideals, same hopes as any of you. Imagine yourself as a young policeman, a lonely dark windy night, and you're just out of college. You hear someone shouting, a group of drunks, at the bottom of the road. As a civilian you can just drive away, report it to the police if you feel public-spirited enough. But he can't do that. He radios for help, then hears the tinkle of breaking glass. What's he do now? His uniform doesn't eradicate the fear, the instinct to run away. And that doesn't ease as you grow older, when you've your family and kids to think about. That is a policeman's lot. Every day, every night, outside pubs, in bars, in the street, anywhere where there are people. And that's on top of the mangled bodies you pull out of car accidents or the faces of old women beaten up by teenage thugs. It's there, even when you're off duty. You can't stop being a policeman by just hanging up your uniform in the wardrobe. And throughout it all, the bobby has to be a normal person to his family, his friends, his kids, the people he goes on holiday with.

'I'm sorry to describe such images after what has been a most glorious meal. But, when you know what your officers go through, try and then imagine how I, and the police force, feel when we hear certain politicians go on about police brutality, about our irresponsibility, about our lack of community.' The screen image of Charlie Soulson suddenly grinned, and he took a handkerchief from his pocket and wiped his brow. 'It's a bit like the gazelle and the lion. Every morning, when the gazelle gets up, he knows that he's got to outrun the fastest lion to survive. And every morning, when the lion gets on the move, he knows he's got to catch up with the slowest gazelle. So, when dawn breaks, both the lion and the gazelle had better hit the ground running, or else they've got problems. Now, that's crime. And that's a policeman's lot.'

'Chief Constable Charles Soulson speaking at a dinner in Manchester last night. Speaking at the same time that drug-related violence once more erupted on the city streets which he and his men are being criticized for not policing.'

Ouch, thought Marshall. That was under the belt. But they were certainly after him. He wondered how big brother was really coping with all that flack. He knew Charles liked being respected, liked being loved. If there was one thing he was certain of, all this would certainly be getting under his pompous and strait-laced brother's skin.

12

RETURN FROM THE NIGHTMARE

National Naval Medical Center
Bethesda
Maryland

HE KNEW THE BRAIN WAS ALL THAT MATTERED TO THEM.

He twisted his neck and watched the two of them approach him across the room. He saw the lead man try not to look shocked at what he saw, but the eyes, hidden behind a gauze face mask, gave him away. They all reacted that way when they first saw him in this most clinical of places, his body a patchwork mass of grafted skin, linked to saline bottles and to a catheter so that his waste fluids could drain out of him without him needing to move.

'If I can stand it, so should you,' he said with that smile on his face that meant nothing more than 'glad to see someone'. This was a lonely place to be alone with your thoughts, especially the nightmares he lived with both in his sleep and his waking moments.

'I wish it were under other circumstances,' said the more senior of the two.

He shrugged and regretted the small action immediately as the pain shot through him. They waited for him to stop panting as the pain eased. It took nearly five minutes. Sudden movement always did that.

'I'm OK now,' he said eventually. 'If you pull those two chairs up and sit in front of me, at the bottom of the bed, I won't have to move much. Hey! Don't scrape the chairs. Even the sound sets me off. Just do it real slow.'

He watched them move the chairs, almost in a slow motion ballet. He tried not to laugh because the pain would be unbearable. But he still had his sense of humour; he knew the sounds wouldn't harm him. The big man would have laughed at his little joke.

'So what's he doing?' the senior man asked when he was finally seated, his white hospital gown wrapped round him.

'Opening doors,' he replied.

'What doors?'

'I don't know yet. Hell, all we know is that he's somewhere in Europe. I guess it's Manchester.' He decided not to tell them about the letter. That was up to Marshall to inform them.

'Why?'

'Because that's where he believes the stuff was going. There or Ireland.'

'But why Manchester?'

'It's a big drugs centre. His instinct will make him push. Until something gives.'

'He could get himself killed doing that.'

'Nothing new to him.'

The second man leant forward. 'There's a lot at stake. Will he keep going until the whole thing is finished?'

'I think so.'

'What if revenge is all he's after?' asked the first man.

'That'll motivate him, but it won't cloud his judgement.'

'We'll never get a better opportunity. Let's hope he doesn't fuck up.'

'He's the best you've got.'

'So everyone tells me.'

'*I'm* telling you.' He suddenly wanted to shout at them, curse them for the horrific thing they had made him party to. The sudden emotion raced through him and exploded in a thousand pain sparks throughout his body. He closed his eyes and tried to shut it down, to cool the temperature in his body, but it was too late and the pain burnt him as though someone had poured lighted gasoline over him. He screamed and the two men stood up, not knowing what was happening. Within seconds the door had opened and two nurses rushed in.

261

'Keep them here!' he shrieked through the discharge of pain that swirled round him. 'Don't let them go. Don't let them go.'

'Sit down again and keep still,' one of the nurses yelled at the two men. 'Just keep still, whatever happens.'

It took nearly twenty minutes for the pain to subside before he could speak again. When the nurses finally left, he spoke to the two men. 'Heat. Can't take excess body heat.'

'I'm sorry,' apologized the senior man.

'Forget it. But you've got to trust him.'

'Even if he's working in the dark?'

'Especially then. Learn to trust your own men.'

'We trust you.'

'It's not enough. He deserves it.'

'We need you to tell us what's happening,' interjected the second man.

'How can I do that? I'm stuck here.'

'We'll bring you information as we get it. About what's happening over there. We'll want to know what he's going to do next.'

'You want me to second guess him?'

'You know him better than anybody,' said the lead man.

'The only thing predictable about him is his unpredictability.'

'We'd like to try anyway.'

'You got someone over there feeding stuff back to you?'

'John Pentanzi in London.'

'Not enough.'

'Are you going to help us?' the lead man asked.

'Got no choice.' He hated them for what they had made him do. The big man deserved better.

The Deputy Assistant Administrator stood up. His assistant, Peter Smith, followed him. 'Good. This is too big a chance to miss out on.'

The two men left the isolation ward.

Ronane lay on the airbed with the paraffin-gauze mattress. He wanted to cry, but knew the tears would run on to his chest and burn the opened nerve ends on his skinless body. He resented what they had done; had lied to Marshall about his death so that he would follow his instinct to England on a wave of savage revenge. In the end it was no good and the tears flowed anyway.

As he screamed in pain, he thought of Betty and the kids and the big man he had sacrificed when he had been tortured by the Texan only a few weeks before. If only he could have warned him, if only he could have stayed loyal to his friend.

This time the nurses heard him scream and left him. The pain was his and they had heard his cries of anguish many times before. They knew there was nothing they could do. In the end, only Ronane could put right what he had wronged.

The Plaza Hotel
New York City

The Texan looked out on the city streets and spat on the window in disgust.

He hated the confinement of the tall buildings, the million staring windows that looked down on the bustling streets and never blinked. He always felt he was under surveillance, that somewhere out there secret watchers followed his every move. He liked the space of the plains that he originally came from. Earth, sky and water. Simple things; things he missed. She had understood him, as ugly and violent as she had been.

He remembered the first time, under the night sky and stars of a Texas wheat field. He was one of the few people outside the family they trusted and he had been instructed to take her to Lubbock and show her where Buddy Holly had lived. She was crazy about the singer and the trip was a present arranged by her parents in Colombia. They had played nothing but Buddy Holly tapes on the long drive. He hadn't told her that there were twenty kilos of cocaine stashed in the trunk; her parents would have had him killed if they had known he was putting her at risk. The shipment had been taken from a local gang who had double crossed the Calis and he had, in his way, wiped them out. But the delivery had to be made and they had supplied him with the stuff anyway. He remembered parking the car and walking to the side of the road to relieve himself. When he returned he found her kneeling on the front seat with a row of powdered cocaine laid out on the dashboard hood. He climbed in and watched her sniff it with a rolled-up dollar bill, then get out of the car, beckoning him to follow her. By the time he had rounded the car she was fully undressed. He fell in love with her body there and then. It was muscular and big. Her breasts were enormous and she lay back on the roadside and opened her legs for him. He had never seen so much hair before, it seemed to pour out between her legs; the thick coarse black pubic hair ran from her belly button all the way between her legs and to the small of her back. It was as if

263

she wore a G-string made of matted hair. He lost control and fell to his knees in front of her, then forced his face into this matted heaven and washed in her juices. She started to relieve herself, but it didn't disgust him, just added to the heat and excitement of the moment. They fucked to the music of 'Peggy Sue' in that Texas evening and both knew they had found their alter egos. They were married three weeks later, and from that moment on she was with him wherever he went. When she was killed by Marshall's bullet, he knew he would never find love like hers again.

He drew the blinds shut and walked back into the hotel room. He was naked, apart from a small, red satin G string that was two sizes too small and stretched tightly across his genitals and into the valley between his buttocks. Nicole Garcia, the girl he had ordered from the escort agency, watched him from the bed. She was pleased to be there; it wasn't often the escort agency got a request for a short, plump, excessively hairy girl. It was nothing unusual for her to turn up at a hotel room only to be dismissed when the client saw her.

He had made her undress as soon as she arrived, told her to wear the stockings, suspenders and thong he supplied. The Texan didn't tell her the bright-green undergarments had belonged to his late wife.

'What the agency tell you, honey?' he asked her as he sat on the edge of the bed.

'That you like big girls,' came the coquettish reply.

'Big and hairy.' He leant forward and gripped her knees. 'Spread them!' he ordered. She felt the pain as his fingers dug into her flesh and she yelped, but did as she was told and displayed her sex widely for him. 'Now that's what I call a pretty sight,' he said, enjoying her shamelessly with his eyes. 'Move it, baby. Show me how you move that little pussy of yours.' He watched her grind her hips. It excited him, even though he knew he was paying for what wasn't as good as he had known. He felt the heat rise in his loins and the pressure of his erection strain against the satin. 'Play it, baby. Play it like when you're on your own.' He watched her slip her fingers into herself, then manipulate herself before she inserted her whole hand. 'Wait a minute, honey,' he said and leant over towards the bedside table where a small mountain of white powder sat next to a jar of vaseline.

He opened the jar and took some out with a table knife that had been left by room service. He spread the vaseline on the table and then mixed some of the powder into it, taking his time and forming a thick jelly.

When he had finished, he held two fingers close together and scooped up a portion of the substance. He watched the girl, still masturbating herself but her eyes had suddenly come alive. He came back in front of her and grabbed her wriggling hand with his free one and pulled it out from her. He rubbed the grey white paste into her wet fingers, then pushed her hand back into her. Some of the powder dropped on the bed and he knelt between her legs and licked it up. Then he watched her in her excitement. The cocaine would spread inside her and slowly bring her alive. It was more exciting than sniffing it. He went back to the table and scooped up some more of the paste, then knelt in front of her again and massaged it into her anus. It was the best way to take it, letting it be absorbed into the bloodstream through the membranes in the colon. It would spread quickly and deeply. She would soon be desperate for a burst of sex as the cocaine lifted her beyond her senses. He felt her squirm with pleasure as he dug deeper into her, then suddenly tighten with shock as he savagely tore at the thick matted hair that stretched between her legs. He suddenly pulled his finger out and she stopped masturbating.

'Go on,' he snapped. 'Don't stop till I tell you.' Then he punched her sharply in the stomach and heard her gasp. But she was learning fast and her hand never stopped moving. He watched her for a while longer until he was satisfied that the cocaine had taken hold. The hunger in her eyes and body told him that as she pushed herself towards him. She was near her first orgasm and he warned her not to, told her to hold herself until he gave the word. Then he stood up and once more reached into the cocaine with his fingers. He released his erection from the confines of the satin G-string and rubbed the white powder into its head and along its length. It wouldn't take long to work now, to give him the highest emotion of pleasure he could possibly achieve.

The phone rang once before he snapped it off its cradle.

'Yeah!' he barked into it, thinking it was the escort agency checking up on how their girl was doing.

'Time to go. Everything's ready,' said a man's voice in Spanish.

'I'll catch a plane tomorrow. Is the stuff in Manchester?'

'Some of it. The rest stays in a safe place.'

'Any news on Marshall?' As he spoke, the Texan continued to masturbate his length. On the bed the girl continued her actions, not daring to come, desperate to explode.

'No. Gone underground. I think the higher-ups are keeping him out of sight till he's calmed down.'

'Don't make no difference. I'll find him.'

265

'Business first. Never forget that.'

'I never did.'

'Nobody knows what Washington's doing.'

'Washington doesn't know what Washington's doing.'

'They're still the best.'

'Only they ain't in England. And if they're that good, how come that shit Ronane's six foot—'

'No names,' the Spanish voice warned him.

'Fuck Washington!'

'Be careful.'

'As always.'

'And don't get too personal. This is for the family.'

'She was family.'

'Then she would understand.'

The phone went dead. The Texan put the receiver back on the cradle.

Then he abused the body of the whore who was the woman he loved and the wife he had lost.

13

SOWING SEEDS OF DESTRUCTION

The Midland Hotel
Manchester

HE MISSED JILL. IT HAD TAKEN ALL HIS WILL-POWER NOT TO RING HER.

He had spent the first day driving round the city and suburbs. It was no longer the place of his youth; very little remained of how he remembered it. When he returned late in the afternoon, Armitage was waiting for him. They went through the new information the older man had collated for him, then had an early supper in the room. The talk was of the work in hand; little was said of the things that had once been personal to them both.

When Armitage left, having reluctantly handed over two boxes of 9mm open-faced bullets, Marshall had gone to bed. For once he had slept fitfully, his jealous green demons rushing through his head as he wondered if she was with someone else. This was her territory and there were things here he knew nothing about. What if there was someone else? Someone more suited to her, of her own age, where laughter was shared and dreams were real and not to be broken. He tried to break it, but the demons persevered and his mind was filled with the vision of her with others, and he tossed and turned and hated her for her youth and extravagance. Then he fought back and remembered the things she had said, the moments that had been happy and mattered to them. When his thoughts were calm, when he felt the pillow he hugged was Jill lying next to him, he finally closed his eyes and slept until the alarm woke him the next morning.

After breakfast he stayed in the room and once more went through the documents he had been given by Armitage. He wanted to make sure he missed nothing. There was no room for slip-ups; he knew he only had one shot at this thing. At noon, bored with the confines of the room, he decided to go out and find somewhere to lunch. He knew where he was going, it was the place this thing had to begin.

There had been no Chinatown when he had wandered these streets as a teenager. Not like it was now. He recalled the bustling warehouses and busy offices by day, which transformed after hours into darkened doorways and gloomy, half-lit streets where cars cruised and whores offered their bodies for a fiver and a bag of chips to be shared. It was the first time he had felt any warmth for Manchester since his return: a surge of reminiscence and rediscovered youth that surprisingly pleased him. He slowed his pace and tried to re-create in his mind the way it had been. Lilly. Her name and face came to him suddenly. The old whore; old to him then, but probably no more than thirty, who had enjoyed taking his virginity in the front seat of a Ford Anglia when he was only thirteen, had giggled her way through the episode while she taught him what to do as she pulled her miniskirt above her waist. Then, when he'd finished, almost ejaculating as soon as he touched her mound, she'd sent him out to proposition punters for her as payment for his freebie. She had been fun, always laughing, always greedy for more business which she paid for with a share of her take or another freebie. Lilly had introduced him to her friends who set up the same business relationship with him. He had been the best of the runners, getting punters or groceries or looking after their kids with a sense of responsibility that they learnt to trust. Good days, when life had never seemed that serious and was to be lived a day at a time.

He reached Freddy Wong's Cantonese Duck Restaurant in good humour. It was after two and most of the diners had returned to their offices. A waiter led him to a table and he settled down to a mixed fried rice and crunched duck platter. As he ate, he watched the waiters and few customers that remained, but there was nothing to learn from the dining area. Just before he finished, a group of Chinese

268

businessmen sat down to eat at a corner table. The restaurant started to fill up with more Chinese, most of them waiters from other areas and businessmen who enjoyed the restaurant when it was empty of Europeans.

'Freddy Wong around?' Marshall asked when the waiter brought his bill.

'You want see Mr Wong?' came the guarded reply.

'Tell him an American wants to see him. A friend of Onionhead.'

The name had no effect on the waiter, who shrugged and went back into the kitchen. While he waited, Marshall toyed with his coffee, swilling it round in the cup as he watched the arriving Chinese.

Ten minutes later, just as Marshall was about to go and ask the waiter if he had passed the message on, the kitchen door swung open and a well-dressed Chinaman came out. A few people called to him as he crossed the dining area towards Marshall. He acknowledged them with a smile and half wave. 'You asked for Freddy Wong?' he said to the big man when he reached him.

'Is he in?'

'Depends on who wants him.'

'My name's Marshall.'

'Would that mean anything to Mr Wong?'

'Not until I spoke to him.'

'This Onionhead you mentioned. A strange name.'

'Mr Wong will know him.'

'Are you from New York?'

'Sometimes.'

'Talking in riddles will not get you anywhere.' The Chinaman looked at his watch, a Cartier Santos. Marshall knew this was not a man to wear a Hong Kong fake. 'I am in a hurry, Mr Marshall. I think we are wasting time.'

'Are you Freddy Wong?'

'If you have anything important to say, be assured it will get to Mr Wong.'

'I know the troubles that Onionhead and the Hip Sing have had with getting supplies from Colombia.' Marshall named the most powerful of the New York Tongs; Onionhead was the leader of a street gang called the Flying Dragons who were loyal to it. The Hip Sing is regarded as the biggest heroin dealer in the city. 'We all know that Benny Ong would love to open a new route that bypassed the Colombians.' Benny Ong, an eighty-three-year-old who also used the name Uncle Seven, had run the Hip Sing Tong since the early

269

forties and expanded out of New York into Dallas, Washington DC, Miami and Atlanta.

'These are colourful names,' commented the Chinaman.

'I can supply exactly the same as the Colombians can.'

The Chinaman thought for a moment, then sat down opposite Marshall. 'Emeralds, Mr Marshall?' Emeralds had been the main export from Colombia before the drug cartels had realized the potential wealth from the product of the abundant cocoa leaves.

'If that's what you want to call it.'

'An amusing tale. Tell me more.'

'From now on I only speak to Freddy Wong.'

'How do you know of Mr Wong?'

'It's my business to know these things.'

'I like crazy men. Gives a spark to the day. So amuse me, Mr Marshall. I am who you want.'

'I know you people are being frozen out. By the blacks. Only it goes deeper than that. You must know they're getting backing. Just like it's happening in New York and Boston and other big US cities. I can tell you it's coming straight from the Colombians.'

'Why would they do that?'

'Because the American market's tightening up on them. The DEA and other administrations are fighting back, using methods that work. They need new markets. Europe's ideal for them. Manchester's the obvious route in. They can control the blacks, just like they do in the US. The Chinese are more difficult. So wipe out the Chinese, take over their supplies from Asia, and control the world market. Of all substances.'

'An imaginative concept.'

'It's an imaginative business.'

'What then? An intergalactic network?'

Marshall laughed. 'You never know. The Colombian drug boys sure have the money to start their own space programme.'

'Who do you represent, Mr Marshall?'

'Myself.'

'And *you're* going to take on the world?'

'I have support.'

'Whose?'

'People of a like mind.'

'And what can you, and your like-minded colleagues, achieve when others have failed?'

'We have two strengths. The first is knowledge which, as you know, is power. Knowledge of the market and the players. Like we

270

know about you, real name Lau Lap Wong, and your involvement with the Triads. About Onionhead. About the Tung On gang of New York, and the Wah Ching of San Francisco and its association with the Cosa Nostra. I can reel off names that even your hierarchy here, in Manchester, have never heard of. Then I also know about the Colombians and the Mexicans and the Peruvians and anyone else involved in this business. Even Mr Abdul Paras of Moss Side.' Marshall saw the flicker of surprise in Wong's eyes. 'On top of our knowledge, we can also supply a vast quantity of a substance that, if flooded on to the streets, would cause a dramatic drop in prices in the marketplace.'

'The world market?'

'Of course. It would flush out those who had the most to lose.'

'Like the Colombians?'

'I don't think it would be long before they had to raise their heads above the parapet. But we want to start here.'

'Why?'

'Because it's a new market. We know the Colombians are putting a lot of their resources into Manchester. This place is important to them. Block them here, make it difficult for them to succeed, win this battle and conquer Europe before they do, then they're trapped in America. The authorities will make it more difficult for them in their own backyard. In time, with your organizations, we can get into America and take over their supply and distribution networks.'

'For emeralds.'

'What else?'

'Why come to me?'

'Because my knowledge tells me that Freddy the Duck is the man. As is your 426, Henry Lip.'

The Chinaman didn't show his annoyance. It was a nickname he disliked. He was equally surprised by the American's knowledge of his superior, Henry Lip. 'I need to know who you are, Mr Marshall. After all, you walk in, unannounced, off the street and expect us to immediately take you into our trust.'

'Will this help?' Marshall reached into his pocket and took out a small sachet. He slipped it across the table to Freddy.

The Chinaman refused to take it and held his hands up. 'Don't they call this entrapment where you come from?'

'Call it whatever you want. But get it checked. You'll find it's the best emeralds money can buy. The highest quality.'

'You're too obvious, Mr Marshall.' Wong stood up as he spoke. 'A dangerous approach in an uncertain world.'

Marshall stood up, leaving the sachet on the table. 'Obvious or not, time's running out. If you want the Colombians and blacks jumping all over you, that's OK by me. But think about it. Then, if you want to take this thing further, call me. I'm staying at the Midland.'

'You mean the Holiday Inn. It sounds like you know Manchester of old.' Marshall was impressed with Wong's astuteness but ignored the comment. 'You've got twenty-four hours to decide whether or not you want to take this discussion further. And if you do, then I'll maybe tell you who I represent.'

'And if we're not interested in buying your emeralds, Mr Marshall?'

The big man shrugged. 'There's a lot more people who want to get into the game. Finding partners isn't that difficult. We think you guys are the best. You got the networks and the loyalty. We've got the means.'

Freddy the Duck watched Marshall leave the restaurant before he returned to his office through the kitchen doors. Two minutes later a waiter came and picked up the sachet and took it through into the kitchen as he had been ordered.

Marshall walked back to the hotel. He knew the Chinaman would have to take it further and he wanted to be there when the phone call for a meeting came.

As he entered the Midland he heard a muffled explosion in the distance; it came from the area he had left ten minutes earlier. It sounded like a bomb, but he didn't worry about it. Whatever it was, it didn't concern him. He knew he would read about it when the evening paper was delivered to his room.

Then he wondered where Jill was and if she missed him as much as he so desperately missed her.

Manchester Town Hall
Albert Square
Manchester

It had been a quiet day on the news front, so the morning papers and television news continued to make a meal of the tragic events at the Crazy Totem Club.

The media coverage coincided with the monthly meeting of the Police Committee and by the time Soulson arrived he knew that

Louise Spencer would have put it at the top of the agenda.

She didn't disappoint him. 'What about this, then?' she wailed at him, waving a newspaper in the air. She looked round at the packed committee room before continuing. She'd expected a full attendance after the recent events. It didn't matter whose side you were on; everyone enjoyed a session of Soulson baiting. 'There's nothing better than waking up to the morning papers and seeing Manchester called Crime City, UK. I want to cancel today's agenda, Mr Soulson. I want you to tell us what you're going to do about all this.' She threw the paper down on the table; a theatrical but effective ruse.

Soulson was aware of the eyes round the table that suddenly swung towards him. 'I agree. A lamentable incident,' he said, nodding sympathetically at Spencer. This was no time for histrionics. He would leave that to her. 'I am more than willing to take the committee through what happened. As long as you accept that it doesn't come under this committee's jurisdiction. I'm telling you because you are concerned citizens in a very violent city.'

'But what are you doing about it?' snapped Spencer.

'Let him tell us about what happened first,' said one of the Tory councillors.

Spencer sat down huffily. 'Just don't take too long.' Soulson took his time as he went through the events at the Crazy Totem Club; he was determined to slow the pace of the meeting and take the emotion out of it. In truth, there was nothing new that hadn't been reported in the papers. As part of his report, Soulson gave them a breakdown of the drugs used and said he was still waiting for the pathologist's report on both the bodies.

'Is that it?' said Spencer impatiently when he had finished.

'Yes. Unless there are any questions.'

'I've got one,' said a Tory councillor. 'Was the sister also on drugs?'

'We'll have to wait for the pathologist to answer that. But from what we know, yes. We believe, and the other dancers verified it, both of them took ecstasy.'

'Who pushes the drugs there?'

'How do you mean?'

'I mean, is it from Moss Side? With all these shootings and stuff going on, do these drugs come from Moss Side?'

'To the best of our knowledge, yes.'

'The papers say that some of the dancers say she went out after the pusher. Because he gave her brother drugs cut with whatever substance it was that killed him.'

273

'That's also what they told our investigators.'

'But, according to the papers, he wasn't black. He was Chinese.'

'Nobody was sure. But there was a Chinaman selling drugs. That's not unusual. A lot of these kids buy a bagful from a main pusher, then resell it to the other kids.'

'Had anyone seen this Chinaman before?'

'No.'

There was silence for a while before another Tory councillor cut in. 'What do you make of all this, Chief Constable? Is the gang war hotting up?'

'We're not sure.'

'But that's always the answer,' interjected Spencer. 'You're never sure.'

'These things take time. But if you're asking me to stick out my chin, then—'

'It'll be the first time you've done it,' she carped.

'Then, I think the drug wars could be starting again. Or . . . somebody wants us to believe they're starting again.'

'Who?' asked the Tory.

'On that, I honestly do not have any idea.'

'Par for the course,' came Spencer's expected comment.

Soulson refused to be drawn. He smiled at her, knowing it would infuriate her. 'If we could get more resources on to this matter, then we would probably move along a lot faster.'

'You've enough resources. How come even London doesn't have the violence we do. We are now the prime drug city in this country. You may not have any more resources than anyone else, but you certainly haven't got any less.'

'Except we do have a bigger problem.'

'So I heard. From your speech the other night. You're good at giving speeches. Especially when you know the TV cameras are there.'

'I say what I feel.'

'Which one are you? The lion or the gazelle?'

Soulson smiled, but was visibly annoyed by the barb. As he collected himself there was a distant explosion.

'What the hell was that?' said a councillor, getting up to go to the window.

'I'm sure we'll find out soon enough,' rapped Spencer, not wanting to let Soulson off the hook. 'I'd like to hear what the Chief Constable is doing about this drug situation.' The table settled down again before she looked back at Soulson. 'Well?'

'I am convinced that this latest incident had something to do with the drug gangs. These acid house parties have unfortunately become part of our culture, but that won't change until we outlaw them and have the legal machinery to close them down and bring swingeing penalties against the organizers. In truth, what happened wasn't anything to do with acid house parties, but with an invasion by one gang of another's territory.'

'The papers mention the Triads,' commented the Liberal Democrat councillor.

'Could be. But I'm sure that's what happened.'

'Doesn't your intelligence show anything?'

'We know there are Triads in the city. And also a supergang in Moss Side. I don't have to tell you that both organizations are almost impossible to infiltrate at the best of times. We can't even use ethnic policemen. The communities we want to learn about are very small. An outsider would stand out like a sore thumb.'

'You need Dirty Harry,' was the wry comment from across the table. 'Soulson's Magnum Force would sort that lot out.'

'Giving policemen guns isn't the only answer,' said Spencer. 'I suppose you'd like that?' she asked Soulson.

He thought of Jimmy. 'No,' he lied. 'Policemen with guns in their hands should only be used as the last resort. It doesn't matter whether it's drugs or terrorism. Moss Side or the IRA. In the end, guns only make the matter worse. And that's when the innocent bystanders get hurt.'

The door opened and a commissionaire came in. He crossed to Spencer and whispered in her ear. When he had finished, she stood up. 'There's been an explosion. A bomb. In Portland Street. Next to Chinatown. There's people badly hurt.'

The meeting broke up and Soulson hurriedly made his way down to where Job was waiting with his Jaguar. On the way to Portland Street, the car phone rang and Job passed the receiver back to Soulson.

It was Armitage. 'You heard about the explosion?'

'I'm on my way there. Anything on the terrorist line?' Soulson referred to a series of telephone numbers that the IRA and other terrorist organizations rang when they committed such atrocities.

'Nothing yet. No-one's claiming responsibility.'

'Meet me there, soon as you can.'

He passed the phone back to Job and closed his eyes. It was probably the IRA. What with the drug wars and Spencer, this was the last thing he needed.

Why the hell did troubles all come at once?

Midland Hotel
Manchester

Marshall watched the scenes of carnage on his television.

Five dead and forty-five badly injured. There had been three devices, all linked by radio to go off simultaneously, in plastic shopping bags at forty-yard intervals along the pavement. The middle device had exploded as a double-decker bus was abreast of it, and three of the victims had died as the force tore a jagged hole in the side of the vehicle. The bus had rocked violently, throwing passengers around its interior, but had not been blown over. If it had, the death rate would have been much higher. The third device had been placed next to a wall which was the back of a Chinese restaurant. The explosion had blown into a storage room. If it had been twenty yards further along, it would have ripped into the main dining area and probably killed many of the Chinese on a late lunch break.

The picture cut to Soulson being interviewed; there was little he could say except talk of the tragedy of the situation. Armitage stood behind him. The *old* team, thought Marshall. Staid. Maybe not so old and staid to have got Marshall over here.

The phone rang two hours after the news programme was over. It was Freddy the Duck. He wanted to meet.

Marshall left the Midland thirty minutes later, crossed the pavement in the thickening fog and walked up towards what had once been Central Station and was now an exhibition hall. He felt the first tickle of a cough in the back of his throat. He hoped he wasn't coming down with a cold. Suddenly he had memories of runny noses and hacking coughs. He cursed quietly under his breath; it was a long time since he had been down with a cold. The black BMW, with tinted windows, was waiting for him and he climbed in to the rear seat. There were three Chinese in the car, two in the front and one in the back. He didn't say anything; he knew they were foot-soldiers sent to transport him to the meeting place. When they didn't blindfold him, he realized they were going to a public place. If the meet had been in a secret hideaway, or at someone's personal home, there was no way they would let him see where he was going, even in this fog. He didn't believe he was in danger, even though these three were probably trained killers. Freddy the Duck would want to know how much he knew. Any danger would come after that information was imparted.

He settled back to enjoy the trip. They skirted Chinatown, which was still closed because of the explosion as the repair teams and police investigators sorted out the mess, and headed south down Kingsway. They left Manchester, passed through Wilmslow and out to the Cheshire village of Alderley Edge. Once through the village, they turned up the steep hill that led to the Edge, a small cliff in the middle of the plains of Cheshire after which the village was named. The car pulled into the parking area for visitors to this beauty spot, which was now empty except for two other BMWs, and came to a stop near the path entrance that led through the wood towards the Edge.

'You got gun?' the minder in the back asked, emphasizing his point as he pushed the sharp end of a knife into Marshall's side.

Marshall shook his head, but the sudden movement caused him to cough. Damn it, the cold was settling in as he swallowed the damp air of the night. He had decided to leave the Glock behind. They would have taken it off him anyway, and there was no guarantee he would get it back even if they did decide to do business with him.

The minder body-searched him in the car, then ordered him out. There were three more Chinese waiting for him, and once more he was frisked. These men were armed; one carried an Uzi sub machine-gun over his shoulder. When they were satisfied he was clean, they signalled him to follow. They led him up the hill, through the woods towards the Edge. The fog was pea-soup now and he stumbled twice over roots that grew into the path.

Freddy Wong was waiting for him on the edge of the cliff face. There was another man present, a short, fat man, but he had a scarf wrapped round his head so as not to be recognized. Marshall realized immediately that this was the leader, the man to whom Wong reported. The guards suddenly stepped back and let Marshall walk the last few yards. He knew there were guns trained on him should he make any sudden and threatening move. He could see the men silhouetted against the greyness of the fog and amongst the trees. He counted four of them; there were probably more he couldn't see. One wrong move and they would cut him down.

'Stop there, please, Mr Marshall,' Wong said when the big man was five yards from them.

They had chosen the spot well. Marshall was illuminated in a small ray of moonlight that brightened the fog as it came through the trees.

'Do you know of this place?' Wong continued.

'Meant to be haunted, isn't it?'

'It is indeed. This is where the witches meet on Walpurgis night. When, it is said, they meet the Devil. That is, if you believe in such things.'

'Do you?'

Wong laughed. 'In the old days they used to throw people off the edge, right here. As a sacrifice. Now they just meet and cackle amongst themselves. In their little coven. Tell me, Mr Marshall. Are you the Devil?'

'No. Just someone who can help resolve your problems.'

'So you keep saying.'

'Who's the person with you?'

'A colleague.'

'How do I know he isn't police?' Marshall knew this was the last place he would find a policeman.

'No more than I know you aren't.'

'I need to know who he is.'

'He will reveal himself if it is necessary.'

'Do I talk to you or him?'

'To me.'

'I have to know who he is.'

'And I said no. You've approached us. You're the one with something to sell. You convince us that we should deal, not the other way round.'

'I presume it's Henry Lip.'

'Presumption can get you killed, Mr Marshall.'

'Maybe. But I want you guys to know that I've done my homework. I'm real, no small-time con artist bullshitting you.'

Henry Lip took the scarf from his head and stepped forward so he stood next to Wong. 'If you don't convince us, Mr Marshall, you will never leave this place alive.'

'I know that.'

'You act like a policeman, not a street corner dealer.'

'We both want the same result. We're just coming at it from different directions.'

'What result is that?'

'The control of drug distribution within Europe. All drugs. Heroin, which you already control . . . and cocaine.'

'And I thought it was emeralds you were interested in,' quipped Wong, regretting it immediately as Lip pivoted round to him, his eyes warning Wong not to cross the line of familiarity.

278

'Come on,' said Marshall. 'Let's deal. To hell with all this pussy-footing around.'

'Who are you, Mr Marshall?' said Lip. 'I will not discuss this further until I know.'

'I'm ex-DEA.'

'How ex?'

'Up to a few months ago.' He suddenly coughed again and felt the phlegm loosen up and choke his throat. He cleared it.

'A bad cough. You should get it looked at. Why did you leave them?'

'I lost belief. I was banging my head against a brick wall. While I was fighting for Uncle Sam and freedom, everyone else was taking the credit. And the money. There were guys out there in the street who were earning more in a day than I took home, including tax, in a year. For every bastard we took in, a thousand just went on living like they were fucking millionaires. That's when I lost my partner. You know what those Colombians did? They stripped him clean of his skin. Peeled him like a fucking banana. Then, while he dripped to death, they went and murdered his family. Two kids and his wife. That's what the bastards did. That's why I lost belief.'

'Why should all that be of interest to us?'

'You ever hear of waste substance?'

'No.'

'It's drugs we seize, then take it to a government incineration plant. Most states have one. That's where we destroy it. Only over the years a few guys have held some back. Taken out some of the shipments, stored it in safe places. It's been small amounts, nothing so it'll get anyone suspicious. On top of that we've interrupted shipments that never got reported. Over the years that's built up to a lot of snow. Best quality you can get. You know how much we got now? Over two thousand kilos. Ready for the streets.' He watched for their reaction. These orientals weren't that inscrutable; he saw the greed jolt them both. 'Now that's a lot of stuff to dump on any market. At wholesale you got £50 million worth of stock. Retail will get you over £100 million.' He let the amount sink in before he continued. 'I've got to tell you, there could be a lot more than two thousand kilos. That's just what they've told me about. I mean, these guys have known me a long time, but they've got to learn to trust me all the way.'

'If you only left the DEA a few months ago, how did you manage to involve yourself with this group so quickly?' asked Wong.

'It's a small community. They knew I was sore at what happened to Ronane—'

'Ronane?' interrupted Lip.

'My partner. When they knew I was upset about his death, they approached me.'

'And then you decided to come to us?'

'Yeah.'

'Just like that.'

'We know all about you. We got files that cover the world. Like I said, my people believe the Colombians are using Manchester to break into Europe. We can't set up the network. We're just a few. But we've got a ready supply. We decided you were the best group to team up with.'

'A fanciful tale.'

'Yeah. I got a million of them.' Marshall coughed again. This continual talking in the outside air was roughing up the back of his throat. The single cough developed into a series of hacking sounds that lasted for a while.

'A bit beyond belief, wouldn't you say?' said Lip, when the big man's coughing fit had finished.

'You don't believe that. Shit, in this game, everyone's finding new ways of cracking the market.'

'Why should we believe you?'

'If you don't, the blacks are going to knock shit out of you.'

'We can handle them.'

'Can you handle the Irish?'

'Why?'

'Who the hell do you think blew up Portland Street today?' Marshall threw in the rumour as fact.

'That was political.'

'The hell it was!' He snorted back the phlegm that was running down his nose. 'The Irish are working with the blacks. Do you really think those guys could organize themselves like they have? Do you? You blind or something? What you've got in Moss Side is a full-scale terrorist army, waiting to be unleashed on whoever they want to have a go at. They got guns, explosives, enough to start a small war with. And you're the fucking first target.'

'Can you prove that?'

'How do you prove anything in this stupid game? By going out and retaliating first. Don't you see how deep this thing runs? It's not just Moss Side. It's the IRA and behind them all the money out of Colombia. That's what you guys are taking on.'

There was silence for a while before Henry Lip spoke. 'This consignment of yours . . .'

'Two thousand kilos.'

'Yes. Is it in this country?'

'No. Still Stateside. But we can get it in.'

'When it's here, that's when we should talk next.'

'No. That way you guys take no risk. We need to know that you're with us. Listen, we don't aim to give you the whole amount now. You don't need two thousand kilos to weaken this market. Shit, you could do that with five hundred. The rest is for your organization to use in other areas. Anywhere in the world. As long as it hits the Colombians and we agree to it.'

Lip laughed. 'I suppose you want payment up front?'

'I'm not setting you up. The stuff hasn't cost us anything, apart from storage over the years. Hell, we know where to keep things where nobody's going to find it. We're gamekeeper and poacher in one. I'm telling ya, this is one straight deal.'

'Then what risk do you expect us to take?'

'Lay the foundations. Start hitting them back. Make them sweat. Show us you're worthy partners.'

'Become terrorists. That's not our way, Mr Marshall.'

'I didn't invent the rules. Or hit that girl and her brother the other night. I presume that was you guys.'

'We didn't invent the rules either. Was there anything else, Mr Marshall?'

'Did you check my sample?'

'Good quality. As emeralds go.'

'I got more. I can give you some. So that you can check the quality.'

'How much more?'

'Maybe three, four kilos. To show you we're serious.'

'We'll think about it. And contact you.'

'Fine. I hope you're going to get me back into Manchester.'

'Don't worry, Mr Marshall. You won't need a broomstick.'

On the way back he told the driver to drop him off in Moss Side. That would get the Triad men talking. What the hell did he want in Moss Side after meeting them? The driver stopped before they drove into the area. Their rule was clear. No Chinese in Moss Side. Marshall hailed a black taxi and told the driver to drop him on Princess Parkway.

He knew the road she worked. He had seen that in Armitage's report. It had started to drizzle and the fog was lifting as he turned down the road. There was a late-night chemist on the corner and he went in and bought a box of tissues, Man Size, and some cough medicine. He left the chemist's, blew his nose and approached the first girl he saw. She was fat and awful and Marshall hoped she wasn't the one.

'I'm looking for a girl,' he said.

'That's why we here, big boy,' she replied, opening her coat and displaying her fat legs squeezed into an opalescent red plastic mini-skirt. 'I'm looking for someone special. Not you, honey.'

'How do you know till you tried?' she said, closing her coat quickly again.

He took a £20 note from his pocket and held it up to her. 'Girl called Shaeron. A friend of mine was with her. From what I hear, she does specialities I like.'

'What you want her for? I can do anything she can. I can do it better. You an American?'

'Yeah. But I want to see Shaeron.'

'You got no taste.' She reached forward for the money.

'Hold on,' he said, pulling the note away. 'You got to tell me where Shaeron is.'

'Down there.' The girl pointed at a group of girls fifty yards along the road, just visible in the grey mist. 'Her in the green coat with the fur collar.'

Marshall gave her the money and walked down the road. There was little business tonight; no cars cruising the streets; no drunken punters out for the last thrill of the night. The girls saw him walking towards them and spread out, putting their wares on show. He walked straight up to the girl in the green coat.

'You Shaeron?' he asked.

'Yeah,' she replied defensively. 'What you want?'

'A friend of mine said you're the best.'

'Your friend got taste. You not a cop, are you?'

'I wouldn't tell you if I was.'

She laughed. 'Well, I ain't a pig neither.' She linked her arm through his. 'Come on, big boy. You better tell me what your friend liked so I can give you some of the same.' She pulled him across the street towards one of the terraced houses.

That's when he saw the unmarked police car on the corner.

He knew it was a police car because Jill Couples was sitting in the passenger seat, next to a young man. He saw the shock in her eyes.

There was nothing he could do. He kept walking, Shaeron's

282

arm now linked through his. She led him into one of the houses. He tried desperately not to look back; wondered what agonies were going through Jill's mind.

They climbed the narrow steps to the middle level where Shaeron lived and carried out her business. It was a big room, dishevelled as he expected it to be, with a large bed at one end and a seating area with a battered old sofa and two armchairs at the other. The television in the corner was as modern as you could get and there was a late-night film playing. It always surprised him how badly these girls lived. They seemed to enjoy the filth they had drowned themselves in. Especially her. He knew her half-brother was rich, yet he allowed her to live in this squalid place and still hustle her body for pin money.

'So what your friend like so much that you got to get some of the same?' she grinned at him as she took off the green coat to display a tight, brown-ribbed wool sweater.

'Whatever you got,' he replied unenthusiastically. A few months ago he would have been dipping into this trough with all the energy he could. Now, all he could think of was Jill's face; the hurt registered in her expression.

'Gonna cost you fifty, if you want the best I got.'

'No sweat,' he said, taking out his wallet and peeling off some notes. He handed them over to her and watched her go to the television and tuck them behind the set. She swung round, lifted her arms and pulled off her sweater. Her breasts were large and dumpy and had seen better days. He hoped she wouldn't take off her bra, but he was disappointed. She unclipped it and her breasts sagged towards her midriff.

'Now that's big, isn't it?' she pouted at him.

'Yeah. Damn big.' He wished he wasn't there. His nose was now running freely, so he took out a tissue and blew it. Damn cold was taking away his energy. 'Say, you got any stuff before we start?'

'What stuff?'

'You know, snow.'

'That's drugs. That's not legal.'

'It's fun. Makes me go on for ever.'

'Gonna cost you more than fifty if you going on for ever.'

'OK. But let's see what you can do before I pay the rest.'

She thought for a moment, then nodded. 'But if you want stuff, that'll be a lot more. And paid up front.'

'Let's do it. How much?'

'Two hundred.'

283

'Expensive.'

'You don't have to have it.'

'Shit, two hundred. That's a lot.'

'That's what it cost me. I ain't making nothing,' she lied.

'What the hell.' He took out his wallet again and peeled off some more notes. She took them from him and went back to the television.

'Where's the stuff?' he asked.

'I ain't giving you that. Not in your hand. This money's for a good time.'

'Hey, we agreed that—'

'Hold yourself, big man. I ain't got no stuff. But maybe someone left some behind. Maybe in that top drawer, over there.' She pointed to a chest of drawers next to the bed.

Marshall grinned at the futility of it; it was her way of not dealing with drugs in case he was a policeman. He crossed over to the drawers and opened the top one. It was nestled there, a small mound of yellowed cocaine, stuck together like soft plasticine. He reached in and picked it out, then went to the table in front of the television and put it on the table. He picked up the newspaper, tore a sheet from it and spread it on the table, then put the slab of cocaine on it.

'That not all for you,' she warned. 'Only enough for one snort.'

'That's all I need, sweetheart,' he said as he took a small, sharp knife from his pocket. He sliced a small piece off the slab, then chopped it over and over until it turned into the finest powder.

Shaeron reached over, her breasts dangling across the table and picked up the remains of the slab. 'You sure know what you doing,' she said as she stood up. Then she turned and walked back to the drawer, where she dropped the cocaine back to a place of safety. At the table Marshall had pulled out another £20 note and was rolling it into a thin tube.

'You want some?' he asked her when she came back.

'Don't need that shit,' she replied. 'You just help yourself.'

It was a long time since he had taken cocaine. In the early days, when he was a lot younger, even in the first few months with the DEA, he had occasionally snorted up. It helped when he was tired and his energy levels were low. Then, when he realized he began to miss it, would have a gnawing sensation in his stomach and get severe headaches, he decided never to touch it again. Sex had been his great liberator. Except now there was Jill and the last thing he wanted was to fuck this awful woman. Suddenly the cocaine had seemed a better way out of his predicament. He also wanted to save a small sample for analysis, to see if it could be traced to its origin. He shrugged and leant forward to inhale the small row of powder in front of him when the door opened without warning.

He was one of the biggest men he had ever seen. He recognized the face from the pile of pictures that Armitage had supplied.

Meet the Devil. Abdul Paras.

'What the hell's this?' Marshall shouted indignantly, standing up from the table, the rolled-up note still in his hand.

Paras grinned. He was used to walking in on Shaeron's punters. To him, they weren't real people, just dick-happy slobs who shelled up cash that kept her off his back. At least this time she only had her tits out; he had often found her in far worse compromising situations. 'Get the fuck out of here!' he welcomed Marshall.

'Come on, I just paid two hundred and fifty bucks for this little outing.'

'You a Yank?'

'Yeah. For what it's worth.'

'Don't make no difference. Just piss off.'

'What about my money?'

'You seen her tits,' Paras joked, then turned to Shaeron. 'You took two fifty off him?' he asked incredulously.

'He wanted some stuff,' she replied, sulky in attitude.

Paras crossed over to the table and looked down on the thin row of cocaine. Then he leant down and blew it away. He stood and faced Marshall, looked down on him. 'No reason to hang around any more, dickhead,' he said.

'What about my money?' repeated Marshall.

'You gave it to her, didn't you?'

'Yeah. For services I haven't had yet.'

'Then it's her money. If you gave it her.'

'I want my—'

'Fuck off. If you want to leave here in one piece.'

The two men glared at each other, then Marshall shrugged and left. As he closed the door he heard Paras laughing and asking Shaeron for the money. Animals. It was their attitude he hated. For all the money they had, they still took small change from the whores. They were pimps by tradition and he was even more convinced that there was a larger organization behind the Nilus Gang. As he descended the stairs, he made a note of the phone number from the payphone in the hall. Outside, he saw no sign of Jill or the unmarked car.

The room service waiter caught him as he came out of the lift at the Midland.

'You've got a visitor,' he warned.

'Who?'

'Police. Showed me a warrant card and said to let her in while she waited.'

Marshall thanked him, ordered a flask of coffee and let himself into the room.

He could tell from the expression on her face that it was going to be an uphill task. He took off his coat and threw it over the back of the armchair.

'I've got a stinking cold,' he said, taking a tissue and blowing into it.

'I hope that's not the only thing you've caught,' replied Jill sarcastically.

'You shouldn't be here,' he said, immediately regretting his facile words. 'It's putting this thing at risk.'

'This thing, as you call it, doesn't give you the right to go round screwing whores.'

He held his hands up to signify calm. 'Nothing happened.'

'Oh yes? How the hell do I know?'

'Because . . . shit, did you see the state of her?'

'I saw her all right. If she's your type, it makes me wonder what you think of me.'

'Come on.' He came towards her to embrace her, but she moved away hurriedly. 'Look, I'm not well. I can do without this.'

'You've got to be joking.'

'It was business.'

'For her.'

'I was after information.'

'I was waiting for that one.'

'Look, have you ever heard of Abdul Paras?' Marshall tried to involve her; snap her out of her preoccupation with the whore.

'Of course. I prepared the bloody report you're reading.' She indicated the papers he had left by the bed.

'That was his sister.'

'You sure?'

'Read your own report.'

'You don't go in with a tart like that and just sit and chat. They're there for just one thing only. Especially slags like that. Christ, was she a fucking slag. Jesus, Marshall, at least go for something better than that.'

'I didn't go for her. I've told you why I was there.'

286

'I don't believe you. You must've done something.'

'Yeah. I snorted coke. And then her big brother turned up and threw me out. The whole thing cost me two hundred and fifty quid. For nothing.'

'You're joking.'

'That's me. The Joker.'

'Is that what really happened?'

'I promise you.'

'What if he hadn't turned up?'

'I wouldn't have done anything. That's why I got her to produce the coke. I was going to snort the stuff, or pretend I was, then act like I couldn't get a hard on. And then get to know the girl.'

'Some girl.'

'Damn it, Jill, you saw what she looked like.'

'Yes. That's what get's you off the hook. I can't imagine you with anyone that rough.'

'Absolutely.' Marshall wondered what she would think if she saw some of the hookers he had been with over the years. Shaeron Paras was in the top half of that league. He went forward and put his arms round her. He felt the sneeze building.

'I'm sorry. I just saw red when you crossed the road with her. I couldn't believe it was you.'

'You should've seen how I felt.'

'I said I was sorry.' She nuzzled him. 'Can I stay the night?'

'Is that a good idea?'

'You don't sound very convincing.'

He laughed. 'I'm not. Anyway you'll be safer here. Every time I look out of the window with that fog it looks like a Jack the Ripper movie.' The sneeze broke and he stepped back to avoid her.

'You really are going down with a cold.'

'Don't I know it. Shit, it'll just knock my energy levels down.'

'You need some medicine.'

'I bought some. It's in my coat.' He watched her walk to his topcoat and take out the bottle he had bought. 'I just hope Roy Armitage doesn't come knocking at the door in the morning.' There was a knock at the door as he spoke.

'I don't believe it,' she said.

'It's OK. I ordered some coffee.' He went to the door, opened it and took the tray from the waiter, who tried to look into the room but was blocked by Marshall's bulk. 'Thanks,' he said and closed the door before putting the tray on the table.

'Don't need coffee to keep me awake,' she chided him.

'I need something. It's been a long day.'

'I know better than to ask you what happened. You'll tell me when you're ready.'

'It's not that I don't trust you. It's just better you don't know in case it compromises you. Anyway, what were you doing there?'

'They pulled us off drugs.'

'They?'

'Higher up. I don't know who makes the decisions.'

'The whole department?'

'The whole Intelligence Unit. After the explosions today, we were called in and told that was what we had to concentrate on. I was sent to Moss Side to see if there was anything unusual. We all had pictures of suspected terrorists.'

'Was there anything?'

'Nothing that stood out. Except for one guy.'

'Irish?'

'I don't know. He was white. Looked out of place. Wasn't the usual sort of punter who hangs round those girls. He was out of place but looked as if he was part of the community. Everybody ignored him as he passed but they knew he was there. If that makes sense? Anyway, I've seen his picture before. I'll have to go through the rest of the files.'

'What's he look like?'

'Small. With red hair. Why?'

'You never know. If you find anything, tell me.'

'Right. Can we go to bed now?'

'Yeah. After I've taken my cough medicine.'

Moss Side Shopping Centre
Moss Side
Manchester

It was high noon when they hit Moss Side.

Two cars and six men. That's all it took. That and the six Czechoslovak Vz 58 automatic assault rifles which they carried. The gun, based on the Kalashnikov AK-47, fires at a rate of 800 rounds per minute as against the AK-47's 400 rounds. Loose one of those off in a crowded shopping precinct and anyone can be forgiven for thinking World War Three has begun.

The two cars, a Vauxhall Astra and an old Ford Granada, had been chosen because they were not out of place in Moss Side. The

288

Astra had 'Go Fast' stripes down the side and the names Stella and Lester printed across the windscreen; common enough names in the area. The Granada, of 1979 vintage, was a tired-looking, paint-faded model which had seen its best years and was no stranger to most of the backstreet car sales lots that proliferated in the city.

The vehicles, with semi-tinted windows so that the occupants were not easily recognized, had come down Princess Parkway and turned down Moss Lane East, just below the big block of flats known as Fortress Moss Side and towards the Moss Side Shopping Centre.

The watchers in the tower blocks noted the cars, saw them pull into the front of the Centre, then dismissed them as local shoppers. They turned their attention back to the streets that led into Moss Side to watch for any danger that might come from there. They didn't see the cars come to a stop under the big concrete awning that covered the entrance, nor did they see the six men with Hallowe'en masks climb out.

Two of the men waited by the cars, their Vz 58s hidden under their coats. The other four walked rapidly into the Centre, a typical 1970s concrete shopping precinct, box-like with a large open central area and squared off shop units with little character facing inwards. What wasn't typical were the rows of steel shutters that lined the top of each unit. At night, with the drug addicts and villains, the precinct became a top security area which was repeatedly vandalized. When they had reached the centre of the open area, the four masked men, who had drawn some amused reaction from the shoppers because of their grotesque Hallowe'en disguises, pulled their Vz 58s from under their coats and opened fire over the heads of the crowd. People ran for cover screaming in panic, as shop windows exploded in a hail of fire, and bullets ripped through the signs and walls and ricocheted around the precinct. The attackers had been told not to hit innocent bystanders and their aim ensured they followed their orders. That was unless they came under attack from any armed blacks.

The attack was too sudden; surprise guaranteed there was no retaliatory action. The four gunmen raced back to their cars, brandishing their weapons in front of them to clear the path. As a final show of strength, the two drivers sprayed their rounds towards the tower-block flats, sending the now advancing watchers sprawling for cover. Then they jumped into the cars and drove away, out on to Moss Lane East, up to the Little Alex pub on the corner of Chichester Street and then northwards back into the city.

The whole thing took less than two minutes; two minutes in

which war was finally declared and Fortress Moss Side invaded.

Abdul Paras, sitting with friends and playing brag in the Club Nilus, exploded with anger when he was given the news by one of his men, who had received it over the CB radio that was the heart of the gang's communications. Storming out of the club to go and see the damage, he never saw the red Ford Escort turn the corner and drive towards him as he ran to the gunmetal-grey Mercedes 500 SEL that was parked outside the club. His driver opened the door as the Escort drew level and one of the passengers shouted at Paras.

As Paras looked up, he saw three men in the car, all wearing Hallowe'en masks. Reacting instinctively, he threw himself on the pavement to shield himself with the Mercedes. His intuition saved his life. The spray of bullets that erupted noisily from the Escort splattered the door and walls of the Club Nilus, winging two of his henchmen who had come running after him. Paras's driver, less fortunate, caught one of the bullets in his neck and collapsed to the pavement. The Escort slowed down as the driver swung towards the pavement so his marksmen could get a clearer shot at Paras, but when he saw more men, this time fully armed, coming from the nearby building, he slammed the accelerator to the floor and drove off, a hail of bullets ramming into the back of the car as it disappeared round the corner.

Then there was silence, just a ricochet of sound as the noise reverberated round the terraced houses.

Paras stood up. 'In fucking daylight!' he screamed. 'They come after us in fucking daylight.' He kicked the wounded driver, who lay clutching his neck, and clambered into the car. He started it and drove off furiously, leaving his henchmen to follow as soon as possible by whatever means they could.

There was no sign of the red Escort, so he made his way to the Moss Side Centre. He slammed the car to a stop against the pavement at the entrance and walked through the precinct taking in the damage that had been caused. One of his men rushed up to him but Paras hit him across the face in frustration, once, then twice again, much harder. 'You meant to be watching you fucking bastard. You meant to be watching. In fucking daylight. Ain't you no fucking eyes?' he railed at the unfortunate man. The others, those who were colleagues of the pummelled watcher, melted into the shocked crowd, not wanting to suffer the same fate.

In the distance the sound of sirens, police and ambulance, could be heard coming towards the scene. Paras left the precinct and ran towards the high-rise flats. Reaching them before the police arrived at the Centre, he took the large, graffiti-covered lift to the fourth floor. Some of the watchers were waiting for him on the concrete walkway; he was aware of their fear of him.

'Didn't no-one see nothing?' he demanded. 'What you doing? Fucking sleeping instead of fucking watching?' He looked round at his men. 'Didn't no-one see anything?'

'There was nothing unusual,' one of the men countered.

Paras whipped round and kicked the man in the shin, then continued to kick him while he writhed on the floor. 'Nothing unusual!' he yelled as he lashed at the cowering figure. 'Shits with guns blasting us up and you saw nothing unusual? You think it's normal for everyone to walk round with masks on their shitty heads?' When he had vented some of his fury, he swung round and stared over the balcony. He watched the police and ambulance men scurrying around below him. 'Give me a gun. A fucking rifle,' he ordered.

One of the men came forward and held out a Heckler and Koch G3A3.

'You know how to use that fucking thing?' Paras asked.

'I know. I practised.'

'Then aim out there.' Paras pointed across the open space to Princess Parkway, a hundred yards away from them. 'Take your fucking aim and hit one of those white bastards in their cars. Make sure you fucking kill someone, or else I fucking kill you.'

The gunman, now classified as a sniper, aimed the rifle towards the slow moving traffic line. He picked a target, held his breath, and unleashed a succession of rounds from the powerful weapon into the three nearest cars.

His aim was lucky and true. He shot dead a doctor on his way to work at Manchester Royal Infirmary, the bullet passing through his head. It was a lucky shot as he had been aiming at the passenger in the back of the car. His other shots, although mostly wasted, managed to injure two other passengers in different cars.

'The cops. They're yelling up. They know we're here,' called one of the look-outs.

'Get fucking moving,' ordered Paras. Then he turned to the sniper. 'If I don't read you killed one of those bastards down there, don't wait around for any fucking medals. All you'll get is what they should've got.'

Then Paras and his men melted into the corridors and flats of the high-rise. Like rats they disappeared when danger threatened, and the police found nothing on the walkway except empty shells from the G3A3 and a watcher whose legs and ribs had been broken

291

by the brutal kicking he had endured.

'I saw nothing. I just fell down the stairs,' was all he would say when the police finally questioned him.

The area between Princess Parkway and Chichester Road, with the shopping centre in between, was cordoned off by the police. The Firearms Unit had been drafted in and, after a search of the flats and the neighbouring buildings, had taken up positions where they could watch for snipers.

Soulson and Armitage walked the short distance between the scene of the car murders and the shopping centre. Having toured the area, as well as the site of the attack outside the Club Nilus, Soulson wanted time alone with his trusted aide, away from the enquiring media lenses and his own subordinates desperate for answers for which he didn't even know the questions.

'I hope this isn't your friends,' he said to Armitage when he was satisfied they were out of range of prying ears and directional microphones.

'Come on, Chief. Not all the Chinese community are involved with the Triads.'

'Or *him*,' Soulson spat the words out. 'I presume we can discount him.'

'He wouldn't do anything on this scale.'

'Is he armed?'

'I would presume so.'

'Do you know if he's armed?' Soulson demanded.

'Not something I asked him.' Armitage skirted the question.

'This is gang war stuff. Tit for bloody tat. Nothing to do with the IRA bombing earlier on.'

'The Home Office may not agree with you.'

'All London's interested in is the conspiracy theory. Blame the bloody IRA for everything. The great cop out. And it makes better headlines.'

'They might be right, Chief.'

'If it is, and this goes on, someone's going to suggest we get the army in here. That's the last thing we want. Soldiers with guns on the street. On bloody search and apprehend missions.'

'It won't happen.'

'If this erupts further, and we're seen to have lost control, there may be no choice. The Home Secretary could be forced to call a state of emergency. No, I don't think it's terrorists. All to do with this drug thing. Just somebody flexing their muscles.'

'Then why shoot innocent members of the public?'

'That's what I can't bloody fathom. But one thing I can tell you, Roy. I'll fight the whole way before I let the army in here.'

Armitage changed the subject. 'I think we should put the Intelligence Unit back on to the drug case.'

Soulson considered for a moment. 'Maybe. We'll see. Let's see what comes up.'

Chief Superintendent Steven White approached them from the Shopping Centre. 'We've found the cars, Chief,' he said as he reached them. 'Near Old Trafford cricket ground. Three of them. The Astra and Granada as described by the witnesses and a Ford Escort riddled with bullets. That must've been the one that hit the Club Nilus.'

'Any clues?'

'There's only a patrol car there right now. He found them. He says they look clean. I've got the CID and forensic on their way there. We're running a bit thin on staff with all this to cover. I hope nothing else blows.'

'What've you picked up here?'

'No more than you heard earlier on, Chief. God knows what's happening. I mean, one lot hit the shopping centre, and the way they sprayed the place I don't think they meant to harm anyone, just give them a frightener. Then, while that lot's getting away, someone else opens up on the Moss Side gang's HQ. Ten minutes later, while our own people are finding out what's been going on at the shopping centre, someone else starts firing at the public and kills an innocent doctor on his way to work. I don't get it. It all happens at the same time, but it's like two separate attacks. Maybe even three. No, only two,' he reflected. 'Otherwise they wouldn't have found all three cars together. Even so, there's no logic.'

'What about a terrorist attack?' asked Armitage.

'Who knows? But I think they did their damage yesterday in Portland Street.'

'I agree,' said Soulson quickly. 'This isn't about the IRA.'

'Maybe the shooting from up there—' White pointed up to the flats '—into the cars was IRA.'

Soulson shook his head. 'Can't see it. The Irish would stand out like a sore thumb in Moss Side. Anything else?'

'Something or nothing. The copper who found the cars. He was on patrol because of a big reception at the cricket ground banqueting rooms. When he found the cars in the car park, mixed amongst the guests' vehicles, he radioed in. We checked the number plates. All three cars had been reported stolen.'

'What was the reception for?'

'You won't like this. It was some society anniversary. I don't know what of, but all the guests were Chinese. Not a European in sight is the report I got.'

Cohn Bourne waited for Stash Maxwell to calm Paras down before he spoke. 'Shooting up the public isn't going to get us what we want.'

The three of them sat in Shaeron's room, where Marshall had been the night before; she had been sent off to the Club Nilus to wait for Paras.

'They got to know we mean fucking business,' came the sulky reply. Paras hated the little Irishman, but knew he needed him, needed the guns and drugs he could supply. His day would come, when he could break the little shit in half and run the organization the way he wanted to. 'They got to know Moss Side is a fortress.'

'Bollocks!' the Irishman snapped back. 'Forget what the papers say. Fortress Moss Side. That's just clever words, to sell papers. We want the public coming here. How the hell are we going to sell the drugs if they're too frightened? This place can be closed to the cops, but let's not knock off our clients.'

'It'll die down,' said Stash quietly, trying to support his leader.

'I hope so. This is the sort of thing that brings the army in. We don't want the army running the streets. This isn't Belfast. This is a place to do business, not overthrow governments.'

'We didn't start it,' snarled Paras.

'I know that. But we're making it worse.'

'Who the fuck was it?'

'We'll find out. Probably the Chinks. But it's not like them to hit back. Not like this. They must be pretty confident.'

'Whoever it is, we can't let them just walk in and take over,' argued Maxwell. 'We got to retaliate.'

'No. Go on in this way and you'll end up with every British squaddie on the streets outside. Martial law. All armed and making sure no-one gets in here to do business.'

'What you saying?'

'Organize. Like we did before.'

'Didn't fucking stop them today,' said an exasperated Paras.

'Tie up Moss Side. Make it so clean that no-one comes in who can harm us. Make it safe for the public. Make sure the authorities don't have any reason to send in the army.'

'Shit to that. If we pull back, every fucker's going to come in.'

'We don't pull back. Just tighten things up.'

'How?'

'Easy. First we get watch-points all over Moss Side. At all the high rise buildings. We have watches, on rotas, teach them to keep their eyes open instead of playing with themselves like those guys did today. They got to make sure that nothing moves in and out of this place without us knowing.'

'You can't block off the Parkway,' said Maxwell.

'Don't need to. All we're interested in is the side roads that lead off it. Them's what we watch. And we get our people out on the streets. Nothing heavy, no fancy uniforms. Just out there, keeping in touch with what's going on. In the pubs and the shops, anywhere there's people. Keep our ears to the ground. Then we set up our own bus service.'

'Where we going to get buses? We don't need that shit,' swore Paras.

'Listen to him, man,' urged Maxwell.

'We don't use buses,' said Bourne. 'Black cabs.'

'Like in Belfast?'

'Just the same. The cabs have our drivers. They just go round on routes that cover the whole of Moss Side. Regular runs, just going round and picking up passengers at regular stops.'

'Why people going to use us?' asked Paras.

'Because we're free. No charge,' Bourne grinned. 'And because everyone who lives here knows that you, Abdul Paras, expect them to use the free service. They don't want to cross you. They're scared enough of you already.'

'What about people going out of Moss Side?'

'Run some cabs into Manchester. But they only drop and pick up people who live here. That way, we can see who comes into Moss Side from outside. We can even pick them up when they get off the buses. We'll know the ones who come here for the drugs and the tarts. Anyone else, anyone spying on us, they'll stand out like a sore thumb.'

'That's good, Abdul,' urged Maxwell. 'And once people round here get used to the service, they'll just use it all the time. And they'll talk in the back. Shit, our drivers can tell us everything that's going on in the Moss.'

'We also tighten up our protection service. Then the shopkeepers and the businessmen tell us what's going on. Listen, all they want is a safe place to make money in. One of the first things we do is find out who the builders are. Anyone from outside the area, we smash their plant, knock down the work they've done. Then we get builders from inside Moss Side to quote for the jobs. It won't take long before all the work's home grown. We might even build our own Belfast Wall.'

'What's that?' asked Paras.

'We built a wall to separate us from the Prods in Belfast, between the Shankill Road and the Falls. It's been standing longer than the Berlin Wall.'

'Fucking good that. Seal the Moss off from Manchester.'

'No chance. They'd have the army in straightaway. You also got to clamp down on the vandals. If you've got any hotheads here, tell them to fuck off and go vandalize Chorlton or somewhere. But keep this place safe and clean. No violence, no shit painted on the walls. Like a doctor's surgery. Only the drugs won't be on prescription.' Bourne laughed at his own joke and saw Paras start to grin. But it was suddenly replaced with a scowl.

'What about that shit today?' growled Paras.

'Forget it. Don't rock the boat any more.'

'They came on to my turf.'

'So what? We'll pay them back when it's time. This is your manor, Abdul. This can be the biggest sting in Europe. Just do it properly. And nobody'll ever bother us again.'

Midland Hotel
Manchester

'Does that prove we mean business, Mr Marshall?' said the voice.

'Killing innocent people wasn't on the agenda.' Marshall recognized Freddy the Duck's voice.

'That was unfortunate, but nothing to do with us. You owe us £240,000.'

'How's that?'

'Four kilos. That's what you promised.'

'I remember what I said.'

'Good. Your cold sounds worse.'

The phone went dead in Marshall's hand. They had fulfilled their part of the bargain; now they expected him to fulfil his. He was pleased. At least they were in the game, even if they didn't completely trust him yet. It was important that they took him seriously.

He went to the window and looked out. The drizzle had been replaced by wispy fog once again as night set in. He watched the dreary scene below him in the square, the lines of traffic now thinned as the last of the city workers returned to their homes and *Coronation Street* evenings in the suburbs. His cold, now well developed, increased his dislike of this dreary damp city.

Oh for Texas. Blue endless skies. Places to hide from the world in. This city he had come to, for all its familiarity, could never be home to him. He had often wondered about coming back; he realized now that Texas was his true home.

The knock on the door shook him out of his reminiscing. He crossed over to the bed, slipped the Glock into the rear of his waistband and went to the door. 'Who's that?' he asked, standing to the side of the door.

'Marshall,' came an American voice, familiar but not instantly recognizable.

'Yeah.' Marshall pulled the gun from his waistband and cocked it. 'Who wants him?'

'It's me . . . John.'

Marshall shook his head in frustration; they had come after him too soon. He leant forward and opened the door. John Pentanzi, from the DEA London bureau, walked in. 'What're you doing here?' said Marshall as he closed the door on his visitor.

'Just visiting.' Pentanzi noticed the Glock in Marshall's hand. 'Thought guns were illegal over here.'

Marshall ignored the comment and threw the gun on to the bed. 'Hey, I'm on vacation. Can't you guys leave well alone?'

'You're meant to report where you're going.'

'Report, report, report. The fucking paperwork's drowning the department.'

'For your own good. There's a lot of bad people out there want to hurt you. It's up to us to protect our own.'

'Like we protected Ronane.' Marshall coughed as he spoke.

The words stung Pentanzi. 'He was my friend, too. My partner before I . . .'

'Yeah. Got promoted. Nice safe job in a nice safe city.'

'Shit to you. Washington stuck me here. I did my stint in . . . Damn you. What makes you so special?'

'Because I'm still out there. Because I'm closer to it. I'm what this department's about. Hitting them where it hurts. Maybe some of you need reminding it's a fucking war, John. And we're not going to win it punching a word processor behind a desk.'

297

Pentanzi gave a deep sigh, then crossed the room and took off his coat and threw it on the bed. 'You got a beer?'

'In the bar.'

Pentanzi opened the small refrigerator and took out a Budweiser. 'Want one?'

'No.'

Pentanzi peeled the flip top and took a swig. 'Why're you hurting so much?'

'Because of Ronane.'

'We've both lost partners before. This is going overboard.'

'It's how I feel.'

'What's the first rule they teach at Quantico? Never get personal.'

'That shit's for accountants and lawyers. Everything's personal for the rest of us.' Marshall sat in the armchair as he spoke. 'How'd you find me?'

Pentanzi came over and joined him. 'Washington said you'd be heading this way. Here or Ireland.'

'Clever Washington.'

'So I just checked the hotels.'

'You tell them?'

'Not yet. Thought we'd talk first.'

'Yeah?'

'There's a lot going on up here. Lot of people getting blown away. You got anything to do with it?'

'No.'

'Then why come here?'

'I just wanted to see my roots. I'm on vacation, remember? Paid for by Washington.'

'Don't bullshit me, Marshall.'

'I don't owe you anything.'

'We don't want to get trapped in what is a British problem.' Pentanzi followed the official line.

'Except the shipment came out of El Paso. That's why Ronane got tortured and killed.'

'Not our jurisdiction any longer. Anyway, what makes you think it came over here?'

'Instinct.'

'Your bloody instinct,' snorted Pentanzi.

'So why does Washington think I'm here? And the shipment?'

Pentanzi laughed. 'Because the saps also believe in your instinct.'

'And you?'

'I'm here to slow you down. For all our good. Including yours.

Once I tell Washington that I've traced you, they'll order you back.'

'Then don't tell them.'

'I can't do that.'

'For Ronane. For everyone on the Honour Roll. They didn't deserve what happened.' Marshall played to his colleague's sense of loyalty.

'You're asking too much.'

'Have you always followed departmental procedure, John? Even when you were in the field? Weren't there times you just went your own way?'

'It was different then.'

'No different from now.'

'What're you up to?'

'No can tell. Unless you just want to hear I'm on vacation.'

'Don't shit me. If you want my support, then I need to know what you've got.'

'I just want your silence.'

'Same thing.'

'If you don't know, then nobody can drag it out of you.'

'Then it's no go,' said Pentanzi firmly.

'Fine. Just remember, you got no jurisdiction over me. Not in England.'

'Crap. If Washington say they want you back, then you respond accordingly. And immediately.'

'I may not be around when you come back for me. That is, unless you already told them.'

'I wasn't lying. They don't know I found you.'

Marshall knew that even if Pentanzi was lying, there was no way he would admit it. The rule was always maintain trust; it was the foundation on which relationships between agents were based. 'Then you won't find me, John. And you know, when I'm closing in on this thing, I can do without you sniffing up my backside.'

Pentanzi laughed suddenly. 'Hell, with that cold you're the one with the sniffing problem. You don't quit, do you, Marshall?'

'Did I ever?'

'Three days. Then I tell Washington.'

'Could need longer.'

'Three days. That's it.'

Marshall was secretly pleased. The answer had told him Washington had already decided he should be left alone in the field for a few days more. Otherwise Pentanzi would have stuck out longer, even offered to help. This way he was a maverick; the DEA would wash their hands of him if things went badly wrong. 'I need some hardware,' he said, pushing his luck.

'You already got that,' said Pentanzi, pointing at the Glock.

'Something heavier.'

Pentanzi reached over and dragged his coat off the bed. He pulled a Heckler and Koch HK-94 Auto Carbine from the special deep pockets sewn into it. The gun, a 9mm with a thirty round magazine, was in two sections and, at six and a half pounds, was one of the smallest and most easily concealed of all the automatic rifles.

'This what you call travelling light?' joked Marshall as he took the weapon.

'Washington doesn't know about this.' This time Marshall believed Pentanzi. 'Make sure it don't bite me back. And watch that cold. Nothing drains your energy like a bad cold.'

After Pentanzi had gone, Marshall checked the HK-94, then slipped into bed. He was sweating heavily and hoped the cold would work its way out in the night.

Once again, her face was the last thing he saw before he fell asleep. She was the only sane thing in this insane world.

Rochdale Canal
Manchester

The fog made it easy for them not to be noticed.

Bourne, as always, arrived first. He was on time, but he knew his contact would wait until he was sure that the Irishman was alone. It was five minutes before he heard the crunch of heavy footsteps on the gravel path that ran next to the canal.

'This thing is getting out of hand,' said Manchester Blue, once he had identified Bourne.

'Fucking right,' cursed the Irishman. 'I've been hearing splashes ever since I arrived.'

'I didn't mean the fog,' came the irritated reply.

Bourne chuckled, pleased with his little joke. 'I tell you what,' he said eventually, 'the Prods, and the whole British government for that, are easy to sort out compared with this lot.'

'What the hell's going on in there?'

'Moss Side? Bloody sooties. They got no organization, no loyalty, no fucking sense. God knows how they make any money.'

'What're you doing with them?'

Bourne tapped his nose. 'That's the trouble with you bobbies. Can't stop asking questions.'

'What do you expect? Nobody, the public or the Home Office, is going to let us keep out of this thing. Jesus, shooting up the public. That's stupid.'

'It got out of control.'

'This isn't Ulster.'

'There's no such place as Ulster. The Six Counties.'

'Forget the rhetoric. You don't let things get out of hand in Belfast.'

'Shove it.'

'How can I? With what's going on. Is what happened official policy?'

'No.'

'Because if it is, I can't stop the—'

'I said it wasn't official. Believe that.'

'So what happened?'

'The Chinks came into the Moss. Trying to teach the sooties a lesson. Shooting at the cars was because the blacks got mad and wanted to hit back. It's their bloody inferiority complex. Think the whole fucking world's out to get them.'

'You sure that's it?'

'That's it.'

'So why're you in Moss Side?'

Bourne paused for a moment, then sighed. He knew he had to tell Manchester Blue the truth. He had to if he expected him to call off the hounds. 'Drugs.'

'I thought the Provos were against that?'

'They were. The old brigade. But it's easier than robbing banks. And it earns more. A lot more.'

Manchester Blue's answer was surprisingly cool. 'Our information is there's no drugs coming out of Belfast.'

'Then believe it.'

'They say it's because it's easier to ship stuff in across the Channel on the ferries. It doesn't make sense to them that drugs should be brought in from one of the highest security places in the world. If I was transporting drugs, I'd be looking for the easiest route.'

Bourne laughed. 'You believe what you want.'

'How the hell did you get into that?'

'There's never been much in Belfast. Not like in Dublin. Run by a family down there. Anyway, they came up to Belfast to try and rope us into a deal. We said no, so they tried the UDA. When we heard about that we threatened the family. They had some sense, because they went back to Dublin. That's when we realized we had no choice. If we didn't do it, the Prods would. That's how it started.'

'Then the last thing you should do is draw attention to yourselves with bombs and shooting at the public,' snapped Manchester Blue.

'I didn't know about the Portland Street bombing. That was another cell. I'm on my own. The rule is no communication between cells.'

'If it goes on, they'll declare a state of emergency and call in the army.'

'You've got to stop that.'

'I'm only one man.'

'It needs stopping. Otherwise we'll increase the bombing. We win, either way.'

'All right,' said a cornered Manchester Blue, 'we'll keep it under police jurisdiction. But don't let anything else happen.'

'I can stop Moss Side. But I can't stop any other cell.'

'That's a cop-out.'

'I don't know who the ASUs are.' Bourne referred to the IRA's Active Service Units whose main responsibility is the planning and implementation of terrorist activity on the mainland. 'They get their orders direct from Belfast or Dublin. They have a list of telephone boxes where they have to wait for calls once a week. Most times nobody rings. That way it's impossible to trace either the caller or the ASU. It's how it is. Doesn't stop you doing your bit.'

'I said we'd keep it under police control. As long as you don't—'

'The Chinks. They need stopping.'

'Not if you're going to keep whacking them.'

'We won't. Not any more. Not unless they come after us.'

'I can't guarantee that.'

'Speak to them. Put them under pressure,' urged Bourne.

'We've already had a meeting with them. Warning them that if the Triads stir things up any further, we'll have to take more drastic action against them.'

'Who were you speaking to?'

Manchester Blue realized that Bourne wanted a name, someone he could go after. 'We had a meeting with some senior members of the Chinese community.' He decided to keep the names out of it. 'We don't know who the Triad leaders are. We just hope it'll get back to them. Anyway, how do you know it was the Chinese?'

'Who else would it be?'

'But you're not sure?'

302

'Nobody saw anything. Just their fucking stupid masks.'

Manchester Blue decided not to tell Bourne where the cars had been found. 'Why would the Chinese come into Moss Side? I mean, things have been pretty quiet for a while.'

'You tell me. You're the bloody police. Unless there's something you haven't told me.'

'Nothing that you don't know,' Manchester Blue lied. At least they didn't know about Marshall. 'I'll see what I can do with the Chinese.'

'Seeing isn't enough. Only doing.'

'Don't shove too hard. We've both got a lot to lose.'

'No. If it goes wrong, I just go home. For you, this is home. You don't have any other choice.'

The Town of Wilmslow
Stockbroker Belt
Cheshire

'Where've you been?' Tessa asked Soulson as he came into the kitchen.

'Just walking,' he said, taking off his overcoat. He came over and kissed her.

'In this fog?'

'I like that. Sort of hides the problems. No, I gave Paul the night off and drove myself home.'

'Do you want some supper?'

'No, thanks. But I'd love a mulled wine.'

She took two glasses and poured red wine into them. Then she reached into the cupboard and took out cinnamon and lemon and added it to the wine. When she had finished, she opened the microwave and put the glasses in, snapped the door shut and punched in the time setting. She was aware that he was watching her closely. 'What're you thinking?'

'That I sometimes forget about you. About the real things in life. I miss not seeing much of you, Tessa.'

'Well, I'm in tonight. We'll have a dad and daughter sort of evening.'

'What's that?'

She shrugged. 'I don't know. Sounds good, though.'

'Are you making fun of me?'

'Of course not.'

'I'm glad you're staying in.'

'Hard day from what I read.'

'Impossible day.'

'What's going on, Dad?'

'Wish I knew. What's the shop floor say?'

'They don't know either. But they are nervous.'

'Why?'

'That someone's going to start shooting at us bobbies soon.'

'I'd like to say that won't happen.' Soulson shrugged and sat down at the kitchen table. 'But I can't.'

'Is all this linked? The bombings and the shootings?'

'Got to be.' The phone rang on the wall. 'Damn it.'

'Leave it.' The microwave pinged and she opened the oven and took out the two glasses.

'You know I can't do that.' He stood up and lifted the receiver. 'Soulson.'

'It's me, Chief,' said Armitage. 'I've arranged the meet for tomorrow. At the farm.'

'Good.'

'Do you want Paul to drive you?'

'No. Anything else come up?'

'The girl. Our courier.' Armitage meant Jill Couples.

'What about her?'

'She was seen coming out of the Midland. Spent the night there.' Armitage didn't tell him it was he who had seen her come out.

'Why?'

'No idea. Didn't think I should push it.'

'Anything else?'

'No. It's all quiet at the moment. The Firearms Unit have secured the area and are staying there overnight.'

Soulson snorted. 'The things we do for the media. I mean, no sniper's going to see anything in this fog.'

'It's best, Chief. Just in case.'

Soulson's eyes followed Tessa as she carried the two glasses to the table and sat down. 'I went for a walk earlier. Did some thinking.'

'And?'

'We need the Intelligence Unit back on the drug enquiry.'

'I'll get that organized for the morning.'

'Good night, Roy.'

'Night, Chief.'

'That sounded a bit harsh,' said Tessa.

'Roy's all right. Just needs pushing now and then.' Soulson sat back at the table and picked up his glass and sipped from it. 'That's good. Bloody good.'

'Even out of a microwave?'

'Beats sticking a poker in a fire.'

She put her arm out and squeezed his hand. 'I sometimes wonder whether you go looking for trouble, or it comes looking for you.'

'What's that mean?'

'That, as long as I can remember, you've always been in the centre of controversy.'

He grinned. 'That comes with the stripes.'

'But other Chief Constables don't get half the flack you do.'

'When push comes to shove, Tessa, maybe I just shove harder.'

'Do you feel alone?'

'What? With you there?'

'That's not enough though, is it?'

'It's all I need.'

'You must wish Mum was here sometimes, or that you had more family instead of just me and Grandad.'

'But I haven't. So why think about it?'

'Even when you go to bed?'

'She's always been with me.'

'Always?'

'Always.'

'After all these years?'

'Never left me. Not Mary.'

'I often wondered why you didn't remarry.'

'Didn't need to.'

'They say that's why you're so unforgiving.' She trod carefully as she spoke.

'Shop-floor talk again.'

'People who believe in you.'

'Do they?'

'Most do. There's few bobbies that don't think you stand up for them.'

'But they still say I'm unforgiving.'

'Because you've nothing else. Just the Force.'

'I've got you.'

'Not enough. The Force has replaced Mum.'

'That's what they say, is it?'

305

'Yes.'

'And you?'

'I agree with them.'

He was silent for a while. She didn't know he was thinking of his brother, the uncle she had never known, the High Executioner in their midst. Wild Jimmy Soulson. If they had anything in common, it had been their love of Mary. He remembered how she had protected him, almost like a son, all those years ago.

'Have you never felt the need for another woman?' Tessa interrupted his thoughts.

'No.' It was the truth. There had nearly been the whore. Years before. She had been no older than twenty; he was a sergeant then. He'd seen her working the strip near Manchester Road. When he had come off duty, he had hurriedly changed into his civvies and rushed back to see if she was still there. After circling her a few times, he plucked up enough courage to proposition her. Five pounds. They had driven to a secluded street and parked in a line of steamed-up cars. But he had panicked at the last minute, couldn't bring himself to enter her. He had pushed her roughly from the car, her pants still wrapped round her ankles, and driven home. It was the nearest he had come to being unfaithful to Mary. No-one would ever have satisfied him as she did. That was something he was pleased about, something to share even in his loneliest moments. In that way she was always alive to him, always his partner as long as he lived.

'Never?' Tessa persisted.

'I like seeing an attractive woman, a well-turned thigh,' he joked. 'I'm not made of stone. But I've got all I want. And you're wrong. You make up for Mary.'

'I'll marry one day. I want kids, Dad.'

'I'm not holding you back.'

'Doesn't stop me worrying about you.'

'I'll make a good grandad. Better than a father.'

'You're a great dad.' She leant across the table and kissed him. 'The best I could have.' She sat down again. 'Why did you pull the Intelligence Unit off the drug caper?'

He chuckled at the way she always changed the subject whenever she got too close. She got that from him, not from Mary. 'I was more concerned about the bombing. Just wanted to see if we could pick something up quickly.' He suddenly remembered Armitage's words. 'Your friend, Jill Couples, she's in Intelligence.'

'She loves it.'

'What's she like?'

'Hard worker. She really believes in her job.'

'Is she married?'

'No. Why? Do you fancy her?'

'Too young for me. She doesn't look like a policewoman. More like someone who likes enjoying herself.'

'Don't believe it. Her work comes first.'

'Has she got a boyfriend in the Force?' he asked cautiously.

'No. She likes having a good time when she's not working. I think there was someone. An American. When she was over there. She's never said much. But I just get the feeling it mattered to her.'

'That's good police instinct. Why do you get on so well with her?'

'I just like her. I never feel she's my friend because I'm your daughter.'

'I forget that sometimes. About the pressure it puts you under.'

'Doesn't bother me. Used to, but not any more.'

'We all have our pressures, I suppose. Time for me to go to bed, love. I need my sleep, ready for the horrors of whatever they're going to throw at me tomorrow.'

'You're lucky. To sleep as easy as you do.'

Nine miles away, Marshall made a phone call, arranged his next move and then went to bed.

He slept like a log.

As always, tomorrow could wait until he woke up and was ready to face the day.

14

THOUGHTS IN MY MIND

Bethesda Hospital
Maryland

THEY HAD BROUGHT THE FILES AS HE HAD ASKED THEM TO, IN THREE large boxes full of printed paper.

Ronane, lying as still as he always did on the airbed, watched the two men carry the boxes in, walking softly on stockinged feet so as not to make any unnecessary noise in this specially prepared isolation ward with the soundproofing material on the walls. Both men wore gauze masks.

The one in front was Peter Smith; behind him came Greg Daly from the El Paso intelligence unit. They were good men, trusted and respected by Ronane. But their first responsibility was to the DEA and that was not lost on him.

'Where do you want everything?' asked Smith.

'In front of me, so I don't have to keep turning my head,' replied Ronane.

The two men crossed the room slowly and gently placed the boxes by the bed. They then carefully lifted two plastic chairs with rubber mounts on the feet and placed them next to the boxes. When they were satisfied they would not have to move again, they eased themselves into the chairs.

Ronane watched with amusement. It was a game he had learned to play with his few visitors. There was no doubt that unnecessary and startling sounds jarred his open nerve-ends, but he enjoyed milking the situation, watching the high and mighty tiptoe round him like mice sneaking past a sleeping cat. 'I'm sorry about all this,' he said.

'No sweat,' replied Smith in the hushed tone that they were used to speaking in. 'They say you're healing pretty good.'

'Getting better.' Ronane didn't add it would take another eight months before his skin grew back over the opened nerve-ends.

'Pretty warm in here.'

'Can't change that. Makes it more comfortable for me.' The heat and humidity eased the pain.

'You ready?' Smith had always been an impatient man.

'Yeah.'

'Where do you want to start?'

'El Paso, I guess. At the beginning.'

Smith nodded and started to leaf through the first of the boxes. When he had found the documents he wanted, he put them on his lap and opened the first file. There was a mound of photographs and he held them up, one after another, for Ronane to look at. 'All these were taken at the border post before and after the attempt to get the drugs through. The close-ups of the corpses are the drug-runners who got shot on the day, including the truck driver. If you look at the general pictures, you might recognize someone you know.'

Ronane saw who he was looking for in the third batch of El Paso pictures. He was there, a bearded, straggly-haired man mingling with the pedestrians as they crossed the border. He was dressed as a Mexican, looked natural as a South American rather than the Texan Ronane knew he was. 'Keep that one,' he said, trying not to let the sudden shock of seeing the perpetrator of his own wounds and the killer of Betty staring back at him. He closed his eyes and thought of vanilla ice cream being eaten as he sat in the snow at the North Pole. It was a silly thing, but the image of all that cold usually helped bring the temperature in his body down. There were a few sharp pains, but nothing he couldn't handle. When he felt more relaxed he opened his eyes. 'It's going to take for ever,' he apologized.

'We've got the time. You just move at your speed.'

'I'm OK now.' He wasn't, but he wanted his mind occupied with new, less painful images.

'Who was in the picture?'

'Just put it to the side, like I said. We'll do this thing my way. I don't want to stop-start my brain, OK?'

Smith nodded and put the picture to one side. Then he continued to leaf slowly through the remainder, only stopping when Ronane singled out the odd one to join the small pile of photographs which he wanted to refer back to. The photos of the dead woman, the Texan's wife, were also added to the pile. Ronane wondered what he'd seen in the ugly woman, but turned his mind away from it when he remembered it was her death which had triggered his own personal tragedy. When they had finished with the El Paso photographs, Smith turned to Daly and told him to read the full report from the El Paso intelligence unit on the raid, the US Customs report and the interrogation file of the Mexican, Ramon Cortez, who had come from Piedras Negras and set this whole thing in motion. Daly read slowly, in a flat monotonous tone as he had been told to. Ronane occasionally stopped him and asked him either to make a note or to reread a section. It was slow progress, but essential if they were to determine what Marshall's game plan was and how they might be of help to him.

Four hours later they stopped for lunch. The two DEA men left the intensive-care unit and went to the commissary while a nurse spoon-fed Ronane and replaced his catheter. He was normally quite chatty with the nurses for he enjoyed their companionship, but today he kept silent, concentrating on the information they had sifted through.

One of the doctors who looked after Ronane joined Smith and Daly at their table. 'Remarkable man, your colleague,' he said as he slurped his way through his vegetable soup. 'Should be dead, you know.'

'Seems to be healing OK,' replied Smith.

'He is. But not because of us. Well, we're playing some part in it, but it's will-power. Sheer determination to live, that's what's keeping him alive. You breed them tough in the DEA.'

'He's one of our best.'

'You should be proud of him. We didn't have enough skin off the rest of his body for a donor graft. So we've used pig skin and a bit of human skin from other sources.'

310

'How long before it grows back?'

'About eight months.'

'That long?'

'At least. We've also got to put him through some very mild exercise routines. Otherwise his muscles will just waste away. The physio's got a good routine with him. Give him pain-killers, then she works on him. Still hurts him, but we've got to do it. Apart from that, and keeping his mind occupied, all we can do is keep him in the right environment and pump dextrosaline and haemecel into him.'

'Haemecel?'

'A blood expander. Thickens it, too.'

'And if that stopped?'

'Then even will-power couldn't keep him alive.'

The DEA men returned to Ronane an hour later. The file number of the photo Ronane had picked of the scruffy Mexican pedestrian in El Paso had been phoned through to Washington. Smith had asked them to fax a copy to the intelligence unit to see if they could match the photograph with their files.

'You're not too tired?' Smith asked Ronane when he was sitting by the bed once again.

'Let's keep going,' Ronane said, eager to stretch his mind, to have something to do while he lay so still.

'You want to move on to San Antonio?'

'No,' Ronane answered immediately. He wasn't ready to cope with the traumas of that horrible time, couldn't bear looking through the pictures they would show him. 'Tell me everything you got on the Irish. About Europe and John Pentanzi's report. Just take me through the whole damn thing.'

'We don't have that much.'

'Come on, Pete. Don't bull me. If you want my help, then give me everything you got.'

'It's outside our jurisdiction.'

'Nothing's outside our jurisdiction. You know that. Shit, we're doing capers even Washington doesn't know about.'

'That's not official.'

'But true.'

'Why do you think we're not passing you all the information?'

'Instinct.' Ronane grinned, that had always been Marshall's answer to anything. 'Don't get me riled up, Pete. Otherwise a No Entry sign goes up.'

Smith thought for a moment before replying. 'Understand there's

311

no conspiracy thing going on here. I mean, Marshall's over there on his own. No support from us. We just want to make sure the department doesn't get compromised.'

'Then pull Marshall out.'

'He won't come.'

'Who says?'

'Pentanzi. He saw Marshall in Manchester. The big man insists he's there on vacation.'

'They can order him home.'

'You know Marshall.'

'Just tell him his furlough's cancelled.'

'He'd ignore it.'

'That there's a job, something important, back in the field.'

'He'd leave the department rather than come back now. No, we've got to leave him there. Support him where we can.'

'What support?'

'I don't know. Just . . . it's damn tricky. I mean, we've got to protect the department as well as Marshall.'

'Shit!' swore Ronane as the awful truth hit him. They knew Marshall would set out to revenge the family. They were throwing him to the wolves and hoping he'd wipe out the mess. And they didn't care, as long as they weren't compromised.

'What the—?' said an alarmed Smith.

But the pain racked Ronane's body; seared through him once again. He screamed, and then closed his eyes and tried to hide the agony, only this time ice cream wasn't strong enough. The attack lasted ten minutes; ten minutes in which Smith and Daly could only sit and wait for him to recover himself.

'Tell me about Manchester and its drug scene. Don't hold back. Otherwise I'll call the nurse and that'll be it.' He needed time to think, to help the big man.

They spent the afternoon going through the European reports. Ronane said little, concentrating instead on trying to get inside his partner's brain as he listened to Smith and Daly alternate as they read out loud. He wasn't too concerned about the department. It was Marshall who needed protection. And maybe from here, from all these thousands of miles away, he could just find the way that could shortcut Marshall's revenge and save him from the danger that Ronane's cowardice and treachery had led him into.

DEA Intelligence Unit
Fort Bliss
El Paso

When the intelligence unit received the fax from Washington, they blew the photo up so that they had a clearer picture of the Mexican pedestrian. Once they were satisfied that the blow-up was not too grainy, they recopied the photo on a 6 by 6 format, studio rostrum Littlejohn camera and enlarged it to fit on to a 22-inch computer screen. Then they ran it through a scanner and broke the image into electronic lines that could be manipulated on the computer screen. They transferred the image directly into the computer and waited for it to appear on the monitor. Three minutes later the face of the Mexican peasant appeared on the screen.

'Pretty blue eyes,' said the leader of the team.

'Yeah. For a Mexican,' came the disbelieving reply. 'He's either wearing contacts or he's dyed his hair. I'd go for the hair.'

'Height?'

'Maybe five-eight, five-nine. About that, from the people round him.'

'Build?'

'Wiry, athletic. Can't tell much because that's the only picture we got. I don't think he was in any of the other snaps. But he seems to lean to the right. Could be nothing, but he might have a rolling walk. Probably putting it on. About one eighty pounds.'

'Hair?'

'With those eyes, probably blond or brown. Skin's dark, but it don't look like make-up in the enlargement. That's natural tan. I'd go for light brown hair.'

'What else?'

'Bone structure isn't Indian. This boy's white. Maybe forty, forty-five years old.' The technician put his hand on the mouse next to the screen, flicked the pointer up to the menu bar, selected the SAVE icon and stored the image. He called it 'Mex/Paso 1'. He moved the pointer to a second menu bar under EDIT and chose the paintbrush icon. As he pressed the mouse button, the pointer changed to a replica of a paintbrush. He moved it across to another icon and chose the thickness of the brush, roughly one-eighth of an inch wide. He advanced the pointer to the base of the pedestrian's neck and then ran the paintbrush along the line of the neck, over the cheeks and ears, over the hair and down the

313

other side of the face. A thick white line appeared on the screen, separating the man's face from the background of the other pedestrians.

'Looks OK,' said the leader. 'Cut it out.'

The technician ran the icon up to the paintbrush width symbol and changed the width to nearly an inch thick. Then he moved the electronic brush over the background area and wiped all the other images off the screen. All that was left was the pedestrian's face. That was saved as 'Mex/Paso 2'.

'Let's get rid of the beard first,' said the leader.

'That might be real,' interjected one of the others. 'I think we should trim his hair.'

'OK. Let's start there.'

The technician changed the paintbrush icon to a rubber eraser image, then slowly worked his way over the top of the man's head, rubbing out, as one would on a piece of paper, the wild long growth of unkempt hair. After he had shaped it to the man's head, he turned the eraser into a thinner brush, pencil-thin, then moved it to the man's hair and slowly drew in a short-cropped style, adding hair where there was now only a skull shape. The team left him to his endeavours; they trusted his experience and judgement.

It took nearly half an hour to give him a neater, more cropped style. He saved the image as 'Mex/Paso 3', then he hit the PRINT button and waited for the image to appear on paper out of the laser printer next to the computer. It took five minutes before the team saw the print-out. After they had discussed it, the leader gave it to one of the junior members and told him to start checking the files for blue-eyed, five foot eight, 180-pound, fairish-haired Cali cartel members, including those with beards. The description probably covered a third of the dealers on the file, but at least it was a starting point. The records computer would produce a list within a short time, a list with index numbers from which they could take photos from the files, or even identikits of those who had never been photographed.

The technician started work on the beard and adopted the same technique he had used on the hair. It took over two hours. He had to match the skin tones where he shaved the beard off, and he matched six different chins from the identikit file. In turn he gave Mex/Paso a square jaw, round jaw, short jaw, long jaw, twisted jaw and double-chinned jaw. Each image was saved and a print made before the lower face on the screen was sliced in half and he started all over again.

When they had finished the last picture, stored as 'Mex/Paso 9', the team broke for a meal and general discussion. There had been no news from Washington, no further photographs to be examined, so the talk was of the picture they had just completed. As they spoke, blown-up copies of all the printed photos were taped on the walls in the large conference room.

An hour later the first of the huge pile of pictures from the files appeared. The team split them into smaller piles and each of the eight men took a section of the large conference table and spread the pictures. It was a slow process, holding up a picture and comparing it with those on the wall, checking the eyes, general features, hair, identifying marks, nostril measurements, lip widths, mouth shapes and all the different attributes that somehow make each face different from its neighbour.

Seven hours later they found the Texan. Light brown hair, one seventy pounds and five feet eight. They didn't have a picture, only an identikit photograph that had been carefully prepared from small bits of information gathered over the years.

'Ty Koons,' said the leader when he spoke on the phone to Pete Smith in Washington the next morning.

'Thought he was dead,' came the surprised answer.

'So did we.'

'You sure?'

'Once we matched the eyes and the lips, the rest just fell into place. It's the nearest we got out of all the pictures.'

'I didn't know we had a picture of Koons.'

'We don't. Just a series of facts and identity reports we picked up over the years and put into an identikit pack. Hell, we must've spent a fortune getting information on that guy.'

'That his real name?'

'Don't think so. But it's the only one he went by.'

'Remind me. It was all so long ago.'

'I'll fax you what we've got on him,' the leader replied.

'Give me a verbal till it gets here.'

'We first heard about him in '74. He was working out of Boston when the Colombians were building up their networks. A tough guy, about eighteen years old, who came from the south and wasn't averse to taking people out for anyone who paid him. The Colombians liked him and he became their Chief Enforcer in the north-east. We came across him then, at least the local law-enforcement boys did. But they never hung anything on him. No pictures, no prints, nothing. Like a ghost figure. And if anyone crossed the Medellins, that was before the Calis became the force they did, he went in and wiped out the

315

trouble. Didn't deal in the stuff, had nothing to do with drugs. Just murdered people, then floated out of sight. He was responsible for the death of three cell bosses in New York, two in Boston and one in Buffalo. Then he disappeared for a while and we heard he'd switched to the Calis. The word was he was recruited by the Fat One, El Gordo himself.'

'I remember now. Meant to be his personal bodyguard.' Jordo Santacruz Londono Don Chepe was the boss who put the Cali cartel at the top of the cocaine network. It was every DEA man's personal ambition to catch him.

'The story is that Koons went down to New Orleans and personally wiped out the cell boss there and seven other members of the gang. All in one night. Then he hit Medellin men in Washington, Las Vegas and Miami. He just ghosted through. No one saw him or knew who he was. Then, about five years ago, he just vanished. By then he'd set up teams of enforcers, mostly South Americans, who looked after the Cali problems.'

'What did you guys think happened to him?'

'No idea,' replied the leader. 'Best guess we had was that he got too big for his boots and the Calis took him out. Or else he just tired of what he was doing, took his money and retired into some small town somewhere.'

'How sure are you that he's the one in the picture?'

'No guarantees, Pete. But the more we matched the better it got.'

'That's if the identikit photo was right in the first place.'

'Nothing else matched so close, Pete.'

'OK. I'll appreciate the faxed report. Makes you wonder, doesn't it?'

'What?'

'What the hell he's been doing for the last five years?'

Bethesda Hospital
Maryland

'He's setting up Europe,' said Ronane.

'That's what we figured,' was Smith's pensive reply.

'You already told Washington?'

'Of course.'

They didn't speak for a while as Ronane soaked in the information concerning Ty Koons. Smith and Daly understood that he controlled

316

things in this room; that he would continue when he was able.

'The guy in the picture . . .' Ronane started, then said nothing more. They didn't urge him to continue; they could tell it was a painful time. Ronane shut his eyes and dreamed of his ice cream. When he was sufficiently in control, when the pain was no longer stabbing through him as he came to face the Devil, he continued. 'That was the guy we called the Texan. The same one Marshall and I met in Mexico City when we ran the poker game. He was the one, Pete. Who did this to me.'

'You knew all along?' came the startled reply.

'Not till yesterday. Not till I saw the picture. I told you he was the same guy in Mexico. But I never saw him in El Paso, not until he came for me in San Antonio. He was just the Texan to us. Just a Cali lieutenant.'

'He's more than that.'

'Yeah,' said Ronane in little more than a whisper. 'He's more. He's the bastard—'

'Don't,' warned Smith, knowing what was coming.

'Koons killed Betty. And the kids.' After all this time, Ronane finally faced the image he had hidden in the recesses of his mind, that moment when Betty knew that she was to die at the hands of the Texan. But there was no emotion in him as he faced the truth; only a cold understanding that Marshall was in danger and that the big man would revenge Betty and the children.

'You OK?' asked a concerned Smith.

'Yeah.' He decided not to tell them about Koons' wife and his own treachery. That would muddy the waters. If they knew it was personal, then they might force Marshall out. Ronane knew his partner had to finish his mission, but it needed his input. Together they could crush the Texan. 'You going to tell Marshall?'

'What do you think?'

'I don't think you should.'

'Why?'

'Confuse the man. He's after a trail of cocaine.'

'And revenge.'

'That'll come second. He's a pro. Believe me.'

'So what's he going to do?'

'Use a diversion.'

'Like what?'

'I don't know yet. Maybe the police. Maybe the Chinese. I mean, from all the reports they're the natural enemy to the Moss Side gangs. He's got to do something like that. Use the tide in his

317

favour. Deflect the forces that are already in play. It's either the police or the Chinese.'

Smith looked across at Daly and winked. This was what they had come for; Ronane, with all his understanding of Marshall, was reading his partner's mind and telling the DEA what to expect next.

But Ronane had already worked out what Marshall was going to do. And the last thing he would do was tell his colleagues.

An hour later Ronane feigned tiredness and asked the DEA men to leave. When he was alone, he pushed the small buzzer that lay next to his hand and waited for the nurse to come.

'I'd like to see the doctor,' he told her, then waited for the nurse to leave the room. He steeled himself once he was alone, then swung both his arms powerfully, ignoring the immense pain that surged through him as he wrenched the needles that connected him to the dextrosaline and haemecel from his arms. The force of his actions knocked the dextrosaline bottle off its stand and it smashed as it crashed to the ground. Then he started to scream as he couldn't contain the pain of his frantic movements any longer.

'For Christ's sake,' said the doctor when he rushed into the room two minutes later, the nurse following him.

'Get her out of here,' Ronane shouted.

'What do you think you're—' the doctor continued as he rushed over to the bottle.

'I said get her out of here. I want to talk to you.'

'We have to—'

'Alone. I've got to talk to you alone. Or I'll just pull this shit down again.'

The doctor stopped where he was, then turned to the nurse. 'Just give us a few minutes. I'll call you.'

'And close the door.'

The nurse nervously left the room, pulling the door gently behind her.

'What're you playing at?' said the doctor when they were alone. 'You could kill yourself.'

'And I will. Unless you help me.'

'You've come too far for that.'

'No. If will-power got me here, then will-power can kill me. I'll rip this skin that's grafting to me off my body. Piece by piece. Right here in front of you.'

'Why?'

'Because my partner needs help. And because you're the only one I can trust.'

'You blackmailing me?'

'Yeah. I'm sorry, Doc. But I'm playing it straight with you. People's lives are at risk. It isn't just you guys who save lives.'

'Is this going to be illegal?'

Ronane smiled through the pain. 'No. But I don't want the DEA to find out. If you tell them, I'll just do as I said. And I'll know if you tell them. It'll get back.'

'You'd do it, wouldn't you?'

'Yes. I would.'

The expression in Ronane's eyes left no doubt in the doctor's mind. 'This Hippocratic Oath can sure get you into trouble,' he said. 'What do you want me to do?'

'Just pass a message. To Manchester.'

'Massachusetts?'

'England.'

'And then you'll behave yourself?'

'Yes, sir.'

'Until you want me to pass the next message.'

'Something like that.'

'You're not bullshitting me? About it being illegal?'

'No. I just want to protect my partner.' He shook his head; it was more than that. 'He's not just my partner. Damn it, he's all I've got left.'

15

GAME PLAN

Midland Hotel
Manchester

IT WAS AFTER TEN WHEN SHE ARRIVED.

Marshall chuckled as he let her into the room. She was dressed like the tinsel whore she was; she must have lowered the tone of the lobby as she walked through it towards the lifts.

'I don't do outcalls,' grumbled Shaeron Paras as she came into the room. 'You promised me five hundred and you better fucking give it to me.'

'Don't worry. You'll get it,' he said, closing the door, clearing his throat as he did.

She crossed to the bed and threw off her short coat. The dress she wore was flimsy and creased, having spent most of its time wrapped round her thighs in the backs of cars. 'I see you still got that cold. I hate the mornings,' she continued whining. 'Never get up till after lunchtime. Not unless it's Saturday and you can work the football crowds.'

'You want a coffee? Or something stronger?'

'At this time of the day?' she jeered. 'Listen, when you rang last night, you said you wanted to fuck all morning. Do you want to get on with it, or just talk?'

'I want to do some business.'

'I told you. That's what I'm here for.'

'Different business.'

She was suddenly suspicious. 'You're not a reporter, are you?'

'No, nothing like that.'

'You sure? I can do without that sort of trouble.' She picked up her coat and prepared to leave.

'Calm down. I'm not a reporter.' He took the coat from her. 'I just want to talk to you. About making money. Lots of it.'

'I work for myself,' she stated proudly. 'No pimps.'

'I'm talking real money.'

'A porno. Hey, I never done it for a camera before.' She wiggled her hips at him, the cellulite on her thighs moving of its own accord. 'You going to make me a movie star?'

'With the money I'm talking about, you can produce your own porno flicks. No, sweetheart, I'm talking more than that. You got that coke on you?'

'No, I left it behind. You should've said when you rang me.'

'You know how much money people make out of selling that stuff?'

'I'm not giving you no money back on last night.'

'Don't want it.'

'You want me to arrange to buy some coke?'

'No. I want you to sell it.'

She pondered his words for a while before she spoke. 'Whose stuff?'

'Mine.'

'Where from?'

'High-grade Colombian. Shipped from the USA.'

'Why me? I'm only a working girl.'

'Because I don't know anyone over here. And you're already handling the stuff. Maybe you can put me in touch with someone who can distribute it for me, out on the streets.'

'I know people could do that,' Shaeron answered cautiously. 'How much you got?'

'Plenty. We're talking mountains of the stuff.'

'Two, three kilos?'

He laughed. 'A lot more. And that's all I'm saying. But if you know someone who's interested, get them to meet me.'

'They got to know how much.'

'Just say more than a thousand kilos.'

'That's a mountain,' she gasped.

The phone rang and he picked it up.

'Me,' said Jill.

'Morning.'

'You alone?'

'Yeah.' He didn't dare tell her that Shaeron was with him; he suddenly hoped she wasn't ringing from the lobby.

'I'm at the office so I can't speak for long. You remember the chap I told you about in Moss Side when I saw you whoring that night?'

'Very funny. Which chap?' He smiled as he realized how quickly he had fallen back into the English vernacular. *Chap*, indeed.

'Small white guy. With red hair. I said he was familiar.'

'Go on.' He watched Shaeron as he spoke; she had drifted over to the window to look down on St Peter's Square. 'I checked through the terrorist suspect files. Nothing there. Except a name that I think went with the picture I saw some time ago. Cohn Bourne. He was an ASU leader.'

'ASU?'

'Active Service Unit. A terrorist cell.'

'You said *was*.'

'There was a Special Branch note that he was now with one of the breakaway units.'

'How positive was the note?'

'Seemed pretty certain. Said he was still dangerous. Just out of the mainstream movement. It was part of my investigation about six months ago. We'd had a couple of bomb threats. I know there was a picture in the file last time I looked. Anyway, I asked if anyone had taken the photos. They told me there weren't any, that Bourne was only a name in the file. I think someone lifted that picture. I know I've seen it before.' There was a rustle on the phone before she continued. 'Someone's coming. I'll speak to you later. Bye.'

The phone went dead before he could answer. He put down the receiver as Shaeron turned back towards him. 'As I was saying, that's why I need someone good. Someone who knows the scene.'

'I got people,' she replied eagerly.

'As long as they know what they're doing. Nobody's going to see this stuff until I'm sure of their credentials.'

'What's in it for me?'

'Get it sorted and I'll make it worth your while.'

'How do I know you ain't bullshitting me? Playing big boy?

Or that you ain't a cop?'

He went to the cupboard, unlocked and opened his suitcase and pulled out his sponge bag. He zipped it open for her to look at. Then he took the knife he carried from his back pocket and sliced a piece of the yellowed substance. He handed it over to her, then zipped the bag and returned it to the suitcase. 'Reporters don't do that.'

She could tell it was cocaine and she slipped it into her bag. 'You owe me five hundred,' she said.

'I've just given you a couple of grand's worth of snow.'

'You said cash.'

He laughed, took out his wallet and peeled off ten £50 notes. He held it out towards her. 'This is a separate transaction,' he said.

'If you want to fuck with me, that's OK.' She reached out and took the money from him. 'Well?'

He shook his head. 'I'd like to,' he lied, 'but I got things to do.'

'Don't matter to me. Anyway, my pussy likes to rest in the morning.'

He leant over and picked up her coat and helped her on with it. Then he crossed over to the door and opened it.

'You a strange bugger,' she said, following him. 'You different from my other punters.'

'Why?'

''Cos they would've fucked by now. Even if it was a stand-up job behind the door.'

'Go on. Before I change my mind. Get out of here.'

She smiled and walked through the door.

'Ring me when you've got something,' he said as her back disappeared down the corridor.

Marshall hired a small blue Vauxhall and drove north towards the hills of Lancashire. It was a pleasant drive once he had left the grimy urbanity of Manchester behind; along winding roads that worked their way through the hills beyond Preston and Clitheroe. There was a motorway now, but he followed the old route, the road map laid out on the seat next to him. Even after all this time it was familiar. He passed the 'dark satanic' mills, now converted into pretty business centres, even apartments looking out on these lush northern valleys. A history of dark industrial revolution now little more than the reminiscent vagaries of old men; just words in hymns of a bygone age. But the countryside hadn't changed.

Rolling hills, sheep wandering the fields, up and down dale, grey, cold-looking stone farmhouses where Heathcliffs still roamed and beat their womenfolk if the supper wasn't ready on time. Marshall laughed at his Americanized view of the past. It wasn't really like that. There would be roaring fires and hot piped central heating and microwaves in the kitchen. Just like New England or Maine. The world really had become one place.

The farm stood on the side of a hill that ran down to the river Hodder. Like most buildings of that era, it had been built into the side of the hill to protect it from the elements. The old stone barn was still there, well roofed, standing next to the house. He parked the car by the five-bar metal gate and climbed over it, stepped gingerly over the cattle grid and walked down the rough path towards the house.

He saw Charles come out of the barn and look up towards him. His elder brother was dressed in a green Barbour, corduroy trousers and black wellies. Marshall stopped as Soulson started to walk up the steep path towards him. He looked just like he had done on the television: a gruff, no nonsense, big-bearded man.

'See you've dressed for it,' said Soulson when he reached Marshall.

Marshall shrugged. There was already mud caked on his black pavement shoes, but that's all he had. 'Hasn't changed much,' he said, referring to the countryside.

'Some things never do.'

'How's Dad?'

'All right. For his age. Never leaves the place. Half blind, worn out after a lifetime of squeezing a living out of this place.' Soulson saw nothing of the Jimmy he had known in the big man who stood in front of him. Apart from the eyes. They were still defensive, still half mocking. He realized he wouldn't have recognized his brother if he had passed him in the street. 'You better come on in. He'll want to see you.'

'You tell him I was coming?'

'No.'

'Later, then.'

'Whatever. You sound like you've got a bad cold.'

'I can live with it,' replied Marshall nasally.

'There's been a bug going round. Fancy a walk down by the river?'

'Why not?'

The two men walked off the path and slowly climbed down the hill field.

'Where's the livestock?'

324

'Cattle went years ago. Then they had to destroy the sheep after Chernobyl. He couldn't bring himself to start all over again.'

'Is he still drinking?'

'Don't forget, do you?' chided Soulson. 'Yes, that never stopped. I sometimes think that's all that keeps him alive. All that alcohol. Pickled his bloody insides and stopped them getting any older. Anyway, this meadow and the house is all that's left for us to worry about. He rents the rest to a neighbour. You worried about your inheritance?'

'Chill out, Charles.'

Soulson laughed. 'There's no English left in you, is there?'

'What did you expect, after all this time?'

'Didn't expect anything.'

'I'm not fifteen any longer.'

'I suppose we're all guilty of living in the past.'

'Not all of us.'

'So why did you want to see me?' Soulson's aggrieved attitude was obvious.

'Because . . . you're my brother. And you got me out here.'

'Roy's given you everything, hasn't he?'

'Everything.'

'So this is a social visit.'

'Partly.'

'Then let's get the business out of the way.'

'What's Roy told you?'

Soulson recounted the reports Armitage had given him. As he spoke, they reached the river bank and continued their walk along it. 'Is there anything else?' he asked when he had finished.

'I think the IRA are involved.'

'Because of the bombing?'

'More than that. Washington believes that's how the drugs come into Europe. Belfast or Dublin, then the continent, up to Manchester and into the rest of England.'

'Long way round, isn't it?'

'No. These guys will do anything to safeguard their supplies. They're making Moss Side bullet-proof. It's the best warehouse for a distribution network into the UK.'

'So this shipment you're talking about is here?'

'Or Ireland. I think Belfast is pretty safe, too. But they'll need it here before long. That's if they're going to hit the streets with it.'

'Then why the bombing?'

325

'Don't know that yet. Unless they were after the Chinese. If the Colombians are supplying the IRA, you've got two organizations who've got a track record of smashing anyone who stands in their way.'

'I didn't think they'd get into drugs,' pondered Soulson.

'Who? The IRA?'

'Who else? Damn it, they should stick to their aim for a united Ireland. All this terrorism, it ruins their chances. And now drugs. God help us.'

'Is that what you believe in? One Ireland?'

'It's their country.'

'That's not a popular view over here.'

'It's my view. Not for publication. And it doesn't stop me doing my job. I'll still chase every IRA bomber I can. And put them in bloody jail.'

'I'd rather go after the Colombians than that lot. I mean, they're fanatics fighting a cause. You can't win against people like that.'

'I suppose you think we've lost in Manchester.'

'Isn't that why you called me?'

Soulson ignored the barbed question. 'Why do you think we're losing?'

'Didn't say you were losing. You've just lost control.'

'Why?'

'Because the politicking seems more important. From what I hear.' Marshall picked his words carefully. 'Policework is about catching the bad guys and protecting the public. Everything else should be secondary to that.'

'But I don't have the resources.'

'Nobody has. Anywhere in the world. But we just do our best. That's why we hold our own.'

'Well, you don't have to answer to a bunch of left-wing loonies like we do,' Soulson said defensively.

'I just said it's not what law and order's about. Don't let it get to you, Charles. Otherwise the day will come when you'll make the wrong decision for the wrong reason. Being a cop's easy. You're a good guy and they're the bad guys. Simplistic maybe, but that's how it is. Just make sure you don't get trapped in the middle.'

Soulson remembered how he had been trapped in the middle; all those years ago when Jimmy was in a mess and Christley had shielded him. That and those awful days on the moors had shaped his attitudes and beliefs. No room for sympathy and understanding after that baptism. 'Have you got a plan yet?' he said, changing the subject.

'Yeah.'

'And?'

'I think it would make your hair stand on end if you knew.'

'I'd like to know.'

'No, Charles. You've got to leave this to me.'

'What if I don't agree with it?'

'Tough. You asked for help. All I'm doing is what we do undercover in other parts of the world.' Marshall decided not to tell his brother about Ronane. This thing had to be work, not a personal revenge.

'Funny, isn't it?'

'What?'

'That we both end up as bobbies.'

'It's a mug's game.'

'So, some would argue, is being a bobby.'

Marshall laughed. 'Hasn't done you any harm. You look pretty fit. For a Chief Constable.'

'Fitter than you. Even if I am older.'

'Crap.'

'Remember how we used to race? When we were kids. I always used to let you win.'

'Like hell.'

'I did. I could still bloody beat you.'

'Try me.'

'OK. From here to the house.' The farmhouse was 200 yards away, all uphill.

'OK. When you're ready.'

'Set, go!' shouted Soulson and the two men raced up the hill, both middle aged and out of condition, their coats flapping behind them as they ran. They slipped as they ran, their feet sliding in the mud as they fought to keep their balance. By the time they were halfway up the hill they were both expended, their hearts pumping. But they were both men of resolve and neither was prepared to submit to the other. They pushed themselves upwards towards the house, the only sound their laboured breathing and the slap of their footwear in the mud. Then, neck and neck with no more than twenty yards to go, Soulson started to laugh. Marshall joined in, the two men now shaking with mirth as they completed their challenge.

'I got it,' shouted Marshall as he touched the barn wall.

'No. No chance,' yelled Soulson as he hit the wall with his

327

hand a second later.

'Damn it, Charles. You always cheated.'

'I didn't. That was a draw. Fair and square.'

'Like hell.' Then he started to laugh again and he put his arm round Soulson's shoulders. For once there was no embarrassment, no animosity. They laughed, at themselves, at the silly enjoyment of it all. They leant against the stone wall until they had caught their breath. 'Damn it, if you did beat me it's only because I'm run down with this cold.'

'I've got something to show you,' said Soulson. 'Come on. Follow me.' He stood away from the wall and went into the barn through the side door.

'Can't help but give orders,' muttered Marshall as he followed him.

It stood in the middle of the barn hidden under a dustsheet. Soulson pulled the sheet off. It was his old 1930 Brough Superior SS 100 motorcycle, gleaming and polished as new. After selling it to buy Jimmy's air ticket in 1965, Soulson had tracked it down and eventually bought it back when he could afford it. He spent a small fortune restoring it. It was important to him and would always remind him of Mary and their little home in Altrincham.

'Remember it?' he said, stepping back as Marshall approached the bike.

'Your old bike. Was it Dad's before that?'

'Good memory.'

'It was a wreck.'

'I had it rebuilt. I got my licence on that.'

'It's beautiful.'

'Had to keep something. Something to remind us of the old days.' Soulson decided not to tell his brother that the sale of the Brough had enabled him to fly Jimmy to America.

'Has he seen it?'

Soulson nodded. 'Yes. Did his courting on it, you know.'

'With Mum?'

'That's what he always says. *I met your Mum on that*,' he mimicked. 'Fancy a ride?'

'Now?'

'As good a time as any.'

'OK.'

Soulson wheeled the bike off its stand and pushed it towards the door. It was a heavy machine, far weightier than the Japanese power bikes of today. Marshall went in front of him and held the door open as his brother pushed the Brough out of the barn. Once on the path,

Soulson held the starter clutch with his left hand and attempted to kick start the bike. It took seven sharp attempts before the big bike roared into life.

'Doesn't that get you going?' said Soulson as he twisted the throttle and the deep sound of the high revving engine filled the valley. 'Like a bloody jet taking off.' He swung his leg over the bike and sat on the black leather, metal-sprung seat. 'Get on.'

Marshall climbed on to the pillion seat; he could feel the power of this huge machine rumbling underneath him. He clung to the side grips as his brother let out the throttle and slowly rattled up the driveway towards the gate. Soulson stopped the bike at the top of the path.

'Open the gate,' he said.

Marshall swung off the bike and opened the big gate, waited for the Brough to come through and clambered on to the pillion seat once again. 'What about helmets?' he shouted above the din.

'They're in the house. We'll be all right. There's no traffic up here.'

He twisted the throttle-lever, fed power to the 1000cc V twin-cylinder, four-stroke engine, and let out the clutch. The heavy machine surged forward, up the hill and along the country road. Marshall relaxed once he realized how good a rider his brother was. The Brough was soon up to 60 mph and cutting through the country lanes with ease. It was an exhilarating ride and the cold air froze their cheeks as they weaved along the road. Marshall coughed relentlessly as the ice-cold air forced itself through his nostrils and down his throat. After five miles Soulson pulled into a muddy lay-by and parked the bike. 'My cheeks are like ice,' he said, rubbing and pinching them as he climbed off the machine. 'Good fun, isn't it?'

'Yeah, great for my cold.' Marshall wondered if he'd passed his germs on to Soulson as they sped along the road.

'Sorry about that.'

'Hell, it's fun anyway. How often do you come out here?' asked Marshall as he swung off the Brough.

'Used to spend every Sunday visiting Dad and cleaning this beauty. It's a bit difficult now. I mean, with all this going on.'

'I'd forgotten how peaceful it was up here.'

'Make you want to come back?'

'No. My home's Texas now.'

'Very different.'

'Yeah. But it's home.' He remembered the last time he had seen it and that awful scene on his bed where Betty and the children lay. The shock hit him as he realized he could never live in that house again, not with those ghastly memories.

'You look as though you've seen a ghost,' said Soulson.

Marshall shook his head. This was not the time to tell his brother about the nightmare he had left behind. 'Just the cold.'

'You know why I'm so committed as a bobby?' Soulson suddenly wanted to unburden himself, to share long-forgotten memories with his brother. He was surprised by his sudden emotion, almost as though there were a feeling of great relief. Mary would have understood.

'No.'

Then Soulson told him about the awful time all those years ago on Saddleworth Moor, when the body of the dead child had strengthened his own resolve. As he spoke, Marshall listened quietly, wondered what it must have been like for Mary to be told all those gruesome details so long ago. 'That's why—' Soulson concluded '—I wanted you out of the way, off to America. I couldn't stand my own double standards.'

'Would you have handed me in?'

Soulson avoided a response. 'It was Mary who fought for you.' He looked at his watch. 'Time to get back.'

'You should've told me she was dead.'

'I shut you off, James. After that Moss Side episode. Just blanked my mind out.'

'Even so, you should've written to me.'

Soulson had no answer, so he shrugged and climbed back on the Brough. Marshall swung up behind him and they went back the way they had come, this time slower as most of the route was downhill and Soulson didn't want to lose control on the damp, leaf covered road.

The police Panda car flashed them to stop when they were only a mile from the farm. It had been travelling in the opposite direction and swung round to follow them.

'It's an offence to ride without a crash helmet,' said the young bobby as he approached them. 'I'd like to see your licence . . .' He recognized Soulson as the bearded man turned round to speak to him. 'Sir. Even if you are a Chief Constable.'

'Sorry, son. There was no traffic up here and we just wanted a short spin.'

'Helmet's for your own safety, sir.'

'You're right. It won't happen again.'

'I should book you, you know.'

'Just some harmless fun.'

'Is that what you'd say to an officer on your Force, sir?' He watched Soulson closely; the Chief Constable smiled and said nothing. 'What would you expect them to do in the same situation?'

'Either book me, or use his judgement and caution me not to do it again.'

The young policeman considered for a moment. 'I trust you're insured and have a licence?'

'Of course. They're in my house. In South Manchester. I can produce them at my nearest police station.'

'That's all right, sir. I know your family comes from these parts. I sometimes stop and see if your Dad's well. Anyway, you've enough problems down your way without me adding to them.' The policeman suddenly hardened again. 'But I'm still cautioning you. Don't do it again, or I'll do you next time.'

'It won't happen again.'

The policeman walked back to his Panda. 'That means you push the bike back to the farm, sir. Please don't ride it.' He climbed into the car and drove off.

'Long way to walk,' said Marshall.

'Not worth the risk. He'll be waiting round the corner.' Soulson thought for a minute. 'No he won't. He wouldn't want to be seen as petty in front of me. Come on.'

They climbed on the bike and gently freewheeled it round the corner. There was no sign of the Panda car, so Soulson gunned the throttle and they drifted down the hill to the farm. The gate was open and Soulson turned into the driveway and came to a stop outside the barn. 'Where'd you get the gun?' he asked.

'You don't miss much,' replied Marshall, stepping off the pillion seat.

'You've had it pressed up against me for most of the ride.'

'It stays with me, Charles.'

'I'm not against that. I don't want you naked in the lion's den.'

'But you're scared I might start blasting off.'

'Crossed my mind.'

'I'm not a kid any longer. I'm used to these things. More than you, or any of your people. I'm not a gangster in a movie, I'm a responsible DEA agent.'

'I'm sorry, James.'

'It's OK. Look, I'd better get back.'

'Roy told you about Mum.'

'Yeah. Too late to say sorry now.'

'Come and see the old man.'

'No. Maybe next time.'

'He's family.'

'So was Mary. You should've written.'

'She mattered more to you than Mum. I never realized that before. Nothing I can do about it now. That's in the past. But Dad's here.'

'No, not now,' Marshall insisted. There was no family; nothing could bring back what he had lost all those years ago. But he couldn't tell Soulson that, not until this thing had finished. Maybe then there could be family; if his elder brother could ever forgive him for whatever might happen next. 'Do you trust your officers?' he asked suddenly.

'Why?' Soulson was taken aback.

'Just watch your back.'

'Do you know something?'

'No. But when there's this amount of money at stake, it's easy to find those closest to you aren't always loyal. It's a common story, Charles. Greed corrupts loyalty.'

'In a way I'm sorry you came back.'

'Really?'

'It was easier not worrying about you. Be careful out there.'

'I always am.' Marshall reached forward and hugged his surprised brother. Soulson returned the embrace, then they separated. Their eyes locked; so much to say, so little said.

From the farmhouse, from a window in the kitchen, the old man watched the two men and wondered who it was his eldest son had embraced. He seemed familiar, but his memory played tricks and he soon turned back to the sink and finished brewing his pot of tea.

Midland Hotel
Manchester

'TEXAN TYCOON MARRIED ROYAL FLUSH. REMEMBER THE ALAMO. ALL IS NOT AS IT SEEMS. PILOT.'

That was all the note said. It had been written out by the hotel telephone operator, Melanie, and pushed under the door. The time of the call was listed at 12.32 p.m. and the caller had left no name or telephone number.

Marshall dialled zero and asked for Melanie. There was nothing she could add, except maybe the call had been long distance. 'You know how it is sometimes,' she said. 'There's a slight echo to your voice.' He asked her if the caller had been a man or woman, and whether he had an accent. 'A man,' she replied. 'Could've been an American. Like you, only not as strong.'

He thanked her and went back to the note. Royal Flush was the girl in Mexico City; the one Ronane had shot dead in El Paso. The Texan was also in Mexico City, but Marshall had not seen him in El Paso. That didn't mean he hadn't been there. And could be they were married. She was an ugly cow and he couldn't see the Texan with her, but then if she had been Cali, it would have helped him higher up the ladder. But why was he a tycoon? Marshall never saw him in San Antonio. Again, that didn't mean he wasn't there. And who the hell was Pilot? Maybe the girl had misheard that. He sat down and went through, in his mind, the events of the last few months. The key was in there somewhere. Only a few people in Washington, and Ronane, knew about the Texan and the Royal Flush.

The phone rang and he picked it up.

'We're ready to collect, Mr Marshall,' said Freddy the Duck.

'But are you ready to play the game like I said?'

'We've proved our credentials. Time for you to show yours.'

'Where?'

'Have you eaten lunch?'

'No.' The phone clicked off in his hand. Marshall looked at his watch; it was after three. He put the receiver down and it rang again. 'Yeah,' he said as he answered it.

'You're a difficult person to get hold of,' she said, a giggle in her voice.

'I'm a popular, fun loving person,' he replied.

'Tonight?'

'Don't tempt me.'

'I've booked a room at the Midland.'

'You're a naughty girl.'

'Bye.'

He put down the phone. He felt warm inside; she had that effect on him. He knew it was risky, but he wasn't prepared to do without her. Energy levels or not, he didn't want to disappoint her tonight. He put on his coat, made up a small parcel, and went out for a late lunch.

The restaurant was full of Chinese, but they were expecting him and put him at a table near the back and well away from the rest. As he sat, he felt the waiter expertly frisk him; the action was so

333

smooth that none of the other diners would have noticed. A small group sat separate from the rest; he could tell they were foot-soldiers. Marshall knew the waiter had searched for a microphone rather than a weapon; he had felt the Glock and ignored it. Marshall ordered his meal as Freddy Wong joined him.

'Your DEA credentials check out, Mr Marshall,' said Wong.

'You reach into high places.'

Wong dismissed the comment with a shrug. 'I also believe you're not out to entrap us.'

'Why?'

'Because you've no link with the police in this country and the DEA are well known for not stepping outside their own jurisdiction.'

'So we've got a deal?'

'Patience, Mr Marshall. This isn't the type of thing one rushes into. Let's just say we're interested in importing . . . your emeralds.'

'So what's next?'

'You said you had a small present for us.'

Marshall put the small briefcase he had brought with him on the table. 'I presume you're not going to open it here.'

Wong smiled, then held his hand up and signalled a waiter over. 'Mr Marshall would like us to keep his briefcase for safe-keeping,' he said to the waiter, who picked it up and went through into the kitchen. 'Four, was it, we agreed?'

'Three kilos.'

'I recall you saying four.'

'I said three or four. That's a street value of nearly two hundred grand. Sterling, for Christ's sake.'

'I'm disappointed, as will be my colleagues. Four emeralds would have been more to our taste.'

'Three or four. That's still a substantial amount to give away. For free. I think that shows commitment, Mr Wong.'

'Please call me Freddy.'

'Freddy. Jimmy. But it also shows that if we can afford to give that much away, there's a lot more coming through.'

'I agree.'

'So what do you suggest next?'

'We need to see more.'

'Only when there's a network in place.'

'We already have that.'

'Only for horse. Emeralds are a different market.'

'But related. We just switch some of our dealers.'

'I need to know where. And how. That's necessary before we

release any more. Giving a few kilos away is different from maybe losing hundreds.'

'All right. In the meantime I will distribute the emeralds you kindly gave us. I will show you how we do it.'

'Cheaper than our competition.'

'Just as we agreed, Jimmy. He'll know we mean business.'

The food arrived and the waiter put it on the table. 'You know I'm armed, don't you?' stated Marshall.

'But you don't mean us harm. Anyway, I'm sure you've looked round the room and seen some of our men. Any sudden movements would rather excite them. Tell me, why did you visit Moss Side the other night?'

'Just for some entertainment. Man's got to live.'

'We can supply you with all the entertainment you need. I suggest, in future, you leave Moss Side to us. We wouldn't like you catching something, would we, Jimmy?'

43 Danzic Avenue
Levenshulme
Manchester

It was a grubby flat; obviously not swept or dusted for some considerable time, with pots and pans overflowing the sink and cigarette stubs piled high in the ashtrays.

The two policemen who had been called to the scene had to break down the door to get in. Responding to a complaint from irate neighbours about the high level of noise, the police had knocked on the door for nearly ten minutes before they decided to force an entry.

It was obvious what had happened. The two men in the flat, one substantially older than the other, were naked. Naked, that is, apart from the high heels and suspenders the younger one wore. They were both flaked out on the bed, their limbs entwined as they lay unconscious to the world. The music, a Lenny Kravitz number, blared from the tape-deck beside the bed. On the table there was evidence of cocaine, four lines of white powder still waiting to be snorted. The scattered white dust showed the men had already gorged themselves on the drug.

'They're alive,' said one of the police officers as he felt their pulses.

'Just fucked and doped out,' replied the other, switching off

335

the tape-deck. 'Better call in.'

'Hold it,' warned the first bobby as he leant over the bed and picked up a wallet. He took out a photograph which had half popped out and passed it over to his colleague. 'Recognize anyone?'

The second policeman took the photo and examined it, then whistled through his teeth. He held the photo next to the older man's face on the bed, then stepped back. 'Now what?'

'I suppose we should just call the station.'

'No. Let someone else take the decision. This could rebound on us.' He crossed to the door with its broken lock and swung it open. There were three neighbours standing in the corridor. 'It's all right now. Just someone passed out after drinking too much and forgetting to switch the music off.'

'Bit early for drinking,' said one of them. 'It's only six.'

'Is he all right?' asked another.

'No problem. Best thing you can do is go back to your flats. And thanks for your help.' He closed the door, went to the phone and dialled a number. 'Hello. Stretford . . . Chief Superintendent Armitage, please.' He looked at his colleague, whose surprise was obvious in his face. 'I'm going to the top with this one.' Then he spoke into the receiver. 'Mr Armitage, please . . . Constable Walmer, F Division, Uniform branch . . . I know, but it's important I speak to him . . . No, I can't speak to anyone else . . .' There was a considerable pause while Walmer waited to be put through. 'Hello, Chief Superintendent Armitage . . . It is important, sir, but I can't talk about it on the phone . . . I'm at 43 Danzic Avenue in Levenshulme, Flat 9. It's an old converted house, mostly students, sir . . . I think you should come down here . . . PC Walmer, sir, and I haven't reported back to the station yet. You'll see why when you get here . . . No, sir, it's no wild goose chase.' He put down the phone.

'I would've rung the station,' said the other policeman.

'He's told me to do that now and say that there's no real problem.'

'What about these two?'

'See if you can find some coffee. Then we'll wake them up.'

'Shit on the end, you see that? Does that mean he's the bloke of the two?'

'You're disgusting you are. Go on, make the coffee.'

The two naked men, still groggy under the influence, were wrapped in coats when Armitage arrived fifteen minutes later. He entered the room and Walmer introduced himself before showing him the two men and the cocaine on the table. 'They've also been drinking heavily, sir. Gin. There's a bottle by the bed.'

'So? Why call me? It's a routine bust.'

Walmer showed Armitage the photograph and the older man's driving licence. 'In view of who it is, sir, I just thought you might want us to handle it differently.'

Armitage whistled. 'Who else knows about this?'

'Only the three of us.'

'What about the neighbours?'

'I told them they'd been drinking heavily, that's all.'

'Why do you think I should deal with this any different than normal?'

'Not saying you should, sir. Except we've had enough bad press on the Force.'

'Are you two safe?'

'All we did was find some drunks having a private party, sir. Not worth an arrest.'

'Have you called in?'

'Yes, like you said. That's what I told the desk. And that we were staying here till they'd sobered up a bit.'

Armitage walked over to the table, knelt down and blew the white powder away. 'Better leave it as you found it, then,' he said. 'When he's sobered up, tell him to go home to his wife. Make sure he knows how lucky he was.'

'Does he know you, sir?'

'I don't think so. And he's not going to remember in that state.'

Armitage drove back to Stretford and went directly to Soulson.

'You're taking a risk, Roy,' said Soulson after Armitage had run through his report.

'Worth the risk, isn't it, Chief?'

'Maybe. We'll see.'

When Armitage left, he pondered the situation. What was it Jimmy had said, *too much politics and not enough policing*. Well, his younger brother didn't have to sit at this desk fielding all those political hand grenades. Wipe out the politicians and there would be plenty of time, and resources, for policing. He picked up the phone and called her. 'I think I'd like a private meeting as soon as possible,' he said.

Louise Spencer walked into his office an hour later. 'It must be important for you to call me into your inner sanctum,' she said loftily.

'Do you know where your husband is?' came the harsh reply.

'Probably at work. Why?'

'Because we've just found him naked in bed with another man. They were both drinking heavily . . . and taking cocaine.'

The colour drained from her face, she gasped and staggered back. Then she swung round quickly and sat down in the chair opposite Soulson's desk. He felt no sympathy; as far as he was concerned she got all she deserved.

He waited for her to collect herself. 'Were you aware of his habits?' he asked finally.

'You bastard,' she cursed him.

'Why? For helping you?'

'You set him up.'

'Oh yes,' came his sarcastic reply. 'We drugged him up, took his clothes off and put him in bed with another poofter.' He saw that hurt so he pushed his point home. 'The other man, a twenty-year-old student, was wearing suspenders and high heels. Apparently your husband was the male in the relationship.'

She knew what he was doing and her face was screwed up with hatred. 'Where is he now? In some police station, I suppose.'

'No. We let him go.'

'We?'

'The police officers who discovered him. They recognized him from this photo and his driving licence.' Soulson slid the picture and licence across his desk to Spencer, who snapped them up with only a cursory glance and put them in her handbag. 'They stayed with him while he sobered up. He may even be home by the time you get there.'

'You didn't let him off because of any finer feelings. Not you.'

'Nothing to do with me. It was the officers themselves. Let's just say they always protect their own. With you in charge of the Police Committee, they see you as one of them.'

'I bet. You'll want your pound of flesh. Won't you, Charles Soulson?'

He shrugged. There was no point in stating the obvious. 'Just ask him to behave in a more civilized manner in future. Next time, things might not turn out as well.'

'I do what I do because I believe in it. I still think you're a bad Chief Constable. That's why I do it.'

'You're entitled to your view.'

'Because you never see the other side. There's little that's human about you. You're just a machine. And you live by the book. If you want to be a good Chief Constable, then you should see the other side. There's a lot of poverty out there, especially in Moss Side. A lot of ordinary hard-working people live there; they're not all drug addicts and pushers. Only you don't see the difference. All you see is the law. And that has to be followed without a damn for human consequence.'

'I didn't turn Moss Side into a drug dealer's paradise.'

'Maybe you didn't. But neither did the thousands of people who live there and try to lead ordinary lives.'

'They're not the ones I'm after.'

'But they're the ones who suffer. You've closed clubs down, objected to every licensing application, even shut youth clubs because you've said there were drugs there. You've pushed kids out on the streets and their parents behind closed doors. You've policed this city with a truncheon, not with understanding. To you it's either right or wrong, black or white. You never look for the grey. Yet that's where most of us live. No point bible thumping when people are frightened to go on the streets where they live. That's why I don't like you, Soulson. Because you do it all by the book. Because you don't care about the public, only the police.'

'Why don't you go back to your husband?' he said dismissively.

'He, like everyone else, has his faults. We should learn to live with those. What happened to you, that made it impossible for you to love, to understand? What made you so fucking perfect? Somewhere, sometime, someone must have really hurt you.' She rose from her chair, turned round and left the room.

He watched the door slam behind her.

As much as he disliked her, he knew there was some truth in what she said. Somewhere along the way he'd lost his way. And he didn't know how to get back.

The Blue Lagoon Club
Fallowfield
Manchester

'Want to score?' the Chinaman asked Dale Richardson.

Richardson grinned. This was his territory. This is where he earned his living. He was used to the odd punter trying to sell drugs on, always at an inflated price. Sometimes they even bought it from him and tried to turn a higher price when they were sure he wasn't around. 'What you got?' he said.

'Snow.'

'How much?'

'How much you want?'

'Give me a kilo,' Richardson joked.

'If you want to push for us, fine.'

'Don't fuck with me.' Richardson's mood suddenly hardened.

'Not me,' said the Chinaman. 'I seen you around here a lot. I can give you a kilo for fifteen thousand. Wholesale.'

Richardson relaxed. The guy didn't know what he was talking about. 'Bullshit. Nobody gets wholesale for less than thirty grand.'

'I know that. And I know you're the dealer round here. That's my price.'

'Show me.'

'OK.' The Chinaman slid further into the corner where he couldn't be seen. He pulled a large, clear plastic packet from his coat. Richardson reached out and put his hand inside the packet, coated the tip of his index finger with the substance and licked it. It tasted and felt like cocaine.

'Where'd you get this?'

'From my people. There's a lot more where this came from.'

'For fifteen grand?'

'We're not greedy.' The Chinaman put the packet back in his pocket.

'You can get a lot more.'

'Except we want everyone to use our stuff.'

'Why should I sell your stuff and make less money?'

'You don't make less. You still get the same mark-up. We take the hit. And the punters come to you because it's still cheaper than anyone else's.'

'You asking for trouble, boy.' Richardson's tone was suddenly threatening. 'Even if you got the stuff, this territory belongs to someone else. They not going to let you take over that easy.'

'Look over there, by the bar.' The Chinaman indicated a corner table where three of his countrymen sat. 'Don't get any ideas. They're armed. And as good as any fuckers your suppliers can produce. So don't come that tough guy stuff with me.' He pushed past Richardson, then swung round. 'Understand one thing. We're coming into this game. At the prices we say. If you're stupid enough to take anyone else's substance, that's up to you. But somebody will be flooding this club with cheaper shit. So you better choose sides.' He smiled at Richardson. 'Otherwise piss off and get a hotdog stand outside Old Trafford. Because that's all you'll be selling from now on.'

Richardson watched the Chinaman walk out with his friends. He went to the payphone and dialled. 'I need to speak to Stash,' he said when the phone was answered. While he waited, he knew there was no choice for him. He'd seen Paras turn on other dealers. He didn't want his face fish-hooked. No, he was going to report in and hope that the Nilus gang would look after him.

Maxwell received six similar calls that night from various parts of the city. A group of Chinese had a big load of cocaine and they were trying to unload it in Manchester. At a price considerably cheaper than the Moss Side supply. The only good news was that one of the Chinese had been picked up by the police and arrested for pushing.

Maxwell called Cohn Bourne. 'It's that sodding Yank Shaeron went to see.'

'Maybe. Let's find out for certain.'

The two men made their plans before going to Abdul Paras. Paras exploded as they knew he would and threatened to kill every Chinese on sight. When he eventually calmed down, Bourne took him through the plan he and Maxwell had conceived. Paras saw the logic and agreed. The only thing he insisted on was that he wanted to deal personally with the man who had originated this whole mess.

'Fine,' said Bourne. 'But only after we've found out what we want.'

Midland Hotel
Manchester

He was restless; waiting for her, knowing she was nearby.

The phone rang and Marshall snapped it off its stand. 'Yeah.'

'How did your meeting with the Chief go?' asked Armitage.

'Fine.' He hid his disappointment that it wasn't Jill. 'Strange, seeing him after all these years.'

'Anything I should know about?'

'No. It was more personal than business.'

'Does he know your plans?'

'Nobody does.'

'Isn't it time you told someone?'

'Has Charles asked you to ring?'

'No. But if something goes wrong, who's going to bail you out?'

'My problem, Roy. The way I said it would be. Was there anything else?'

'No. Just keeping in touch. You sound terrible.'

'Bloody cold. It's getting worse.'

'Well, make sure you get a good night's sleep. Sweat it off.'

Marshall put down the phone. He didn't want it to ring again, not unless it was her. Five minutes passed before there was a knock on the door and he opened it.

It was the room service waiter with a single rose. 'I was given this for you,' he said.

'Who?'

'Room 354,' the waiter smirked.

Marshall grinned, grabbed his key and was about to leave the room when he remembered his weapons. He picked up the Glock and slipped it into his overcoat. Then he took the holdall which contained the Heckler and Koch HK-94 and left the room with it.

He heard her laugh through the door when he knocked.

'You took your time getting here,' she said. 'Don't you want any fun and games?'

'How long have you been here?'

'About an hour.'

'So why not ring me?'

'I wanted to get ready.' She swung her arms round him and kissed him. 'Do I smell nice?'

'Fresh. And clean.'

'For you, big man.'

He dumped the bag and coat on the floor and returned her embrace.

'Let's go to bed,' she said, then stood back. 'Are you up to it?'

He sniffed. 'I'll make sure I'm up to it.'

He was up to it, but the demons returned. He closed his mind to them; tried not to think about others she dressed for, wore make up for, smelt fresh for.

'I ordered some champagne,' she said across his thoughts.

'Aren't we meant to drink it before we go to bed?'

She giggled and he loved the warmth of it. 'I'll open it now,' she warbled as she jumped out of bed and picked up the bottle.

He watched her, saw the firmness of her body as it moved around the room.

'I've booked the room for two nights,' she said. 'You'd better help me, because these prices are more than a simple working girl can afford.'

'We'll sort it out.'

'How's work going?'

'OK.'

'Anything I can help with?'

'No.' Then he remembered the note and how he had decided to ask her help in deciphering it. 'Well, there's one thing.'

'What's that?'

'It can wait.'

'No, tell me now, while I'm filling the glasses.'

'I got a note today. A phone message the telephone operator took.' He leant over and took the sheet of paper from his discarded jacket pocket. He spread the note on the sheet and reread it as she joined him in bed with two champagne-filled glasses. She spilled some on the note and he wiped it, smearing some of the writing.

'Sorry,' she apologized.

'No problem.' He took his glass and held it next to hers. 'I don't want to be on top of you, don't want to be under you, just want to be inside you.' He tipped his glass and poured some of his champagne into hers. Then they both drank.

'This it?' she said, picking up the note.

'Yeah.' He looked over her shoulder as she read it. 'You're in the Intelligence Unit. Make anything of that?'

'Who's Pilat?'

'Pilot.'

'It says Pilat,' she insisted.

'The drink smeared that.'

'Like Pontius Pilate.'

Marshall sucked in breath sharply. 'Maybe it was that. Maybe she mistook it for Pilate.'

'Who do you know who's washing his hands over you?'

'Somebody in Washington. Trying to help. Someone who feels guilty.'

'Who else would know about all this stuff?'

'Only one person.'

'Who?'

'Ronane.' *It couldn't be. Not Ronane.* He remembered he'd once called Ronane by that name. It had been a joke between them, all that time ago in Washington. 'Jesus Christ!'

'Can't be. I mean—'

'The only person who knew all those things was Ronane. He couldn't have told anyone else. He was in too much pain before he died.'

'Go on,' she prodded him.

'Jesus Christ!' he exclaimed again. 'This fucking cold's muddling my mind.'

'What is it?'

'I just don't believe—' He quickly collected himself, then told her about the poker game, the Texan and the ugly woman. He took her through the events in El Paso that led to San Antonio. She knew what happened there.

'Why tycoon?'

'It's a name. Ty Koons. Big enforcer for the Calis. That was the Texan. Shit, I thought he was dead. We all did. So that was him. Damn it, I stood right in front of him. Ty Koons, as close as you are.'

'You can't be sure.'

'Only Ronane and me knew the guy as the Texan. Our nickname for him. We coded everyone like that.'

'The Irish and the Alamo?'

'Don't know. Except we both believed the IRA were involved in this shipment. If Koons was organizing it, then he could be over here.' Marshall suddenly sat back and let out a deep breath. 'Shit.'

'What?'

'He was after revenge. He thought I killed his wife, so he came after my partner. Jesus! He was the guy in San Antonio.'

'What about Ronane?'

'He's got to be alive. Maybe crippled, but alive. Dear God, that's a cruel and dirty game.' He suddenly hated Washington for their treachery; there was no need after all these years of service.

'They wanted you over here, risking you because you believed you were avenging Ronane.'

'I was set up. Except Ronane's got me this message. He's trying to help. He's no Pontius Pilate. God, he must feel awful, knowing what happened to Betty and the kids. Poor Ronane.'

'*All is not as it seems.* What's that?'

'Just warning me that I'm on my own. Don't trust Washington, don't trust anybody.'

'That doesn't include me, does it?'

'No. You're the only one.'

She reached over and stroked the curls on the back of his head. He moved his head gently, enjoyed it for a moment, let it relax him. But his mind was full of compassion and dread for Ronane, for what he may have become.

'You could walk away,' she broke into his thoughts. 'Just pack your bags and go home. Go and find Ronane.'

344

'I'm in too deep now. Like a snake that's got hold of its prey. My jaws won't let go. All I can do is swallow.'

'Nobody would blame you.'

'I would. And so would Ronane. Damn it, he must hate himself. So damn alone, sitting wherever he is, believing he's thrown me into the lion's den.'

'You really love him, don't you?'

The big man nodded. 'Apart from you, he's the nearest I've got to family.'

'Are you going to tell me what your plans are?'

'No. The less you know, the less danger you're in.'

She put her glass down and hugged him with both arms. 'Let's go to sleep. I want to feel your arms round me again.'

He put his drink down, switched off the side light and wrapped himself round her. It wasn't long before they were aroused by the closeness of their naked bodies.

It was a gentle lovemaking this time, measured and considerate in its slow movement, two bodies as one in a floating vacuum of shared sensuality. There were no new positions, no gimmicks of eroticism. Just him on top of her, glued together with heat and sweat and fifteen minutes of love before it was over and they finally rolled apart.

They said nothing for quite some time.

'Jealousy's a terrible thing,' he said eventually.

'Don't start again.'

'It fucks up your mind. I'm in so deep, so close to the heart of this thing. Then, when I should be concentrating on what to do next, my emotions take over. All I see is my jealousy, my weakness over you. I'm scared I'll be like that one day when someone comes after me and I won't recognize the danger.'

'Then don't do it. Learn to believe.'

'Wish it were that easy.'

'We're all what we are, big man.'

'Meaning?'

'Hold back. It wasn't meant—'

'You were trying to tell me something?'

'I wasn't,' she protested. She could never tell him how she wanted her freedom to love him, yet lead her own life. She knew he could never cope with that. 'You expect too much of me. I love you. Isn't that all that matters? To have love?'

'Not that easy.'

'Why not? It's not my fault you imagine me with other men.

It's like some sort of fantasy, like it turns you on.'

'Shit to that.' He sat up in the bed.

'It is. You make yourself old.' She regretted it as she said it.

'Nice one, Jill.'

'What do you expect?' As much as she regretted her words, it was difficult to stop now. 'He was the same. Always going on about my age.'

'Who?'

'My bloody stepfather. Who do you think?'

'Why bring that up?'

'Why not? You will.' She moved to the end of the bed, away from his physical contact. 'What're you going to do?' she defied him. 'Beat me like he did?'

'You can't hide behind him for ever.'

'That's crap.'

'Is it? I don't think so. It's the way you are.'

'Maybe I want more than you can offer.' She saw that stung him, but she couldn't stop herself. She knew he was right, that she always rebelled when someone got close. She couldn't tell him he wasn't the only one, as much as she wanted to hit out at him. None of the others had mattered as much, but she realized he didn't matter enough. 'Life isn't a John Wayne movie, you know. For all that you think.'

'What's that supposed to mean?'

'Stop frustrating me,' she screamed. 'You know what I fucking mean.' She resented him for his cool, for making her appear stupid and out of control. She lashed out at him and he easily protected himself from her frail blows. 'Don't make fun of me. Don't think I'm nothing.'

He waited for her to quiet, felt her wrap the sheet round herself as she turned away from him.

'That really gets to me,' he complained.

'What?' came the surly reply.

'Just being able to turn over and go to sleep after a row.'

'No point in staying awake. All we ever do is go on shouting.'

They didn't say good night after that. Marshall lay still, angry with himself for letting the emotion cloud his instincts. He fought to bring himself under control, willing his powers of concentration to focus on the task at hand. He conjured up Ronane's face, tried to imagine the pain he must have endured. It took him half an hour to push his thoughts away from the still, almost lifeless form lying next to him.

For once Marshall didn't sleep. He was fitful through the night, his mind full of Ronane and the terrible things he must have suffered. It dawned on him that his partner, under torture, must have told them where Marshall lived, possibly about the letter from Manchester. That meant they could know about Jill and who she worked for. He felt no anger for he knew each man had his breaking point; a threshold beyond which you revealed your soul. But that was nothing compared to the anguish that Ronane now suffered, knowing he had put his partner in great danger and possibly brought about the death of his own family.

Now it was about revenge. And that is what he would exact from those who had irreparably wounded Ronane.

Then he cursed her iciness and wished there could be a love between them that wasn't engulfed in rancour and jealousy. He slid over to her and put his arm round her.

She didn't move.

He couldn't tell if she was asleep or not.

He stayed as still as she was.

Jill couldn't sleep either. She hated his jealousy. It constrained her, took away her independence. Why was it always like this? Why did she come to hate all those who tried to change her from what she was instead of letting her be herself?

The two figures lay side by side and waited for the morning to come and break the lie.

Marshall's room was a mess.

They had come looking for him during the night, broken into his room with the intent of hurting him. When they found he was out they had ransacked his drawers, ripped the sheets and his clothes.

The room service waiter had noticed Marshall's door ajar at four in the morning. When he checked the room, and saw the state it was in, he took the lift to the third floor and knocked on Room 354.

'I need to see Mr Marshall,' he said to a drowsy Jill when she eventually answered the door.

Marshall stepped out from behind the door. 'What's up?' When the waiter told him, he slipped into his clothes and went to his room. He checked it over, but the only thing he took was the cough medicine.

'Want me to call security?' asked the waiter.

'Not till the morning. They've taken nothing, just made a mess,' replied Marshall. 'I'm going back to bed.'

He returned to Jill's room, swigging from the medicine bottle and told her what he had found.

'Who?' she asked.

'Chinese. Or Moss Side. I don't know. At least they don't know I'm up here with you. I'm going back to sleep.'

'Doesn't anything get to you, big man?'

'Yeah. You.' He put his arms round her and they both drifted back to sleep.

He called security the next morning and told them he had been out all night and returned to find his room vandalized. He added that nothing was missing and could they please find him a new room. And yes, he would expect a discount in view of their lax security.

Jill had gone to work and he was established in his new room when the phone rang. It was Shaeron.

'I called last night,' she said. 'You weren't in.'

He knew she was lying, otherwise the switchboard would have told him that someone had called. He had already arranged with them to monitor all his calls, even if they didn't leave a message. So it was Paras, more probably some of his men, who had broken into his room. 'I was out for the night,' he replied.

'Hope she was worth it. You could've seen me.'

'There you go. Did you talk to anyone about my proposition?'

'I got someone who could be interested. He wants to meet you.'

'Bring him to the hotel.'

'He wants you to come here. My place.'

Marshall paused, then, 'OK. This afternoon.'

'He said he wants you to bring some stuff.'

'Why?'

'To prove you're genuine.'

'I'll see you about three thirty.'

Marshall put down the phone and broke into a coughing fit. The cold worried him; he knew he would need all his strength if they came against him. He decided to rest on the bed until it was time to go. He dialled room service and ordered beef sandwiches. It was important to build his energy.

Did you feed a cold and starve a fever? Or was it starve a cold and feed a fever? He never could remember. Anyway, he felt hungry and the sandwiches would at least take away the gnawing sensation in the pit of his stomach. Marshall climbed onto the bed, feeling extremely sorry for himself, closed his eyes and drifted into sleep.

Giulio's Terrazza Restaurant
Nicholas Street
Manchester

They sat at the window table watching the group of young girls, local office workers, rush past to some secret place where excitement would be crammed into the one-hour lunchbreak that broke the monotony of their work-day.

Tessa laughed as the Italian waiter placed her spaghetti bolognaise in front of her.

'You wanna some black pepper?' he asked.

'No, thanks,' she said and continued to giggle as the waiter withdrew.

'What's so funny?' Jill asked. Giulio's Terrazza in Nicholas Street was a favourite of theirs and they met at least once a month to eat, sometimes in the evening before going out to a club, often during a lunchbreak.

'Remember how we used to sneak out from school and go to those lunchtime discos.'

'We were lucky we never got caught,' Jill acknowledged as she cut into the calves' liver in front of her.

'My dad would have killed me,' Tessa continued. She sensed her friend's unease; had known her for too long not to catch Jill's change of moods. 'We were really lucky. Nobody ever rang home to see if we felt better. I'm just glad that we never needed sick notes for afternoons off.'

'What did he say that time you got hurt?'

'I'd forgotten that. Bastards,' she cursed. She was fifteen at the time, a schoolgirl who kept her skimpy party clothes and high heels in a second school satchel so that her father would never find them. She'd been dancing at one of the local lunchtime discos in Manchester, having skipped out from games classes, when a group of young men, teenagers in jeans and leather jackets, had surrounded her and a girlfriend as they danced. The girls had been frightened, but kept dancing as the men jostled them. One of them, the leader, had grabbed at Tessa and she pulled away, cheekily telling him to keep his hands to himself and that he was nothing but a yob. Her manner incensed him and he started to hit her across the face and chest, cutting her lip as he pummelled her. The others formed a defensive ring round the two girls so that no-one could help them.

It was an ugly scene and Tessa was soon knocked to the floor. Before she could get up, the teenager kicked her twice in the stomach with his Doc Martins before the thugs ran away. When she got home she told Soulson that she had been attacked by some men on her way home from school. She lived in fear for weeks, frightened that the truth about her injuries would emerge. But she was in luck; no-one reported the incident at the disco and things eventually returned to normal. From that moment, Tessa had finally become her father's daughter and vowed never to lie or be compromised again.

'If you saw them again you could run them in.'

'I did once.'

'You never.'

'Pulled him for speeding. In a yellow Mini. Rusty old banger. Didn't realize who he was till he got out.'

'Which one?'

'The one who hit me.'

'Did you book him?'

'No. He didn't recognize me. Wouldn't expect him to, would you? Just another silly schoolgirl.'

'You should've had him.'

'He scared me. Made me feel I was fifteen again. Would you believe it? One look at him, tatty little yobbo in an old Mini, and I wasn't wearing a bobby's uniform any longer, just a bloody gym slip.'

'You let him go?' Jill was amazed.

'With a weak little warning about driving safely and looking out for others.'

'He was probably more scared than you.'

'He probably was.'

They ate in silence for a while before Jill spoke. 'Do you know why your Dad pulled the Intelligence Unit off the Moss Side thing?'

'No.'

'Decision came from the top.'

'Doesn't mean he knew anything about it.' Tessa was suddenly defensive. It had always been their policy never to compromise themselves over their police duties; both had secrets best kept from the other. 'Why do you want to know?'

'It just seemed strange. Whip us off it, then stick us back on. Everyone feels we should also be giving the Chinese villains a hard time, but it's all aimed at the blacks.'

'We never discuss it. All I get is through the grapevine.' Tessa leant closer to Jill. 'What's the matter with you?'

'Nothing.'

'Like hell. You've been jumpy ever since I got here. What's so important about Moss Side?'

'Nothing to do with that.'

'Then what is it?'

'I just feel everything's getting on top of me.'

'Since when?'

'Since he arrived.'

'Who?'

'My American.'

'He's here?' Tessa was surprised. 'When?'

'Few days ago. I didn't tell you, but I met him again when I went on holiday over there.'

'And he followed you over?'

'You could say that.'

'I thought you loved him.'

'I do. But you know what I'm like, Tessa. I can't stand being trapped. He's the only guy who ever got through to me. I love being with him. But I miss my freedom. I miss having my own space. And, much as I . . . it's all getting too heavy.'

'I don't understand you, Jill. If you love him?'

'I don't want to be tied down.'

'Because he's older?'

'Maybe.' She suddenly smiled. 'He's not that old. Beats any of the young guys I've been with. Knocks them into a hat, with their posey clothes and their "I'm going to give you a good time",' she mimicked. 'The other night this guy ran his hand over my knee and said, "What's a joint like this doing in a girl like you?"' They both laughed. 'Cheeky sod.' Then she was suddenly serious. 'Trouble is I liked it. I mean, they're fun, make me feel good. It doesn't mean too much, even when I go to bed with them. Don't look so shocked. It's the way I am. I like my work. I like my independence. I'm not ready to settle down. Not yet, Tessa. But it's what he expects.'

'You can't blame him.'

'I know. He's lovely, really. I mean, I respect him, find him sexy, he understands what my work means to me.'

'Isn't that enough?'

'Can't be. Otherwise I wouldn't feel like this. Damn. I need him and yet it's the last thing I need at the moment.'

'What're you going to do?'

'I don't know. And it's not just that.'

'What?'

'His life. It's full of danger.'

'What sort of danger?'

Jill shrugged. 'Now's not the time to talk about it. Except that I don't know if I can go on facing it. Maybe it'll sort itself. Maybe it'll reach its own conclusion.'

Moss Side
Manchester

Marshall drove the hired blue Vauxhall into Moss Side half an hour earlier than he was expected. He first noticed his tail when he swung on to Princess Parkway. It was a green Vauxhall, similar to his own; the driver was black, but unrecognizable at that distance. He slowed to let him catch up, but the green car matched his pace and the distance between them remained the same. By then it was too late to intercept the follower as Marshall turned into the road where Shaeron lived. He drew up to the pavement, noticed the Vauxhall stop at the corner in his rear-view mirror, then climbed out and locked the car. He checked the boot was secure, the HK-94 was hidden there, and crossed to the house.

One of the working girls called to him from across the street and he waved back before he pushed through the front door and climbed the stairs. He knocked at Shaeron's door and waited.

'You're early,' she said, alarm in her eyes. She was naked and held a sheet round her ample body. The fishy smell of stale sex and hash smoke filled the room.

'Makes no difference, does it?' he said, pushing past her into the room. He stopped when he saw Paras hurriedly getting out of bed, dragging his purple satin trousers on furiously. 'Sorry, didn't know you had company,' he apologized.

'I never said you could come in,' she hissed at him.

'I can wait outside,' he said.

Shaeron looked helplessly at Paras. She knew he was angry and that he would beat her when they were alone. 'Not my fucking fault,' she screamed across at him.

Paras pulled on a gold shirt and came round from behind the bed. 'Get your fucking clothes on,' he ordered her.

'I told him three—'

Paras ripped the sheet from her, spinning her round till she fell on the bed, her floppy body spreading out under her. 'Get

352

fucking dressed. Then fuck off on the street. Go on,' he bellowed. She whimpered as she scrambled off the bed and started to dress. Paras ignored her and turned to Marshall. 'You the fucker who's been selling cheap shit on my streets?' he demanded.

'I haven't sold anything. I'm here to do a deal. If you're the man I'm meant to meet.' He turned to Shaeron. 'Is he the guy?'

'Fuck her. You speak to me, shithead.'

'This is not the way to cement a business relationship.'

Paras took a deep breath as he collected himself. Bourne had told him to take it easy and find out what Marshall had to offer. *Where the fuck were they?* 'OK, OK. Shit, man, you startled me, bursting in here like that. You meant to be here at three thirty.'

'I said I'm sorry.'

'You got the fucking stuff with you?'

'We need to talk first. About whether you can distribute it.'

''Course I can fucking distribute,' Paras bellowed. Then he swung round to Shaeron. 'Are you dressed yet? Go on, fuck off.' She rushed past him towards the door and he kicked her with his foot as she shot past, sending her reeling. She scrambled up and squeezed out of the room, still half undressed, carrying the remainder of her clothes in her arms. Paras kicked the door shut behind her. 'Fucking slut,' he yelled after her. Then he swung round to Marshall. 'Sit down. We got to wait for my partners.'

Marshall crossed the room and sat in front of the TV, took out a tissue and blew his nose.

'Don't give me your fucking germs,' threatened Paras, then went to the window and looked out. 'Here they come. About fucking time.' He went back to the door and held it open, waiting for whoever was coming. After a while Bourne and Maxwell entered; they were both obviously surprised to see Marshall already there. 'He fucking came early,' grumbled Paras as he came back to where the big man sat. If he had his way, he would have cut the American's face to ribbons. This whole thing was a waste of time anyway.

'You're early,' said Bourne as he sat next to Marshall.

'So I keep being told. Who're you guys?' Marshall was surprised the Irishman was there. If he was a Republican, or even a UDA man, they must be at a critical stage of their plan for him to show himself. He listened to see if the Ulsterman dropped his 'H's. It was one way of identifying whether a man was a Catholic or a Protestant. Catholics were better educated and tended not to drop them.

'We're all partners. We're here to deal.'

'How do I know you're not cops?'

'Do we look like police? I'm only five foot four. The rozzers don't accept recruits at my size.' He turned and pointed to Paras. 'Does he look like a cop? Anyway, who says you're straight?'

As Bourne finished speaking, Marshall was convinced he was a Catholic from his accent. That meant he was dealing with the IRA. 'Do I sound like a cop?' he asked insolently, accentuating his Texas accent.

'Yeah,' said Paras sarcastically.

Marshall stood up. 'This is crazy. I bring you a great deal and all I get is insults.'

'Slow down,' said Bourne.

'What for? Are you guys up to this or not?'

'We hear you can shift a thousand or more kilos,' continued Bourne.

'I got enough for this crummy operation. I need good guys, not dopeheads like him,' he indicated Paras.

'Fuck you!' roared Paras, lunging towards Marshall. 'Don't call me a fucking dopehead.' He lashed at Marshall, who ducked easily, then stamped on Paras's naked left foot. Paras swore even louder and grabbed his foot, yelping in pain as Marshall stamped on the other one. Paras fell backwards into an empty chair. Maxwell moved round to protect his leader, but Marshall pulled the Glock from his belt, cocked it and pointed it at the threesome.

So easy to do it now. Just pull the trigger and end this thing. He felt the urge rise within him. Then he remembered the Texan and Ronane. And the job he had come to do. Kill them and the El Paso shipment would resurface somewhere else. *Shit, it would be so easy to finish it now.*

'You're crazy,' shouted Bourne. 'We want to deal.'

'Then fucking prove it.'

'Put the gun away. Come on, let's talk.'

Marshall waited for a minute, then uncocked the Glock and sat back in the chair, the gun resting on his knee. He watched Bourne quieten Paras, then sit opposite Marshall.

'We already have a large supply,' started Bourne.

'Yeah. We soon have everything we want.' Paras looked away as Bourne gave him a warning glance.

'Then you don't need me,' answered a wary Marshall.

'Except for one thing. Competition isn't going to do any of us any good. And our supply could run out. Which means we're prepared to deal with more than one supplier.'

Marshall knew the Irishman lied. Suppliers liked monopoly situations. 'I can't guarantee that. That's up to the people behind me.'

'Are you dealing for the Medellin cartel?' came the loaded question.

Marshall shrugged, non committal. 'Doesn't matter who. As long as I come up with the goods. I would've thought a bigger concern was keeping the cops out of Moss Side.'

'They're no problem.'

'Meaning?'

'That they're no problem.'

'I heard they busted your ass in a big raid.'

'They got fuck all. Did us good. Cleared out all the other gangs and left us to run the patch. The danger comes, not from the boyos in blue, but from outside competitors. Listen, we've got to know you're genuine.'

Marshall reached into his topcoat and took out a plastic bag. It was full of cocaine, processed and ready for the streets. He tossed it on to the table. 'Two kilos as a sample. That's over a hundred grand on the streets. Take it. Do what you want with it. If I wasn't serious, I wouldn't be giving you that for free.'

Bourne sat back in his chair and watched Marshall for a while before speaking. 'This thing needs to go higher.'

'Who do you represent?'

'Powerful friends.'

'IRA?'

'Don't involve yourself in what doesn't concern you.'

'I need to know who we're dealing with.'

'Well, we both agree on that. If you want to take this further, then we'll meet again. Gives me a chance to talk to my people. You're staying at the Crowne Plaza. We'll call you there. As soon as we have something.'

'When?'

'Pretty quick. Probably in the next few hours.'

Marshall stood up and pocketed the gun. Paras watched him, the hatred pouring out of his eyes. 'About the sample,' said Marshall, pointing at the cocaine. 'Even if we don't deal, you keep it. It'll remind you of what you missed.' He walked out of the room without another glance, pulling the door shut behind him.

'Should've fucking killed him,' said Paras, still massaging his feet.

'And then you wouldn't know if he supplied the Chinese.'

''Course he fucking did. They hit us all over town last night.'

'Then we need to find out. Listen, he's just a front, setting up the deal. Knock him off and there'll be others following. Only they won't come to us, they'll go straight to the Chinks. And that's not going to do us any good. It's a shame we didn't find anything in his room last night.' Bourne stood up, then turned to Maxwell. 'Did you do like I asked?'

'Yeah. They went straight in when he left the hotel.'

'Good. Maybe we'll get lucky this time.'

The green Vauxhall followed Marshall back to the hotel. The driver, still at a distance, was definitely black. It had to be one of the Moss Side team. Marshall decided to ignore it, although there was something vaguely familiar about the man and the way he sat at the wheel.

He went to his room and found nothing disturbed. The cold was knocking him out and he undressed and stepped into the shower, turned the temperature up so that he would sweat heavily and spent fifteen minutes under the near-scalding water. Then he dried himself, dressed and dialled Jill's room. The line was engaged, so he went up to see her.

He knocked on her door but there was no reply. He turned the handle and the door opened. He walked in to find the room waiter tied and gagged on the bed. There was no sign of Jill. The waiter's face was bruised from a beating he had taken and his eyes were dark and puffed. Marshall untied him and loosened his gag. The waiter, relieved at being found, started to cry and Marshall waited for his tears to subside. He saw the phone had been left off the hook.

'What happened?' he asked, when the waiter had collected himself.

'Two men caught me going into your room,' said the hapless man. 'They bundled me in there and asked what I knew about you.'

'What sort of men?'

'Big. Black. In black leather coats.'

Paras. 'Go on.'

'They wanted to know where you spent last night. I didn't tell them, then they laid into me. I couldn't take it any longer, they were disgusting what they did to me. I told them. I'm sorry. I thought they were going to kill me.'

'You brought them up here?'

The waiter nodded.

'Was she here?'

'Yes,' he said softly. 'They held a gun to her, forced her to go with them. Then they tied me up . . .'

'How long ago?'

356

'About half an hour.'

That's when he had been in the shower. Damn it, he could've helped if he had come straight up to see her.

'I'm sorry,' whined the waiter, starting to cry again.

'Not your fault.' Marshall took a wad of notes from his wallet and gave them to the waiter. 'Get off home. Don't let anybody see you like this. And don't talk about it to anyone. OK?'

The waiter nodded and Marshall left to go back to his own room. He knew he would have to wait for the call from Bourne. He cursed himself for agreeing to let her stay in the hotel. He tried not to face the consequences of what might happen to her.

There was little he could do but wait for them to call the next shot.

Rochdale Canal
Manchester

The call had startled Manchester Blue. It was the first time Bourne had rung the office and asked for a meeting so early in the evening.

It was just after six when he arrived to find the Irishman waiting for him. He stayed under cover of the Victorian iron bridge as Bourne told him about Marshall, about the drugs for the Chinese and the kidnap of the girl.

'This is getting out of hand,' Manchester Blue said when Bourne finished.

'Don't I know it. Has this Yank got anything to do with you?'

'No. We don't work that way.'

'Then why's his girlfriend a copper?'

'What're you talking about?'

'The girl we nabbed at the hotel. She had a warrant card in her bag. In your Intelligence Unit. Jill Couples.'

'I know her.'

'What's she doing with this Marshall character?'

'I don't know.' He hoped she hadn't told them about his involvement with Marshall.

'If you're conning us . . . if you were, we'd come after you with—'

'Don't threaten me. I'm telling you, I don't know why she's with him. I'd know if we were involved in an undercover operation. Me, of all people.'

'You got no ideas?'

'Maybe she's bent. Helping this Yank set up over here. Bent

coppers do happen, you know,' he joked sarcastically. 'You say she was staying in the hotel?'

'Yes. In her own room.'

'She wouldn't be able to afford that on her own. Not in a luxury hotel like that. And we certainly wouldn't put someone undercover in there. Christ, we have enough problems justifying our budgets. I reckon she's bent. Fucking him and fucking us at the same time.'

'If we find out different, then you'll never escape us.'

Manchester Blue ignored the threat. 'What're you going to do?'

'Find out what he's up to. See if he's involved with the Chinese. That's the only thing that's kept him alive. The last thing we want to do is take on the Triads in a head to head. We can beat the army, we can beat the police. But there's no guarantees we can beat the Triads. They've no soul, the Chinks. No soul and no fear of death. Worse than the fucking UDA.'

Midland Hotel
Manchester

'Is everything all right?' asked Soulson over the phone.

'One or two problems, but nothing I can't handle. Why?' replied Marshall, surprised that his brother had rung him.

'Just concern.'

Marshall sensed how difficult it was for his brother to show feelings after all these years. 'Thanks, but don't worry. I'm playing to rules I understand.'

'Ring Roy . . . or me, if you need anything.'

'I'll do that.'

'Dad saw you through the window.'

'What did he say?'

'Didn't recognize you. Asked me who the big bloke I was hugging was.'

'And?'

'I said it was a close friend. Someone who'd lost his wife. When this is over, you've got to see him.' Soulson knew his words were wasted.

'I met some of the Moss Side people today.'

'Who?'

'No names on the phone. Except one of them said your lot were no problem. Sounds like they've got someone who's feeding them information.'

'Are you sure?' Soulson was taken aback by Marshall's observation.

'That's how I read it.'

'I trust all my senior men. They've been with me a long time.'

'Just telling you what I heard.'

'I'll bear it in mind. Be careful.'

'Bye.'

The phone went dead and Marshall sat back to wait for Bourne's call. It came twenty minutes later, just after seven thirty, when he was in the middle of a coughing fit and had just taken some more cough medicine. He regretted it as he picked up the phone; he was starting to get drowsy.

'Drive out of town on the M56,' Bourne instructed him over the line. 'When you come to the Manchester Airport turn off, go to the airport. At the end of the dual carriageway, there's a big roundabout. Take the second on the left and pull in about a hundred yards down. There'll be a black taxi there. Signal him three times with your lights. He'll pull out and expect you to follow him. Stick behind him until you get to your destination. You'll know when to stop. I'll meet you there. And bring your passport. But don't think you're going on holiday.'

'Where's my girl?' asked Marshall.

'Your police friend, you mean?'

'No. My girl.'

'That's what she keeps saying. Funny, I don't believe her.'

'Remember this. There's a lot of heavy armour and money behind me. Don't harm her. Otherwise you got no deal.'

'I hear what you say,' came the mocking answer. Bourne had already decided not to let Paras' men loose on Jill. He had questioned her himself, soon getting her to admit that she and the American were lovers and had started their affair in America. She said she knew he was involved in some criminal activities and had first given him the idea of coming to Manchester. He had learnt of the gang wars through her and felt he could profit from the situation. Her primary concern wasn't to be part of any criminal activity but to be with her lover. Bourne found her story wanting but believed the gist of it. But his instinct was to safeguard the girl until they had determined Marshall's true intent. After that, if they didn't deal, the girl was Paras's problem. 'Make sure you don't get to the roundabout until eight thirty. On the nose.'

Marshall left the hotel twenty minutes later and set off on his directed route. Behind him, the green Vauxhall picked him up and stayed the customary distance. He kept to the speed limit when he reached the motorway, holding the speedometer at seventy. He turned off at the Manchester Airport junction and followed the instructions until he found the taxi waiting for him. The black cab pulled out in front of him and he followed it round the back country lanes that surrounded the airport. They eventually turned into an unguarded gate on the south side of the airport where the private and charter aircraft were parked. The gate had been unattended for years, in spite of repeated warnings that the airport was now open to terrorist attacks, due to cutbacks from the airport authority in an attempt to shave costs.

The taxi stopped in front of a row of trailer buildings, next to the vast black hangar where the charter companies and flying schools were based. There were a few cars scattered round the car park, but the taxi had pulled up next to two which were parked in the unlit area at the side of a building marked Northern Executive Travel Services.

Marshall parked next to the black car and climbed out as Bourne came round the parked cars to meet him. His two companions, both white, waited in the shadows.

'Brought your passport, boyo?' asked Bourne.

'What've you done with Jill?'

'She's in a safe place.'

'How safe?'

'For the moment. As long as you behave yourself.'

Marshall knew it was a waste of time pushing. 'Where're we going?'

'To meet those who make decisions. I hope you're not carrying that little armed toy, are you?'

'I've got it.'

'Leave it behind. I don't think the customs men will appreciate it.'

Marshall opened his door and put the Glock in the glove compartment, locked it and the door. Even if they went for the gun, they wouldn't think about searching the boot where he had hidden the HK-94. The black car reversed and drove away as Marshall followed Bourne and his henchmen into the hangar, past the various small jets and propeller planes parked there, and out on to the tarmacked apron area where a small twin-engined Cessna Golden Eagle was waiting for them, its engines already turning over as it lashed the air with its three-bladed propellers.

Marshall followed Bourne up the steps into the six-seater plane

360

and the last of the henchmen climbed in and pulled the stairs up. The plane started to taxi immediately on to the taxiway and towards Runway 24.

'What about customs?' Marshall shouted above the engines, anything to keep talking and not worry too much about Jill. Bourne would know where she was, but it wasn't advisable for Marshall to show too much concern.

'We've been cleared outbound,' replied Bourne. 'The only people who worry about who's going in and out of Ireland are Special Branch. They'll have our names on a manifesto which the pilot cleared before we got here. Mind you, it won't be so easy when we get to Harbour.'

'Where's Harbour?'

'Harbour Airport. Belfast.'

The plane rolled on to Runway 24 and the engines powered up to their maximum rpm as the Cessna accelerated along the runway and lifted into the air 2000 feet later.

The pain hit Marshall about fifteen minutes later as the plane passed 16,000 feet on its climb to 24,000. Although the Golden Eagle was pressurized, its cabin pressure rose to 8000 by the time the plane had reached maximum altitude. And that wasn't good for a man with a serious cold. Marshall felt his sinus spread across his cheeks as the pressure changed. What was a gentle ache became a searing pain. He used his tissues to try and clear his nose, but that had little effect. He leant back in his seat and closed his eyes. He hated claustrophobic enclosures at the best of times and had never enjoyed travelling in what he called toy planes. The loud noise aggravated his senses and he tried to calm his inner self to absorb the pain. Here he was, flying into the eye of the tiger, and all he was worried about was his cold.

At the airport the man in the green Vauxhall watched the plane take off before he drove round to the north side where the main terminal was. He rang air-traffic control and said he was expecting a private plane. He gave them the registration number and the duty officer confirmed that the plane had arrived and already departed. He then added that the plane was bound for Belfast.

The man hung up and redialled an international number. When he got through to his superior, he made a full report of all that had happened.

Lindow Common
Wilmslow
Cheshire

Manchester Blue had only just walked in the door when the phone rang.

'I'll get it,' he shouted as he picked it up in the hall.

'We need to meet.' It was a voice he knew but didn't expect.

'Now is not a good time.'

'I'll see you at Lindow Common in fifteen minutes. Just opposite the Boddington Arms. In Wilmslow.' The phone clicked off.

Manchester Blue knew it had been a car phone and he opened the front door. The tail lights of a car disappeared round the corner. They must have been watching out for him; that's why the phone had rung as soon as he entered the house.

'Your dinner's nearly ready,' she shouted from the kitchen.

'I forgot something,' he replied. 'I'll be back in about half an hour.'

He closed the door hurriedly, jumped in the car and drove off before she could question him further. The Common was only five miles away and he drove slowly. There was no point in getting excited. Meetings called at short notice usually generated their own excitement.

There were no other cars in the small car park as he pulled in and switched off the engine. He saw a man's silhouette, topcoated with a cloth cap, against the night sky and he climbed out of the car and walked in that direction.

'You've not been in touch,' said the familiar voice.

'There's too much going on. I can't take the risk.'

'That's our decision, not yours,' said Henry Lip.

'This is no time for rash actions.'

'Tell that to the people who're trying to blow us up.'

'That was a political act.'

'Not according to our informants. There's no IRA terrorist cell. It's to do with the drug war.'

'You know more than I do.' Manchester Blue knew he was under scrutiny. *What the hell were they up to?* He suddenly realized his life was in danger; that how he behaved now would have a direct bearing on whether or not he would ever walk away from this lonely place. 'What've you got?'

'My sources—'

'What sources?'

'I'm told there's an American involved. A major supplier.'

'That's news to me.' So they knew about Jimmy. *Why bring it up now?*

'That he's supplying cheap drugs. To anyone who'll take them.'

'I would've heard.'

'Maybe you have.'

'Come on. We've been together for too long.'

'I hope that counts for something. I would hate to think we couldn't trust you.'

'I know where my loyalties lie.' Manchester Blue moved it up a notch, became indignant. 'Who stopped the police raiding you when they went into Moss Side? A few of the senior men wanted to hit the opium dens and known heroin pushers. I stopped them.'

'If you pick up anything on the American, contact us. The usual way.'

'Anything else?'

'No. I hope we can still trust you.' The threat was unsaid; they wouldn't tolerate him lying. 'You've done well out of us over the years.'

'So have you. I don't want to risk anything. There's too much at stake.'

'Go home now. And contact me if you hear anything. You can leave the rest to us.'

Henry Lip melted into the darkness as a perplexed Manchester Blue walked back to his car. *Where the hell was Jimmy?* He had rung him before he left the office, but there was no answer from the American's room. The whole affair was getting out of hand and Manchester Blue felt the ground grow unsteady under him.

Airspace over Belfast City
Northern Ireland

He had started to control himself and his thoughts were filled with concern about Jill when the pain exploded in his head. The plane had started its descent and the cabin pressure sharply changed. Marshall wanted to scream, to help relieve the pressure on his sinus, but knew he must not allow the Irishman to see him suffering. He kept his eyes closed and gritted his teeth, grinding them harder as the plane descended and the cabin pressure returned to sea-level.

363

The pain never eased; there were hot steel needles slashing through his eyes and cheeks and nose as the plane finally touched down. It was a smooth landing, but the only relief came from the reduced noise as the pilot pulled the throttles back and idled the twin Lycoming engines. The pain still throbbed through his head as the Cessna taxied to a stop beside the small terminal.

Harbour Airport is not where most visitors to Belfast land. The main airport is ten miles to the west at Aldergrove. Harbour is no more than a mile from the city centre and is owned by the Shorts Aircraft Manufacturing Group. The small terminal is used by corporate and private aircraft and the occasional shuttle service. It has the normal customs and police facilities, and there was nothing unusual about this incoming flight. One of Bourne's colleagues was a well-known national hunt jockey and Marshall was told that he was to identify himself as a business manager for an American company interested in promoting the jockey in North America.

The transition through customs and immigration went as smoothly as could be expected. Marshall noticed the police wore guns and flak jackets. This wasn't the Britain he had once known. They found a Ford Granada waiting for them outside the terminal. The driver, a New York Yankees baseball hat rammed on his head and with a scarf wrapped round his neck, stayed in the car as they climbed in, Bourne in the front, and they drove into the city, crossing the Lagan River at Queen's Bridge.

'See them cranes,' Bourne pointed across the river at two big dockside cranes. 'Two of the biggest in the world. That was the Harland and Wolf dockyard. They built the *Titanic* there.'

Marshall nodded. Next to him, the jockey and the third man chattered on about a race meeting they had attended and ignored Marshall. He didn't want to speak, the excruciating pain was only just starting to ease.

It was ten in the evening but there was plenty of life on the streets. He concentrated on controlling the pain while he looked out of the window. It wasn't like anything he had seen before. It was a suburb of a place, but had the air of an occupied territory. Armoured personnel cars drove slowly by while ordinary people went about their ordinary evening's pleasure. He recognized his first police station by its fortress appearance: high barbed-wire topped walls with gun turrets and armoured doors. Not the sort of place that would welcome you if you were lost and wanted to ask the way. The officers on duty had the customary Sten guns strapped across their flak jackets as they watched for the first sign of danger to threaten them.

'We haven't got long before we get back for the shipment,' he heard Bourne say quietly to the driver.

'BRITS WANK - IF YOU WANT PEACE PREPARE FOR WAR' said the white-painted graffiti on a wall as they entered the heart of the city. Belfast was a place where normality and violence were not integrated, but lived side by side.

The pubs were packed and noisy as they drove up Victoria Street, past the Europa Hotel which had been bombed more times than any other building in the city, into Donegal Street and on to the mainly Protestant Crumlin Road. When they passed the Mater Infirmorum Hospital, the car turned right past Girdwood Park and into a small estate, mostly of the older terraced house type. They pulled up outside a corner house and Bourne got out, signalling the others to do the same. The driver walked towards the house and there was a familiarity about him that Marshall couldn't place.

'Take the car home,' Bourne told the jockey. 'And thanks for the plane ride.'

Marshall followed Bourne into the house. The men who opened the reinforced door as they approached were both armed with automatic rifles. This was Fortress Belfast he was about to enter.

As the door closed behind him he saw the driver, standing halfway up the stairs, turn and remove his scarf and baseball hat. He recognized the cruel grin before the man spoke.

'What the hell you doing here, Marshall?' said the Texan.

'You sure get around, don't you?' Marshall croaked. The phlegm in his throat tasted bitter and he held back a cough.

'You know him?' asked a surprised Bourne.

'Yeah,' said the Texan. 'He's DEA.'

'You fucking shit!' screamed Bourne, swinging round and hitting Marshall with the back of his hand. Before Marshall could react, the two gunmen were next to him with their automatics pointed at his chest.

'Cut it out,' ordered the Texan as he came down to face Marshall. 'I want to know what he's doing here.' He turned and walked into the living-room. 'Bring him in here.'

The gunmen prodded Marshall to follow the Texan. He entered the room with Bourne behind him. It stretched the entire length of the terraced property and there was a door in the wall which was half open. It connected to the next house and Marshall realized most of the terraced block was probably connected and would be like a maze if security forces attacked any of the houses. The inhabitants would simply scurry through the connecting doors and escape from any one of the twenty houses that linked the block. Two women and a young, unkempt man were in the room, sitting on the chairs. They looked bored, the look of those with nothing to do. The Texan signalled them to leave and they resignedly got up. Marshall realized they were Hispanics, probably Colombians.

'I told you to keep out of sight,' said the Texan to the man in Spanish. The man shrugged and pushed the women out of the room. 'We need to speed things up,' he replied in Spanish. 'Otherwise we'll have problems back home. The last thing we want now is the DEA involved.' The man left the room.

'Is he clean?' asked the Texan.

'Yes,' replied Bourne.

'You frisked him?'

'No.'

'Then do it. Don't take anything for granted.'

Bourne faced Marshall and frisked his body, then, in an uncontrollable flush of rage, hit him hard in the testicles so that Marshall collapsed on the floor.

'I said cut it out!' shouted the Texan. 'Get up, Marshall.' He watched the big man struggle to his feet. He moved forward and pushed Marshall into a chair. 'You'd better tell me what you're doing here.'

'I'm dealing with these people. Not you.'

'Wrong, buster. This is my show.'

'You're Cali, right?'

'Nothing you don't already know. So what's that make you? Still DEA? Or you gone private? Medellin, maybe?'

'Private.'

'Crap. Not you. Not you, cocksucker.'

'Go to—'

'Don't shit me. You're minutes away from having your head blown away.'

'No way.'

'Why not?'

'Because if you're wrong, and the market's flooded with what my people supply, your investment's blown. Your Colombian friends won't like that.'

The Texan ignored the statement, but realized that Marshall had understood Spanish. 'Why should you go private?'

'Because my partner got killed and no-one did a damn thing about it.'

'That guy Ronane. From Mexico City.'

'Yeah. Ronane.' It was a whisper. 'And his family. They mattered to me. I don't know who did it, but I know I was being followed by DEA agents. Now why the hell were they tailing me at the same time that Ronane got taken out? And then you know what they did? They took out the agents who were tailing me.'

'That's a crazy story.' The Texan looked across at Bourne, who shrugged.

'Crazy or not, that's what happened. Maybe they thought we were on the take.'

'Were you?'

'Like hell. And neither was Ronane. But why tail us? What other reason could there be, unless they were waiting to see if we were making contact with the narcotics suppliers? Shit, I can't make sense of it myself. But that's how it went.'

The Texan pursed his lips and blew out slowly. 'Maybe one of the suppliers came after him.'

'Then why was I being tailed? Why not take me, too?'

'That's your problem. But a new drug supply is mine. They say you've got a thousand kilos to unload.'

'That's right.' Marshall started to cough. Maybe the Texan might just believe his story. 'Who's supplying you?' cut in Bourne.

'DEA agents turned private. Waste substance. Stuff that's been stashed away over the years.'

'That rumour's been round for years,' added the Texan, giving some credence to Marshall's story.

'It's no rumour.'

'You haven't got a distribution network.'

'The Chinese have.'

'So it was you,' acknowledged Bourne.

'Who else?'

'That's a fancy story, Mr Marshall,' said the Texan. 'Tell me, would you sell the whole stock to us?'

'If the price is right.'

'It could save your life. And that girl we picked up.' The Texan turned away. He hated the big man for what he had done to his wife, but this deal was too big to screw up now. Instinctively he didn't believe him, but there was too much risk to his own plans if he blew him away now. He had to hold Marshall, keep him alive and out of sight until he had completed his immediate task. 'OK, Marshall. I'm giving you the benefit of the doubt. You stay here, as our house guest, for a few days. I got something else I got to finish first.' He turned to the guards. 'Put him in a cell. And watch him all the time. If he does anything that makes you nervous, then waste him. You got my authority for that.' His last words before he left were for Marshall. 'If you're shitting us, then understand this. The stuff we imported is already on its way to its destination. Manchester or otherwise. So don't waste your time, or ours, chasing what isn't there any more.' The Texan grinned suddenly, a cruel smirk flashing across his face. 'Fuck us up, Marshall, and I'll let those animals loose on your lady friend. You have a good day now.'

The Texan left with Bourne. There was nothing Marshall could do to help Jill while he was here and he decided to concentrate on his predicament. As he was trained to, he went over the details of the last few hours. If there was one thing he was certain of, it was that the shipment hadn't been completed. Paras had said something about *soon* having everything they wanted. It was that instinct again, even through this awful cold, telling him the game still had time to run. He remembered Bourne's words when they first arrived in Belfast. *'We haven't got long before we get back for the shipment'* is what he told the Texan. That meant they were on their way to complete the deal. Probably with the Colombians he had just seen.

If this thing was IRA controlled, surely they wouldn't take the risk of having Colombians around. Not when they were under almost certain surveillance by the security forces.

He smiled at the guards but met a blank resistance. So he smiled even more, then started to cough. 'Say, do you feed a cold and starve a fever, or is it starve a cold and feed a fever?' he said when the coughing had stopped. 'I never could remember. But I sure could do with something to eat.'

16

PULLING STRINGS AND . . .

Bethesda Hospital
Maryland

SMITH READ PENTANZI'S REPORT THREE TIMES TO RONANE GOING over each detail slowly.

Ronane hadn't spoken once throughout the readings, apart from asking Smith to repeat the process each time he finished. The first reading gave Ronane the basic information of what was occurring in Manchester. The second was so that he could pick out the pertinent facts which he considered would be important to Marshall. When Smith read the lengthy document the third time, Ronane had become Marshall, had replaced his own instincts with those of his friend. It wasn't a difficult transition; lying in bed for all these solitary weeks had given the little man the ability to transcend his own consciousness.

'Want me to run through it again?' Smith asked when he finished.

'No. Except that newspaper report about the Chinese guy being arrested.'

Smith leafed through the sheets until he found the section.

A Chinaman was arrested by police last night for selling cocaine.

369

This comes at a time when the Chinese Triads in Manchester are under investigation after another oriental was seen at the scene of a murder last week when a girl had her throat cut in the street. The oriental was alleged to be responsible for passing a poisoned mixture of ecstasy to the girl's brother in a night-club. The brother died while he was dancing with her.

Smith looked up from the newspaper. 'I don't know what bearing this could have, except that the war between the Chinese and blacks has blown up again, and because Marshall has twice visited a Chinese restaurant known to be owned by a senior Triad member.' Smith looked up at Ronane. 'Think there's something there?'

'Don't know.'

'You know what's going on, don't you.' Smith wasn't asking a question but stating a fact.

Ronane nodded. He had known for a while; Pentanzi's report had simply fleshed out the skeleton. His only problem was how much to tell Washington. He knew Marshall needed support. His message through the doctor would have helped, but what if Washington decided to dump Marshall.

'You going to tell me?'

'Sure. It's what I said he would do. Go with the tide. Use it to resolve the situation.'

'How?'

'He's using the gang war. Offering the Chinese help. But he's also opening doors into Moss Side. He's got them all thinking he's got something they want.'

'Arms or drugs. That's all.'

'Or information.'

'Maybe. Only then he'd have to tell them he was DEA.'

'That's right. Or ex-DEA. They both think he can help. This trip to Belfast.' Ronane remembered that Pentanzi, having followed Marshall to the airport, had stated the big man had gone willingly to the plane. 'That ties up with us thinking the IRA, or UDA, are backing the Moss Side boys. If Ty Koons is over there . . .'

'What gives you that idea?'

'Why not? If it's the same shipment out of El Paso, and it's the Calis supplying the Irish . . . hell, it's his baby. All the way through Mexico, via El Paso. The only spanner in the works is that the Chinese are suddenly pushing cocaine. Now that's not their bag of tricks. Not in Manchester. And they've been doing that ever since our boy got there. Which means everybody thinks he's supplying it. He's set himself up as an alternative source. And that's all that's keeping him alive. The Chinese because they expect him to supply them . . . and the Irish because they want to block him bringing any more in.'

'Why go to Belfast?'

'To meet the top men. Or take him out.'

'After they've questioned him.'

'Yeah,' Ronane whispered softly. Ty Koons. He knew how to question, how to peel the skin off until you screamed for him to stop. Ronane felt the heat rise in his body and he clamped down on his sudden rush of fear. 'He needs support,' he hissed through clenched teeth as he felt the pain burst through to his nerve-ends.

'Why? There's nothing we can do.'

'Keep him alive and he'll take out Ty Koons.'

'We've got no links into Belfast.'

'If they don't kill him in Belfast, they'll bring him back to Manchester. That means they didn't find out his source. We've got to help then.'

'Out of our jurisdiction.'

'Fuck that! Kill Ty Koons and you break one of the biggest links into Europe.' Ronane realized he had said the wrong thing. It was well known within the department that everyone preferred the drugs to channel into Europe rather than North America.

'Forget about Europe,' replied Smith, confirming Ronane's view-point. 'Koons is a different matter. But we don't know he's there.'

'Yes, we do.'

'Only guesswork.'

'No.' The pain was now reaching full intensity. He pushed himself further. 'It was Koons who did this to me.'

'We know that.'

'Don't matter. Because . . . the woman we took out in El Paso. She wasn't just Cali, she was married to Koons. He cut me for revenge. But it was Marshall he wanted. Only the big man got away. So don't tell me that Koons isn't after him. Except . . .' This was the moment that Ronane had always known he would have to face one day. '. . . it wasn't Marshall who took her out. It was me. I shot the bitch. And I was so scared, so shitless for Betty, that I told Koons it was . . . Marshall . . . who killed his woman. That's why he'll go after the big man. As soon as he knows where Marshall's supplies are coming from.'

'Damn you, Ronane. You could've said.'

'There's more. The Manchester police knew him from when he was a kid there. His brother's the Chief Constable. They sent him

371

a letter, asking him to help with their drug problem.'

'And he went back.'

'His brother needed help.'

'Fuck his brother. He could compromise the whole department. And you knew. And never said.'

But Smith's anger was lost on Ronane as he screamed with pain. Smith threw the report down in disgust and hurriedly left the room to call Washington. He never heard Ronane's last words before he passed out. 'Help him. Get someone to help him or I've killed him as well as Betty. For God's sake, somebody help him.'

A nurse came through five minutes later and popped Ronane with a syringe full of tranquillizer. The last thing he saw before he faded into unconsciousness was the Texan with the microtome in his hand approaching the bed. Only it wasn't Ronane in the bed, but Marshall. Ty Koons leant down and started to scrape away Marshall's face, blistering the skin from the flesh and turning it red raw. The blood oozed out and ran down his neck and on to his chest, then spread over the sheets and saturated the bed in a deep red foaming eiderdown. There were no features left on Marshall's face, no lines or lips or nostrils or ears. But his eyes were still there, still staring upwards. The Texan slashed savagely at the big man's eyes, but the microtome had no effect. He heard Koons yell in furious frustration, before turning and looking at Ronane. There was a huge grin on his face before he faded into nothing. Marshall's eyes turned slowly towards Ronane. His partner looked at him and mocked him for what he had done. He knew then that Marshall would never forgive him for the awful destruction his cowardice had unleashed on those who loved him the most.

Wilmslow
Cheshire

After they had eaten supper Tessa went to bed, needing an early night as she was on the 6 a.m. shift in the morning.

Soulson settled down with the files he had brought home, work fallen behind with, but his mind centred on Marshall and the sudden acceleration of events in the city. He rang the hotel twice to speak to his brother but there was no answer from the room.

It was midnight when Armitage rang. 'We've got problems, Chief. I'm on my way to you.'

Soulson put the kettle on while he waited. When Armitage

arrived ten minutes later there were two cups of coffee already on the table.

'A reporter who owes me called. Spencer's called a press conference in the morning. He doesn't know why.'

'Any ideas?'

'She could be about to blow the whistle.'

'No. She'll want to protect her husband.'

'Unless she's thinking of turning it against you.'

'I've been giving it some thought, too. I know I acted rashly.' Soulson sighed, everything he touched right now turned sour. 'It may be hard to believe, but I didn't want to see the police rubbished because the Chair of the Police Committee can't control her husband's little peccadillos.'

'If she blabs, you'll come out worse.'

'I could ring her.'

'What, appeal to her better nature?'

'I don't think Louise Spencer has a better nature. I never threatened her, Roy. Not once. Except she'll make it sound like I did. Our silence for an easy ride with the committee. What the hell was I thinking of?'

'There's more. Jimmy. According to the Special Branch lists, he left Manchester for Belfast on a private plane.'

'What for?'

'God knows. He was with an Ulsterman called Cohn Bourne, and a couple of national hunt jockeys going home after a race meeting. The plane was hired by one of the jockeys. Bourne's reason for going back, according to the Special Branch list, was to see his family. He's no-one special.'

'And Jimmy?'

'Said business trip on his card.'

'He should've rung us.'

'Why? Your brother's not exactly kept us informed as to what he's doing.'

'Dear God.' Soulson put his head between his hands.

'Not finished yet. Jill Couples didn't report on evening shift. No phone call, nothing. The duty officer rang her digs. She's not been in for two days. I checked the Midland. There was a room booked in her name. But she wasn't there.'

Tessa came through the door. Woken by the front-door bell when Armitage arrived, she had come down to see who it was. Without intending to, she found herself in the role of unwitting eavesdropper. The shock of hearing her friend was missing had propelled her into the sitting-room. 'What's going on, Dad?'

The two men turned to her, surprised that she had overheard.

Soulson stood up and moved towards her. 'Nothing, chick. Just standard police work.'

'Why's Jill missing?'

'That's what we're trying to find out.'

'What was she involved in? These bombings? Is that why you're interested in the Special Branch report?'

'I'm not a suspect, Tessa. To be questioned like that.'

'Except she's my friend. I even had lunch with her yesterday.'

'Did she say anything?'

'I wasn't interrogating her. It was friends out together.'

'Anything out of the ordinary?'

She shook her head, exasperated. 'You don't let up, do you, Dad? No. Apart from wanting to know why the Intelligence Unit was pulled off the drug investigation.' She watched for a reaction but got none. 'I think I'm entitled to know.'

'As a bobby you're entitled to know what I tell you. And no more,' snapped Soulson.

'I'm also your daughter. That gives me certain rights.'

'Not where this is concerned.'

Tessa swung round to Armitage. 'Tell me, Uncle Roy. What's going on?'

Armitage shrugged. 'It's between you and your Dad.'

'You're in trouble, aren't you?' Tessa asked Soulson. 'That's why Spencer's called a press conference tomorrow.'

'We don't know that,' said Armitage.

'Why should she think you threatened her?'

'Because that's how she is,' grumbled Soulson.

'Whatever her faults, she only does what she thinks is right.'

'Oh, you approve of Louise Spencer, do you?'

'No, but I think she's entitled to her view. In the end, the police have to be responsible to someone.'

'Who's she responsible to, apart from her own political ambitions?'

'The public.'

'You're too naive, Tessa. Like your Mum. Just think the best of everyone.' He saw his words stung Tessa, and he reached out for her. 'I'm sorry, love.'

She pulled away. 'You once said Mum stood for all that was good. Doesn't that matter any more? Wasn't that what you were about, Dad? All those years ago, when you told me how you stood on the moors. Remember that, how you said it changed you, how you wanted to be a good bobby. What happened, Dad? What makes people think you're threatening them?'

'Forget it.'

'No. Because I'm right. And, deep down, you know I am. Mum would understand that. Anyway, I'm going in to work. To see if I can help find Jill.'

'There's nothing you can do.'

'Beats praying, Dad. Is that what you were going to do?'

'That's very unfair.'

'Is it? As unfair as me finding out, by listening at the door, that you've got a brother. My uncle.'

Soulson shook his head in despair and turned away from Tessa. 'Tell her, Roy.'

'No, you tell me,' she shouted at Soulson. 'Who is he?'

'Marshall. Jimmy Marshall. He got into trouble with the police a long time ago. When he was a teenager. Just after you were born. We sent him to America to keep out of trouble. He lived with an aunt of ours, took her name.'

'Must've been serious for him never to be mentioned.'

'Serious enough.'

'Then why's he back here?'

'He's an American drug agent. He's working on something with us.'

This time Tessa decided to keep her information to herself. Jill's American had to be her Uncle Jimmy. He wouldn't harm her. 'And that's how Jill's involved.'

'Yes.'

'Why?'

'Jill was our contact with him.'

'And now she's gone missing.'

'We don't know that for sure.'

'But you're more concerned about what Louise Spencer's going to say than about your brother or Jill, who's one of your officers. That's awful, Dad.' Tessa stormed out of the lounge as the two men looked helplessly at each other.

'You'd better ring Spencer,' suggested Armitage.

'All I do these days—' came back Soulson '—is fix fences and cover my tracks. She could be right. It's not what being a bobby's about. I think I'll leave Spencer to her own ends. Who knows, maybe she just wants to tell them what a great Chief Constable I really am.'

Drug Enforcement Administration
700 Army Navy Drive
Arlington

'Why do you think he didn't tell us?' The Deputy Assistant Administrator was angry, but didn't want Smith to know that.

'God knows,' Smith replied over the phone. He had rung as soon as he came out of Ronane's room. 'Maybe he wanted Marshall to avenge his family and thought we'd pull him out if we knew.'

'You're damn right we would've pulled him out.'

'This could work in our favour,' said Smith. 'If the Texan is Koons, and it looks like it, then we could wipe him. That would be a big blow to the Calis. And, if it goes wrong, we dump this whole thing on the British police.'

'Except Marshall's in there.'

'He's the one guy who could get Koons. And you know the fall-out he generates. He'd take half the Irish dealers with him. And anyone else who was involved.' Smith waited for the silence to end. He knew the idea appealed to the administrator.

'Tough way to earn a living,' the administrator replied eventually. 'We need Marshall out alive at the end of this thing. Then there's no links back to us.'

'You saying we should support him?'

'No,' came the studied reply. 'Just that we need him back alive.'

'We've no contacts in Belfast.'

'Then let's hope he gets back to England in one piece.' The administrator put down the phone.

Then, like Pontius Pilate, he washed his hands and went home to the smart suburb of Georgetown to have tea and cookies with his wife and three children.

17

...SNAPPING THE UMBILICAL

Housing Estate
Girdwood Park
Belfast

THEY HAD STRIPPED MARSHALL OF HIS CLOTHES INCLUDING HIS UNDER-wear, and kept him locked in a small, windowless room under the stairs. Little more than a cupboard, the only furniture was a sleeping bag which he huddled into to keep warm. The hard, stone floor had made him stiff as he slept, and he had only woken when seized by a coughing fit. The phlegm had loosened in his throat and he felt the worst was over. He coughed and spat up mucus throughout the night; and the release in his throat made him feel better. There was no bulb in the airless room, no electric wires that he could use to his advantage in escaping from this cell. The only source of light came from a small hole in the wooden door through which his captors kept watch over him.

He had no idea of the time when they opened the door and woke him; they had also taken his watch the night before. One of the guards threw a large bath towel in and told him to wrap it round himself. When he emerged from the cell he noted that the hall curtains were drawn, but not enough to hide the fact that the sun was out.

'I'd like my clothes,' he said.

'You look fine as you are,' chuckled one of the guards. 'We thought you'd be wanting some breakfast.'

He was led through the lounge where he had last seen the Texan, through the door in the wall and into the adjoining house. Two children, the eldest no more than four, played on the stairs. They giggled and pointed at the half-naked man and his two armed guards. Marshall was led along the narrow passageway and into the small kitchen at the rear. He noticed the area under the stairs was a replica of the room he had spent the night in and realized there were many cells along this row of terraces. Of the Colombians there was no sign. They had probably been told to keep out of sight.

The smell and sizzle of cooking hit him as he entered the room. The woman, small, black-haired and about twenty-five, was wearing a pinny of the sort he remembered from his youth and she turned from the electric stove and smiled at him. 'Eammon thought you'd appreciate a good honest Ulster breakfast,' she welcomed.

'I did that,' said Eammon, the taller of the two guards.

'More like he didn't want to sit watching over you and miss his own breakfast,' joked the second guard.

Eammon pulled up a chair at the small table and beckoned Marshall to sit.

'At least give the poor man a coat,' said the woman. 'He'll be freezing to death.'

Eammon nodded to his colleague, who left the kitchen. Eammon sat opposite Marshall, the automatic resting on the table but pointed at his captor. Not a good move, thought Marshall. These boys weren't pros. But, experts or not, he knew they would be prepared to pull the trigger.

'What's for breakfast?' he asked the woman as she shovelled food from the oversized frying pan on to the three plates that were on the draining board.

'A proper Ulster breakfast. Bacon, fried eggs, sausages, fried potatoes and soda bread. I hope you're not one of those dieting Yanks, are you?'

'No way. Sounds good.'

The second guard returned with Marshall's jacket and he slipped it over his shoulders. The guard joined Marshall and Eammon at the table and he kept his automatic on his lap, once again pointed at Marshall. The woman placed the three plates on the table, then went to the sink to wash up the cooking utensils.

It was a long time since he had enjoyed such a breakfast, reminiscent of the ones Mary used to cook. He splattered brown sauce, something not to be found in America, over the meal and dug in with relish. For a while he didn't give a damn about where he was and who was guarding him; his hunger and the sheer enjoyment of this large greasy meal totally absorbed him.

The woman gave them big mugs of tea when they had finished and then left to tend to the children.

'Your kids?' Marshall asked Eammon.

'They are,' came the proud, satisfied reply. Eammon leant across the table, the automatic still pointed at Marshall's chest. 'So what's a DEA man doing chasing drugs in Ireland?'

'Ex-DEA.'

'You've no chance,' said the second guard. 'Drugs is everywhere.'

'I agree.'

'First time I went inside, I didn't know nothing about drugs. But you can get it easier in there than you can get a pint on the Lisburn Road when they call last orders. I mean, if you can get drugs with all them screws watching and all those barred windows, then you're not going to do much good trying to stop them outside buying it in the streets, are you?'

'How did they get it into prison?' asked Marshall, his DEA instincts refusing to desert him.

'The wives and girlfriends wrap this stuff in small plastic bags and hide it under their tongues. Then, when they visit the prisoners, they pass it over while they're kissing and hugging. The men swallow it, then come back into the cells. They don't eat nothing. Then, next morning, they crap on the floor and lift the package out of the mess. Then they put the shit in the slop bucket and no-one's any the wiser. Easy.'

It was a tale Marshall had heard many times before. He tried not to think about it especially after the breakfast he had just eaten. 'You're right,' he said. 'That's my new motto. If you can't beat them, join them.'

The door opened and the woman came back in. 'I'll need the kitchen,' she explained. 'The kids need feeding.'

'Come on, then,' said Eammon, picking up the automatic and standing up. As Marshall pushed his chair back, the two youngsters toddled in. He stepped back, and when they were in front of him and clambering on to the chairs, he suddenly reached out and grabbed them both, collected them into his chest like a shield and stepped back against the wall. The second guard scrambled up and also picked up his gun. The woman, now at the sink, reached for a big kitchen knife and rushed towards him, but he lunged at her with his right leg and hit her just below the knee. She fell to the floor screaming.

'Shut up,' he yelled, not wanting her to alert anyone else who was in the house. 'Or these kids get hurt.'

She stopped and stared at him, the knife still in her hand. He stepped back towards the door as the children started to cry, but they were too frightened to struggle. Eammon decided to take the initiative and pointed his automatic at Marshall's knees as he moved towards the big man. Marshall moved his grip and held the two children's heads in such a way that they were forced together.

'I'll crush their heads before you pull that trigger,' he warned Eammon. 'Don't for a moment think I haven't been trained to kill.'

'Leave him, Eammon,' the woman shouted. 'For God's sake, don't.'

Eammon faltered, then slowly lowered his gun.

'Where's my clothes?' asked Marshall.

'In the next house,' said Eammon.

'Where?'

'Just behind the door where we kept you.'

'Anyone else around?'

'No.'

'Don't lie. Otherwise your kids are dead.'

'Only my mother. Upstairs,' said the woman.

'And the Colombians?'

She looked at Eammon, who shrugged. 'They were moved out this morning,' she said to Marshall.

'Where to?'

'I don't know.' Marshall had no reason to disbelieve her. 'What were they doing here?'

'They're with the Yank.'

'They meeting the IRA?'

'Don't know what you're talking about. Please don't hurt my kids.'

'OK. I need my clothes. But first put down your guns. On the table.' He watched the two men do as he ordered. 'Now step back, against the sink.' When they had complied, he moved round to the table and, holding the children with one hand, scooped up the automatics with the other. He backed towards the door again. 'I'm taking the kids with me.'

380

'No.'

'Until I get my clothes. You stay here for five minutes. Then I don't give a shit what you do.'

'Don't take my babies,' she appealed to him.

'Stay in here and they'll be safe. Understand?'

The woman nodded and Marshall backed out of the kitchen. He turned and ran down the corridor and into the next house; had some difficulty opening the connecting door as his hands were full of children and weapons. He kick slammed the door shut behind him and hurried into the next corridor. He was as surprised to see the man standing there as the man was to see him. It wasn't every day that a naked man brandishing weapons and babies with a towel trailing behind him burst into your corridor.

'Hold the children. Quick, for fuck's sake,' yelled Marshall.

The man, recognizing the children, took them off the big man. 'Who're you?' he asked incredulously.

'We've got a problem,' said Marshall, looking at his pile of clothes and pulling his underwear and trousers on hurriedly. The man started to put the crying children on the floor. 'Don't put them down,' Marshall yelled. 'Get them out before the bomb explodes.'

'Fucking hell,' yelped the man, turning and scuttling out of the front door.

Marshall finished dressing and raced out of the back door, into a small stone yard with high brick walls. Eammon saw him through the kitchen window, and satisfied the children were safe opened his back door and started yelling. Marshall, now carrying only one of the automatics, came into a narrow alleyway and, having no idea of where he was, sprinted towards the opening to the street beyond. He heard Eammon shouting behind him as he turned the corner and ran into the man still holding the babies. The startled man, realizing he had been duped, was not able to do anything except run after Marshall, calling to others in the street as he ran.

People were taking notice of the commotion and some men started to run after Marshall. He didn't want to fire the automatic, because that would draw police attention. So he waved the gun frantically as he ran, warning those near him that he was armed and dangerous.

He made it to the next corner without being stopped. An old yellow Renault 4 had pulled into the kerb and a young woman was unloading her shopping. He pushed her aside, saw the keys were still inside and slid into the car. He turned the ignition and started the engine as the girl threw herself at him, swearing profusely as he tried to steal her car. The pursuing crowd were now getting closer. He punched her across the face and knocked her out of the car. Then he grappled with the strange gear shift that stuck out of the dashboard at him. He crunched it a few times before he slammed the car into gear and accelerated away from the kerb. A hail of bullets raked the back of the car, smashing the rear window, and he ducked. Then he careered round the corner and drove frantically away from a furious Eammon who was brandishing an old Sten gun.

He had no idea where he was, so he drove along until he found a sign that directed him to the city centre. He ditched the car there, leaving the gun inside and asked the way to Victoria Street. Once there, he made his way to the Europa Hotel and the phone booths in the lobby. He rang the international airport and asked details of the next flight to Manchester. It was a British Airways flight, but the earliest available seat was at 4.50 p.m. It was only ten in the morning, but he had no alternative but to wait. He used his American Express card and reserved his seat. With more than six hours to kill, he decided against booking into a room; a few phone calls by his pursuers could easily discover his whereabouts. He had to go walkabout; mix with the shoppers and coffee bar crawlers and hope he wasn't noticed. Not easy when you're six foot plus, unshaven and look as though you've spent the night in a sleeping bag under a staircase.

There was nothing else he could do. Just hope that luck ran with him as he got through the day. At least the cough had improved. Things were finally looking up. He tried to push Jill from his mind, not wanting the panic to spread through him as he thought of her hopelessness. He believed she was still safe. They wouldn't harm her until they knew where he was. He knew too much and they would want to trade her safety for his silence.

Town Hall
Manchester

The press conference called by Louise Spencer was impact aimed at the tabloids.

The room was packed when she strode in, flanked by two of her fellow Labour Party councillors. When the murmur had died down, she held up the report prepared for Soulson by Chief Inspector Mailer of the Motorway Unit on the Rover 216Si.

'I have copies here,' she said, 'of a road test carried out on the instructions of Chief Constable Charles Soulson. The car, a Rover 216, was delivered new to the test ground. It was driven by the head of the police Motorway Unit to see if it was suitable for use as the new replacement car for the Chief Constable. The test took six hours, during which, as you will see from the copies my colleagues will hand out, the car took a hammering that no vehicle would be expected to last through. In my view, because Mr Soulson does not want a smaller car than the Jaguar he enjoys at present, the Rover was systematically driven beyond its normal expectations and deliberately wrecked so that it could be deemed unsuitable for the Chief Constable. This was done with Mr Soulson's full knowledge. It is just another example of the disregard he holds this police authority in. It is misuse of public funds at a time when our cash is low and our resources are suffering.'

Her two colleagues took the stack of files and distributed them amongst the reporters. When Spencer saw they all had copies, she continued. 'At a time when we have vicious street battles between the narcotics gangs, when terrorist explosions are killing Manchester citizens and people are frightened to go out of their houses, I suggest that Mr Soulson devotes his energy to policing this city instead of protecting his little empire and the trappings that go with it. That is my belief and my commitment.' She paused for a moment, wanting her next words to have the full impact she planned. 'In view of the terrorist situation, and the recent cowardly attacks on police officers, I am in sympathy with the fact that the Chief Constable could be in considerable danger. If he believes, as he says he does, that a larger, more robust and powerful car is necessary so that he can escape any terrorist attack, then I am prepared to accept his view. But it has to be his decision. Let him choose the car he wants, as long as it's British. Then, once he's got his car, I hope he pulls back from these silly games and gets on with policing this great city before it blows itself apart. Thank you.'

The reporters bombarded her with questions, but she refused to answer any. Her final comment to the journalists was, 'If you have any further questions, I suggest you ask the Chief Constable.'

Then she was gone from the room.

'That was a bit of something over nothing,' a local reporter commented to the tabloid journalist next to him.

'Maybe. But can you see tomorrow's headlines? Christ's cop crucified for dream car.'

383

The Front
Moss Side

It was a lesson they had learnt from Belfast.

Link the house with connecting doors and it became a fortress. On the first floor of the Club Nilus, a door had been built into the connecting wall and went through to the rooms above the next door shop. The door was reinforced with steel, as was the door that led out of the room. The windows had steel shutters above them, ready to be slammed down within seconds if necessary. A row of steel shutters ran around the room, above the pelmet rail. If they were lowered, the room would become a vast safe which would take many hours to break into. The rest of the house had similar protection, not to mention the permanent armed guards who were posted at all vantage points across the five houses that linked together and formed the Front.

The doors that protected the safe were locked. There were over 800 kilos of street-ready heroin in the safe.

When the additional 200 kilos arrived from Ireland, the shipment that had started in Colombia, passed through Mexico and El Paso, worked its way across the Atlantic in the bodies of the Quigleys and found its way to Moss Side in tranches of 200 kilos, would finally be ready for distribution in Manchester and the rest of England.

There were also detention cells, similar to the one Marshall had found himself in in Belfast, in the buildings. Jill Couples was held in one of these rooms. Unlike Marshall, she had been allowed to keep her clothes on but was the continuous target of vile and suggestive taunts by her captors. She ignored them, but knew that they would be allowed to exercise their prerogative at some stage. She kept her mind off them, especially the big man who had threatened her with a knuckleduster as he tried to find out what her relationship with Marshall was. They told her Marshall was a prisoner in Belfast and that she would soon be left to their whims. The one thing she did overhear was that the safe upstairs was where the drug shipment was now held, and that a last shipment was due before they began distributing the candy in the streets. By careful conversation she determined where the safe was, and how it was protected. The boastful guard enjoyed telling her what she didn't know; it somehow proved his manhood over her.

She sat in the darkness of her cell and saw Marshall's face in her mind. With a childlike belief she knew he would come after her. When she conjured his image, she somehow felt very safe. Then she remembered how they had made love and how the pain of his age and her experience had affected him. He didn't understand her, then she realized with a start that she didn't understand him. Generations apart; different minds and different people joined together by physical love and a pathetic need borne out of loneliness and the inability to give of themselves to others. That's why they were good at what they did, because it demanded less of them than the giving of their souls. She still believed he would come for her, but that was because it was his duty, and that was something he would never forsake. She calmed herself. Whatever happened, she must be prepared for it. That was also her duty. He would expect it of her.

She closed her eyes and thought about San Antonio. For a brief moment they were happy there. But even that happiness was built on fear and need. What was it that made her run for cover every time she came close to surrendering herself; this feeling that it was always greener on the other side? It never worked out that way. She thought of her mother and the man who had played at being her father. Then, as the shame filled her, she turned and thought about her present predicament. Would they harm her? Would they ever let her go, when her use as a hostage was over? What had they planned for her once they had what they wanted?

In truth, unknown to her, the plan conceived by the Texan had taken root and its deadly seed was about to flower.

Town Hall
Manchester

Soulson and Armitage, having been given a verbal report of Spencer's conference by the police press officer, drove to the Town Hall for a hastily arranged meeting with the Chair of the Police Committee.

'We don't need him,' Spencer pointed at Armitage as the two police officers entered the committee room. 'This is between us.'

'Please, wait outside, Roy.' Soulson was overly polite where Spencer had been deliberately rude. 'I shouldn't be long.'

Spencer waited for Armitage to leave the room before she continued. 'Follows you like a bloody lapdog.'

'Loyalty and subservience don't always go together,' replied Soulson as he crossed the room and sat opposite Spencer. 'I heard about

385

your press conference.'

'That makes us even.'

Soulson laughed. 'You cheapen my rank.'

'No. You don't need any help from me on that score.'

'For a car? Do you really think I protected your husband so that I could get a new Jaguar?'

'Why did you protect him?'

'In truth?'

'In truth.'

'I really don't know. I only once before did something like that. A long time ago.'

'And did you call your debt in?'

He couldn't tell her about his brother, about the danger Jimmy was in. Or the girl. They were all in deep because he'd called his debt in. 'Yes.' His honesty with her surprised him.

'I thought so.'

'I learnt my lesson. It'll never happen again.'

'You expect me to believe that?'

'I don't need to behave in that fashion.'

'You've put me in an impossible position. Fuck you, Soulson. That's a dirty way to force me out.' The tears welled in her eyes and she fought them back. She turned away from him, hated him seeing her distress and hopelessness.

'Did you believe I'd trade the car for my silence?'

'You stupid man.' Her frustration changed to anger. 'I was going to tell them what happened. But I couldn't. I couldn't destroy him. I know what I married, what he is. But he's mine. And for that I'll stand by him. So I hit back at you. Stupid and childish, but I had to hit back at you.'

'What're you going to do?'

'What do you think? Resign. I'll find a reason.' She was startled as Soulson stood up to go. 'You've won, haven't you? Fucking bastard.'

'Don't resign.' He was surprised as he heard his own words.

'Why? So that you've got a hold over the police committee?'

'No. What happened to your husband will never come out. I promise you that. I don't agree with your ideas or your principles. But I can fight you. Straight. And beat you. You know, my daughter stood up for you last night. Had a go at me, even though she thinks you're an idiot. I'm sorry this ever happened. But you're lucky. By chance, your husband's name was protected. But don't resign. Don't give me that satisfaction.'

386

He turned and left the room, was jaunty in his walk for the first time in many months.

'What happened, Chief?' asked Armitage when he joined him outside.

'Nothing, Roy. Nothing's changed. Now let's see what Intelligence has got on Moss Side and if there's any news on that missing bobby.'

Runway 06
Manchester Airport

British Airways Flight BA 5288 touched down four minutes early and taxied in to the terminal. The first drops of a heavy drizzle were falling and specking the tarmac.

Marshall watched the turbine propellers turning on the ATP and heaved a sigh of relief. He had spent the day hiding in crowds and shop corners, waiting to be discovered by the army of watchers he knew were looking for him. But his luck held. He eventually caught a bus to the airport, not wanting to take a black cab. He knew they were commonplace IRA transport and would have hated being driven back to the place he had escaped from. At one stage he was sure he was being followed, but nothing came of it. His tension had continued when he boarded the plane. He didn't expect it but the IRA had done stranger things than blow up aeroplanes in mid-flight. Which is why, as he saw the terminal through his window, he felt an immense surge of relief. Yet he was still surprised the IRA had not spotted him at Belfast Airport.

Maybe things were not as they seemed. He suddenly recalled the Irishwoman's words in that small Belfast kitchen. Perhaps the IRA weren't involved.

As the plane stopped by the terminal, he saw an Aer Lingus 737 parked at the next stand. The baggage was being unloaded from the hold on to a luggage train. A small white van with a revolving yellow light on top pulled up next to the hold. The sign on the side read Northern Executive Travel Services. Marshall remembered the company; it was the name above the building where he had parked his car. The plane sighed to a stop and the passengers stampeded for the entrance. But Marshall stayed where he was, watching the van. It stayed where it was, at a slight distance from where they were unloading the Aer Lingus. It was as though it was part of the scene but not really belonging to it. Then one of the baggage loaders pulled two large suitcases from those being unloaded and set them to one side. The loader walked away and continued loading the train. The white van drove closer and the driver stepped out. It was Cohn Bourne. Marshall watched him load the two suitcases into the van and drive off. Bourne drove to another stand where he parked.

Marshall leapt up and pushed his way through the crowd, ignoring the objections of the other passengers. When he reached the door, he raced down the covered ramp until he was in the terminal. He looked round for a door on to the ramp, but they were all locked. He ran along the terminal pier, pushing past passengers who were disembarking from other planes. He saw a doorway half open, left by a careless airport worker, and he went through it.

Nobody saw Marshall come on to the ramp. He ducked past the workers who were unloading the planes and ran towards where he had last seen the van parked. It wasn't there and he ran back the way he had come, knowing Bourne would soon be crossing the main runway to the other side of the airport where the private aircraft were parked.

He saw the van with its yellow revolving light waiting near the runway for permission to cross to the south side. There was a jet spooling up to take off on the runway. He knew he had to get to the other side. Bourne was his best chance to get to Jill.

He ran out into the night, ran like he never had before, straight for the runway over 300 yards away. He dodged under a taxiing Boeing 727 and sprinted on to the grass strip that ran alongside the runway. It was an 80-yard dash to the tarmac and he stopped at the edge. An American Airlines 747 was on final approach, no more than an eighth of a mile out, its lights filling the runway as it started to flare on its final act of descent. Marshall ran across the 50 yards of the runway, rolling into the wet grass on the far side as the 747 streaked on only seconds after he had scrambled across. He knew the van would be cleared across as soon as the big plane passed it and he closed his mind to the breathless pain that cut into his lungs and forced his legs to push his heavy weight towards the big hangars 200 yards away.

The 747 turned off the runway and ground control cleared Bourne across to the south side. He drove across and along the winding, blue-lit taxiway towards the same hangars.

By the time Marshall reached the hangars and had worked his way past the parked planes outside the big building, Bourne had parked the van and unloaded the two suitcases into an old Ford Cortina. He had glanced over at Marshall's Vauxhall, remembered the gun in the glove compartment and gone over to it. He tried the doors, and when he confirmed they were locked, he went back to the van, pulled out a jack handle and smashed the Vauxhall's passenger window. He pulled the lock up, opened the door and tried the glove compartment. It was locked, so he rammed the jack handle against it, over and over again, until the flimsy lock snapped and the compartment fell open. He took the gun and slammed the door shut.

'That's my property,' said Marshall as he stepped out from the darkness of the hangar.

Bourne was startled by the big man's appearance, but collected himself quickly, primed the Glock and aimed it at Marshall. 'Prepare to die, you American bastard.'

Marshall ducked behind the Cortina as Bourne fired. The Irishman walked calmly towards the car, knowing that Marshall was trapped by open space. As soon as he moved clear of the car, Bourne would drop him. Marshall stood up, his hands held high. 'You're not IRA, are you?' The truth of it was suddenly so clear; the heightened excitement of near death had cleared his senses. 'You're fucking independent.'

Bourne laughed. 'Clever shit, aren't you? Think you know everything. You know fuck all. It's not the IRA you should be worried about. It's the fucking police. They're putting the Chinks under pressure. Don't think you'd be left alone if you walked away from here.'

'Someone's been feeding you information.'

'Oh, that's bright.'

'That's why you're always one jump ahead of everyone.'

'Except they didn't tell us about you.'

Marshall had to keep Bourne talking. It was his only way out. 'They don't know about me. I told you, I'm the genuine article.'

'Maybe, maybe not. But it doesn't matter any more. We've got all we need.'

Marshall knew the Irishman was going to kill him; the suitcases in the car boot contained the last of the El Paso shipment. Bourne smiled and aimed directly at Marshall's torso.

The short burst of automatic fire stopped Bourne in his tracks. Two sets of headlights snapped on, illuminating the ground where the Irishman stood. 'Drop the pistol,' barked a voice from the blackness behind the car lights. 'Drop it, or we drop you.'

Bourne swung round and fired two rounds, then rolled behind the car as gunfire erupted round him. Marshall stood his ground, hoping his inaction would spare him.

'Hold your fire,' called the voice and the shooting stopped. By this time Bourne had crawled, shielded by the car, towards the hangar and, realizing no-one was shooting at him, opened a small door and sprinted through it.

'After him, get him,' yelled the voice and two gunmen raced past Marshall and into the hangar.

By now Marshall had recognized the Chinese accent. 'Somebody want to tell me what's going on?' he bluffed, holding his hands up to signify he was unarmed.

'You don't seem to be a very popular man, Mr Marshall,' came the familiar voice of Freddy the Duck. The Chinaman stepped into the brightness of the headlights. 'Always in trouble.'

'He was breaking into my car,' said Marshall, lowering his arms.

'So it would seem,' smiled Wong. He spoke to one of his men in Chinese and waited as the man walked over to Bourne's Cortina, opened the back door and lifted out the two suitcases. 'Perhaps he was going on holiday and liked your car better,' he continued when the cases had been deposited in front of him.

'It's part of the shipment I promised you.'

'Then why did he have it? Or do you like doing deals with as many people as possible? Like selling the Eiffel Tower over and over again.'

'That's my property.'

'In his car?'

'He got greedy.'

Wong laughed, then leant over and flipped the catch on one of the cases. The white powdered contents in clear plastic bags didn't need explanation. He closed the case and stood up. 'My property now.' He turned to Marshall. 'Where's the rest of it?'

'In Moss Side.'

'Then who was that man?'

'Part of the Moss Side team.'

'Wrong colour. Or hadn't you noticed.'

'He's the guy who organized them. Irish.'

'Does that mean what I think it does? That he's IRA?'

'He'd like you to think that.'

'Why?'

'Helps his case. He and some friends went independent. But they like people to think they're still involved. Helps frightens them off.'

The two gunmen returned from the hangar and spoke to Wong.

390

'Did they get him?' asked Marshall.

'Unfortunately not. He ran across the runway and my men saw some airport vehicles out there so they couldn't follow him. Do we need him to get the rest of the shipment?'

'No,' came the flat reply.

Marshall turned and walked to the van.

'Where're you going?' he heard the voice behind him.

'To finish what I started.' Marshall stopped and turned back.

'Will the IRA come after us?'

'Does that make you nervous?'

'No more than usual. We have been fighting the world for thousands of years. Just another boil to be pricked.'

'No, they won't come after you. I told you, they don't even know what's been going on.'

'Any more than I do. Time to come clean, Mr Marshall.'

'I told you. I'm a DEA operative.'

'Outside your jurisdiction.'

'Partly. I'm working with the Manchester police. Following a big shipment from America to here. Part of that cache is in those suitcases.'

'Who are you working with?'

'Chief Constable Soulson,' Marshall said after a long pause.

'That's rather far-fetched,' was the sarcastic reply.

Marshall knew he wasn't believed. 'And Chief Superintendent Roy Armitage. That's all.'

'You'll need a better story than that.'

In for a penny, in for a pound. 'Charles Soulson is my brother. We've lived separately since we were kids. I was brought up by an aunt in America. Marshall was her name and I adopted it. My brother, through Roy Armitage, asked me to come over. To help with the investigations.'

'What investigations? This town is controlled by the gangs.' Wong knew that his source had lied; that the man he trusted to inform him about police activities had deliberately misled him.

'He wanted to use American methods.'

'Not something you expect from Charlie Soulson.'

'I was already trailing this load from El Paso to Ireland and into Manchester, so I said yes. I thought it was the Colombian gangs working with the IRA. I was wrong. The Irish group is a breakaway unit, probably ex-Republicans. More interested in profit than politics. They've been using Colombian money to organize and set up distribution networks in England and then into Europe.'

391

'That's a wild story.'

'Wild enough to be true.'

'Do you know these Colombians?'

'Yeah. The link is an American. Guy called Ty Koons. He's over here now. In Moss Side. There was a Colombian in Belfast. With a couple of women. I think they were part of the organizing group. They may be here, but they've probably drifted somewhere into Europe. To set up new lines of distribution.'

'You lied before. Why should I believe you now?'

'Because this thing's near to an end.'

'I can take my profit and leave you to your fate, Mr Marshall.'

'Come on,' Marshall urged. 'That's only twenty per cent of what you could make.'

'Which is better than a hundred per cent of nothing.' Freddy the Duck considered before continuing. 'Are you going in after the drugs?'

'Yeah.' Marshall decided not to tell the Chinaman about Jill. There was little point in confusing the issue. 'I need those cases to get in there.'

'A sprat to catch a mackerel. More like caviar at that price. Risky, don't you think?'

'I need something to bargain with.'

Wong smiled. 'You're either a fool, or a very brave man. I'll take you for a fool. Fools can be lucky. But I want something in return. Otherwise you can walk away, but not with any of that stuff.'

'What's the trade-off?'

Freddy the Duck took Marshall's arm and led him into the darkness away from the rest. What he told Marshall shocked the big man. He didn't know it ran that deep. And he was being asked to be Executioner once again. Did it never end, this blood trail that had become his life? He suddenly felt very tired; this awareness in him that he was little more than a hired gun. It somehow cheapened all he had achieved in the past, made so much of his life worthless.

But Jill came first. And Ronane. He agreed to the Chinaman's conditions. He went back to the van, took the suitcases and put them in the Vauxhall's boot, next to the HK-94. Then he drove away from the airport.

'What was all that about?' asked one of the gunmen as they watched Marshall drive off.

'Just family business,' replied Wong. 'Time to pay off all debts.'

Police Headquarters
Stretford

Armitage hurried up to Soulson's office as soon as he received the report. 'Special Branch have reported that Jimmy came off a flight from Dublin, but didn't go through Special Branch or customs.'

'He can't have disappeared into thin air.'

'We've also got a report of what sounded like gunfire on the south side of the airport. Airport police investigated and found nothing. And a pilot of a landing jumbo radioed in that he missed a man running across the runway. All this took place at about the same time.'

'Special Branch have got Jimmy's name on file. It won't take long before they trace him to the Midland.'

'That'll take hours. You want me to go and see him?'

'No. He knows how to look after himself.'

'Heard from Tessa?'

'No.'

'Anything else I can do?'

Soulson shook his head. 'Just be available. I'm staying here late. Just in case something else blows.'

'I'll be downstairs, Chief. If you want me.'

Soulson watched the door close behind Armitage. It was all going awfully wrong. It was hard to believe this was happening in an English city.

He felt the emotion rise in him and fought it down again, grinding his teeth as he felt the migraine take hold. Whatever he had done had been from his sense of duty. The result could well be the destruction of his family. He regretted the years without Jimmy; a time of being alone and living with the grief that followed Mary's death. He realized he was wrong about Jimmy, that he had been too inflexible. *Damn it, I was his brother, not his father . . . or his keeper.* And Tessa. He had missed her growing into womanhood because of his own loneliness and the drive that pushed him to concentrate on his position rather than his values as a man and a father.

But there was nothing he could do. He had unleashed the whirlwind, and all he could do now was wait and see which way it blew.

The first call came from John Pentanzi. 'Where the hell you been?'

'Misbehaving. You promised three days.'

'Ain't broken it,' Pentanzi lied. 'But I'm kind'a bored and could do with some fun.'

'Get you into trouble.'

'Like you said, it's time I got out from behind a desk.'

Marshall knew Pentanzi had been ordered to watch over him. He didn't mind; Pentanzi was a good agent and would be a valuable ally. 'OK.'

'What's the dress?'

'Chic Moss Side. You staying in the hotel?'

'Two floors above you.' Pentanzi gave him the room number.

'Don't think that makes you superior to me. I'll come up in twenty minutes.'

Pentanzi laughed and hung up. Marshall dialled a number and waited for the phone to be answered. 'Shaeron . . . It's the Yank, Jimmy. I want to speak to that brother of yours . . . Don't hang up, or he's in trouble. I want you to tell him to get Koons for me . . . Yeah, Ty Koons. American guy. I'll ring back in ten minutes. If he can't get him, then get that dopehead brother of yours to come to the phone. If Bourne hasn't already told them, I've got the shipment.' He hung up, then opened his coat and took out the HK-94 and started to check it. He wanted to make sure the hardware worked. There was a knock on the door and he threw his coat over the gun and answered it.

It was a young woman in police uniform. She looked so much like Mary that it took his breath away. So this was little Tessa.

'Uncle Jimmy,' she said.

His hairs stood up on the back of his neck. She even sounded like her. God, how had Charles coped all these years with this replica of the woman he had loved, always reminding him, always making him realize what he didn't have. 'Hello, Tessa,' he said huskily.

She came into the room. 'How do you know?'

'Because you are your mother.' He closed the door and followed her into the room.

'Where's Jill?' she asked.

'In Moss Side.'

'I thought you'd know. You're her American.'

'Does your Dad know . . . ?'

'He doesn't know I'm here.' She quickly explained how she had overheard the conversation between her father and Armitage. 'It was all a bolt out of the blue, to say the least,' she concluded. 'Can you get to Jill?'

'Yes.'

'Can I help?'

'Maybe.' He was still amazed by the similarity. 'Christ, you look like her.'

'I want to help. She's my friend.'

'Whatever I do has no official sanction.'

'The uniform is just what I was working in.'

He went over to the bed and removed his coat. She gasped when she saw the HK-94. 'This isn't for traffic violators, Tessa.'

'I know what goes on in Moss Side. I don't care what you do, as long as we get Jill out.'

'OK. I've got things to do. Just grab a seat and . . . wait.' Marshall picked up the phone and dialled. 'It's Marshall.'

'Who's Ty Koons?' said the Texan.

'Don't shit me, Koons. Ain't got time for that.'

'When did you find out?'

'Always knew,' Marshall lied, but knew that would intrigue Koons. 'I already heard from Bourne.'

'I got two suitcases of yours. I want to trade.'

'For the girl?'

'Of course.'

'Bring it down here.'

'Come on, Koons.'

'That's how it's got to be,' came the firm reply. 'You want her more than we need the stuff.'

'Where?'

'Hang on,' said Koons as he covered the phone and spoke to Stash Maxwell. 'You know Princess Parkway?' he said to Marshall after he had the information he wanted.

'Yeah.'

'What you driving?'

'A blue Vauxhall. Cavalier.'

'You be there at ten. Just cruise the south-bound lane. Slow. If we miss you, skip round and do it again. When you see us, you stop and get out of the car. I know you'll be armed, so don't get any funny ideas. Someone'll come out and check the suitcases. If they're satisfied, then we'll release the girl and you let the guy take the cases. If I was you, Marshall, I'd get the hell out of Manchester as soon as I swapped.'

Marshall put the phone down. It was a risky meet, but he had little choice. He turned to Tessa. 'Different from the way you normally do business, isn't it?'

'I want to help.'

'Too dangerous.' He'd already compromised her mother and father once; he didn't want to be responsible for her.

'I want to help Jill.'

'Forget it, Tessa.'

'No. I can't just walk away. I'm still a policewoman, not just family.'

'Your father wouldn't . . .'

'Nothing to do with him.'

'He wouldn't agree.'

'I don't care. I don't need looking after. I've got to help somewhere.'

'He's going to love me for this.' Marshall grinned, she had Mary's pluck. And Charles's. He looked at his watch. Then he quickly told her what he had arranged with the Texan. 'We've got two hours before the meet.' Then he explained his plan to her. 'Can you manage that?'

'Is that all?'

'Yeah. It'll give us the space we want.'

'But I—'

'That's it, Tessa.' Marshall was firm. 'You don't know how to use weapons and you've never been in this kinda situation before. Any more than that and I'll be worrying about you, instead of getting Jill out of there.'

'All right,' she agreed reluctantly.

He let her out, telling her to ensure that she followed his plan as he had specified. He asked her to deliver a police radio and a portable phone to Pentanzi's room before she went to her final rendezvous. 'I know this isn't the way things're done here,' he said. 'But we don't have time to do it any other way.'

'I understand. If it's the only way.' Halfway down the corridor she turned back to him, knowing he was watching. 'What was she like, Uncle Jimmy?'

He liked the way she said that. *Uncle Jimmy*. 'Beautiful. And perfect.'

'Did you love her?'

'I was only fifteen at the time.'

'But did you love her?'

'With all my heart. Until Jill, she was the only woman for me.'

Tessa smiled the smile he remembered so well, and then was gone. He closed the door, finished his preparations and left his room. He didn't want to be there in case anyone came calling; too many people knew where he was. He heard his phone ringing as he walked down the corridor, but he ignored it. His plans were made and he didn't want anything to change them.

Marshall climbed the emergency stairs to Pentanzi's floor and knocked on his door. The man who opened the door was not the smart urban London agency chief that he knew so well, but an unkempt tramp of a man who would happily grace any dustbin.

'Shit, John,' Marshall said as he entered the room. 'You even smell like a hobo.'

'I found a couple of room service trays in the corridor and smeared the food over my clothes. Then I got the dirt out of a flowerpot, went in the shower, and smeared it all over my body. When it dried, I just rubbed it, and some ketchup and baked beans and Marie Rose sauce, into my body. Then I got dressed. Goddamn bathroom's a mess.' Pentanzi grinned at Marshall. 'Hell, I wouldn't even get into a Salvation Army hostel smelling like this. But I sure as hell will get into Moss Side and mix it with those down and outs there.'

Marshall told him what had happened in Ireland and the plan that was forming in his head. 'Do you think it's a bit wacky?' he asked when he finished.

'No. We've had worse. Anyway, that's your way. Just follow your instinct, big man. It's what you know best.'

'You've been reporting back to Washington.' It was a statement, not a question.

'I guessed you knew.'

'You were in the green Vauxhall.'

'Just watching your tail. But all that's happening now, that's my contribution.'

Marshall believed him. He wanted to ask about Ronane, but now was not the time. 'You better get going.'

Pentanzi, the big jolly black giant, suddenly burst out laughing. 'It's damn good to be back in the field. Hell, I hope I don't get arrested going through the lobby. I'd have a shit job explaining this one away.'

Police Headquarters
Stretford

Soulson put the phone down. It was the third time he had called Marshall's room in the last twenty minutes. He wanted to warn him, even pull him back from what he had unleashed. But there was nothing he could do. His brother was wreaking his own vengeance, doing his job in the way he knew best. He suddenly envied him; envied the freedom to resolve the law in his style and manner.

He stayed at his desk. There was nowhere else to go. Nothing else to do. He'd try again in ten minutes. Maybe Jimmy would be back by then. He picked up the phone again and called Armitage.

'Better stay put in case anything else breaks,' he said. 'And keep Paul Job on stand-by. To be used as we need him.'

He replaced the receiver and suddenly sneezed, then cursed before the second one came. The last thing he wanted was to catch a cold when hell was about to break about him. Then he remembered his God and he knelt beside his desk and prayed.

Princess Parkway
Moss Side

Thursday night and the weekend had already begun for some. The traffic was heavy and the headlights cut through the steady drizzle that was falling as the revellers and prossie hunters and drug seekers searched for nirvana in the night.

Marshall turned on to the Parkway near the big brewery, cut into the inside lane and drove at a steady twenty miles an hour. The passenger seat was soaked as the drizzle came in through the window that Bourne had smashed at the airport. He watched for any sign of recognizable movement on the pavement, but there was nothing on the first run. It's what he had expected, after all they would want to ensure he wasn't setting them up. He completed the two mile run, then swung across a junction and drove back to repeat the exercise. There was no reaction on the second trip.

He saw the Texan on the third trip, about halfway down the Parkway where the burnt-out shops from the riot stood. But Koons was hidden in a shop door and made no attempt to signal Marshall. He had been lit up by the lights of an oncoming car as Marshall drew level and the big man made no attempt to let Koons know he had seen him. He hoped that Jill was nearby, that Koons hadn't set up an ambush. He saw no unusually parked cars in the side streets waiting to drive out at him. And Koons knew Marshall was a pro, that he would fight to the death and probably destroy the shipment if he were attacked. Marshall counted on that for his safety from a sniper's bullet or sudden attack. He didn't accelerate as he passed the group of drunken tramps further down the road; there was no danger there, no hidden gunmen.

He was making his fourth pass when Koons stepped out and signalled him to the kerb. As Marshall pulled in, he spoke into the police radio microphone which was wedged between his legs. 'Car 54, where are you?' was all he said. Then he switched the radio off so there would be no sound of static and let it drop to the floor. He pulled into the kerb, the HK-94 a comfort under his right arm.

Six ordinary police patrols and one member of the Nilus Gang who was monitoring the police frequencies heard the transmission. No-one took it seriously; there was always some bored bobby muttering something cheeky into his radio as he did his rounds.

The message was received and understood by Tessa, now in her police uniform and driving a Panda car that she had sneaked out of the yard behind the station in which she worked. It hadn't been difficult; she had simply walked through the office, checked which vehicles were logged off service, taken the keys from the board in the duty room and driven out of the yard. She eased the Panda towards Princess Parkway, increasing her speed so that she wouldn't arrive too late.

Marshall climbed out of the Vauxhall, shielding himself from Koons with the car. 'Hold it there,' he ordered, bringing the HK-94 into view. 'Let's talk the trade through.'

'You're a crazy fucker coming in here on your own,' said the Texan.

'I'm rigged to the suitcases. Two grenades on wires. If I go down, I pull the pins and you lose your shipment.'

'Where you going to get two grenades?' sneered Koons.

'Same place I got this,' replied Marshall, waving the barrel of his automatic rifle.

'You sure got balls, dickhead.' The Texan looked round, saw nothing to alarm him, then signalled a car which was parked across the road on the northbound carriageway. The car drove off, turned at the first junction and joined the southbound lane, coming to a stop twenty yards before it reached the Vauxhall. Two men got out, both in black leather coats, carrying Uzi machine-guns. A second car went past Marshall and pulled in twenty yards further on. Two further leather-coated men got out. 'I hope you're not thinking of crossing me, Marshall.'

'We agreed the deal.'

'Switch the engine off.' He watched Marshall lean in and turn the key to silence the engine. 'We got to check the candy.'

'When I've seen the girl.'

Koons shouted behind him and Paras stepped through the boarded-up doorway of a burnt out shop. He checked the street, then turned and pulled Jill out from the entrance. Her hands were tied behind her back, but apart from that she looked as well as could be expected. Marshall's heart surged, then he ignored her. At this time he needed all his wits about him. He noticed Bourne standing in the shadows where Paras had been.

On the north side of Moss Side, a Nilus sentry saw a Panda car streaking towards Princess Parkway without its siren or flashing lights. He paused for a while, not sure whether to report it or not.

'Bring the girl towards the car,' said Marshall. 'The stuff's in the back seat.'

'What about the wires?' asked Koons.

'I'm not going to blow her up, am I? I'll let them go when she's in the car. And I want those jokers,' he indicated the car in front with the armed men, 'out of here.'

'OK.' Koons turned to Paras. 'Take her over, only keep her between you and him.' He yelled at the car in front to move away and they did as ordered.

Paras shoved Jill who stumbled but caught her balance. Paras laughed and shoved her again. 'I'm going to come and personally cut your fucking heart out when this is over,' he yelled. 'Nowhere you going to hide.'

'Speed it up, dopehead,' returned Marshall.

'Fuck you,' came the roar.

'Just do like I said,' warned Koons.

The Panda sped towards Moss Side.

Sixty yards down the road, a black tramp detached himself from the group of drunks huddled in a burnt-out shop to keep dry and warm.

'You go on like that, and I won't be able to save your hide, Marshall,' continued Koons.

'Come on, let's get it done.' Marshall watched Paras reach the car with Jill. He didn't look at her, avoiding her eyes until they were out of here. 'Open the front door so she can get in.'

'Not till we get the cases,' yelled Koons.

'Open the back door as well,' Marshall told Paras. 'Take out one case, then put her in.'

Paras turned to Koons for confirmation.

'Do it,' said the Texan. He stepped aside so that he had a clear shot at Marshall and pulled out a Browning Hi-Power automatic pistol. 'My insurance,' he told Marshall. 'In case you change your mind.'

Paras leant in and took one of the cases out. Then he shoved Jill into the front seat, banging her head as he did. Marshall heard her yelp in pain as Paras laughed loudly and stepped back between Koons and the car.

Tessa, now a quarter of a mile away, hit the siren and accelerated past a slow-moving line of cars down Princess Parkway.

'Get the second case,' yelled the Texan, moving so as to keep his gun pointed at Marshall.

A radio crackled from the shop behind, then someone yelled, 'The cops are coming!' Koons looked up sharply as he heard the siren at the same time.

Down the road the tramp screamed at them. 'Goforit goforit, nownownow,' yelled Pentanzi as he pulled his own HK-94 from under his smelly coat and fired a short burst towards the group near the Vauxhall. Koons rushed forward, colliding with Paras who dropped the case and hit Jill in a rage across the face as she tried to shut the door. Marshall fired at Koons and missed, then dived into the car and turned the key to start the engine. 'Get down,' he ordered Jill as the car engine burst into life. As he slipped the car into gear, he saw Koons grab the second case from the back seat. He accelerated away as gunfire burst around him. Koons had managed to drag the suitcase from the back and he was running with Paras towards the safety of the shop. Marshall slowed as he reached Pentanzi, who dived into the back, then accelerated sharply. The car that had been parked in front now came out of a side street with one of the gang shooting at them with his Uzi from the front passenger window. One of the bullets nicked Pentanzi in his arm as he tried to return the fire and he dived between the seats. Marshall swung the car across the central divide, bounced it across the grass and concrete slabs, then drove northwards towards the city centre. His action, and that of the car following him across the centre island, caused consternation amongst the drivers hell bent on a good night out and there were a series of accidents on both carriageways. Pentanzi, realizing he was not badly hurt, knelt on the back seat and fired out of the back window at the following car, the bullets smashing the glass as he

401

shot through it. He hit the driver in the shoulder and the vehicle lost direction, veered to the left and smashed into a row of parked cars. From across the road, a second burst of gunfire erupted towards the Vauxhall, but then all was quiet and they were safe. Marshall kept his foot pressed to the floor. Jill lay very still in the passenger well, her hands still tied behind her back.

'Fuck it!' swore Pentanzi. 'The guy was wearing shades.'

'What?' yelled Marshall.

'The crazy fucker was driving with shades in the middle of the night.'

'Check Jill, for Christ's sake.' He saw Pentanzi lean into the front well and prod Jill, then feel her for damp patches which could be blood.

'She's breathing OK. Just knocked out,' said Pentanzi as he untied her hands.

Marshall realized the savage punch from Paras must have knocked her out. He reached between his legs and pulled out the police radio. 'Mancunian Way,' he said, then switched it off again. Tessa's police car had been a good diversion; Koons and Paras must have believed there was a big police raid under way. It had taken the heat off Marshall, otherwise he was certain they would have come after him. Right now the rats were running for cover. At least he hadn't needed to con the Chinese. Except he wanted that shipment. That was why he was over here. The shipment and to get the man who had tortured Ronane and killed his family.

'You OK?' he asked Pentanzi, remembering he had been hit.

'No sweat,' came the muffled reply as Pentanzi pulled back his arm and checked his wound. The coat and extra padding had deflected the impact; there was only a small graze on his skin.

Tessa, having seen the commotion outside the shops, swung east off the Parkway and drove to meet Marshall under the Mancunian Way flyover.

Meanwhile Marshall arrived at the rendezvous. Jill had come round by now and he held her as she told him her saga. She had been taken directly to the Front when she was kidnapped. She knew the area intimately from her surveillance days and she told him about the layout of the house and the safe.

'You're going back, aren't you,' she said, suddenly frightened for him.

'We agreed I'd finish what I started.'

'They'll be expecting you.'

'Maybe. Maybe not. But they won't move anything with all this ruckus going on. Now's the time. When it's all there, in one

402

place.' He picked up the portable phone and made his call. 'If you want it, that's where it is,' he said into the mouthpiece. 'I'm going to hit them in three hours. At one thirty. This is what I suggest you do.' He went through his plan, then switched off the phone.

'What do you think?' asked Pentanzi.

'Could just be the two of us,' replied the big man softly, not wanting Jill to hear.

Tessa arrived and immediately took charge of Jill. 'There's police cars coming from everywhere because of the shooting,' Tessa told him. 'I'll get her and the Panda back, then meet you at the hotel.'

Marshall watched Tessa move off; saw Jill's face in the rear looking back at him. He waved, then blew a kiss. They held each other's eyes until the darkness swallowed them.

'Nice woman,' commented Pentanzi. 'What you going to do?'

'Fuck knows.' He didn't need to add *when this is over and if we make it*. Then he remembered the deal he had with the Chinese. That could blow everything; how could she come to him after he had completed it. *Damn you for bringing me here, for forcing me to destroy you*.

They moved the bullet-ridden car deep under the concrete pilings where it was well hidden from passing traffic, and settled down to make their plans and wait until it was time to move.

'Christ, you smell,' said Marshall.

'You should try it from my side,' came the wry comment.

Police Headquarters
Stretford

Manchester Blue was sitting in his office when the call regarding the shootings and multiple car accidents in Moss Side came through. He listened, then said he would make his way there.

'Damn you, Jimmy Soulson,' he cursed as he slammed down the receiver. 'You buggered me from the beginning. It was all your bloody fault.'

He picked up the phone and called the duty officer. He instructed him to get Paul Job to bring the Jaguar to the front door. Someone would have to go out and help Marshall.

The phone rang again while he waited. An Irishman had been killed in the crossfire. The description of the dead man fitted Bourne.

A sense of relief flooded over him.

403

Maybe he was safe now.

Maybe his awful nightmare would finally end.

The Front
Moss Side

They drove the Vauxhall with its smashed windows and bullet-holed wings back into Moss Side. The watchers were in disarray and it was impossible to monitor who was moving in and out of the area. The police had opened up Princess Parkway to through traffic although many of the banged-up cars were still littered along the side. The pavement area was cordoned off as forensic officers shifted through the debris looking for empty cartridges and other clues. The sight of another smashed up car caused no interest as Marshall parked the Vauxhall three streets from the Front.

'You sure they'll come?' asked Pentanzi for the third time.

Marshall didn't reply; Pentanzi didn't expect him to.

'Too many cops. Could put them off,' continued Pentanzi.

'I'd like to be around to see Washington squirm when they find two dead DEA agents in Manchester with machine guns in their hands.'

They saw the first Chinese five minutes later. He drove an old Ford Escort and parked thirty yards away. Marshall got out with Pentanzi and ambled along the pavement towards it. The Chinaman got out and waited for him. Marshall recognized him, he was one of the waiters from Freddy the Duck's restaurant.

'You the only one?' asked Marshall when he reached him.

The waiter grinned and opened the door. There were eight more Chinese crammed in there in a horizontal position, one on top of the other. Behind them an Astra pulled in and parked. Marshall could only see a driver, but he knew where the rest of the team were. He nodded to the Chinaman and walked past him towards the street that led to the back of the shops on the Front.

The Club Nilus was closed for the night. So was the shabeen at the opposite end of the small block. The two agents stayed in the shadows of the wall opposite the rear of the Club Nilus. They could see guards on duty at various windows, but there was only one sitting at the base of the scaffolding that ran up the back. The drizzle had formed a fine mist which helped them stay hidden from the watchers.

It was Pentanzi's world and he stepped out from the darkness, to all intent and purpose an alcohol-sodden tramp looking for a warm place to spend the night.

'Don't ham it,' muttered Marshall as he saw his partner stagger across the road.

The guard sat on the planks that ran across the scaffolding, protected from the rain by wooden planks on the second level, his legs swinging loosely as he watched the drunk. He was wrapped in a black raincoat and the bulge under the gabardine was proof that he was armed. 'Get the fuck from here,' he shouted at Pentanzi.

Pentanzi stopped in the middle of the road, reeling as he tried to focus on the guard. 'What the fu . . . ? What the fu . . . ?' he slurred.

'Piss off, you drunken lush.' The guard laughed at Pentanzi who fell forward on his knees and scrambled across the road. 'Ground got unsteady on you, shithead? Think there's a fucking earthquake going on?'

Pentanzi reached the pavement and pulled himself on to his feet, stood there swaying as he looked at the guard. 'What the fu . . . ?' he breathed again, then lurched towards the guard, retching as he did. The guard scrambled backwards, trying to get out of the way of the onrushing tramp. But it was too late and Pentanzi crashed against him and sent him reeling backwards, trying to grab the metal scaffolding to stop him as he did. The gun, an automatic pistol, fell from his coat and clattered on to the planking. Before the guard could recover, Pentanzi picked up the pistol, a Smith and Wesson automatic 659, and whipped it across his skull. The guard looked at Pentanzi in surprise, then held his hand up and touched where he had been hit. He looked at his hand, saw the blood on it and pulled himself to his feet to fight the tramp. Pentanzi hit him again, twice across his forehead, before the guard finally keeled over and crashed on to the planking. Pentanzi pistol-whipped him once more for good measure, then leant over and picked him up by the shoulders and set him against the scaffolding so that he still looked as though he was on watch. When he turned Marshall had crossed the road and joined him on the scaffolding.

'Took your time,' kidded Marshall. 'Out of practice, I guess.'

'Smart ass.' He held the 659 up for his partner to see. 'Fancy iron. You don't usually get these outside the US of A.'

'Courtesy of the Colombians, I guess.'

The scaffolding, which was Paras's escape route from his bedroom, was the weak spot of the fortress. Not something the two agents were aware of; to them it was just a way in to the building.

'Could've done with a vest,' said Pentanzi as he started to climb up the scaffolding looking for a window that was open.

'That desk job's made you soft,' replied Marshall, following him.

They reached the third-floor level without finding a window. It was a difficult climb; the drizzle mixed with the grease of the city that had collected on the metal structure made it a slippery ascent. There was a ledge on the third floor. It carried on round the building to a small lit window. They surmised it was an attic room. Marshall led the way and carefully stepped along the ledge, Pentanzi just behind him. When he reached the window, he eased himself forward to look in.

Shaeron was naked on the bed, her legs wide open and pointing at the ceiling. Paras, also naked, straddled her. She gripped his shoulders, her eyes wide with fear and her mouth twisted in considerable pain as he fucked her and kept slapping her round the head. The scene fascinated Marshall; it was the last thing he had expected to see and it suddenly reminded him of his own weaknesses and the awful things he had done to hookers. In the rippling black and cruel muscled body that he saw inflicting shame and violence on the girl, so he saw what he had become and how terrible his own weaknesses had been.

'What's going on?' whispered Pentanzi from behind.

Marshall collected himself. Paras had to be taken out, but quietly so as not to alert others in the house. A shot through the window was out of the question. It had to be with their bare hands. He turned his head away from the scene and told Pentanzi what they must do.

'Wait for the fireworks,' counselled Pentanzi.

'No. We're going now.'

He leant forward and carefully tried the window. It was closed, but not latched. In the room, Shaeron was now crying, begging her brother to stop. But that excited him more and he slapped her around the mouth as he increased his intensity. She yelled once more and Paras laughed.

It was now or never.

Marshall smashed the single pain with his foot and, holding his coat over his head, burst through the window. As he rolled on to his feet, freeing the coat so he could see, he felt the HK-94 slip from his grip and fall to the floor. Paras turned to see what was happening, although his body, so close to his orgasm, kept pumping away at Shaeron. His eyes opened wide when he recognized Marshall and he tried to pull out from her. Pentanzi burst through the window and fell in a heap next to Marshall. The sudden shock of discovery, added to the pain she was enduring, sent Shaeron into a panicked spasm and she wrapped her legs round Paras, trapping him momentarily as he tried to free himself. He swung round and reached across the table and put the fish-hooked knuckleduster on his right hand, then tried to free himself again. But she had him snared between her legs; the pain was still in her as was his penis.

'Let go, you fucking bitch,' he yelled, then slashed at her with his right hand. He missed her face as she jerked back, but cut across her breasts, splitting the flesh. The blood and fat and tissue and milk ducts that led to the nipples spilt across her chest and the bed. She screamed and twisted violently, hurting his manhood as she turned it like a corkscrew. 'Let fucking go!' he thundered again and lashed at her, this time tearing into her face with the evil weapon. She died as he slashed at her, her body suddenly slackened and her legs fell away. Paras pulled away from her and turned towards the men.

But Shaeron unwittingly had given them the time they needed.

Pentanzi threw himself at Paras and wrapped himself round the man, pinning his legs and arms so that the gang leader couldn't move. Marshall, his gun now lost in the jumble of the untidy room, hurled himself at the struggling duo and hit Paras across the head. It had little effect and the struggling man managed to get his right hand free and slashed at Marshall, tearing though his coat and grazing some of the muscles in his upper arm. Marshall grabbed his arm and tried to hold it, but the gang leader was more powerful than the two men combined. With his natural strength, and the adrenalin of violent sex and the fight for survival raging through him, Marshall knew they couldn't hold him much longer.

He put his knee over Paras's arm, pushed his weight down to hold him for a moment, then grabbed his head and dug his thumbs into the gang leader's eyes. Paras screamed, but Marshall gouged deep into his skull, his thumbs burying into his head as though he was nothing more than a bowlful of jelly. The blinded Paras exploded off the bed, the sheer force of the man breaking Pentanzi's grip and Pentanzi rolled backwards on to the floor. But Marshall hung on, gripping tighter, digging deeper into Paras's skull with his thumbs. The gang leader stood up, naked and powerful and tried to lash blindly at Marshall, but Marshall was too close for the punches to have any real effect.

Pentanzi got off the floor and rammed his fist hard into Paras's naked groin, grabbed his testicles and screwed them round and round until the gang leader collapsed on to the floor in incredible pain. Pentanzi saw Shaeron's stockings by the bed, and he grabbed one and wrapped it round Paras's neck as tightly as he could and strangled the huge man, pulling it tighter as the nylon mesh dug into his flesh as deep as any wire garotte. They held him like that for nearly three minutes before they were convinced he was dead.

Marshall stepped away first and looked for his gun. He avoided Pentanzi's eyes; what they had done was not something either of them was proud of. With the HK-94 back in his possession, he went to the door and listened for any sounds from outside. The commotion from Shaeron and Paras had not drawn any attention, it was obviously something the occupants of the house were accustomed to.

'Want one of these?' asked Pentanzi, holding up some grenades. Marshall nodded and Pentanzi brought two over and gave them to the big man. 'There's a box by the bed. Enough of these to start a war.'

'Bought by Colombian money,' said Marshall. He switched off the room light, then opened the door. He felt Pentanzi slide into position behind him. There was no-one in the dimly lit hallway and he stepped out into the corridor and slowly descended the stairs.

The second floor, with its three doors closed, was as Jill had described it and the two men eased their way to the first. If Jill was correct, this was where the safe was, on the floor above the Club Nilus. There were sounds of movement from the first floor balcony and Marshall stopped. His arm was now throbbing where Paras had slashed him and he rested the HK-94 on it as he tried to ease the pain.

The first sounds of distant shooting began one minute after they had stopped on the stairs. Within moments activity, in the form of running feet and doors slamming, erupted above and below them. Marshall leapt on to the first-floor landing and blistered the walls with a short burst of bullets, knocking one of the guards, who was trying to close the steel safe-door, against the wall with the force of two bullets that entered his back and his left shoulder. With Pentanzi now covering his rear as men ran down the stairs, Marshall climbed over the fallen man, who unknown to them was Stash Maxwell, and entered the safe. Pentanzi loosed one burst off towards the staircase and the gang members scattered as they hit the landing.

The Texan, in his boxer shorts and half asleep, saw them first. Resting on the sofa in the corner of the room, he had been wakened by the explosive sounds outside. He lurched towards his Uzi and sprayed a burst towards them, hitting Pentanzi in the leg but missing Marshall. The big man dived behind a steel desk as Pentanzi crawled towards him. Marshall covered him with a burst that made the Texan duck behind the sofa. Pentanzi, his leg bleeding profusely, slid into the small space next to Marshall. In the distance, the sounds of gunfire were increasing.

'Why don't we miss extra time and call this a tie,' said the Texan, as affable as ever.

Marshall looked round and saw the steel shutters which could turn the room into a fortress. He looked at the boxes piled in the corner, next to the suitcases he had taken from Bourne. That was the only place big enough to hold the narcotics. And probably weapons for the gang.

'You suggesting we split the proceeds and get out of here?' replied Marshall.

Koons knew he had seen the suitcases. 'Shit to that,' he said. 'Let's just walk away, Marshall.'

'Ronane wouldn't approve of that.' Marshall knew that Pentanzi's movement was limited, it was almost impossible for his partner to flank the Texan.

'I lost somebody too. Call it equal.' For all the detached coolness of the Texan's voice, Marshall sensed he was eager to resolve the situation and get out of here before he was trapped.

'You mean that ugly cow you called your wife?'

'Ease off, man,' warned Pentanzi.

'Not very charitable, Marshall.' Koons's voice didn't give away the anger that he felt. 'Listen, if we stay here, we're both gonna get hit. Let's throw our hands in and walk away.'

'I don't trust you, Koons.' said Marshall.

'Get your friend to slide his weapon out, then you and I stand up. We drop our hardware and walk out of here in separate directions.'

'Why should I do that?'

'Because you've got the stuff. And you've fucked up any plans we had here. You're out of your jurisdiction, Marshall. Stay here any longer and you're going to compromise the DEA. I never did believe you were acting under orders. This was always your private game.'

'How do I know you've got no other weapons?'

''Cos I'm naked, dickhead. You think I'm going to shoot you with my prick?'

'OK.' Marshall looked at Pentanzi, who was surprised. 'Slide it out, John.' Pentanzi shrugged, then pushed his weapon out into the open. 'I'm standing now,' said Marshall. 'But I'm pointing straight at you.'

'OK.' The Texan's head appeared followed by the rest of him. His Uzi was directed at Marshall's stomach. So easy just to squeeze the trigger.

'Walk into the centre of the room,' instructed Marshall, cutting across his thoughts. 'Then we approach each other. With your free hand, you catch hold of my muzzle, and I'll do the same with yours. On the count of three, we'll both push the muzzles aside. Then we let go our own guns, so that we're holding the other by its barrel. Then we drop them. Got that?'

'Sounds pretty DEA manual,' bantered Koons.

The two men stepped out from their respective shelters and crossed the room, their weapons still aimed at each other. When they met they took the other's muzzle with their free hand and completed the manoeuvre as Marshall had stipulated. Once free of each other, they slowly lowered the weapons, holding them by the barrels, to the floor. They slid the guns across the room, away from each other. Then they both stood up.

'You all have a good day now,' said Koons, still grinning as he hurriedly stepped towards the door that led to the next house, opposite the one through which the DEA men had entered.

Marshall pulled the Glock from inside his coat. 'She really was an ugly cow.'

'Fuck you,' yelled Koons just before he saw the pistol. He started to run towards the door, but Marshall shot him in the left thigh and he fell, twisting on to his back as he did. Marshall crossed over and pointed the gun at his head.

'I just want to know,' Marshall asked. 'You really Ty Koons?'

The Texan's eyes mocked Marshall. 'Shit to you, dickhead.'

And Marshall knew he would never know for certain. He pulled the trigger and wiped the sneer from the Texan's face.

He helped Pentanzi to his feet. The London bureau man hobbled back to the door they had come from. From outside the shooting was getting nearer. 'Your Chinese friends are getting in,' said Pentanzi.

'Guess so. All clear outside?'

Pentanzi checked the corridor. 'Let's go.' He led the way, his automatic cradled in his arm as he limped towards the stairs.

Marshall followed him to the steel door, took out the two grenades, pulled the pins and tossed them on the pile of drugs and weapons. Then he closed the door and helped his partner back up the stairs. The explosion from inside the safe rocked the house and blew a hole in the wall below them. Then the room caught fire.

They climbed the stairs and, with extreme difficulty, worked their way back to the scaffolding and down to the street below. Marshall stopped at the first-floor level, pulling Pentanzi into the shadows of the scaffolding. On the street he could see Freddy the Duck waiting by the blue Vauxhall. There were three men with him; from their watchful stance Marshall could tell they were armed and waiting for him.

'Got to keep going,' whispered Pentanzi behind him. 'If the cops get us, the department's in deep shit.'

'Fuck the department. Those guys, down there, are waiting for us.'

'You're going to have fun telling them you just blew up their supply.'

'How do you feel?'

'Shaky.'

'Christ, I should've kept one of those grenades.'

'No point talking to them, I guess,' asked Pentanzi, but the look on Marshall's face answered him. 'Guess not. You always were a charming bastard.'

Marshall puffed his cheeks out and blew slowly, exhaling a swirl of condensed air into the cold night. The gunfire had died down to the occasional dull plop from the front of the Club Nilus and the main sounds were of people shouting and running in the darkness. He guessed the Moss Siders had found Paras and that the sight of their dead leader would have broken their spirit. They would be frantically trying to get away now, desperate to escape the Chinese who waited at their door and the police who would soon appear. As if to answer his question, a lone siren wailed in the distance.

'Come on,' hurried Pentanzi from behind him.

Marshall, knowing there was nowhere to go, no more time to waste, swung carefully down to the next level, the HK-94 levelled towards Freddy the Duck. He could see the Chinaman, a soft-edged shape in the mist, was getting restless. He eased himself through the wooden slats of the scaffolding's base boards on to the pavement, hugging the steel structure so as not to attract attention.

He heard Pentanzi curse softly before he slipped and fell through the wooden planks on to the pavement beside him. The sound, a crashing cacophony of falling man and wood, attracted the Chinaman's attention and he shouted a warning to his men as he took cover behind a parked car. Pentanzi yelped with pain as he landed on his injured leg and collapsed into the gutter.

A spray of ear-splitting machine-gun fire erupted around the two DEA men as Marshall pulled Pentanzi deeper into the

411

protection of the scaffolding. Bullets ricocheted off the steel structure, but all missed the two men. Marshall and Pentanzi returned the fire, scattering their bullets over a wide area and sending the Chinamen for cover.

'Can you run?' Marshall shouted at his partner.

'I won't get very far,' came the answer. 'You get outta here.'

'No.'

'Get going, Marshall.'

'Fuck off.' As if to reinforce his point, Marshall let off a volley, which was returned immediately, ripping into the wall behind them and gouging chips of brick out of the wall.

'Marshall,' shouted Freddy Wong. 'We have matters to settle.'

Marshall could smell the smoke from the building behind; the fire was beginning to engulf the structure. 'Nothing left, Mr Wong,' he returned. 'It's all going up in smoke behind me.'

'That's not what you promised.'

'Can't help the fire.'

'You promised me a narcotics supply. If you can't meet it, then you must pay.'

'Look at it this way, you're back to the status quo. No more black supergang. You're in charge of your own territory again.'

'I always was, Marshall. It was always written that we would win.' Freddy Wong shouted an order in Chinese and a hail of bullets exploded round the DEA men once again. They returned the fire, then Marshall took two wooden planks and held them up as a shield. 'Follow me and stay close,' he told Pentanzi, then started to slide along the wall and away from the scaffolding. A few bullets thudded into the wooden slats and Marshall heard Pentanzi painfully keep up behind him.

Through the mist he heard people running towards him, the fusillade of shots still thudding into the wood that protected them. He lifted the HK-94 above the plank and, without looking, sprayed a burst towards the oncoming group. He hit one of them; he knew that from the scream of pain as someone fell to the road. Another burst, this time over his head from Pentanzi's gun, joined in and their attackers, after a few shouts, fell back to the protection of the parked cars.

'Where we fucking going?' asked a pained Pentanzi.

'Hang in there, John,' returned Marshall. He wanted to get away from the scaffolding and the corner of the building. Out here, protected by the mist and the line of parked cars, they weren't trapped like rats any longer.

A much shorter barrage of shots rattled into the plank and over their heads. The lone police siren that they had first heard was now joined by others, all getting closer. Someone yelled in Chinese and the shooting suddenly stopped, followed by more running feet, the slam of car doors and the squeal of tyres as they roared off. Then there was only silence; just the distant toll of police sirens urgent in their approach.

Marshall peeked over the plank, and seeing nothing untoward in the mist picked himself off the pavement and laid down his wooden shield. He knelt next to Pentanzi. 'Can you make it to the car?'

'Yeah.'

'Come on,' urged Marshall, taking his partner's arm and helping him carefully to his feet. 'Let's get out before we—'

'Compromise the agency,' joked Pentanzi, flinching through the pain as he pulled himself up.

'Hey, you're beginning to sound human,' retorted Marshall. The two men hobbled towards what was left of the blue Vauxhall.

Freddy the Duck stepped out from behind a parked car. Another Chinaman, one of his bodyguards, stood next to him, an Uzi aimed straight at Marshall.

'We had an agreement, Mr Marshall,' said Freddy Wong.

Marshall, still clinging to Pentanzi, couldn't bring his HK-94 to bear on the two Chinese. It would have made little difference; the two DEA men would have been cut down before they could react. 'Still had, until you opened fire.'

'You blew up my property. Property you promised me.'

'That's my job. Kill me and my people will come after you.'

'I doubt it. It was always outside your jurisdiction. They'd wipe their hands of you.' The police sirens came closer and one of the gunmen spoke urgently to Wong in Chinese. Freddy nodded, then continued. 'It was remiss of me to lose my temper. But you made a promise, then broke it. How do I know you will keep the rest of it?'

It was the opening Marshall hadn't expected. 'I could never let you have the drugs,' he replied. 'That's what I'm about. You got to trust me on the rest.'

'I have little choice. It is the only way.'

Freddy the Duck walked away into the night, his bodyguard following. Then the sirens got closer and police cars and fire engines pulled into the street.

'What the hell you promise him?' asked Pentanzi as a black Jaguar pulled up at the kerb.

'Nothing that involves Washington,' replied Marshall as he saw Armitage and Paul Job get out of the car and run towards them. 'I've done my duty for the department. Now it's family business.'

'Let's get you out of here,' yelled Armitage to Marshall. He and Job helped with Pentanzi, leading the DEA men to the black Jaguar and assisting the injured man into the back. Marshall climbed in after his partner and the two policemen in the front.

'What're you doing here?' Marshall asked Armitage.

'We were sent to help.'

'Coming out of hiding, huh?'

Armitage didn't comment.

As they drove away, the Club Nilus turned into a blazing inferno. The fire was spreading through the walls into the next-door building. By the morning the Front would be nothing more than a burnt-out shell, a row of terraced ghosts to the power that is cocaine.

The marked police cars ignored the black Jaguar as they passed it. After all it was one of their own. Everyone knew the Chief Constable's car.

Marshall looked out of the window. It all made sense to him now. He said nothing, felt nothing.

He drove out of Moss Side for the last time.

Midland Hotel
Manchester

She was waiting in his room when he got there, by the window with a cigarette in her hand. Tessa was with her, sitting on the end of the bed. A police radio lay on the bed.

He didn't say anything at first, just packed his HK-94 in the cupboard. He hadn't come straight to the hotel; they had driven to a police surgeon's home where Pentanzi had the bullet removed and was patched up. He had lost little blood and, after the wound was sewn up, was allowed to return with Marshall, whose own wound was minimal. The whole episode had taken over an hour before the two DEA officers were driven back to the Midland Hotel. Pentanzi, having had a shower at the doctor's, was now presentable, and caused little interest in the lobby as Marshall helped him towards the lifts. Armitage and Job had returned to make a full report to Soulson. Marshall left Pentanzi in his room to call Washington and went to his room to find the two women waiting for him.

'Are you going to tell us what happened?' Jill asked testily when

414

he had put the weapon away. The tension of her ordeal made her snappy and distant from those around her.

'Didn't you pick it up on the radio?' he countered. He was worried about her, but wished he was alone. It was always like that after the heat of danger; he needed time on his own to bring himself back from the awful deeds he was so good at.

'Only that there was another gang battle,' interjected Tessa, trying to bring the heat between them down. 'And the Front burnt down.'

'That's what happened.'

'I'm sure you had something to do with it,' came Jill's sarcastic response.

He ignored the barb. 'Are you OK?' he asked.

'Thought you'd never ask.'

He shrugged, then turned to Tessa. 'Can you give us a few minutes?'

'No, don't go, Tessa,' begged Jill. 'There's nothing you don't know about.'

Tessa shook her head and left the room.

'Why're you having a go at me?' Marshall asked.

'What do you want? A medal for coming after me?'

'Come on,' he urged softly, kneeling in front of her. He tried to take her hands in his, but she pulled away.

'You just don't know what I went through.'

For all her toughness, he realized this was only the second time she had faced mortal danger; that moment when every law-enforcement officer realizes the uniform isn't any protection against those who mean harm. He wanted to protect her, but the horrors were also within him. 'Come on,' he repeated.

She turned her face away, desperately fighting to hold back the sobs. He put his arms around her shoulders.

'Tell me what they did,' he urged.

'No.'

'Paras. The big one. Did he . . . ?'

'No-one touched me. I was just frightened. I thought . . .' her voice faltered.

'Go on.'

'I thought they were going to kill me.'

'Did they threaten you?'

She shook her head. 'I was alone. Just locked away.'

'Didn't they come in there with you?'

'No.' Her protestation grew louder. 'Why?'

'Not like them. Their sort don't leave girls alone.'

'Damn you, Marshall.' She swung round and faced him. 'Is that what you want to hear? That they came in and beat me up? That they raped me?'

'Don't be crazy.'

'You're the crazy one. For God's sake. What is it with you? Why must you always believe the worst? Isn't it enough that I was frightened for my life?'

He knew she was telling the truth; why couldn't he just accept and believe and trust? But the demon had risen within him. 'I know what these animals are like,' he continued, hating his jealousy as he spoke.

'Go to hell, Marshall. You just can't cope with real people. We're not all whores. We don't all live the way you do, always expecting the worst.' She leant forward and held his head with her hands and stared into his eyes. 'Look at me. Look into my eyes. Look at the truth.' Then she spoke deliberately and slowly. 'Nothing happened. I was just frightened for my life. Don't you understand that, big man? Just 'cos you don't care for yours.'

'I'm sorry.'

'You've got to trust.' She regretted her lies as she spoke. She'd never been faithful to him, not in all this time. But that was her way; she knew she loved him. Maybe it was time to change. She slowly took her hands away from his face. 'You've got to trust.'

'Yeah. So damn easy.' He remembered why he was there; that there was more to do. 'You'd better get some sleep, huh?'

'Is that it?'

'I love you, Jill. But this thing isn't over.'

'What else is there? You did what you came here for.'

'Ends . . . don't happen that easily.' He stood up. 'One more thing to do. Then I'm going home.'

'What about me?'

He said it again. 'I love you.'

'I love you, too. Is that enough, big man?'

'You tell me.'

'Do I come with you?'

'I'll tell you when I'm leaving.'

'I'm frightened.'

'Of what?'

'Everything. Being with you, not knowing if you can cope with us. Damn, that's not all the truth.' She stopped herself.

'Go on.'

416

'I love you, but I don't know you. The life you lead, all that violence. I don't know if I could live with that. Not now I've seen it. It was bad enough in San Antonio. I tried to block it out of my mind. What's happened in the last few days has brought it all back.'

'I'm leaving the DEA.'

'You can't. It's all you know.'

'I'm tired. It's all finally got to me.'

'I don't know if I can take it. I like what I do. I couldn't live my life the way you do.'

The look between them was soft and lost. They both knew there were no easy answers.

When Tessa came back a few minutes later, Marshall was already gone. She found Jill lying back on the bed, her eyes open and fixed on the ceiling. She could tell she didn't want to speak, so she sat quietly on the chair by the window. She looked out as the last few shreds of darkness hung on to the city skyline. The drizzle had finally stopped and the wind pushed the clouds along away from the city at a hurried pace.

She wondered where her father was and why he hadn't visited Moss Side.

Then Jill started to cry and Tessa went and comforted her.

Saddleworth Moor
Manchester

Dawn was breaking over Saddleworth Moor when the Jaguar pulled up on the soft shoulder of the A635, the narrow open road that snaked between the villages of Holmfirth and Greenfield.

Paul Job parked behind the shot-up blue Vauxhall and climbed out. There was no-one in the car, so he looked out over the moor. He saw the big man standing a hundred yards away in the mist, looking out over the bog. He went to the car and told Soulson.

'Wait here for me,' said Soulson, then he and Armitage slid down the grassy embankment and made their way through the soft bogland towards Marshall.

'Why here?' said Soulson when they reached his brother.

'Because this is where it all started.' Marshall turned to face them. 'Where was it?' he asked Soulson.

'Down there.' His brother pointed at a patch of bog to the

417

south. 'Couple of hundred yards away.' He stared at it for a while, he'd come here many times before, on his own. The place still fascinated him, drew him to it because of its memories. Then he cleared his mind and turned to his brother. 'What's going on, James?'

'The thing was finished last night. I rang you because I needed to talk before I went home.'

'You're leaving?' He didn't show his disappointment.

'Yeah. Isn't that what you want?'

'Things need to quieten down again.' Soulson avoided the direct question. 'What about the girl?'

'Jill? I don't know.'

'You still running away?'

'Not everyone's a Mary, Charles.'

'Washington called,' said Armitage. 'They want you both to go home as soon as possible.'

'I met him once,' added Soulson. 'Mr Pentanzi.'

'Yeah,' nodded Marshall. 'He said.'

'It's probably for the best. Everything's under control except for Special Branch. They're looking for you because you dodged them when you came back from Belfast. Damn it, Jimmy. I still don't know why you wanted to meet here.'

'To settle all debts. Manchester Blue mean anything to you?'

The two policemen looked at each other. 'No,' said Soulson.

'You know what fucked us up all along? Bloody Irish. We all thought it was the IRA. Even Manchester Blue.'

'Who's Manchester Blue?' asked Armitage.

Marshall ignored him. 'There was no IRA involvement. Bourne, the Irish organizer in Moss Side, was part of a breakaway group who were setting up their own little empire. Small time crooks trying to be big. Guns and drugs. Supported by the Colombians. They could've become the biggest network in Europe. If their plan had succeeded.'

'Which it didn't,' said Armitage.

'That's right, Roy. You know why? Because they didn't know about me.'

'Nobody knew about you.'

'Only you and Charles. That's what upset them.'

'Upset who?' asked Soulson. 'Cut the riddles, James.'

'It's a dangerous game, playing both sides against one another, hoping to pick up the pieces afterwards.'

'James!' said an exasperated Soulson.

418

'It was only a gang war. Narco-terrorists, trying to muscle in on each other's territories. Nothing political about it at all. Just the Colombians using the blacks to screw up the Triads and force them out of town. It was Bourne who made everyone think it was the IRA. That put a different light on it. And, like we all believe, you don't mess with the Republicans. They're not just gangsters, they're fanatics. Don't know what surrender means.' Marshall paused, then turned his attention to Armitage. 'They even conned you, Roy.'

'They conned everyone,' came the measured reply.

'Would you have stuck with them if you didn't know they were IRA?'

'What the hell are you going on about?'

'You know damn well. Bourne had a contact in the Force. High up. Someone who knew everything that was going on. So he made you believe he was a Provo. You were so fucking scared of them, that you told them anything they wanted. Until I came on the scene. What were you hoping for, Roy? That I'd knock them off and get you off the hook?'

'Don't be daft,' snapped Armitage.

'I've got it chapter and verse. Your friend, Freddy the Duck, filled in all the bits. How you've been on the take for all these years, warning them about raids, making sure they never got caught. I know about your gambling debts and the tarts you screwed supplied by Wong. You were in too deep to stay an honest cop. Death or dishonour. You had no choice.'

'You're talking through your arse.'

'I hope you can substantiate this, James,' said Soulson.

''Course he can't.' Armitage shook his head in anger. 'I'm not wasting any more time here.' But he didn't move; the Glock that quickly appeared in Marshall's hand ensured that.

'Put it away,' ordered Soulson. 'Before this gets out of hand.'

'I even know about Christley.' Marshall saw the surprise on Armitage's face. 'You and Christley were taking from all the hookers and pushers in Moss Side. I know, I was there. Even in those days I knew what was going on. That's why Christley agreed to cover me when I got into trouble. Then he had such a strong hold over you that he had you informing to his mates, the IRA. I know the story, Roy. When he retired and went back to Ireland, you took over his role, bloody Manchester Blue.'

'Crap.'

'Not crap. The Chinese rumbled that a long time ago. They knew all about Christley, even his codename. Only it didn't matter in those days. They weren't bombing the mainland. Harmless information about nothing. What happened then, Roy? Did Bourne become your contact? Had you been supplying the Provos info for all those years, or did Bourne stumble on to your involvement with Christley and use it against you?'

'I never gave information to them.'

'You did to Bourne.'

'Sod you, Jimmy. You caused it. All those years ago.'

'You were bent before that.'

'Pennies from hookers. Every bobby had his hand in the till.'

'Not all of us,' interjected Soulson.

'No, you were bloody perfect. If it hadn't been for the mess he . . .' Armitage pointed at Marshall '. . . got us into, none of this would've happened. Christley had it all against me, once we got Jimmy out of there. You killed that bloke, didn't you?'

Marshall ignored him. 'Doesn't make what you did right.'

'I saved your fucking life.'

'A long time ago.'

'One night Christley got pissed. He told me he had this codename, Manchester Blue. It was fucking harmless. The troubles in Belfast hadn't even started. When he left the Force, he never asked me to give info to the IRA. Then one day, when the blacks and Chinese were at each other, I get a phone call from an Irishman, saying he was a Provo and he wanted to talk to Manchester Blue. Said I owed them. For what happened all those years ago. I presume Christley had told them everything. I had no choice.'

'You had a choice,' replied Soulson to his oldest friend. 'You just took the wrong one.'

'I didn't know he wasn't a Provo.'

'Doesn't matter.'

'Get off your high horse, Charles. You were part of getting Jimmy out of that murder rap as much as I was. If this comes out, it'll blow you out of the water. Especially when Spencer gets hold of it.'

'You're just a fucking crook,' yelled Marshall. 'Because of your marriage, you soon got into the Chinese mobs. Christ, you must have had a good thing going.'

Armitage shrugged. 'Pull me down and you pull everyone down. Including yourself. You prepared to do that, Jimmy?'

'You should've left me to go inside. Then I wouldn't have come back to haunt you.'

'You fucked your brother once. You going to do it again?'

Marshall's voice was flat when he eventually replied. His mind had already been made up. 'Last night, with Pentanzi, I wiped out over a thousand kilos of cocaine that was being stored in Moss Side. We also closed down the Moss Side gangs and cut off the route the Colombians had laid into Manchester. It'll happen again, somewhere else, but at least we slowed it down.' He turned to his brother. 'I couldn't have done it without the Triads. They thought I was going to give them the cocaine for their help. When they lost that, they came up with a new deal.'

'You after part of the action, Jimmy?' said Armitage. 'That how they do it in America?'

'Your life for their support,' came the chilling answer.

'No,' gasped Soulson immediately.

'I gave them my word.'

'No.' Soulson suddenly remembered how Armitage had supported him when Mary died, how he had been the only friend he had ever turned to. 'No,' he repeated.

'He's a dead man, either way.'

'Leave it, James.'

'They want him because he didn't tell them about me. He set them up and hoped I'd fuck the lot of them.'

'I said no.' He suddenly wished he was armed. To Soulson, it was brother against brother. Armitage had always been closer to him than James.

'They're probably watching us now. He won't make it back to Manchester. Even in your car. Let it go, Charles. This time, in this place where you formed your beliefs.'

'Your way, not mine.'

'It's the way the world's become. If I let him go, then they'll come after me.' Then Marshall raised the gun and pointed it at Armitage. 'As easy as turning off an electric light.'

'Damn you, James,' was all a stunned Soulson could say.

'I'm damned if I do it, and I'm damned if I don't. Some fucking choice.'

They stood like that, a still tableau on the lonely moor. In the distance Paul Job saw them and he scrambled down the embankment towards them, his revolver in his hand.

Then Marshall lowered the gun. 'Fuck you, Charles.'

'Leave him to the law.'

'This is the only law,' said Marshall looking at the gun. Then he threw it into the bog. 'And I'm pissed off with it.'

'Maybe you've got some sense in that head of—' commented Armitage.

421

Marshall turned, clenched his fist and punched Armitage, knocking him to the ground. 'Shit to you.'

Paul Job had nearly reached them, and he approached Marshall with his gun aimed at him.

'You've done the right thing,' said Soulson.

'I don't need your blessing, Charles. He was your friend because it suited him. But he didn't give a damn about anyone. Maybe once, a long time ago.'

'Chief?' queried Job as he approached them.

'It's all right, Paul,' said Soulson. 'Go and wait by the car.'

Job hesitated, then holstered his revolver and retraced his steps towards the Jaguar.

'Why?' Soulson asked Armitage.

'Why do these bastards, any of them, ever do it?' interrupted Marshall. 'Fucking greed, that's why.'

'I thought . . .'

'That I was like them. Just imagined the worst of me.'

'That was a long time ago.'

'No. It's still the same. He causes the trouble, I get you off the hook, and all you're worried about is him. You're like a social worker, Charles. Find someone who's bleeding to death and ask him who did it, because that person's got a problem. Fuck the victims, they just happened to be in the way.'

'You held back from shooting him.'

'Does that make me OK in your eyes. Hey? Make me a white man in your eyes.' Marshall laughed savagely. 'You have no idea. You think I did it for you. Saved that shit for you.' Marshall lashed out at Armitage with his foot, kicking him in the chest and sending him sliding in the mud. 'I did it for me. Because I'm tired of what I am. A fucking battering ram used by everyone else. A fucking hired gun. That's all I am. All I ever was.'

'You're a good law enforcement officer.'

'Yeah. Then fuck you all.'

Marshall turned and walked away.

'What about Roy?' Soulson shouted after him.

'What about him?' Marshall yelled over his shoulder. 'He's your problem now.' Then he turned and climbed the embankment and walked past Job towards the blue Cavalier.

Soulson felt an enormous sense of failure as he watched his brother drive away. He turned and looked at where the children's bodies had been discovered all those years ago, the night he had committed himself to his job. Then he remembered Mary and how

422

she had protected James. He realized, after all this time, after all his experiences, that he knew as little now as he did as a young bobby. Worse still, he understood even less.

'You won't be able to prove a thing,' Armitage said as he pulled himself to his feet. 'Otherwise we bring everything down, including you.'

'I'll take that risk. And I'm sure Freddy Wong will supply whatever evidence I need.'

'Supping with the Devil now, are you?'

'If I need to. The one thing I promise you is that everything you see from now on will be from the inside of a prison cell.' He signalled Job to come over, then walked to where Marshall had thrown the Glock and picked it up.

'You're fucking yourself, Charles. You're no different from Jimmy. Just deadbeats. Useless for nothing except doing what you're told. Never amount to anything, you two. Bloody deadbeats.'

Soulson shrugged. There was no deal with Armitage. Whatever the consequences. It saddened him and he suddenly understood his brother. 'Chief Superintendent Armitage is under arrest,' he told a surprised Job. 'Escort him to the car, with your gun at the ready, and call for back-up.' *Deadbeats or not, this time they had been on the same side.*

The two brothers had walked off the moor and back to their lives, out beyond the mist and secrecy that had swirled around them and finally drawn them together, then wrenched them apart.

Ringway International Airport
Styal
Manchester

He'd rung Tessa and told her the flight number.

She promised she'd tell Jill immediately.

'Bye, Uncle Jimmy.'

'Bye, Tessa.'

'Do I really look like her?'

'More than you'll ever know.'

Then he'd driven to the airport and left the battered blue Vauxhall with the car rental company. The receptionist had been shocked by its appearance, but there was little she could do but report it to her superiors. He felt sorry for her when he saw the tears well in her eyes. It was her first day at work and she was already frightened she'd lose her new job.

He didn't see Freddy the Duck in the main concourse, but he knew the three Chinese watching him would report that Marshall had flown back to America. He knew he was safe; they just wanted to make sure he left their patch.

The big man waited until the last call before he picked up his hand luggage and walked through immigration.

He looked back once for her, but knew she had decided not to come.

Maybe she'd follow.

Maybe his demons would finally go to sleep.

Saturday morning
Moss Side
Manchester

Yvonne Tessler watched her thirteen-year-old son Mikey wheel his BMX bike out of the back yard, hop on it and cycle down the road to meet his friends.

She waved a last farewell then closed the kitchen door. Her husband had gone to buy some wood for the built-in wardrobe he was building in the baby's room. She stopped at the bottom of the stairs and listened; she heard the baby gurgling away, playing with his toys in his cot.

She smiled, it was a good life, and went back into the kitchen. As she made herself a cup of tea she thought about her life. It wasn't that bad. They'd been told she'd never have any more children after Mikey but then, miraculously, she'd found herself pregnant after all these years.

Maybe life was really going to get better. The horrific news on the morning programmes had shocked her at first, but then, when she thought about it, she realized that this drug thing could come to an end now that the police were taking control. Maybe the Moss could be the way she, who had always lived there, wanted it to be. A place of homes, a place to be happy, a place to bring up children the way she wanted to, just like they did in the adverts on the telly.

She poured her tea and revelled in her dream.

Two streets away, on a corner hidden from the main road, Mikey pocketed the £10 note, stuffed the small package under his jumper and raced away to deliver it to the address he had been given.

The young man who had organized the delivery watched Mikey disappear on his BMX. Then Stash Maxwell turned and walked back to his house to prepare another shipment. He walked with a limp, the result of the final battle at the Front. It was a bitch, but he had customers to supply, money to be made.

Around him, business in Moss Side went on as usual.

Bethesda Hospital
Maryland

Smith called in and reported the events in Manchester, as passed on by Pentanzi. Ronane, suspended in his bed wrapped in gauzes, listened without comment.

'They're home and dry,' concluded Smith. 'The English police say we were there to help, but that the gunplay was between the rival gangs. John's wounds aren't too bad. And the department didn't get compromised.'

'Marshall say anything?' was all Ronane asked.

'Yeah. That he's coming straight back. Something about seeing you.' He saw the tears well in Ronane's eyes. 'He said he was going to leave the department. Get out of the business. Can you believe that shit? The son of a bitch.' Smith shook his head. 'Battle fatigue. Where the hell else is he going to go? Guess he's going to go on making trouble. He's a good agent. You always said he was one of the best.' Smith checked his watch. He had a meeting scheduled in half an hour about a shipment that was due through Corpus Christi. *People got hurt and files got closed, but this damn thing went on like it always did.* 'I got to get back to the office. Say, I spoke to the doctor before I came up. He says you're mending fast. That you'll make it OK.'

The little man lay quietly for a while after Smith had gone. So it was over. Marshall was coming home. He was a good friend.

But there was an emptiness in Ronane, a void that no-one would ever fill. He missed his family, missed the kids laughing and shouting at each other when he arrived home, missed Betty most of all.

At least he'd helped pay Marshall back. Betty would understand why he had stayed behind.

He sighed, knowing the terrible pain he was about to endure, and sat up in the bed. He yanked his arms so that the needles that connected him to the bottles sprang out from his raw flesh. The pain seered through him, but he was beyond caring now. He slid off the bed, walked for the first time since he'd been in this place. His legs buckled, but he forced himself up again. Then he ripped the skin transplants that had been growing over his arms and his chest and the other flesh-opened areas, wrenched them, tore them where they had been healing. This time he felt the pain and he screamed in agony as it took hold of him.

He walked slowly to the window, steeling himself against the searing, all-consuming pain. He reached up, unlatched it and pulled it open. The cold outside air burnt into his nerve-ends as it flowed into the sealed room.

Then he stood on the chair near the window and stepped through it and fell to his death and to Betty and the only place he wanted to be.

His last thought was of Marshall and he knew the big man would understand.